D1048457

John Suchet is an award-winning television journalist and newscaster. As an ITN foreign correspondent he has reported from every country in Western Europe, as well as America, Africa, the Middle East and the Far East. In 1986 he was awarded the Royal Television Society's Journalist of the Year Award for his reporting from the Philippines, and in 1996 was voted Newscaster of the Year by the Television and Radio Industries Club. He was a frequent presenter of *News At Ten*. He now presents all ITN news bulletins and is the regular presenter of the Lunchtime News and senior presenter on ITN's 24-hour News Channel. Since publishing *The Last Master* trilogy, he is increasingly asked to give talks about Beethoven at theatres and concert halls around Britain. He also has his own Beethoven website at www.madaboutbeethoven.com.

The three volumes of *The Last Master* have been widely acclaimed. The *Sunday Telegraph* describes them as 'an admirable picture of a creative life' and the *Mail on Sunday* praises their 'great seriousness and integrity', while the *Daily Telegraph* regards the trilogy as a work that 'will probably do more to further understanding of the composer than any professorial paper'.

Also by John Suchet

THE LAST MASTER: Passion and Anger
THE LAST MASTER: Passion and Pain

The Last Master

Passion and Glory

Volume three of a fictional biography of
LUDWIG VAN BEETHOVEN

by
John Suchet

WARNER BOOKS

A *Warner* Book

First published in Great Britain in 1998
by Little, Brown and Company
This edition published in 1999
Reprinted 2000

Copyright © 1998 by John Suchet

The moral right of the author has been asserted.

All rights reserved.
No part of this publication may be reproduced,
stored in a retrieval system, or transmitted, in any
form or by any means, without the prior
permission in writing of the publisher, nor be
otherwise circulated in any form of binding or
cover other than that in which it is published and
without a similar condition including this
condition being imposed on the subsequent purchaser.

A CIP catalogue record for this book
is available from the British Library.

ISBN 0 7515 2752 1

Typeset in Bembo by
Palimpsest Book Production Limited,
Polmont, Stirlingshire
Printed and bound in Great Britain by
Clays Ltd, St Ives plc

Warner Books
A Division of
Little, Brown and Company (UK)
Brettenham House
Lancaster Place
London WC2E 7EN

For Bonnie, *unsterbliche Geliebte*

Contents

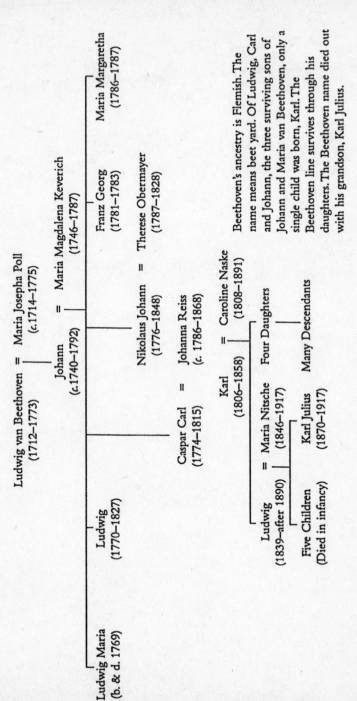

Ludwig van Beethoven = Maria Josepha Poll
(1712–1773)   (c.1714–1775)

Johann = Maria Magdalena Keverich
(c.1740–1792)   (1746–1787)

Ludwig Maria (b. & d. 1769)

Ludwig (1770–1827)

Caspar Carl = Johanna Reiss
(1774–1815)   (c. 1786–1868)

Nikolaus Johann = Therese Obermayer
(1776–1848)   (1787–1828)

Franz Georg (1781–1783)

Maria Margaretha (1786–1787)

Karl = Caroline Naske
(1806–1858)   (1808–1891)

Ludwig = Maria Nitsche
(1839–after 1890)   (1846–1917)

Four Daughters

Many Descendants

Karl Julius (1870–1917)

Five Children (Died in infancy)

Beethoven's ancestry is Flemish. The name means beet yard. Of Ludwig, Carl and Johann, the three surviving sons of Johann and Maria van Beethoven, only a single child was born, Karl. The Beethoven line survives through his daughters. The Beethoven name died out with his grandson, Karl Julius.

Cast of Characters

Continued from Volume Two

Beethoven, Karl van (1806–58). Beethoven's nephew and the only child of the three Beethoven brothers. Following his brother Carl's wishes, Beethoven assumed guardianship of the boy on his father's death, but a lengthy court battle ensued as his mother Johanna fought against being excluded from his upbringing. Beethoven developed an overwhelming love for the boy and constantly attempted to establish a father-son relationship with the sole Beethoven of the next generation.

Beethoven, Therese van, *née* Obermayer (1787–1828). House-keeper to Johann van Beethoven in Linz, she became his wife in 1812, despite Ludwig's strenuous efforts to prevent it. She had an illegitimate daughter from a previous liaison.

Braunhofer, Dr Anton. Physician who attended Beethoven during the last years of his life, after the rupture in relations with Dr Malfatti.

Breuning, Gerhard von (1813–92). Son of Beethoven's lifelong friend Stephan von Breuning by his second marriage. Gerhard became close to Beethoven during the composer's final illness. Beethoven nicknamed him 'Hosenknopf', Trouser Button.

Broadwood, Thomas. Member of the British family of piano-makers. Beethoven met him in Vienna and he sent the composer a magnificent six-octave instrument with the heavier British action, which suited his playing.

Franz I, Emperor of Austria (1768–1835). Former Holy Roman

Emperor forced by Napoleon to give up the title. At the Congress of Vienna in 1814 he introduced Beethoven to the allied heads of state, including Tsar Alexander.

Galitzin, Prince Nikolas Borissovich (1794–1866). Russian prince and great admirer of Beethoven's music. He commissioned three quartets from the composer, which became opp. 127, 130 and 132, and with opp. 131 and 135 form the Late Quartets.

Giannatasio del Rio, Cajetan (1764–1828). Teacher who owned a boarding-school in the Landstrasse suburb, which Karl van Beethoven attended. His daughter Fanny kept a diary with reliable details about Beethoven, his nephew and the guardianship battle.

Glöggl, Franz Xaver (1764–1839). Kapellmeister at Linz. During Beethoven's fraught visit to his brother Johann in Linz in 1812, Glöggl became well acquainted with him and asked him to compose a set of *equali* for trombones.

Goethe, Johann Wolfgang von (1749–1832). Germany's greatest poet and playwright. Beethoven set many of his poems and texts to music, the best known being the incidental music to *Egmont*. The two met only once, in Teplitz in July 1812, but the relationship was uneasy. Beethoven felt Goethe was in thrall to the Imperial court; Goethe wrote to his wife that Beethoven had an 'absolutely uncontrolled personality'. In later years Beethoven tried to rekindle the relationship, but Goethe did not respond.

Holz, Karl (1798–1868). Government official and accomplished violinist, often playing second violin in Schuppanzigh's quartet. For a period in Beethoven's final years he acted as assistant and secretary. The canon *Wir irren allesamt*, which Beethoven sent to Holz from his deathbed, was the last complete work he composed. (In performance it lasted barely thirty seconds.)

Liszt, Franz (1811–86). Hungarian pianist and composer. Beethoven met him and heard him play when he was eleven years old, and predicted a great future for him. It was Liszt who led the campaign for a monument to be erected to Beethoven in the Münsterplatz in Bonn, where it still stands.

Mälzel, Johann Nepomuk (1772–1838). Inventor of the panharmonicon and other mechanical instruments, as well as developer of the metronome. He made ear trumpets for Beethoven, and persuaded him to compose a piece for the panharmonicon, which became known as the Battle Symphony, later orchestrated and performed to great acclaim during the Congress of Vienna.

Moscheles, Ignaz (1794–1870). Composer and pianist from Prague. For a number of years he acted as Beethoven's assistant, before moving to London.

Palffy, Count Ferdinand (1774–1840). Court theatre director who purchased the Theater an der Wien in 1813. Instrumental in persuading Beethoven to resurrect his opera *Leonore/Fidelio*.

Schiller, Johann Christoph Friedrich von (1759–1805). Renowned poet and playwright. Beethoven never met him but greatly admired his poetry. He knew Schiller's lyric poem 'An die Freude' while still in Bonn, harbouring ambitions to set it to music, which he finally accomplished in the Ninth Symphony.

Schindler, Anton Felix (1795–1864). Lawyer and violinist. He was in very close contact with Beethoven during the composer's final years, acting as assistant and secretary with more zeal than any of his predecessors. After Beethoven's death he sanitised much documentary evidence to preserve his master's reputation, destroying many of the conversation books and falsifying others. Beethoven did not admire him as a man, but came to rely on his dedication and efficiency.

Schmerling, Leopold von. Viennese lawyer who handled Beethoven's court battle for guardianship of Karl.

Schubert, Franz Peter (1797–1828). Austrian composer. Given that the bulk of his output was composed before Beethoven's death, it is inconceivable that the two did not know each other, at least by sight, though there is no absolute proof that they met. Schubert's natural shyness and Beethoven's unpredictable attitude towards other composers probably mitigated against it. Nevertheless on his deathbed Beethoven studied the scores of many of Schubert's songs and professed admiration of them. Schubert was a pall-bearer at Beethoven's funeral and his own deathbed wish was to buried alongside him, a wish that was fulfilled.

Sebald, Amalie (1787–1846). Singer from Berlin. Beethoven met her in Teplitz in 1812 and grew very fond of her. Amalie looked after him during his illness there, and the intimate nature of their notes to each other led, at one time, to her being considered as a candidate for the Eternally Beloved.

Seibert, Dr Johann. Chief surgeon at the General Hospital, brought in by Doktor Wawruch to perform the abdominal operations on Beethoven during his final illness.

Umlauf, Michael (1781–1842). Viennese conductor and Kapellmeister at the Kärntnertor theatre. He conducted *Fidelio* during the Congress of Vienna and the first performance of the Ninth Symphony, with Beethoven at his side to give him the *tempi*.

Unger, Karoline (c. 1803–77). Contralto at the Kärntnertor theatre. She sang in the first performance of the Ninth Symphony.

Wawruch, Dr Andreas Ignaz (1773–1842). Beethoven's principal doctor during his final illness, who wrote a detailed report on its progression. Given that Beethoven died in his care, it was inevitable he would be criticised for his treatment in the years following Beethoven's death. Seen from today's perspective his treatment was not inappropriate, given that Beethoven was already terminally ill when Doktor Wawruch first attended him.

Weissenbach, Dr Aloys (1766–1821). Surgeon and poet from Salzburg who wrote the text for the cantata *Der glorreiche Augenblick* which Beethoven composed for the Congress of Vienna. Beethoven's relationship with him was short but highly amicable, no doubt influenced by the fact that Weissenbach too was deaf.

BOOK ONE

Chapter 1

1812

The rain pounded on the roof of the carriage. Ludwig van Beethoven rested his head back and closed his eyes, allowing the regular rhythm to flood his head and calm his nerves. Conversation with the other passengers was impossible and he was grateful for it.

Over and over again he relived the few hours of passion he had shared with Antonie Brentano. Her face hung in his mind, soft, gentle and smiling, but with a sadness that seemed etched on to her features.

Again – it must have been for the hundredth time – he felt the crumpled piece of paper in his pocket. He did not need to take it out and read it: he knew it by heart. *Give me hope . . . that one day we will live our lives together. Only hope.*

He wished now that she had not written it. It meant she was not ready to accept the inevitable – that they would never be together.

I must try to make her understand that, he thought. But how? He remembered she had made him promise to write to her. Hadn't she given him her pencil? He felt it in his pocket.

At the first stop, in Schlan, he had an angry exchange in the coach station.

'We have only four horses, sir. They cannot take the mountain route. And in this weather that is the only route possible.'

'Esterhazy left. I heard you say so.'

'His Excellency had a team of eight, sir. They can manage the mountain road.'

'Then I will take the lower road.'

'There is no road, sir. With all this rain it has turned to mud.'

Ludwig threw extra coins on the desk. 'I want to leave now. I want to get to Teplitz. Do you understand?'

The man scooped up the money and shrugged his shoulders.

Three hours later, in the town of Laun, Ludwig found himself once again in an argument. He was tired now and his head was aching. A dull heaviness hung like a thick curtain in his ears and he knew that, at any moment, the dreadful noises would begin. By leaning forward and letting his gaze flit between the clerk's eyes and mouth, he could understand what the man was saying.

'Sir, the road through the Waldtor forest is impassable. The rain has turned it into a quagmire. Not only that, you cannot travel at night. There are bandits in the woods. I cannot risk your safety, or the safety of my driver.'

'I want to leave now, do you understand? I *must* get to Teplitz.'

'Sir, there is an inn just two doors up from here. Take a room there and leave in the morning. It will be safer and the rain may have —'

Ludwig took out more coins. 'I want to leave now.'

'Then I shall have to give you an extra driver, sir. For your own safety. It will cost you an additional five florins.'

Just outside Laun the coach turned north on to the road that passed round the western end of the Mittelgebirge mountains and ran through the Waldtor forest. It was jerking and shaking on the uneven road, and the rain still pounded on the roof. Ludwig heard the coachman's cry pierce the night as he cracked the whip over the horses' backs.

In his head Ludwig heard the softness of Antonie's voice, which alone seemed able to penetrate the fog in his ears. Yes, I loved her, he thought, a tremor of happiness coursing down his spine. But it is a love that cannot endure, that must now be put aside . . .

He must have dozed because he was woken by a sharp crack, followed moments later by a sudden lurch as the carriage shuddered to a stop and jolted to the side. Ludwig fell against the wall. He heard the coachmen shouting and felt the carriage shake as they manoeuvred their way off it. The door opposite opened and an angry face peered in. 'Broken axle, sir. I knew it would happen in all this mud. You'll have to get out while we repair it. Here, give me your hand.'

Ludwig reached up but the weight of his body was too much. He could not grasp the coachman's outstretched hand.

'All right, I'll have to come round. Pull yourself clear of the door.'

The door to Ludwig's right fell open and the driver said through it, 'Come on, sir. Out this way.'

Ludwig rolled over and tumbled through the door. He scrambled to his feet.

The coachman cursed loudly. 'Damn it, sir, if you'll forgive my impertinence. Never should have come. Now, go and stand under that tree while we fix the axle.'

Ludwig tramped through the mud and stood against the thick trunk. The rain filtered through the leaves, falling on to his hair and shoulders. A shiver ran through him. He wondered what time it was. Probably after midnight.

He watched the men's laboured movements as they lifted their boots high to walk round the carriage. Working as swiftly as the rain would allow, they removed the wheel, then unfastened the splintered axle. Tossing it to the side, they reached under the carriage and pulled out a new one.

Ludwig wondered what would have happened if they had not been carrying a spare, or if the second coachman had not come too. He shivered again as he remembered the warning about bandits.

He looked down at his boots, sunk deep into the mud, and pulled his coat tighter around him, but it was sodden and cold and he let it fall open again. His head was hurting with each beat of his heart. He wanted to be warm and to feel the comfort of a mattress underneath him. In his mind he saw the chambermaid enter the room and light the fire, the glow of Antonie's skin as she hung her wet clothes in front of it . . .

The men took their position underneath the carriage and, with a nod from the leader, grunts and straining, they lifted it. The leader slipped the wheel swiftly on to the new axle and tightened the nut that held it in place.

Each man then laid a board under the two back wheels. One put his shoulder against the back of the carriage and indicated to Ludwig to do the same.

At a shout from the head coachman, Ludwig and the other man pushed against the carriage, and suddenly it was upright. Mud sprayed on to Ludwig's face and he wiped it off as best he could with his sleeve. The carriage drove on a little until the coachman was sure he was on firmer ground.

The other man nodded to Ludwig and they walked to rejoin it.

'We must stop at Bilin,' the head coachman said. 'Check that the wheel is on firm. We'll stay till morning. Then the last leg to Teplitz.'

Ludwig's head. 'No. After you've checked the wheel we must go on. I want to get to Teplitz tonight. Tonight, d'you hear?'

'That's madness, sir. It'd mean we'd arrive in the middle of the night. If we have no more problems with the carriage.'

The rain was coursing down Ludwig's forehead. 'We keep going. Until we get to Teplitz.'

Ludwig slept again, he did not know for how long. At one point he heard the distorted sound of voices, which he assumed meant they had reached Bilin. Soon the carriage was rocking again.

He realised, after a while, that the ride had become smoother. A faint glow of light shimmered behind the still heavily falling rain. They were, at last, descending the hill to Teplitz. The coachman slowed the horses to walking pace. Ludwig felt the steady rumble of cobbles beneath the wheels. With a shout from the coachman, it halted.

He climbed out, dug into his pocket for coins, which he gave to the two men. He nodded at them, picked up his bag and, in the early hours of Sunday morning 5 July, entered the Hotel Zur Eiche, the Oak Tree.

A candle flickered on the desk, illuminating a bell. Ludwig picked it up and rang it. A clerk, rubbing his eyes, appeared.

'Beethoven. I need a room.'

The clerk looked in the book that lay open in front of him. 'I am sorry, sir. We have nothing. We are full.'

Ludwig could not make out the words. 'What? Speak up, man. I am hard of hearing. What are you saying?'

'We are full, sir. We have nothing until Tuesday. But there is another hotel, sir. Down the hill. The Goldene Sonne. They have rooms. Your carriage will take you. Meanwhile I will put your name in the book for Tuesday.'

Ludwig walked out of the hotel but the carriage had gone so he strode down the hill, the rain still coming down in sheets.

Tired, soaked to the skin and with a pounding headache, Ludwig entered the Goldene Sonne, let his bag drop to the floor and walked to the desk. 'I need a room. Until Tuesday.'

'We only have a small one, sir. Will that do?'

'What? Yes, anything. Bring me hot water.'

The clerk led Ludwig down a narrow passage and unlocked a door.

Ludwig kicked off his boots, threw his coat over a chair and lay on the bed. He did not hear the clerk return with the water. He was woken several hours later by the pale greyness of the day filtering through the window.

Outside the air was warm and oppressive. Rain fell steadily. Opposite was a small park with a square, squat building at the end. A sign read 'Steinbad', Stone Baths.

Ludwig entered the building, wrinkling his nose at the smell of sulphur. He paid and took a towel from a woman, who handed it to him without looking up.

There was a large bath with two or three smaller ones on one side. At least a dozen men were in the bath already, some conversing, others lying back. They ignored Ludwig as he stepped into it. The heat of the water flowed over him and he slid down, allowing his head to float on the surface. The bubbles rose up around his ears, the regular rhythm calming them. The water slowly penetrated his thick hair, warming his scalp.

A feeling of utter weariness came over him. The dreadful journey, the drama of the breakdown, the few hours of sleep after his arrival . . . and the incessant rain.

He did not know how long he slept. He was woken roughly by the woman he had paid shaking his shoulder. 'You must leave. We are closing.'

He dressed quickly and stepped out into the evening. The rain had stopped but the air was so damp he felt as if he could reach out and squeeze drops from it, and it was chilly, more like February than July.

Suddenly he felt hungry. He remembered passing a tavern on the hill and walked up there.

The tavern was thick with tobacco smoke and throbbed with a steady, lively hum of conversation, punctuated by a sudden laugh or shout. The noise did not worry Ludwig. He ordered red wine and a bowl of broth. As he drank he watched the people crowded in large groups round the small tables. Animated, long-haired, dressed colourfully, arms waving. What were they arguing about? Life and death? God? Good and evil? Ludwig smiled to himself. These were Bohemians, and the contrast with the strict formality and polite discussion of Vienna could hardly have been greater.

The wine soon calmed him and he began to ponder what he would write to Antonie.

First thing in the morning Ludwig went to the desk and asked for several sheets of paper.

Back in his room, beads of sweat broke out on his forehead as he thought about what he had to do. He threw open the small window, untied the top of his shirt and sat on the bed, his hands clasped between his legs. How to tell her? What to say? Somehow he had to make her understand.

He looked at the little table, the sheets of paper sitting defiantly pristine. He took out the crumpled letter and the pencil Antonie had given him from his coat. He read the letter again and tossed it on the bed. How he wished it was musical notes he was about to write. But words. Words!

He sat at the table and clenched his lips.

> My angel, my all, my very self – only a few words today, and even with pencil –

He cursed silently. Should he start again? No. He wanted to get his thoughts down right now.

> (with yours) only tomorrow will I know definitely about my lodgings, what an awful waste of time – Why this deep sorrow when necessity speaks – How else can our love endure except through sacrifices, through not demanding everything from one another? How can you alter the fact that you are not wholly mine, I not wholly thine – Oh, God

He threw down the pencil and took the few short paces to the window, breathed in the sultry, damp air. The sound of the rain falling through the leaves made a gentle rustling in his ears. Quiet and still and calm. He looked up and saw a bird on a branch, its head drawn down into its plumage, which shone dark in the rain. Fortunate creature, he thought. No need to struggle, to fight with life . . . No heartache and sadness.

He sat at the table again and, without looking at what he had written, turned the page.

> Look to nature in all her beauty and let her calm your heart about what must be – Love demands everything and rightly so, and that can only mean *me with you and you with me* – you forget so easily that I would have to live for myself and for you, only if we were completely united would you feel as little pain as I –

He sat back and looked at his words. Surely he was right? The only way their love could endure was if they were able to be together, and that was impossible. Antonie was married to Franz and they had children. Should I have written that I would have to live for us both? he wondered. Yes. I must make her understand what it would mean. He reached forward and underlined 'for myself and for you'. If I am to go on working – and there is so much work still to do – how could I possibly play the role of husband and father?

He resumed writing.

> My journey was terrible. I did not get here until 4 in the morning yesterday. Because they were short of horses the coach took a different route, but it was a dreadful road. At the one to last stage they warned me not to travel at night, that I would have to go through a dangerous forest, but that spurred me on – and I was wrong. The coach, of course, had to break down on the dreadful road.
>
> Esterhazy took the other more usual route and had the same trouble with 8 horses that I had with four. Yet to a certain extent I got pleasure as I always do when I overcome a problem –

He paused. He wanted some wine. Should he ask for some to be sent to the room? He decided against it. He would finish the letter quickly, ending it with what he hoped would be fitting sentiments.

> Now swiftly from external matters to internal ones. We will surely see each other soon. There is no time now to tell you what I have been thinking about these last few days regarding my life – if our hearts were only united I would not have to have such thoughts. My soul is so full of things to tell you – Oh – There are times when words are simply no use – be cheerful – remain my only true darling, my all, as I am yours. The rest is for the gods to decree, what is to be for us and what should be –
>
> your faithful
> Ludwig

He read the last sentences again. Maybe he was giving her too much hope. No, he thought. It will do. I will see her soon in Karlsbad and I will be able to tell her exactly what must now happen.

With a long sigh he pushed to one side the two sheets of paper he had filled.

Then he left the hotel and went to a small inn two doors down where he ordered a carafe of wine. He waved away the menu but ate the bread the waiter brought in a basket. The wine quickly created a sensation of lightness in his head. The ringing in his ears, which had intensified while he was writing, faded slowly.

Later, as he walked across to the Steinbad, a shiver ran through him, more in anticipation at the heat that would shortly flow around him than from the air, which though still damp was warm.

In the hotel he sat in an armchair in the entrance area, opposite the mailbox, into which he would shortly place his letter. He stood, steadying himself for a moment on the back of the chair, and walked to the mailbox, above which, pinned to the wall, was the postal schedule.

It took a moment for his eyes to focus on the print, and then his heart sank. Only on Mondays and Thursdays did the imperial mail coach go to Saaz, Karlsbad and Eger, leaving at 8 a.m. What was today? Monday. The next post for Karlsbad was not until Thursday morning.

Walking past the clerk's desk, he picked up several more sheets of notepaper and returned to his room. He sat heavily in the chair and pulled a clean sheet towards him. He tried to think clearly.

Monday evening on 6 July
    You are suffering my most precious one – only now have I discovered that letters must be posted very early in the morning. Mondays – Thursdays – the only days when the mail-coach goes from here to K. – you are suffering – Oh, where I am you are with me, with me and I can talk to you – if only we could live together, what a life it is!!!! now!!!! without you – Pursued by the kindness of people here and there, which I think – which I no more want to deserve than do deserve – humility of a human towards humans – it pains me – and when I regard myself in relation to the universe, what I am and what is He –

who is called the Almighty – and yet – herein lies the divine in mankind –

He threw down the pencil. What was he trying to say? It had seemed so clear only a few moments ago. Yet to find the words . . .

He walked to the door and opened it. 'Wine. A carafe of wine!' he shouted down the corridor.

He sat down again, slightly calmer, and continued writing.

I weep when I think you will probably not receive the first news of me until Saturday – as much as you love me – I love you even more deeply – do not ever hide yourself from me – Goodnight – taking the baths has made me tired – Oh go with, go with –

His head was spinning. He scratched out the last few words.

Oh, God – so near! so far! is our love not truly sent from Heaven? And is it not even as firm as the firmament of Heaven.

Exhausted, he got out of the chair, kicked off his boots and lay down. He fell asleep instantly.

A pale yellow glow filtered through the window-panes. The sun, at last, was penetrating the thick damp air. Ludwig's head was heavy and he wanted to turn over and go back to sleep, but sleep would not come.

He remembered what he had written to Antonie the night before. Sadness swept over him. Fate. Finally I love and am loved, and it cannot be.

He could smell the aroma of freshly roasting coffee. He walked to the door. 'Coffee!' he called. A memory of the night before stirred. He looked at the table, at the empty carafe.

He had not finished the letter; the last words were only half-way down the page. *Auch so fest, wie die Veste des Himmels.* Even as firm as the firmament of Heaven. His lips turned up in a small smile of satisfaction. The words had a fine ring and they scanned like poetry.

Yes, he thought. She will understand.

A chambermaid knocked, opened the door, and put a jug of coffee and bread on the table. He sat down, examined the lead of Antonie's pencil, then sharpened it.

Good morning on 7 July – even lying in bed thoughts of you force themselves into my head, my Eternally Beloved, now and then happy, then again sad, in the hands of Fate, to see if it will heed us – I can only live with you wholly or not at all, yes, I have even decided to wander helplessly, until I can fly into your arms, and say that I have found my haven there, my soul embraced by you to be transported to the kingdom of spirits – yes, sadly that must come – you will accept it more readily, knowing I am true to you, that never can another woman possess my heart – never, never – Oh, God, why do we have to be so far apart from what we love? And yet my life in V. now is such a wretched existence – Your love makes me at once the happiest and unhappiest of men – at my time of life I need stability, calmness of life – can that exist in a relationship like ours?

He sat back and sighed. He left his room and went to the desk. 'I need a stamp,' he said to the clerk.

'Certainly, sir. Where is it for?'

'Karlsbad.'

'Two kreutzer, sir. And, if you hurry, you will catch this morning's mail-coach.'

Ludwig's jaw dropped. 'This morning's mail-coach, did you say? But it's – it's – Tuesday. The post only goes on Mondays and Thursdays. I saw it myself. On that schedule, on the wall. Over there.'

The clerk smiled indulgently. 'Except in the summer, sir. It says so at the bottom of the schedule. In the summer months, May until September, it leaves every day at eleven a.m. Though, I admit, you could hardly call this summer, with all the rain we've had.'

Back in his room Ludwig snatched up the pencil.

Angel, I have just been told that the post leaves every day – and so I must close, so you can get the letter immediately – be calm, only through reflecting calmly about our existence can we reach our goal to live together – stay calm – love me – today – yesterday – what tearful longing for you – you – you – my . . .

He was writing rapidly now, the words spread out across the page, just one or two to a line. He knew, even as he wrote, that he had been too honest. That he could never send the letter.

Love – my all – Farewell – Love me still – never misjudge the most faithful heart of your beloved

    L.

    ever mine

    ever thine

    ever ours

He ended with a flourish, stacked all the pages together and made to tear them in half. At the last moment he paused, tossed them on the table and sighed. He folded them and put them into an envelope.

Maybe, he thought, I will show the letter to Toni. Then I will destroy it.

Chapter 2

Ludwig's legs ached as he trudged up the hill. He had to hold his bag high to stop it dragging on the ground and it hurt his arm. A steady afternoon drizzle was falling. He walked into the hotel Zur Eiche and dropped his bag at the desk. 'Beethoven. I have a room.'

The clerk shook his head and turned down the corners of his mouth. 'We are full, sir. Completely.'

Ludwig stood a moment to allow the words to filter into his brain. The clerk spoke again. 'Her Imperial Majesty the Empress, sir. She is in the Schloss. Her staff is staying here. We are honoured.'

Ludwig looked wearily at the clerk, who went on, 'The Duke of Saxe-Weimar is also here. Then next week His Majesty the King of Saxony with his retinue. His Excellency Prince Wittgenstein –'

Ludwig balled his fist and brought it down hard on the desk top. 'I am Beethoven. I have a room.'

The clerk took a step backwards and turned to an older man, who had come out of a smaller room on hearing the noise.

'May I help you, sir?'

'Beethoven. I have a room booked. I came before. They sent me down to the Goldene Sonne.'

The man smiled. 'I wish we could see the real sun. Such a pity, with so many important people here for the Congress.'

'Is my room ready?'

'Of course, sir. Would you sign here?'

Ludwig took the pen, dipped it in the pot and wrote in the register, *Beethoven, Kompositeur, Wien*. The senior clerk took a small sheet off a pile and sat down.

'May I have your travel pass, sir? For the police register.' Ludwig took the document from his inside pocket and handed it to the clerk, who smoothed out the wrinkles with his hand and copied from it on to a form.

He handed Ludwig a key. 'We'll hold on to your pass, sir. Don't forget to collect it when you leave. Now, your room is on the first floor. Down the passage on the right. I'm sorry we have no room overlooking the gardens.'

Ludwig climbed the steps, entered the room and walked to the window. To the left, and almost near enough to touch, was the tall blackened monument to the Great Plague. He shuddered. Was there a town in Austria or Bohemia without such an edifice with grim-faced saints, hands up in benediction, and on the base the dark staring skulls of the dead?

To the right, running the length of the square, stood the castle, really nothing more than a large long building three storeys high, a tower at the near end, a church at the other. Beyond it another church, onion-domed. Ludwig smiled. This was Bohemia: two churches in the main square and a castle that in Vienna would pass unnoticed.

Outside the castle sat two ornate carriages – belonging to the Empress, no doubt. Few people were in the square, preferring to shelter indoors from the rain.

Ludwig breathed in the air through the open window. The rain gave it a freshness, heavy with the scent of midsummer flowers. Impulsively, he walked quickly down to the main entrance and outside.

High to his right were trees and foliage – the castle gardens, the largest area of green in the town. Dismissing his fatigue, he strode up the incline into the park. He was alone. He lifted his face and felt the rain bathe and cleanse it, wiping away the grime of the city and the dreadful journey.

He walked towards a large lake. A flock of herons sat lazily on a mound in the middle, their wings held away from their bodies so that the rain dropped off them on to the ground. Ludwig saw the silvery shapes of fish in the water, heedless of the danger that lurked above.

As he walked he thought of Antonie. Should he go on to Karlsbad to see her and Franz? Maybe it would be better . . . No, he thought, it is better I go. I will be able to tell her. She will understand.

He shivered as a gust of wind blew off the lake, then turned and headed back to the hotel.

It would be another week before Goethe arrived, if he

remembered correctly what Bettina Brentano had said. He had forgotten where he would be staying, but he knew it was not at the Eiche. He would wait for Goethe to contact him. Meanwhile, there was the Symphony in F, the eighth, to work on.

The weather would surely change soon. He knew that the main baths were close to his hotel, down a small incline on the other side of the square. They would be less shabby than the ones near the Goldene Sonne.

Yes, he thought, two or three weeks in which to work, take the waters, meet Goethe . . . and then on to Karlsbad.

The hot sulphurous water bubbled round Ludwig's head. It beat against his eardrums, rhythmically and insistently like a timpanist playing faster than a pair of arms ever could. He closed his eyes to concentrate on the sound. Slowly the pressure built up against his ears and the beat of the water began to hurt.

He sat up quickly, sending water over the side of the bath. The pressure intensified. It felt as if something was pushing against his ears – *inside* his head. He screwed his eyes tight, anticipating what would happen next. A slow, steady build-up of noise, a tone that would become a shriek and split his head like a meat cleaver. *Why should this wretched fate befall me? Why should I, a composer, a musician, a man who knows nothing but music, be so accursed?*

The chill air above the steamy heat of the water settled round his shoulders and he lowered himself again, keeping his ears above water this time. Slowly, the pressure faded, leaving nothing but the familiar dull heaviness.

Cold, wet Teplitz. Go and relax in the warmth and beauty of Bohemia, Doktor Malfatti had said, and here he was, experiencing the worst summer in living memory. But he was away from the city – away from the demands of publishers, the requests to play at soirées, and Archduke Rudolph's pleas for composition lessons. As the days passed he felt ever more relaxed, and he was soon to meet Germany's greatest poet, and then on to Karlsbad to see Antonie.

He sat for a few more moments, then climbed out of the bath. The air felt even chillier and he wrapped one towel around his waist and flung another over his shoulders.

There was a cavernous feel to the marbled hall, and its walls shone with condensation, rivulets of water tracing irregular paths down the thousands of mosaic tiles. He glanced across at the huge mural on the wall – a Roman man and woman sitting opposite one another in a bath, both with black, curly hair, hers tied up with a ribbon, looking directly, and without any trace of embarrassment, at each other. The upper curve of her breasts was visible above the side of the bath.

Ludwig dried himself and dressed quickly. Outside the rain had stopped and the sky was a pale, apologetic blue, but the air was still chilly. He started up the hill to the Schlossplatz. A noise filtered through to him and he knew at once it was music and that it was not originating inside his head. He walked towards the sound, which was cacophonous, accompanied by a heavy beat. At first he could not place it.

He noticed other people were walking in the same direction, smiling, nodding, revelling in the absence of rain, if not yet the warmth of summer. He turned up into the Schlossplatz and the music flooded over him. A stand had been erected on the side of the square facing the castle and a band of musicians – twenty or so – was playing.

Ludwig recognised the music now. It was known in Vienna as Turkish music, military marches, mostly, accompanied by cymbals and drums. Occasionally the cymbalist would exchange his great discs for a tambourine, lending the music an exotic, Eastern flavour. It was music, Ludwig knew, that appealed immediately to audiences, as they tapped their feet to its enticing beat.

Two men were arranging wooden chairs in straight rows and people were sitting down. Others stood around in small clusters. Ludwig watched a group of small children, imaginary muskets on their shoulders, marching up and down, knees raised high, dissolving into laughter when they tried to wheel round.

He walked towards the Eiche and stopped behind the Plague monument. The musicians, their cheeks blown out, puffed into their instruments. The scene reminded him of the wedding dance he had witnessed outside Heiligenstadt, which had given him the inspiration for the third movement of his Pastoral Symphony. He doubted he would receive the same stimulus from the music he was hearing now.

But he was *hearing* it. He liked its roughness – crudeness almost. Again, as in Heiligenstadt, here were musicians enjoying themselves and an audience choosing to stop and listen. Wasn't that what music should be for?

Suddenly the musicians stopped. Their director beckoned

them to stand. The audience did likewise, turning their heads. Ludwig followed their gaze. The Empress, with her retinue, was walking out of the castle towards the stand. She held her head at an upward angle, acknowledging with the slightest nod the bows of the people. Her heavy eyelids contributed to a look of haughtiness, and Ludwig stiffened his spine.

Knowing he was half hidden, he leaned against the monument, arms folded. He had not seen the new Empress before. The previous Empress, who had come to his concert with her young brother-in-law Archduke Rudolph all those years before at the Burgtheater, had died, tragically young, five years previously. There had been some surprise that Emperor Franz had remarried so swiftly, and while the people of Austria had accepted Maria Ludovica as the new Empress, they had not taken her to their hearts.

Ludwig knew that the nature of the music would change. He shook his head as wrong notes marred the sound, the drummer beating ever more loudly and the director's face – Ludwig could tell from his hunched shoulders and stiff arm movements – masked in panic.

The applause was polite, the spontaneity gone out of players and audience alike. Ludwig let out a sigh, turned and entered his hotel. He ignored the clerk's look of surprise that he had left the square while the Empress was still present, collected his key and went upstairs.

The dull thud of the drummer permeated his room and his ears. The quiet and calm of his surroundings, though, soothed him. In his head he could hear music, his own music. Strings, first violins, playing gently, taking their beat from the regular pulse given by the drum.

He pulled towards him the folder containing the first movement of the Symphony in F. He took out a clean sheet. No drum, just wind and strings, the wind giving the beat, regular and persistent. Gentle, he wanted it to be gentle. Timpani would give it an urgency he did not want it to have.

Two beats to the bar, staccato semiquavers in the wind, *pianissimo*, chords. And in come the strings, a delicate melody, as fine as filigree, *pizzicato*, *pianissimo*.

The notes flowed from him on to the paper, accompanied by his tuneless singing. Through the heaviness that hung like a thick velvet curtain behind his ears, he could hear the notes as clearly as if the orchestra were in the room. At the top of the page he wrote 'Movt. II Alleg. Scherz.'

He stopped writing. The rest would flow without effort. He wanted wine; the sulphurous bath water had given him a thirst.

He stood up and walked to the window. A sudden squall had blown up, sending large drops of rain almost horizontally across the square. The Empress, all dignity gone now, was hurrying towards the castle, head bowed, holding her dress clear of the ground, one of her ladies-in-waiting struggling to keep an umbrella over her elaborately coiffed head. People were darting in all directions to seek shelter. The players were hurriedly putting their instruments into boxes.

Ludwig watched the scene for several minutes. Slowly the rain and wind subsided, the clouds began to part and the sun valiantly sent down a few weak, watery rays. At the far end of the square, beyond the dome of the church, was the slightest hint of a rainbow.

But it was too late for the music: the musicians had long since gone.

Ludwig left his room and went downstairs. He placed the key on the hook and noticed an envelope bearing his name in flowery writing propped underneath it.

His stomach churned. Another pleading, tearful letter from Antonie. Oh, God, he hoped not. But even as he thought it, he knew the writing was not hers.

He broke the seal and extracted a folded sheet of thick paper, luxurious to the touch. He took it to the light of a window and read it.

17 July 1812

Most Excellent and Highly Esteemed Sir

It would do me the greatest honour to make your acquaintance during my stay in Teplitz and discuss the great artistic works which you have given to the world.

I flatter myself that you have seen fit to honour my own humble efforts with your divine art.

I am residing in the Goldenes Schiff. Might I suggest a meeting there two days hence at 2 p.m.?

I remain your servant, Sir,

Goethe, W. J. v.

Chapter 3

Ludwig felt nervous as he walked towards Goethe's hotel, despite the glass of wine he had swallowed before leaving. Germany's greatest poet – Europe's greatest poet – so many of whose verses he had set to music, and for whose play, *Count Egmont*, he had written accompanying music; appointed to the court at Weimar, ennobled by the Emperor, an artist in his early sixties at the height of his powers.

And I, thought Ludwig, pulling his coat more tightly around him, who have had to struggle every day of my life, whose music is sometimes applauded, sometimes mocked, with few friends I can call my own, who has been loved just once . . . and who is cursed with an affliction that will surely one day destroy the art that is still within me.

The first sight of Goethe did nothing to calm his apprehension. He was a tall man, who stood with his back as erect as a soldier, his head held high, his full stomach testifying to a comfortable life, his legs thin, and feet that seemed surprisingly small, given the weight they supported.

He bowed to Ludwig; Ludwig returned the courtesy, but kept his eyes raised.

'A great honour, Herr Beethoven. Your music is known to me.'

Goethe's voice was strong and deep, but the heaviness in Ludwig's ears had not dissipated – if anything, the brisk walk down the hill had worsened it – and at any moment the dreadful noises might start. Should he tell Goethe right away?

To Ludwig's relief, Goethe continued, 'I have heard, my good Beethoven, of your sad affliction. Shall we sit in this room over here? I have told them we are not to be disturbed.'

Ludwig's shoulders sagged. Immediately he felt all the more inferior in Goethe's presence. If only . . . *if only fate had not been so cruel to me, I would be able to stand beside any artist and be judged their equal.*

He followed the poet into the small anteroom, where they sat in two plush chairs facing each other, a small round table between them. The furnishings gave the room a dull, heavy feel, which Ludwig knew would cut out extra noise and make conversation possible.

Goethe looked round, a tentative smile playing at the corners of his mouth, as if he was not quite sure what to say. He smiled and coughed, his hand held to his mouth. 'Dreadful weather. Absolutely dreadful. For July.'

Ludwig nodded. 'Same in Prague. Nothing but rain. The ground was so soft my carriage broke down on the way here.'

Goethe raised his eyebrows.

'The wheel broke off, in the middle of the night. In the Bilin forest.'

'You should not have travelled at night.'

Ludwig looked down at his hands. 'I insisted. I wanted to get here. I . . . It was a mistake.'

Goethe raised his eyebrows even higher.

Ludwig waved his hand impatiently. 'It doesn't matter. I arrived safely. Have you studied my *Egmont* music? Have you heard it?'

Goethe was looking over Ludwig's shoulders, his eyelids slightly lowered over his eyes. 'In the middle of the night? Dangerous forest, that. Often walk in that direction. You really travelled through it in the middle of the night?'

'I did not come here to talk about my journey!' Ludwig said, rather more sharply than he intended. 'I arrived safely.'

'You were fortunate, most fortunate. Now, what did you ask me? Yes, my *Egmont*.' He put a slight emphasis on the 'my'. 'I have heard it, yes. Most impressive, if I might say so. Most impressive.'

'Impressive?' Ludwig echoed weakly.

'Impressive. Dramatic. Perhaps in places a touch too dramatic. Melodramatic.'

'*Melodramatic?*'

'Of course I do not mean to criticise. In fact, the audience at the performance I attended were quite enchanted.'

'Enchanted?'

'You are a fine composer, Herr Beethoven.'

'Yes. Thank you. I admire your poetry. You can do with

words ... I have no facility with words. My language is in notes.'

'Ah, words. When I write, it is as if they are like pieces of stone that I carve into any shape I want. Choosing the best piece, selecting it over the others, so that I have exactly what I need.'

Ludwig was warming now to what Goethe was saying. 'I do the same with notes.'

'But your choice is smaller than mine. You have only the keys in the scale.'

'No, no.' Ludwig shook his head vehemently. 'No, no. It is not just the notes themselves. It is what lies *behind* them. I hear what no one else can. Like you with words. It is not just the sound of the word, is it? It is more than that. Only one word is ever perfectly right. Is that not so?' He shook his head again, frustration on his face. 'I'm sorry. I find it difficult. I cannot –'

'In God's name, Beethoven, you are right. I have never heard it expressed like that. But you are right!'

Ludwig smiled. 'Shall we not order wine? Should we not drink to our discovery? Brothers in art?'

A look of disapproval came over Goethe's face and his lips turned down. 'No, no. I must work. So much work to do. But shall we meet tomorrow? I am walking to the edge of the Bilin forest. In daylight. Will you join me?'

The two men walked through the Schlossgarten: one tall, erect, arms scarcely moving at his side, hair silvery and waved; the other, more than twenty years his junior, hands either thrust into his pockets or folded in front of him, body bent forward as if each pace he took led towards an invisible target.

Ludwig was aware that they made an incongruous sight. He saw how passing strollers never failed to acknowledge Goethe, either with a smile and small inclination of the head or a full bow. Goethe either responded with a barely perceptible gesture or made no acknowledgement.

It did not irk him that the only people who looked towards him did so bemusedly. What did it matter? I do not ask them to acknowledge *me*, he thought, just my music.

He soon wished he had not agreed to take this walk. It was impossible to talk with the great poet. The open air felt like a vast emptiness against his ears. Normally it was welcome, the only sounds being the song of birds; but now it was forbidding. There was so much he wanted to discuss with this man, but how could he while they walked like this? He was grateful that Goethe seemed to recognise this and did not try to make conversation, but he was weighed down with disappointment at the fruitlessness of it.

They had left Teplitz behind and were walking along a country lane; ahead of them, in the distance, the dark shapes of the trees of the Bilin forest. He wondered whether to tell Goethe that he wanted to turn back, but before he could do so he heard the other man say, 'Come, I know a tavern close by. Let us sit for a while, then we will return. That will be enough walking for one day.'

Ludwig gulped the beer that was put in front of him, careless of the foam that spilled on to his hand and aware of Goethe's disapproval. The other man was pouring water from a jug, careful not to let the blocks of ice splash into the glass.

Ludwig braced himself for what he knew was about to happen – the dreadful, inevitable reminder of his fate. The effort of the walk and the cold draught of beer had made his heart thump and his head throb. Soon the whistle would start in his ears.

Goethe was dabbing gently at his forehead with a handkerchief. Ludwig knew he would try to make conversation. He drank another mouthful of beer, beginning to feel already its more welcome effect. He braced himself as Goethe turned to him, his eyelids slightly lowered, his head held upwards as it seemed always to be.

'Oppressive, isn't it? The air. As if it wants to rain again but can't quite bring itself to. Such weather for July.'

To his relief Ludwig heard him clearly. 'I've been sent here for my health. Hah! I shall return to Vienna more ill than when I left.'

'That is not good for you,' Goethe said. 'So much beer without food. After a long walk.'

Ludwig put down the stone mug firmly, hoping Goethe would notice the deliberate gesture, but he had already turned away.

'We will get the carriage back,' Ludwig heard him say. 'It stops here in fifteen minutes. The air is too stifling for another long walk.'

It was not a question and Ludwig felt no need to respond. All he wanted was to drink his beer, allow the sounds in his ears to subside, then walk back to Teplitz alone, stopping to sit by a stream or under a tree and listen to the sounds he wanted to hear – those of his own music filling his head.

'So sad about young Schiller, do you not think?'

Goethe's question took Ludwig by surprise. 'Schiller?'

Goethe nodded. 'Only forty-six when he died. He was ten years younger than I. Fine poet.'

Ludwig nodded vigorously. '"To Joy". "*Bettler werden Fürstenbrüder*. Beggars become the brothers of Princes." It is a fine line, a noble idea.'

Goethe smiled. 'Did you know he replaced that line? In a new edition of his works published not long before he died. "*Alle Menschen werden Brüder*", he wrote. "All mankind will become brothers".'

Ludwig heard him clearly, as if the subject matter had banished the sounds that interfered with ordinary speech. He turned Schiller's words over in his head. *All mankind will become brothers.*

'Yes. All mankind. *All* mankind. Better. Much better.'

Goethe snorted. 'No, no. Too general. Too idealistic. I'm afraid poor Schiller –'

'You're wrong!' Ludwig exclaimed, pleased to see the effect his words had on Goethe, whose eyes widened in surprise. 'Idealistic, yes. But is that not what art is for, to express the ideal? Otherwise what purpose has it? And what finer ideal is there than for all mankind to become brothers? All equal before God. No distinction between beggars and princes. That is what Schiller is trying to say.'

He saw the skin of Goethe's throat move as he swallowed. The poet's eyelids drooped again. 'We agree that it is idealistic, then. We differ as to whether it is worthwhile. All nature has its order, whether it is animals or humans. It is not for the artist to say otherwise.'

Ludwig's head swam: he wished he had the words to argue rationally with Goethe. He knew that in his eagerness, he would not express himself properly. 'It is an ideal. That is what he is saying. To strive for. And we artists must express that ideal to show people what to . . . to strive for. Don't you see? Don't you understand?'

'I understand, my dear Beethoven, that it is easier to speak of such lofty matters on a diet of water than it is on a diet of beer. Shall we take the carriage and return to Teplitz? Come, I see it approaching.'

Ludwig said nothing on the short ride back to the Schlossplatz. The jolting of the carriage caused a pain in his head. He could already taste the wine that would soothe his nerves and take away the awful noises. *All mankind will become brothers.* Was there any more noble or honourable sentiment? How wrong Goethe was!

As they walked back through the gardens to the Schlossplatz, the familiar greetings began again. Goethe acknowledged them more freely this time, as if to convince him, Ludwig thought, that it was pointless, impudent even, to question the words of someone so highly regarded.

Ludwig looked at his feet as he strode alongside Goethe.

Goethe said, 'So tiresome, all these salutations, do you not think? Quite interferes with one's solitude. Mmmh?'

Ludwig smiled. 'Do not trouble yourself, Your Excellency. Perhaps the greetings are intended for me.' He did not look up to gauge the other man's reaction.

That evening in a short letter to his wife Christiane, who was taking the waters in Karlsbad, Goethe wrote:

... Today I met the composer Beethoven. A more ardent, spirited, profound artist I have never met. I can fully understand why the world marvels at him so.'

Ludwig sat once more in the bubbling water, the powerful odour of the sulphur curiously pleasing now that he had become accustomed to it. Goethe had asked him to come to the Goldenes Schiff to play the piano for him, and he had accepted. Not because Goethe had promised they would be alone, but because he had said in his note that he wanted to discuss the possibility of writing a new work for Ludwig to set to music.

He stood up and the water cascaded off his shoulders. He coughed and swallowed. A slight soreness at the back of his throat made him grimace. He walked to the stone basin set into a side wall and held the battered metal cup under the steady stream of water that came up from the earth. It had a strong, brackish flavour. He swallowed a couple of times, swilled more water around his mouth and spat it out.

What was he to make of Goethe? The man had a certain arrogance – the single quality above all others that Ludwig detested – but then why shouldn't he? The greatest poet and dramatist alive, appointed to the court at Weimar, did he not have the right to feel superior to those ordinary mortals about him? Ludwig had thought about their argument over Schiller's words. He suspected that, in fact, there was little difference of opinion between them. If only I could express myself better, he thought, we would have ended up agreeing. I know that. Yes, I will go and play for him, communicate in my language, and tell him how honoured I will be for him to write a poem or even a play for me to set to music.

When he arrived back at the Eiche the clerk handed him a letter and he knew immediately who it was from.

> My dear Ludwig
>
> Franz and I are so looking forward to seeing you. We hope you will come soon. We have heard that it is cool and damp in Teplitz. Here it is finer and the waters are excellent. We are at the Aug' Gottes, number 511 auf der Wiese.
>
> We have some news to tell you, which I know will please you as much as it pleases us. Do come soon.
>
> > Your good friend
> > Antnie Brntno

'My dear Beethoven, you have lost your colour,' Goethe said. 'You should go to Karlsbad. My wife is there and has written to me and told me the sun has made an appearance.'

'I am going. Soon. Very soon, probably. Now, first, I shall play for you my setting of your "Mignon's Lied". I made the setting a year or two ago with another of your verses. Breitkopf published them. Will you permit me?'

Goethe inclined his head and Ludwig walked to the piano. He played the gentle opening chords, threw back his head and sang the words as he played.

> Do you know the place where the lemon trees grow,
> With their dark green leaves the orange trees glow,
> Where gentle breezes from the blue skies waft,
> And the myrtle and laurel stand tall and aloft?
> Do you know that place, do you know it well?

Ludwig strained his voice to hold the high note at the end of the sequence, then, his fingers playing the insistent chords, he sang the couplet that rounded off the verse.

> It's where you and I my love will dwell,
> Where you and I my love will dwell.

There were more verses but Ludwig was anxious to see Goethe's reaction. He lifted his hands from the keys and turned to face the poet.

Goethe's eyes held a sparkle that was almost mischievous. 'My dear Beethoven, your piano playing is considerably better than your singing. I regret that even my words cannot improve the quality of your singing.'

Goethe's remark at first cut into Ludwig's head as the sounds of his music receded. When its sense became clear he felt hurt. But Goethe was smiling. 'Do not take offence, my friend. You have enhanced my own humble efforts most exquisitely.'

'Are you pleased with it? I have heard it sung properly, by a soprano, and I believe –'

Goethe held up his hand. 'I do not doubt it at all. Now, will you do me the honour of playing me one of your pieces for the piano? Your fame both as composer and pianist has spread to Weimar, and I shall surely be asked to describe your skills when I return.'

Ludwig turned to the piano again and played the opening unison phrase in bass and treble that opened the sonata in F minor. The same phrase again, answering in a new key, and the trill that ended it. The trill again; staccato notes in the bass; the trill again. A huge descending arpeggio run in the right hand, answered by a rising arpeggio in the left; massive *fortissimo* chords – three times – and after more chords, accompanied by an insistent beat in the bass, the extraordinary phrase, dotted crotchets and semiquavers, that seemed to rise from the depths of the ocean.

Tunelessly Ludwig sang with it, that phrase that had come to him unbidden and fully formed, that was the bedrock of the movement.

On he played, his fingers performing the huge semiquaver *forte* runs in a blur. He sensed Goethe close to him, watching his hands soaring across the keyboard, but he did not look up. And that theme again, alternating with chords, and the semiquaver runs.

He shook his head to emphasise the chords, alternating, syncopated between the two hands. Finally a run of semiquavers in the right hand, the main theme rising again in the left, but crossed over the right hand and higher up the keyboard, then down into the bass again, deeper, deeper, closing, not with crashing chords but with a *piano pianissimo*, the keys barely stroked, a small chord in the treble, a single F at the extreme bottom of the keyboard.

He sat still, his fingers holding down the keys, allowing the sounds to fade away in his head. He turned to face Goethe, who had returned to his chair.

Goethes eyes were wide, his lips slightly parted. He roused himself and said, 'My dear Beethoven, that was most exquisite. Yes, really most exquisite. Passionate, I believe, is the appropriate word.'

'The publisher gave it the name "Appassionata".'

Goethe laughed. 'He was perfectly correct, my friend. It is an appropriate name.'

'The second movement proves it to be wrong. That is different in nature altogether.'

He turned to the keys again but Goethe said, 'No. No more, Beethoven. That is enough for me to digest. Come, the rain has stopped. Let us walk in the Schlossgarten.'

'Can we not talk? I want to talk about a work with you. You said you would write something –'

'Later, later. Come now, I need to breathe some fresh air.'

Ludwig sighed deeply, unable to disguise his disappointment. Really, Goethe reacted to his music no differently from anybody else. He saw only the virtuosity and fury. He did not see *behind* the notes, as Ludwig had hoped he would. Surely an artist as great as Goethe would be able to do that, to discover the inner meaning, the essence of the music? But no, his reaction to *Egmont* had proved he was unable to do that, and now he had demonstrated it again.

Ludwig trudged after him and up the short hill into the Schlossplatz. Without speaking the two men walked into the garden towards the lake.

'It has been a pleasure making your acquaintance, Beethoven,' Goethe said, finality in his voice. 'I shall await your future compositions with interest.'

Ludwig heard the words and the unspoken message behind them was as clear as daylight to him. He shrugged his shoulders. 'You may write to me in Vienna. I am on the Mölkerbastei. Baron Pasqualati's house. I hope –'

But Goethe had been distracted by movement close to the garden's entrance, through which they had themselves walked. He pointed. 'Look, Beethoven, Her Imperial Majesty. We must pay our respects.' He increased his pace, walking swiftly along the path towards where the Empress was acknowledging the bows of the people, who stood aside to allow her to pass.

Ludwig was exasperated but followed him. Suddenly Goethe stopped. He caught the Empress's eye, stood aside and executed a low bow, sweeping his right arm in front of him and holding it extended away from his body.

Ludwig saw the Empress stop, turn, and begin to speak to the poet. He had had enough. Enough of Goethe, enough of all this ridiculous protocol, of incessant greetings, of bowings. With his right hand he pushed the top hat firmly back on his head, folded his arms in front of him and walked past the Empress, staring straight ahead.

The next day Goethe wrote to his wife:

> . . . Beethoven's talent amazes me. He plays exquisitely. But unfortunately he has an absolutely uncontrolled personality. Admittedly he is not wrong in finding the world detestable, and yet by so doing he does not make it any more pleasant either for himself or for others. At the same time he deserves to be greatly forgiven and greatly pitied, for his deafness is increasing . . .

Ludwig left for Karslbad the following afternoon. In a letter to the publisher Herr Härtel, of Breitkopf and Härtel in Leipzig, he wrote:

> . . . Goethe delights far too much in the court atmosphere, far more than is becoming for a poet. How can one criticise other virtuosi in this respect when even poets, who should be regarded as the foremost teachers of the nation, can forget everything else when confronted with that glitter?

Chapter 4

Ludwig wondered if Goethe would keep his promise and write something for him. He hoped so. The man might not be exactly what he would have expected, but his power with words was undeniable.

Words. He thought of the letter he had written to Antonie, which now sat at the bottom of his bag. How inappropriate his own words were! He had tried to express what he felt, to explain why their love could never be. But sitting at the piano for just a few minutes and playing for her – as he had at the house in Vienna when she was ill – would express it so much better.

He looked out of the carriage window at the mountain range that formed the border with Germany. Germany! A pit opened in his stomach. Was it not time to return to his home, the Rhineland, and see Bonn again? And the Rhine, and the Siebengebirge. And the Drachenfels.

I'll ask Steffen, he thought, the pit deepening as he remembered their last encounter. He had not seen his old friend since that business over Carl and Johanna. He rested his head on the carriage wall.

His brother Carl was seriously ill with consumption. How much longer did he have? What would become of Johanna and the child? Johanna! He shuddered at the thought of her, already the cause of so much friction in the family. Had he been alone in believing that Carl had done the right thing reporting her to the police for stealing money? How *could* she have done it? And she the mother of Karl, the first of the next generation to bear the name of Beethoven.

What if there were more children in the next generation? They would belong to his other brother, Johann. He sighed loudly, oblivious of the glances of the other passengers. Johann, a prosperous apothecary in Linz who intended marrying his housekeeper. His housekeeper, who already had a child by another man!

How could my brothers have so besmirched the Beethoven name with their choice of women? he thought, running his fingers raggedly through his hair.

Finally his thoughts turned to the woman with whom *he* had fallen in love. So different from Johanna or this house-keeper. Calm, gentle, beautiful, an angel. *My angel, my all, my very self . . .*

And our love cannot be. Am I any better than my brothers? Tears pricked behind his eyes at the thought. The woman I love I cannot have. He took a handkerchief from his pocket, wiped his eyes and sniffed.

Of course I am better than my brothers. I, at least, am a moral man. Antonie and I expressed our love to each other. And now it must end. I fell in love with an angel and I must tell her it cannot be.

Such misery. He gazed at the mountains again. Far beyond them lay his homeland, where once he lived free of respons-ibilities and pressures. Free with his art, to compose and perform his music. What was life now but one crisis after another? Family problems, financial problems, problems over where to live, problems with publishers, with players . . . and one problem above all others, which affected him alone, which set him apart, which meant he could never be *normal*, the direst problem a musician could have . . .

He started as he felt a hand on his knee. A sympathetic female face was looking into his. Her words penetrated the fog in his ears. 'Do not worry. You will see your family again soon. I am sure.'

Ludwig's heart pounded as he descended from the carriage and walked along the Wiese to the Aug' Gottes. The street ran on both sides of a narrow river whose name it bore, affording a picturesque promenade for those wealthy citizens of the empire who had come to take the waters.

There was an aura of smugness about the town. Ludwig felt it as soon as he stepped on to the pavement. Ladies strolled in pairs, acknowledging each other with polite nods, eyes quickly taking in another's apparel to see if it outshone their own. Colourful parasols hung from delicately folded arms, or were held up to ward off the gentle spray from the many fountains that seemed to pervade the air. There were fewer men: they were either taking the waters or conducting business.

The Wiese river – the name, meaning 'meadow', harked back to an earlier era when it spilled on to the flat grassland that sloped up and away from it – was broad and long, beginning in a wide arc as it descended from the high lake that was its source, and ending in the lower part of the town where the bath-houses stood. The Aug' Gottes – the Eye of God – stood tall, smaller buildings butting up against it on both sides. It had, Ludwig saw, an ornate front, stone mouldings surmounted by small cherubs clutching harps or blowing into celestial trumpets.

Suddenly he longed for the simplicity of Teplitz and the Eiche, the tavern in which he had drunk, the laughter and the smell of tobacco ... He suspected it was different here. Before he reached the desk of the Aug' Gottes, he had come to the conclusion that Karlsbad had been turned into a far-flung outpost of Vienna.

It was late afternoon. Franz would be in a business meeting and Antonie was probably resting with Fanny after spending the morning taking the waters.

'Your travel pass, sir.'

The clerk's words took Ludwig by surprise and it was a moment before they registered with him. The clerk repeated them more loudly.

'Yes, I heard you,' Ludwig snapped. He put his hand into his inside pocket. It was empty. He sighed. 'It's in my bag. I'll give it to you later. Give me my room key.'

The clerk made a note, handed Ludwig a form and said, 'Please fill this in and bring it back to me with your pass. And, sir, a lady left a letter for you.' He turned, took the key and letter out of a cubby-hole and handed them to Ludwig.

Ludwig clutched his bag in one hand, the key and the letter in the other. The room was small and at the back of the hotel, but it looked out on to the rising meadows on which sheep grazed. It would be quiet, and for that Ludwig was grateful. He was glad Antonie had written, otherwise how would he have arranged to see her?

He crossed to the window and threw it open, breathing in the air – a curious mixture of sulphur and the strong aroma of summer grass. The sun was low in the sky, casting a warmth over the countryside. There was none of the chill damp of Teplitz.

He opened the envelope and took out the single folded sheet of hotel paper.

My dear Ludwig

I hope your journey was not too arduous. Franz, who is looking forward to seeing you, attends meetings most of the day. I shall come to your room at six and we can talk. Fanny will be sleeping.

In haste
Toni

The weariness that had been creeping up engulfed him. He wanted to kick off his boots, lie on the bed and sleep. He was glad that Antonie was coming to see him, yet dreaded their encounter. Nothing must happen – he must not allow it. What had already happened between them was in the past. He must be strong.

He needed to think. Sleep was impossible. Perhaps a vigorous walk across the meadow would help him throw off the fatigue that was draining him, and a stop at a tavern to taste the bitter flavour of red wine . . .

'Dear Ludwig,' Toni said, leaning forward and kissing his cheek. 'It is so good to see you again. But what a small room they have given you. I shall complain.'

'No. It is fine. I prefer it.'

She smiled. 'Come and sit down and let us talk.'

He watched her move the two upright wicker chairs close to each other. The voice that he recalled so well, its timbre soft and gentle, was so soothing to his ears. But there was a matter-of-factness to it now that he did not remember.

'First, tell me how you are.' She took his hands in hers for a moment, then let them go.

'Teplitz was cold and wet. It might as well have been November.'

'It has been bad here, too, but it looks as if it has changed at last.'

'I almost caught a chill. But the baths were relaxing. I worked more on the symphony. And I met Goethe.'

'Of course. Tell me all about it. Did it go well? Does he like your music?'

'He does not understand music. And he is pompous, arrogant.' He shrugged his shoulders. 'It does not worry me. He is a fine artist. But he has taken on too many of the ways of the court.'

Toni chuckled. 'And that does not appeal to you. The Empress is there, isn't she?'

Ludwig nodded. 'He insisted on bowing to her in the Schlossgarten. I did not, which upset him. And it is about to get worse. Princes, kings, dukes – they are all coming to Teplitz to discuss the war against France, how to help the Tsar now that Napoleon has invaded his country.'

'Franz says Napoleon has made his biggest mistake ever. Russia will prove too much for him. He says it is the one country in Europe it is impossible to conquer.'

'Maybe he is right. Maybe not. Everyone thinks they know what that man will do next, and they are never right.'

Antonie leaned forward expectantly. 'Ludwig, how is your hearing? It seems to be fine. Maybe the rest –'

Ludwig interrupted, 'No better, Toni. Still the awful noises. Still trouble hearing what people say. It is fine now. Your voice is – I can hear your voice. And we are in a small room where it is quiet. Outside . . .'

'Oh, you poor man.' She took his hands again. 'I am sure by the time you return to Vienna you will be rested and it will be better.'

They fell silent. Ludwig's mind raced. What should he say? How could he tell her? The words were not there. They just would not come. He felt her squeeze his hands and again let them go.

Then she spoke. 'Ludwig, dear Ludwig, do you remember I said I had some news for you? In the note I sent to you at Teplitz?'

Ludwig looked up sharply. He had forgotten that line at the end of her letter. 'I am having another child. Isn't it wonderful? Franz and I are so pleased.'

Ludwig took a few moments to digest her words. Then panic flitted over his face, but Antonie was smiling. 'No, Ludwig. You have nothing to be concerned about. Just tell me you are pleased for Franz and me.'

Ludwig relaxed and grinned at her. 'It is wonderful news, Toni. Already you look radiant. I am happy for you. For you both.'

She cast her eyes down and Ludwig saw her press a handker-chief to them. When she looked up she had recovered her composure. 'Ludwig, what happened between us will always be precious to me. I admire you more than any other person. I believe you are a great artist. Greater than anyone else. Mozart, Bach. Greater than the poets. Goethe's name will not be known as yours will be. For the rest of my life I will treasure our – our – love. Soon Franz and I must return to Frankfurt. You will not forget me, will you, Ludwig?'

'No, Toni,' he said. 'There will be no one else. Ever. Just my music.'

Chapter 5

'I am sorry, sir,' the clerk said, with an edge to his voice. 'You must get your travel pass. Everyone who comes to Karlsbad has to register with the police. You should have given it to me as soon as you arrived.'

'It is in Teplitz, I told you. Why don't you contact the Eiche? They will confirm it. Ask them to send it.'

'They will not do that, sir. You have to collect it yourself. I am sorry, but without it you will have to leave. Police orders.'

Ludwig trudged up to his room. He kicked off his boots and lay on the bed. Antonie's face formed in his mind. He looked across to where they had sat. The chairs had been moved back to their original position by the chambermaid.

In his head he could hear Franz Brentano's voice. 'Goodbye, Ludwig. And look after yourself. We shall all miss you.' Ludwig had bowed formally to Franz and Antonie, and patted little Fanny's head. 'And you shall be the first in Vienna to know of our new arrival,' Franz had continued.

He swung his legs off the bed, put his boots back on and left the hotel. He turned down a side-street and strode off across the rising meadow. It was late afternoon and the sun was going down. The first chill of evening was beginning to break through the warmth, but Ludwig untied his shirt and enjoyed the feel of the air against his skin.

It had been easier than he had expected, seeing Franz again. Antonie's pregnancy had altered everything. What a totally unexpected turn of events, and how fortuitous! Franz, always so busy almost to the point of neglecting his wife, now solicitous and caring; she, flushed and glowing and enjoying his attention. And little Fanny was responding to the waters, breathing more easily.

Ludwig paused, then sat under a tree and looked down on the town. It was late summer, and many of the prosperous visitors had already left. He could barely believe that he, too, was now to depart.

Not long before an appalling piece of news had reached Karslbad, which had dominated the conversations round the coffee tables and in the bath-houses. The town of Baden, south of Vienna, which Ludwig knew so well, had been almost completely destroyed by fire. Archduke Anton's palace, Count Esterhazy's palace, the Augustine cloister, the main theatre, the Frauenkirche – the church which had stood for so long – as well as more than a hundred other buildings, had all been lost.

The town authorities in Karlsbad, knowing of Ludwig's presence, had persuaded him to give a concert in aid of the people of Baden. He had agreed and, with the Italian violinist Giovanni Polledro who also happened to be in the town, had played to a highly appreciative audience in the colonnade of the main spa building. The mayor and members of the council had publicly thanked him for helping them raise nearly a thousand florins – and now the police were telling him he had to leave!

He knew that a single word dropped in the ear of the mayor would suffice, but, in fact, he was ready to leave. He had seen Antonie and had the conversation he had so dreaded, but which had gone so unexpectedly well. And Franz had talked of all their plans for when they returned to Frankfurt . . .

The candlelights of Karlsbad twinkled below him in the half-light of dusk. He should walk back, he knew, but he did not want to hear voices or see faces. In his head, music revolved – a snatch of the violin sonata he had played with Polledro, the discord he had written for the brass in his new symphony, a furious run on the piano . . .

The birds had stopped singing and a bat swooped erratically, diving so low that he had to move his head. Ludwig stood up and the muscles in his legs ached. A warming bath in the sulphurous waters, followed by a carafe of red wine to ensure a good night's sleep before the journey back to Teplitz in the morning – that was what he needed.

He walked back down the hill, tying his shirt as he went. He was shivering now, astonished at how quickly the warmth in the air had yielded to the chill of night. He walked through the colonnade where he had given the concert and turned the large iron handle on the double doors. It was locked. The baths were closed.

He threw up his hands in despair, then let his arms fall limply against his sides. He returned to the Wiese, where candlelight danced invitingly in front windows. Holding one hand in front of his face as a disguise and hoping no one would talk to him, he went to the bar, ordered a carafe of wine and a pipe of tobacco, then sat at a small table at the back of the tavern.

He sighed with pleasure at the welcome taste of the wine, ignoring the pain in his throat when he swallowed. Moments later, he pulled deeply on the thick, pungent tobacco smoke, closed his mouth and breathed it out, calmingly, through his nose.

Every jolt of the carriage wheels sent a shaft of pain through Ludwig's head. His throat hurt and his skin was sore. His forehead was damp and clammy to the touch, chilly under his fingers, yet it felt to him as if it was burning.

After what seemed like an eternity the carriage drew into the Schlossplatz. Ludwig climbed out, almost dragging his bag across the cobbles, and went into the Eiche. The familiar face of the clerk looked up at him. 'Your travel pass, sir. We kept it for you. Will you be staying with us again?'

'What?' Ludwig could not hear the words clearly through the throbbing in his head, but the clerk's expectant smile made it obvious what he was asking. 'Oh, yes. At the back. I want total quiet.'

'That's fine, sir. The season is over and most people have left. And what a dreadful season it has been. We have never known such awful weather. Even the poor Empress and the kings and the dukes all returned home with coughs and colds. I shall keep your pass and register you again with the police. May I ask how long you will be staying?'

But Ludwig was already walking towards the stairs. The room was the smallest he had yet stayed in, but the little window looked out on to flat pasture. A peasant was bundling up hay, a dog at his heels. He wore a leather jerkin, tied with a stout cord against the early-autumn air.

Ludwig kicked off his boots, undid his shirt, lay down and pulled the blankets closer around his shoulders.

He slept the night through and awoke surprisingly refreshed. The throb in his head had lessened and although his throat was still sore some strong coffee would cure that. He threw open the window and breathed in. The air smelled dank, acrid

– the remains of a bonfire, no doubt, the ashes now sodden in the early-morning dew. A heavy mist hung low over the pasture, the bundles of hay showing through only as ghostly dark shapes.

He went downstairs and asked the clerk to have hot water and coffee sent up. Then he sat waiting for it, wondering what to do. How long had he been away from Vienna? Long enough certainly. He should think about returning. But work on the symphony was progressing: maybe he should stay to complete it.

The problem, he knew, was his health. There had been no improvement: the reverse, in fact. He did not feel well. He had not felt well since leaving Karlsbad. Was a fever threatening? If the weather did not improve, and it was unlikely to now, he might well succumb. And what would that mean for his hearing?

It seemed as if Doktor Malfatti was no better than Schmidt or anyone else. At least he had warned Ludwig that his hearing was unlikely to improve, just as Ludwig had suspected all along. And he could hardly blame Malfatti for the damp and the cold that had made his stay in Bohemia so wretched.

As he closed his eyes now, the whistle was in his ears. But it was tolerable. No dreadful crashing sounds and no unbearable pain. But if the fever came again, what then?

He drank the scalding coffee, splashed water on his face and arms, dried vigorously and dressed. He pulled on his jacket and boots, went downstairs and glanced at the clock: just after six. It was not yet light and the square was empty. He turned and walked up towards the Schlossgarten.

In the half-light and empty of people it seemed a different place from when he had walked there with Goethe . . .

Instead of going round the lake, he continued straight, enjoying the effort of climbing the incline. Soon he was walking in the thick woods that covered the hill as it rose away from the town. Above him he heard the warning cries of birds, angry and fearful that their territory had been invaded. Several times a sudden movement in the undergrowth caught his eye: probably a fox or a small deer scampering to safety. Even among the trees the thick mist penetrated, like a heavy blanket.

After a while he came out into a clearing, to find bundles of hay lying tied up like those he had seen from his window.

He sat at the base of a tree, ignoring the damp that penetrated his clothes to his skin. He wiped his forehead; it ran with rivulets of the moisture in the air.

He became aware he was growing hungry, so he stood up, brushed off the blades of grass that clung to his breeches and began the walk back through the forest.

At the Eiche he sat at a table in the small dining room and devoured a plate of ham and a side plate of eggs, topped with a dark sauce. When he left to return to his room, he saw a young woman sitting close to the reception desk. She caught his eye and, to his dismay, bounded over to him.

'Herr Beethoven. Amalie Sebald, soprano, from Berlin. You do not remember me, I know, though I have made your acquaintance. I have come to pay my respects to Europe's greatest composer.'

Ludwig did not know how to react. His first feeling was of relief that her voice was audible. That she was from Berlin meant her accent was accessible to him, and her words – spoken with disarming honesty – were flattering.

'We have met?'

'Yes, sir, and I shall not put any strain on your memory by reminding you. But I am here in Teplitz, with my mother, and I told her I would not miss the chance of renewing our acquaintance. May I invite you to the Schiff, where there is a piano, and I will sing for you?'

'The Schiff?' Ludwig frowned, then remembered that it was where Goethe had stayed, and where indeed there was a piano. 'Thank you, but really I have work to do.'

'Come, sir, please accompany me.' She spoke conspiratorially, but still clearly. 'It is much nicer there than here. Do not mind Mama. She is unwell and in bed so you will have no ceaseless chatter to cope with. We will talk only of music.'

Despite himself, Ludwig was smiling. Amalie was pretty and pert, her hair parted in the middle and gathered in bunches, which bounced with the lively movements of her head when she spoke. Her eyes shone animatedly and she clasped her hands in front of her each time she finished a sentence as singers do when they perform.

She had turned and was already moving towards the door. He followed. In fact, he rationalised, it *would* be relaxing to sit at the piano and play for a professional singer. So different from when he had tried to accompany himself in front of the great Goethe!

Amalie's voice, he quickly discovered, was light and airy, with a tremulous vibrato. She knew his songs well, and he noticed that she chose only songs of love: 'Adelaïde', which Leni Willmann had sung so beautifully, so long ago; 'To Hope', the song he had written for Josephine Brunsvik – his first instinct had been to say no when Amalie suggested it, but why should he mind? – and then, to his great delight, 'Mignon's Lied'.

She sang the last two lines of the first verse, her voice tripping lightly over the chords, an almost tangible smile in her voice, and on to the final couplet of Goethe's poem:

> That's where, that's where our path doth lead.
> Oh heav'nly Father, grant our need.

Ludwig stood up quickly, put his hands on her shoulders and kissed her fleetingly on both cheeks. She flushed, pointing over his shoulder.

A small group had gathered at the entrance to the room, their faces wreathed in smiles as they applauded. Amalie took her dress in both hands and curtsied.

To Ludwig's relief the impromptu audience left the room then, not asking for more music, and he sat in a plush chair. The music still revolved in his head. Amalie's voice, he knew, would not hurt him, but he did not want to have to talk.

A young man in a starched shirt and flowery waistcoat, his long dark hair almost touching his shoulders, walked towards them and put a tray down on the table. Coffee steamed on it and sugar-coated cakes glistened. Ludwig nodded his thanks, noticing that the waiter looked at Amalie and that she turned up her eyes at him coquettishly. He felt a twinge of envy.

Amalie poured the coffee and handed Ludwig a cup. His throat was still sore as he swallowed, making his eyes water.

'Are you all right, Herr Beethoven? You look . . . you seem . . .'

Her voice was as light as when she sang, and gentle on his ears, but in a different way from Antonie's. There was no depth to it; it was the voice of a young woman for whom the lessons of life still lay ahead.

He cleared his throat, ignoring the pain. 'I have not felt well for some days, and the journey from Karlsbad did not improve me.'

'You must stay in bed and I will bring you food,' she said, an earnest frown knitting her brows.

Ludwig refused politely, then asked, 'How long will you be in Teplitz?'

'Only another week. Mama would like to stay longer, but I have to return to the Singakademie. Actually,' she lowered her voice, 'I shall be pleased to return to Berlin. It is very . . . provincial here, isn't it?'

'It is. But I like the Bohemians. So different from the formality of the Viennese.'

'Are you staying long, Herr Beethoven?'

'I must return. I have work to do. I will take the waters a little more, then I will return to Vienna.'

He saw her eyes shine and her lips part as if something had occurred to her and she was trying to make up her mind whether to say it. He was convinced then that she would ask him to compose something for her.

'Herr Beethoven,' Amalie said, 'you must forgive my impertinence, but in Berlin your name is often spoken – especially at the Singakademie where Herr Zelter, the director, has made us learn your songs. He has told us that you are losing your hearing. We did not believe him. How can you be a musician if you are losing your hearing? And I can tell from our brief meeting, and the way you played the piano, and the way we are talking now, that it is not true. And when I return I shall tell them so.'

Chapter 6

When Ludwig awoke the next morning his skin was on fire, his head pounded and his ears howled. The fever had struck. Strangely, he was not unduly worried. It had been threatening for some time. The emotional strain of seeing Antonie again and saying farewell to her had drained him. The concert with Polledro – although everyone had assured him to the contrary – had not been a success. The man had a tenth of the talent of George Bridgetower, and Ludwig himself had not felt inspired.

Ludwig was no stranger to fever: how often had he been laid up in bed in Vienna, kind Nanette Streicher looking after him, making sure the doctor attended regularly?

Ignoring the pain in his head he got out of bed and went over to the window. It was the half-light before dawn and again the mist was thick. He opened the window and the air felt like a soothing face-cloth against his skin.

His skin was burning and he was now shivering uncontrollably. He climbed back into bed, and fell immediately into a deep but fitful sleep.

His dreams were wild and troubled. Antonie's lovely face, looking at him so longingly, transmuted before his eyes into the face of a whore, her lips bright red and smudged. When she spoke her voice was Johanna's, mocking him as she thrust the face of her child in front of him. His brother Carl, feeble and racked with pain, his cheeks flushed like their mother's in her final illness, pleaded with him to rescue Karl from his wicked, immoral wife.

He awoke late in the evening to find that the worst of the fever had passed. His skin, although still hot to the touch, no longer burned and the pain in his head had subsided.

He climbed from the bed, put on his breeches and boots and walked to the door. He suddenly felt weak and a wave of giddiness swept over him. For a moment he thought he might fall, but the unsteadiness passed.

He was aware, as he descended the stairs, that although there was no pain in his head, the heaviness inside his ears was worse.

When he reached the desk, the clerk's mouth opened but no sound came out. He repeated the words and as they reached Ludwig's ears they brought with them an intolerable whistle.

Ludwig leaned on the desk and looked at the man, who took a small pace backward. 'I . . . I am pleased to see you have recovered, sir. The chambermaid said you were unwell. We were going to call a doctor.'

'No, no doctor. I need food. And wine.'

'Certainly, sir. I will have some brought to your room. What would you like?'

Ludwig realised that the clerk's words were becoming clearer, which lifted his spirits. 'Just some soup. Soup and wine.'

'Of course, sir. I will arrange it.'

Ludwig went back upstairs. He had found it easier to hear the clerk the more he spoke. Was his hearing really worse, or was it just the immediate after-effects of the fever? It had to be the fever. Whenever he was ill it was always his hearing that paid the price.

That night he slept deeply, undisturbed by wild dreams.

He awoke feeling as if all the strength had gone out of his body. He tried to stand up, but his legs buckled. Why was he so weak? He wanted more than anything to walk again in the forest, feel the fresh air on his face. But he did not have the strength.

Instead, he began work. His ears, as dull as they were the day before, could hear nothing, yet in his head he heard the full orchestra. Grabbing a sheet of manuscript paper, he wrote on the top 'Movt. IV, Allegro vivace' and, as a reminder, Timpani in F, an octave apart.

Hah! he thought. That will provide them with their first surprise. No one had ever done that before – not Mozart, not Haydn. Simply, it was never done. Both tuned to the same note, but an octave apart? A waste of harmonic potential, they'll say. And in the middle of a piece? You cannot do it.

But I am deaf, I will reply, and what matters to me therefore, as much as harmony, is rhythm. He wrote a lithe swift phrase, beginning with triplets and turning almost on a single note, repeated a semitone higher. '*Pianissimo*,' he said, scribbling *pp* on the paper.

The phrase continued, answered by high descending staccato crotchets, the phrase again, quieter, quieter, '*Piano-pianissimo!*' he shouted, writing *ppp* this time. And – suddenly –

He shouted, 'C sharp! Yes, C sharp!' He wrote unison octaves of C sharp, *fortissimo*. C sharp! Why? In a movement in the key of F. Unrelated, alien. A sustained minim to bring the music almost to a halt, before the main theme takes off again *fortissimo*.

He threw down the pen, exhausted. He had the shape of the final movement of the Symphony in F. The rest could wait. The surprise he had wanted, the shock, was there. C sharp!

He must have drifted into a light sleep, because a faint knock on the door woke him. A chambermaid brought in a tray. The smell alone made the saliva run in his mouth. She handed him a note.

> Dear Sir!
> To help the famous musician's faculties to function even when his health suffers, I offer him this humble fare.
>
> A. Sebald, soprano

He gasped and smiled, then signalled to the maid to wait. Grabbing the pen, he wrote on the bottom of the note:

> Frln Sebald
> I demand you send me a bill. I demand it. Meanwhile I thank you, and give you strict orders not to repeat your kindness.
>
> L van Bthvn

The next day the same thing happened. This time Amalie's note said:

> My tyrant commands me to send him the bill – which is:
> One chicken – 1 gulden
> The soup – 9 kreuzer

Ludwig scribbled on the bottom of it:

> Tyrants do not pay. But the bill must be settled all the same. And that could be done most easily if you would come yourself, NB with the bill, to your embarrassed tyrant.

His heart skipped as he folded the paper and handed it back to the chambermaid. He should not have written that, but he wanted to see Amalie again, with her smiling face and laughing eyes, and he wanted to talk with her. He wanted to test his hearing, to know if he could hold a conversation.

That afternoon, feeling stronger than he had for days, he decided to go out. He walked on to the meadow he could see from his window. The ground was stubbly under his feet and he relished the cracking sounds as he trod down the stalks that were left from the harvest. The cool air felt good on his face. He walked to a tree that stood on a small mound and sat on the bare earth. All around him was silence. Autumn was yielding to winter. The birds had migrated. The clouds, dark and heavy, threatened yet more rain!

He sank his head in his hands, listening to the whoosh of waves crashing on the shore, each crash coinciding with the beat of his heart. He screwed his eyes tight shut and forced the sounds of his symphony into his head. Slowly, distorted at first, they became clearer, until finally he could hear the whole orchestra.

But when he stood up the sounds so dear to him dissipated and the whooshing returned, giving way moments later to a sharp, high-pitched whistle. By the time he had returned to his room he knew he had not yet shaken off the illness.

Amalie's note was abrupt, telling him it would be improper for her to come to his room. He let out an exasperated sigh. Had he upset her? He had not meant to. God, he thought, why do things always go so wrong?

He decided it was time to take action. First he lay on the bed and slept lightly for an hour. It had the effect he desired, and he got up feeling a little more refreshed. His head still hurt, but he could cope with it. Amalie had stopped sending him food, for which he was grateful, but he wanted to be sure he had not offended her.

He walked to the Goldenes Schiff and wrote a note to her, telling her he was downstairs and waiting for her. When she arrived, her smile told him he had worried unduly. She stood before him, hands clasped, head inclined.

'Amalie, I wanted to thank you for the food. You were most kind.'

He braced himself for her voice, hoping so much that it would penetrate his ears.

'It was nothing, Herr Tyrant. I was pleased to do it. I was looking after Mama here, and you there.'

He could not make out her words.

'Come, let us walk a little, Amalie. I want to speak to you.' He took her arm, ignoring her slight resistance, and led her to the door. They walked slowly up the hill towards the Schlossplatz. 'Amalie, my hearing is worse. Forgive me if I offended you with my note. I wanted only . . . I fear it is going for ever. Soon I might not be able to hear music. You were not offended, were you?'

There was a bench on the grass set back from the hill and she walked to it. He followed.

He sat and looked at her and smiled. He reached into his pocket and brought out five florins. She recoiled. 'If you do not take them, *you* will offend *me*, and I will compose a song for you that is impossible to sing!'

She smiled and took the coins. 'Herr Tyrant,' her face suddenly fell, 'Mama and I leave for home in two days. If you are well enough, I would like very much to sing for you again.'

She was speaking close to him and mouthing her words distinctly.

'If I am well enough, Amalie.'

Why could he not shake off this wretched illness? His head pounded again with a pain that was almost unbearable. He dreamed that he was playing the piano and Amalie was singing, her hands folded demurely. Her mother was sitting in a chair, but she was grotesque: at one point she hauled herself out of her chair, came over to him and rapped his fingers. 'Evil man!' she hissed. 'To make such a suggestion to my daughter.'

He forced himself awake. He did not know how long he had slept. It was dark outside. Which night was it? Had he lost a day?

He fell asleep again. He was aware at one stage of someone in the room, but he could not open his eyes.

How much longer he slept he did not know, but when he awoke finally he felt better. He sat up and he screwed up his eyes against the glare of daylight. The noise in his ears was dreadful, – whooshing, whistling, and so was the pain.

Enough, he thought. I must return to Vienna. I must see Doktor Malfatti. He will be able to do nothing but I cannot go on like this.

He stood up, steadying himself against the bed. The weakness again.

Then he saw two letters on the table. He looked at them.

One was a note from Amalie: he recognised the writing and the envelope said simply his name and hotel. The other was in a larger envelope with stamps and a full address. There was a vague familiarity about the writing but he could not place it. He turned it over and his heart sank. It was from his brother Carl.

He opened Amalie's note first.

My good and most worthy Herr Tyrant
  Your poor servant is so sad to hear that you are again unwell, made all the more so by the fact that she can no longer render you assistance.
  Mama and I leave by the next stage for Berlin. I shall for ever remember the time we made music together.
  I do hope your health improves swiftly, and with it your hearing. I have no doubt it will.

Your servant in music
Amalie Sbld

He drew a deep breath. Sweet Amalie, without a care in the world and with a singing voice that would always be admired. Soon she would marry and have a family, and live a *normal* life.

With a heavy heart he opened the other envelope and unfolded the single sheet of paper.

Vienna, 15 Sept., 1812

Brother
  I hope this finds you well. My health continues to deteriorate and I feel weaker with every day. Our brother Johann has written that he is to marry in October.
  I am convinced this marriage, if it is allowed to take place, will bring shame on the family and the name of Beethoven. Will you travel to Linz and stop him? My health forbids me from undertaking such a mission, and I know he greatly admires you and will be more likely to heed your advice.
  My wife Johanna believes we should not interfere, but she is a truly stupid woman, as you realised, sadly, before I did. My son Karl is in good health and a fine young Beethoven.

Yr brother
Carl Caspar

BOOK TWO

Chapter 1

'So, brother Ludwig, you choose to travel to the provinces and your fame travels with you.' Johann van Beethoven tossed a newspaper in front of Ludwig.

It was the *Linzer Musik-Zeitung*, the local music paper. Ludwig picked it up and read the paragraph Johann had ringed in red crayon.

10 October 1812

Now we are fortunate to have the long-wished-for pleasure of having within our city the Orpheus and great musical poet of our time, Herr L. van Beethoven; and if Apollo is favourable to us we shall also have an opportunity to admire his art and report on it to the readers of this journal.

'Well, they won't,' he said gruffly.

'Come now, Ludwig. They do you the honour of mentioning your arrival and you treat them with contempt. I notice that they did not see fit to mention your brother, the great apothecary of the city, who tends to the sick and wounded.'

The sound of Johann's voice grated on Ludwig's ears. He was still tired from the journey to Linz. It had taken almost two days from Teplitz and he had decided not to stop overnight in Prague. Johann, surprised by his unexpected arrival, had not made him welcome, obviously surmising the reason for the visit.

Ludwig's hearing had worsened in a way he had not anticipated: previously the noises in his ears had accompanied the pain in his head, and the dullness and heaviness had allowed words to penetrate, albeit shrouded in a thick fog. Now the noises were still there, although they had lessened, as had the pain. But Ludwig was aware of a new tenderness in his head, as if his nerve endings had been exposed. He heard voices as distorted and jagged sounds. Johann's voice had always been shrill and surprisingly high-pitched for such a large man. Now it sounded coarse and rough.

'Johann,' he said, deciding it was better to broach the subject right away, 'my hearing has worsened. I have a lot of trouble hearing voices. You must speak clearly, and instruct everyone else to.'

Ludwig felt a slight relief at having raised the subject that he had for so long resisted acknowledging. He looked towards the paper again, flattered now that he had been mentioned in such terms. 'Who is responsible for that?' he asked Johann.

'The venerable Kapellmeister of Linz, His Excellency Franz Xaver Glöggl. He receives details of prominent arrivals from the police.'

'It is impossible to travel without having one's tracks followed.'

Johann went to look out over the main square of Linz towards the fountain. When he turned back to Ludwig his face was serious. 'I know why you have come here, Ludwig,' he said, raising his eyebrows, which drew attention to his right eye, with its slipped pupil and drooping lid. 'Look, I am thirty-six years old. I am a busy man. I run a successful business, which occupies me every moment of the day, and frequently at night if there is an emergency. I need someone to keep house for me, cook my meals –'

'I understood she did that already.' Ludwig could not disguise the contempt in his voice.

'So what does that matter?' Johann cried. 'Have you done any better, my famous brother?'

'She has a child already.'

Johann nodded, and Ludwig thought he detected a slight sagging of his shoulders. 'Yes,' he said, in a quieter voice. 'The father left her. He lives in Vienna. It was not her fault.' Johann moved away from the window and sat in a chair. 'Anyway, it is none of your business. I am not just your youngest brother any more. I am a grown man.'

Ludwig did not want to continue the conversation; Johann's voice was hurting his ears. But it was evident from his brother's face that there was more he wanted to say.

'I have been very successful, you know, Ludwig. More successful than Carl, much more. And probably more successful than you. My comings and goings might not be written about in the papers, I may not be famous throughout

Europe, but I have become a wealthy man. A pillar of society.'

'And if you take up with your . . . your *housekeeper*, what will they say then?'

Johann smiled, his face given a certain slyness by his drooping eyelid. 'That shows how little you understand, my brother. She is a local girl. If I marry her, it will go down well.'

'If that is the only –'

'Ludwig, you do not understand how things happen here. This is not Vienna. In Vienna I would be nothing. But here, everyone knows the Zur Goldenen Krone. It is the foremost apothecary shop in Linz. Remember, when I first came here I had nothing. I was in debt. But I worked hard. I remember when we were children Father used to call me lazy. "You will never make anything of yourself," he used to say. Carl was always running around as if he had important things to do, but it was just an act. He fooled everybody. And you . . . Father said he didn't understand you. Mother said so too. But at least you could play the piano and impress people –'

'Enough, Johann.'

'No, I will not take orders from you the way I used to. I am successful, despite what they all said.'

'You are not popular, is that true? That is what Carl told me.'

'Hah! He did, did he? Jealousy, that is all that is.'

'You sold medicines to the French. The invaders.'

'Are they not human beings? If they are ill or wounded and they come to me for bandages, can I refuse? And I assure you I was not the only one. How do you think the coffee-houses made so much money, and the taverns and restaurants? By selling to the people of Linz? These bourgeois provincial burghers who walk around as if they are so important. It taught them a lesson, having the French army billeted here. And, anyway, we are not Austrians. We are Germans.'

Ludwig did not know what to say. He was sorry Johann had brought up such painful memories of the past, but in a way it cleared the air between them.

'When will I meet your – the woman you – What is her name? I don't believe you have told me.'

'Therese. Therese Obermayer. You will like her. I know you will.'

*   *   *

Ludwig stood at the back of the cathedral, gazing around him in awe. The sun was sending shafts of light through the upper windows, illuminating a million tiny motes that flitted in the air like minuscule insects. There was a smell of mustiness and incense. The side walls of the cathedral, which were divided into a series of alcoves, were the most ornate he had seen. There were, too, marble statues adorned with gold filigree, elaborate gold decorations at the tops of pillars, a gold-fronted pulpit and, the crowning glory, the huge altar. Above it hung a Renaissance painting of Jesus Christ, standing in a bucolic setting, flanked by pillars; and above that a sumptuous golden carving of cherubs, flowers, tiny animals, all gazing up at a stone figure of the risen Christ, topped with golden spears of sunlight reaching up to the domed roof of the cathedral. Ludwig caught his breath at the elaborate beauty. In the front pew an elderly woman knelt at prayer. The walls of the cathedral seemed to enclose an area of extreme piety, reverence and devotion.

He was reluctant to move, to break the spell it had cast on him. He also marvelled that here, in the cathedral, his ears seemed to be at rest. Soon the peace would be shattered by voices, but at least in this building he would be able to find peace.

He looked over his shoulder towards the one artefact that had so far eluded him and which he knew would be there. Half-way up the wall, on a wooden platform supported by thick beams, sat the organ. It was smaller than he had expected. Sooner or later he would play on it, but alone, with no priest to decide when and what he should play. He was pleased to find that Linz took such an interest in music. A musical newspaper, a Kapellmeister with an office in the cathedral. It was exactly what he needed to immerse himself in as an antidote to the domestic crisis he was confronting with his brother.

He walked through the arch that led to a small passage with rooms off to the side and located the Kapellmeister's.

When he went in a small man, red-faced and bald, his white cassock billowing like a sail, leaped to his feet and walked towards him, hands outstretched. 'Herr Beethoven, what an honour. Please –' He directed Ludwig to a chair and pulled one up himself.

Ludwig allowed a small smile to lift the corners of his mouth. Kapellmeister Glöggl was clearly nervous – overawed even – and Ludwig found that appealing. There was none of the stiff formality of Vienna, the wigs and frock-coats, the nobility conscious always of rank.

'If – if I had had more notice, I would have arranged for my choir and musicians, all my –'

Ludwig held up a hand. His initial worry about hearing Glöggl's voice had dissipated. The Kapellmeister's voice was rich and mellifluous; he spoke as if at any moment his speech would become song. And he leaned towards Ludwig and enunciated clearly. He must know, thought Ludwig.

'We are so honoured to have you in our humble city. May I ask how long you intend staying?'

Ludwig shrugged. 'I don't know . . . It depends. I am with my brother.'

'Ah, yes. Herr Beethoven the apothecary. He is a well-respected burgher of this city. But not a musician, I fear.' Glöggl coughed discreetly. 'Herr Beethoven, do you have any plans? Will you grace us with your musical genius while you are in our city? I can arrange everything.'

Ludwig had taken an immediate liking to this man, who was so full of admiration for him, and he had expected the request, albeit not quite so soon. He had already thought about it. If he gave a recital, it would surely improve the standing of his brother – reflected glory. But if he performed once, he would be asked to perform again. And the truth was that with such an obvious worsening in his hearing he was not sure how well he would be able to play.

Glöggl caught his hesitation. 'Oh, I am so sorry. Do please forgive me, Herr Beethoven. How precipitate of me. But you do not know what an honour for a simple trombonist like me –'

'Trombonist?'

'Yes, that is my instrument. I am orchestral director, of course, but before I took up that arduous duty, I made my living as a trombone player and teacher.'

'It is a fine instrument. Not used enough.'

'And, sir, that is a charge of which you yourself are not guilty. Your symphony in C minor, fourth movement, three trombones. Three! To produce a sound that is unrivalled.'

Glöggl, arms waving, sang the opening theme of the final movement of Ludwig's fifth symphony.

Ludwig was warming rapidly to Glöggl, who took such a conspicuous interest in his music.

'Ah, yes, sir. You shall hear our trombonists, Herr Beethoven.

We have four in Linz, all taught by me. Does Vienna have more? I doubt it. They will play here, in the cathedral, on All Saint's Day. I shall be writing a sequence for them . . . a simple sequence . . . just harmonies.'

'Why will they –?'

'The service for All Saints, sir. On November the second. At the solemn moment when we remember all the martyrs to our faith, with the congregation on its knees, I shall have our trombonists play an *equale*. Perfect, do you not think?'

'An *equale*?'

'Such as they play at our funerals here in Linz. It is traditional. Four trombones, of equal weight, playing a sequence of harmonies –' He leaned forward, shaking his head. 'So moving, sir. And within the walls of this sacred building . . . Ah, yes. I hope my poor and feeble effort will do them credit.'

Ludwig's mouth twitched. 'Can I hear one of these . . . *equali*?'

'Oh, yes, Herr Beethoven. Indeed you can. It will do me the greatest honour. Will you allow me to arrange a soirée and my men of brass will play for you? My good friend Count von Dönhoff I know will oblige. And, sir, do not concern yourself. I shall not ask you to play. No one will. You will be our honoured guest, and it is you who will listen, not play.'

Chapter 2

Ludwig was astounded. His brother's fiancée was undoubtedly the most stupid, imbecilic individual he had ever come across. She was at least ten years younger than Johann, with the voice of a girl who was not yet out of her teenage years. Her accent was thick with the lilt of the Austrian countryside. Ludwig had trouble hearing her and when he told her to speak up it made no difference. Her face was round, almost plump, as was her figure. She wore a peasant skirt, which billowed from the waist, and above it a white cotton blouse.

So far, all Ludwig had been able to get her to say was: 'Therese Obermayer, sir, and greatly honoured, sir, to make your acquaintance.'

'Have you nothing else to say for yourself, woman? Mmh?'

Johann snapped, 'She is nervous, Ludwig. Can you not see that? Anyone would be, meeting you for the first time. You are not the most welcoming of individuals. Go now, Therese. Prepare lunch.' He landed a sharp slap on her backside as she turned. She yelped and hurried from the room, clearly relieved at her release.

Ludwig's mouth hung open. Finally he looked at his brother. 'You are going to give that woman the name of Beethoven? You cannot. You must not.'

Anger flared in Johann's face. 'Do not talk like that to me, Ludwig. You are not our father. I intend marrying her. It will be a convenient arrangement. She will keep house while I run my business. She is from Linz so she will bring more people to my shop.'

'But – but – she will be mother to your children. That woman! It is not possible, do you hear, Johann? I will not allow it!'

Johann could not control himself. '*You* will not allow it! Ludwig, if you continue like this, I will order you out of my house. *Do you hear?*' His face was close to Ludwig's and he was exaggerating his mouth movements.

A wave of sadness flowed over Ludwig. First there was Carl and the dreadful mistake he had made. And now Johann was going to make a mistake just as bad.

He stood up, forcing strength into his knees, which had weakened during the quarrel, and crossed to the window, which overlooked the Hauptplatz towards the old Danube bridge. To the right, a little downriver, men were unloading a vessel, their backs bent under barrels and sacks. He thought of Bonn and how, as a child, when he and his brothers were playing in the sandpit on the bank of the Rhine, he had watched men doing the same.

'I am sorry I shouted,' he heard his brother say, 'but you drove me to it. You must leave me alone to make my own decisions.'

Ludwig shook his head. 'You are making a decision you will regret for the rest of your life. It is my duty as your elder brother to warn you.'

'The date is set,' Johann said flatly. 'November the eighth. The banns have been posted. There is nothing to stop it now.'

Kapellmeister Glöggl rubbed his hands with glee. 'Herr Beethoven, sir, I cannot tell you how happy . . . Please do come in. Our host will . . . Here he is. Sir, this is Count von Dönhoff, a senior burgher of our fair city and one of its most generous benefactors.'

'Sir, your servant,' the Count said, in a clear strong voice, bowing his head but not too deeply. He had an open expectant face, which Ludwig liked. 'Welcome to my humble establishment, where I hope you will do us the honour of eating and drinking with us, after you have heard the music that the Kapellmeister has arranged for you. Will you come through to the music room?'

Ludwig followed the two men into the salon, where a small group of people stood and applauded, all smiling faces directed at him. It was good to be among musicians and music lovers after the trauma of trying to deal with Johann's problem.

'My son Franz,' Glöggl said, 'and my four men of brass, Halter, Grossmund, Nagel and Baum. They will play an *equale* for you before we eat.'

Ludwig smiled at the men, who all held their trombones. Young Glöggl, Ludwig thought, was a smaller version of his father. His eyes flitted across the room to the piano, which was covered in a sheet.

'Gentlemen, let us begin with the music right away. Herr Beethoven, this *equale* was composed by Johann Rudolf Ahle in the free city of Mülhausen a century and a half ago. We played it in our cathedral last month at the funeral of one of our prominent citizens.'

Ludwig sat in the chair that was brought to him, crossed his legs and folded his hands on his lap. How rare, he thought, to be listening to music, instead of being urged to play it! He tilted his head back and watched the four musicians blow into their instruments to warm them and test their slides.

Then they brought their trombones up to their shoulders and, at a nod from the lead player, began.

There was a moment's pause before the sound, deep and sonorous, swept over the room. If Ludwig had had any concern as to the effect on his ears it was soon dispelled: the music, regular and unchallenging, was soothing and consisted of pure chords, linked by an occasional short sequence from the lead player. There were no unexpected key changes or contrasts, or any variation of dynamics. For what it was, it was fine, and the players were performing it well. But . . .

At the end there was restrained applause, the listeners' response to the music's funereal quality. Kapellmeister Glöggl hurried to the front of the seats. 'If you will permit me, Count, Herr Beethoven, we will now hear one of my own humble efforts.' He turned and placed some new music on the stands. He stood in front of the players, hands raised. Then he began to conduct.

The chords this time were linked by small flourishes, taken in turn by each of the players. Long, sustained chords, interspersed with sprightly little runs. Glöggl's arms moved with total regularity, swinging out in unison. His body did not move so the trombonists played with clockwork precision, minim and crotchet chords divided by quaver runs.

Applause, as polite and uniform as the music, greeted the final chord. Glöggl's face, when he turned, was flushed with excitement and pride, as if he had just led a performance of one of Mozart's great symphonies in the Burgtheater.

The sound of the applause was, as usual, harsh on Ludwig's ears and he half closed his eyes against it. Instantly the Kapellmeister was at his side. 'Herr Beethoven, we have not offended you?'

'Just my hearing, Glöggl. It causes me problems.'

'Then we shall offer you the finest food and wine in Linz, sir. Count Dönhoff has arranged a meal befitting Europe's most celebrated musician in the dining hall. We shall not delay. Will you accompany us, and while we eat we can discuss the music? Your opinion would be valued above words.'

Ludwig said nothing for a moment: his ears had to come to terms with the changing sounds assaulting them. Then just as Glöggl began to speak again, he said, 'I need a little air. I shall walk for a few minutes.'

'I understand, sir. And may I join you, to ensure–?'

'No. Thank you, Kapellmeister. I prefer to be alone.'

Count von Dönhoff's house was one of the largest on the Hauptplatz, on the other side of the square from Johann's apothecary shop. It was an October evening and the air was cool with the onset of winter. What a year! Ludwig thought. Nothing but rain . . . and misery. He took a deep breath as the face of Antonie Brentano came into his mind. So soft, so gentle, so unattainable.

How deeply I loved her, he thought. Yet every time he thought of her, he could hear rain. Prague and the Charles Bridge . . . The rain splashing down on the umbrella and running down their faces as they kissed . . .

My angel, my all, my very self . . . He remembered the tortured letter he had struggled over, still lying at the bottom of his bag.

He stubbed his foot against a cobble as Antonie's image yielded to the fleshy peasant face of Therese Obermayer. Johann. Nikolaus Johann. Always the laziest of the three brothers, more concerned with his dress and how he looked than with matters of importance. Yet now look at him. A leading citizen of Linz – but at what cost? By trading with the French he had harmed his own reputation and sullied the name of Beethoven. And now he intended sullying that exalted name still further.

I must stop him! *I must.* It is my duty.

A solitary carriage rumbled across the square, the driver's shoulders hunched against the cold night air. The noise of the wheels clattering over the cobbles would soon begin to hurt Ludwig's ears. He turned back to the house. He needed to hear another kind of sound. A purer, sacred sound, which he alone was capable of creating.

He climbed the stairs and walked into the entrance hall. From the right he heard the steady hum of conversation, punctuated by the irregular clatter of cutlery on plates. Normally he would loathe such an occasion, with its formality and the difficulties it would present with conversation. But here in Linz it was different. He liked the unpretentious Glöggl and Dönhoff was transparently honoured that Ludwig had come to his house – with him there was none of the fawning of Prince Lichnowsky or the correctness of Prince Lobkowitz. Here was a man who listened to music because he loved it, not because it was a necessary social activity.

Without thinking he went towards the music room. There was nobody in it but the candles on the walls still burned. He closed the door behind him and walked towards the piano in the corner. He pulled off the cover and dropped it in a crumpled heap by the wall. He stroked the dark wood, which glowed in the candlelight. He caressed the ivory keys with his fingers, again looked round the room to check that he was alone and sat on the stool.

Plain chords at first, such as the trombonists had played. A flat, the warmth of the black keys. Slowly his fingers wandered, the notes of the chords spread out, themes growing underneath them. He was not performing or even testing new ideas. He was simply talking. His language.

Some themes he allowed to go, some he developed. One moment he would play on the beat, the next off it. Key changes occurred every few bars, and never to a related one. *Forte, piano, forte, piano* – just like in conversation.

Now I am the equal of anyone, he thought, as he played. I can converse, discuss, argue, agree, make jokes, be serious . . . and my hearing causes me no problems.

His back was arched, his arms outstretched as his fingers caressed the keys. The next moment he had hunched forward, head low, fingers rising and falling in chopping movements, left hand crossing over right.

In his head he heard the music he wanted to play and knew that he was creating it with his fingers. Was he hearing what he played? What did it matter? He could hear the music in his head. And he played more, his hands spanning the keyboard. My music. *My* music. Music I will never write down or give to a publisher. Not structured, like a formal composition.

Suddenly he remembered that he was supposed to be having dinner. He had most likely caused offence, as he often had in Vienna. There he did not mind; sometimes he wanted to. Here it was different. He liked Glöggl and Dönhoff, and the trombonists who had tried so hard. And as he thought of them a wave of hunger and thirst swept over him. A glass of wine, after playing for so long at the piano! The speed of his playing increased, a long slow *crescendo* that culminated in a series of chords, all major, through the keys chromatically, ending with a massive chord with all ten fingers two octaves apart.

He kept his hands on the keys to allow the sounds – the glorious, rich sounds – to fade in his head. And as they faded the curtains slowly came down, the familiar oppressive silence. But there was no pain and no dreadful noise.

As he entered the dining hall a harsh noise swept over him. Everyone was standing and applauding, their faces wreathed in smiles of appreciation.

A weakness came over him as the sound rocked him. He wanted to tell them to stop, that they were hurting his ears. But in fact – and unusually for him – he was grateful for their appreciation. They had made no request of him, not pleaded with him to play, so he smiled, and thanked them. Then he put out his arm to steady himself, but his hand came down on the edge of a serving table and a small pile of dishes fell off it, clattering to the ground and smashing. He looked down in horror, the sound jangling in his ears. Glöggl was immediately at his side, his grip strong and reassuring on Ludwig's arm.

'Come, sir. Be seated and drink some wine.' Ludwig allowed himself to be led to the table, took the glass of wine that was put in front of him and sipped it. He reached for a jug of water that stood close but a servant anticipated his move and filled a glass for him. Ludwig drank it thirstily and followed it with more wine.

He was aware that Count Dönhoff, opposite him, was on his feet and beckoning for silence. 'I shall say just a very few words, so as to allow you to eat and drink without delay. We have been privileged to hear tonight the flowering of the greatest genius the art of music has produced. That is what I believe. And when we are all old men we will tell our grandchildren we heard it. Herr Beethoven, our debt to you is incalculable. Will you all please raise your glasses to the great genius in our midst?'

Ludwig wished Dönhoff had said nothing, but his words had been so genuinely spoken that he found himself smiling.

'And,' Dönhoff continued, his face spreading into a grin, 'I for one will have a permanent reminder of his genius. I have been informed by my servant, sir, that a number of strings on my piano have broken, unable to cope with the demands those final chords put upon them. And they shall not be repaired. I will preserve my piano in exactly the state you left it.' He added, 'But I shall replace the crockery!'

There was a burst of laughter, in which Ludwig gladly joined. 'I apologise for both your piano and plates,' he said, as the laughter subsided. 'But I appreciate your kind – and unnecessary – words. Now, do not let me hold up the dinner any longer.'

Servants handed out plates covered with cold meat and filled glasses.

'May I ask your opinion, sir, on my men of brass?' Glöggl asked – remembering, to Ludwig's delight, to speak close to his ear and firmly.

'Highly commendable, Glöggl. Highly commendable. They enjoyed their playing. Nothing is as important as that. Ignore wrong notes. I tell them that in Vienna constantly. What matters is the spirit of the music.'

'Yes, yes. Quite. And my own . . . my poor . . . my rather feeble –'

'Glöggl, you are as fine a musician as I have met. Shall I tell you why? Not because of your skills or your artistry, but because you enjoy music. D'you hear?' Ludwig sipped his wine. 'You *enjoy* it. Nothing is as important as that, as I said. So be proud of what you have written.'

'Thank you, Herr Beethoven. I shall compose an *equale* for All Saint's Day with renewed vigour.'

'You shall have an *equale*, Glöggl, in return for your hospitality,' Ludwig replied.

'Sir, you do me – and, indeed, this town – more honour than you know. May I tell the assembled company?'

Ludwig put a restraining hand on the Kapellmeister's arm. 'No, Glöggl. Not now. I do not want to be the centre of attention again.' His face clouded as a thought entered his mind. 'Tell me, Glöggl. A little bit of advice in return. My brother intends to make an ill-turned marriage. He is –'

Glöggl moved closed to Ludwig and spoke clearly but so that no one else could hear. 'I know, Herr Beethoven. We all know. The whole of Linz knows. She . . . she has a reputation.'

Ludwig caught his breath. So his suspicions were not ill founded. 'What can I . . . ?'

'Difficult, most difficult. But I understand your concern. Why don't you talk to the Bishop? He might be able . . . since he has to give consent to all marriages. Yes, talk to the Bishop. I will arrange it for you.'

Chapter 3

'My dear sir,' the Bishop said, 'I understand your concerns perfectly. But, if I am not mistaken, both parties are consenting adults. They desire this marriage.'

'She has a child already. The father is in Vienna.'

The Bishop shifted in his seat. 'It is a sad state of affairs, I grant you. But as far as I can see there is no doctrinal reason why they should not marry. They are not contravening any of God's laws. As far as the laws of man go . . .' His words drifted off. Ludwig concentrated for a moment to be sure he had heard correctly.

'What are you suggesting?'

'It is not for me to say, but if it were to be found that she was married previously a second marriage would be impossible. Unless the divorce was in order. In any case, divorce or no divorce, that would prevent the marriage from taking place in church. I am sure your brother is a devout man, and if he were not able to marry in church, maybe . . .'

Again he lifted his shoulders, then looked away as if to indicate there was nothing more to be said.

Ludwig's mood fitted perfectly the composition of the *equale*. In fact, he decided to explore the genre a little further than he had intended and compose three pieces. Three *equali* for four trombones.

Solid chords to open the first, to be played in perfect unison, joined not by runs but by equally plangent passages for a solo trombone, key changes, unison runs, a *crescendo* to a *forte* discord, a second *crescendo* to a second discord, then a repeat of the minor opening; a brief development section ending on two mysterious chords, paving the way for the second *equale*.

The major key now, from darkness into light, despair into hope. Again, unison chords, whose sounds, Ludwig knew, would reverberate off the ancient walls of the cathedral. Key changes, but never to the expected key. A brief minor section, but the major returns. Death to resurrection.

Still the major for the third *equale*. Positive now, confident chords, an affirmation of the afterlife. The briefest of the three. All three together would take only a few minutes to play. But everything that was Beethoven was there: interrupted cadences, unexpected key changes, emphasis off the beat, sudden changes of dynamics . . .

He looked at what he had written. Wenzel Schlemmer the copyist would be proud of him. It was neatly laid out, perfectly legible. He would give it to Glöggl to copy into four parts. There would be ample time for rehearsal before 2 November. Hah! How they wish in Vienna that I was always so obliging, he thought.

Ludwig felt ill at ease sitting opposite the man in a uniform of dull grey, edged with green, that looked as if it had been out in the sun for too long. His face was pinched and dour, the desk in front of him covered in a disordered mass of papers, and Ludwig knew before he had uttered a word that his voice would match his appearance: small and strained.

'My brother, the apothecary on the Hauptplatz, wishes to marry a woman who may have been married before and who has a child. I am the senior member of the family and I wish to prevent it. It is unsuitable. His Grace the Bishop advised me –'

The official held up his hand. 'Do you believe, sir, that the council has the power to do such a thing?' The voice was that of an oboe with a worn reed.

'If he has contravened the law –'

'He has not, sir,' the official said, with sudden force. 'I know the young lady in question. She has not been married before. She is a Linzer, born and bred in our city and proud of it. You people from Vienna, you think –'

'I am not from Vienna. I am from Bonn.'

The man waved his hand dismissively. 'There is nothing I can do for you, sir. And if an offence against the law has been committed, then it is the concern of the police.'

Ludwig wanted to banish the voice of this man from his head. As he left he summoned the deep burnished sound of the trombones to replace it.

Ludwig sat at the back of the cathedral, watching Glöggl rehearse the four trombonists. The pieces were not difficult to play, all in the middle register and demanding nothing further than sixth position on the slide, arm extended with elbow locked. What was difficult was playing the chords in perfect unison. There must be no stray sound from any of the four instruments.

Glöggl was talking to his musicians, drawing their attention to certain passages in the manuscript. Heads nodded, questions were asked and answered. He raised his arms. Two trombonists lifted their instruments to their lips. Yes, Ludwig thought, rehearse them, Glöggl. Make them see into the music, beyond the notes.

Moments later, the full sonority of the opening chords swept over him. His breathing became shallow and he felt a tingle creep over his skin as the trombones played the *crescendo* towards the discord. Perfect. *Perfect*.

From the minor to the major. No vibrato. Good. Ludwig saw the intensity of the players' faces. This is how music should be made, he thought. The musicians must *want* to play well.

Such small pieces, and destined never to be heard outside Linz. My gift to the city.

There were two men, one sitting, one pacing the floor with a hand under his chin. This second man, the senior of the two judging by the shreds of ribbon that decorated his chest, looked sideways at Ludwig. Two tall hats, round and shiny black with small peaks, stood on the table at which the other man sat. It was he who spoke to Ludwig.

'Are you alleging that a crime has been committed, sir? If you are, we shall have to investigate.'

Ludwig said nothing.

'We shall need details of your allegation.'

There was a howling in Ludwig's ears, so intense that at first he believed it must be coming from outside but as it was not troubling the two policemen he knew that his ears were flaring up again.

Johann. Johann and his ridiculous, *immoral* intentions. Stupid, ignorant Johann and his – his strumpet of a housekeeper.

'Herr Bethoffen?' the policeman said, looking down at the paper to check the name. 'Your allegation, please.'

'She . . . my brother . . . He wants to marry her, but I am sure she is already married. Her husband is in Vienna.'

'Then he cannot marry her. It is simple. Do you have proof of the former marriage?'

'Wait.' It was the other policeman. He had stopped pacing and was leaning towards Ludwig. 'You believe she has not told him?'

Ludwig nodded.

'If that is the case, she has misled him in a criminal fashion. We would have to arrest her and question her. And if the allegation is found to be true, we would apply for an order for her to leave the city by a certain date. If she does not obey it, we would have to expel her.'

Ludwig swallowed. 'Expel her?'

The policeman nodded. 'It is the Obermayer woman, isn't it?'

'Yes. She has a child.'

'We know that. She is . . . How shall I put it? She is not unknown to us.'

Ludwig sat up. 'Then we must stop this marriage, whatever happens. My brother cannot marry a – a – criminal.'

In the days that followed Ludwig avoided Johann. He spent part of each day in the cathedral, listening to rehearsals for All Saint's Day, and the rest in taking long walks.

The noises and heaviness in his ears were as bad as he could remember and he knew that his hearing was deteriorating irretrievably. It was as if this summer had put the seal on any hope of recovery.

For hours he walked along the banks of the Danube, up-river towards the woods. The water flowed sedately past him, on its long, leisurely pilgrimage to Vienna and beyond, with none of the ripples and sudden eddies of the Rhine, none of the mysteries that lurked deep in the legendary waters of Germany's greatest river. And the woods . . . Ludwig did not bother to climb the hills: they presented no challenge.

What if when I leave, he thought mischievously, instead of going east to Vienna, I travel in the opposite direction and return to the Rhineland, where my spirit resides?

He knew it was impossible. He had made his home and career in Vienna. It was where Europe's finest musicians and wealthiest musical patrons lived and worked. And, anyway, he was ready to go back. The summer had been long enough – cold, wet, miserable and fraught. There was just this final matter to clear up with Johann.

The door burst open and Johann's face was a mask of fury. 'You! What have you done? Are you trying to ruin me?'

Ludwig recoiled, but quickly recovered his composure. Relief swept over him that, at last, this matter had come to a head. He had – foolishly, he knew – retained the smallest hope that Johann would have come to his senses and realised his folly.

'Johann. You must listen to sense.'

'Sense? *Sense?* Ludwig, I do not understand the way your mind works. I have never understood and I never will. And I am not alone. Father did not understand it. Or Mother. She used to weep, Ludwig. Did you know that? No, of course you didn't, because you never thought of anyone but yourself.'

Ludwig saw flecks of foam at the corners of his brother's mouth. He shot out of the chair. 'Don't you dare talk to me like that!' he shouted. 'You are nothing but an ignorant stupid dolt, Johann.'

'You have the nerve . . . Ludwig, you have such a high opinion of yourself because you can play your stupid music. You can play it but you can't hear it, can you, Ludwig? Because you're *deaf*. That's why you're so impossible to live with and why everyone runs away from you. Haven't you noticed?'

Ludwig saw a red mist in front of his eyes. 'You, Johann. Vile and base and consorting with – with strumpets, prostitutes, the lowest of the low. You're –'

Johann lunged forward and seized him by the shoulders. 'Damn you, Ludwig! You *and* your meddling ways. You get out of my house now! Now! I don't want to look at your face again. And I only pray it will be years before I do.'

Chapter 4

The journey from Linz to Vienna took two days, with an overnight stop in Melk, a town on the Danube dominated by the huge bulk of a Benedictine abbey.

Ludwig paid no attention to his surroundings. He did not accompany the more devout among his fellow travellers who climbed the hill to the abbey to give thanks for their safe arrival and pray for a safe onward journey. Nor did he accept the offer of a room for the night at the coaching inn.

His head was full of the minor chords of the first *equale*. He wished he had remained in Linz long enough to hear the *equali* performed in the cathedral, but it was not to be.

Each time he thought about it he felt a wave of anger. It was the fault of that damned policeman. He had bungled the inquiry. Instead of asking discreet questions and establishing the facts, he had summoned Johann to the police building and interrogated him.

Johann had been furious, invoking the name of the mayor, the councillors, the Bishop – every city dignitary he knew – and had succeeded in humiliating the man. He had vowed on the Bible that Therese had not been married before and obtained sworn statements from the mayor and the Bishop to back him up. Finally he had dragged Therese herself to the building, tears streaking her cheeks, puffy-eyed and pale from sleepless nights, to rebut the allegation.

Ludwig had seen neither Johann nor his fiancée before he left – it would have led only to more angry words. He had heard enough to know that their wedding would go ahead. It would take an act of God, nothing less, to stop it.

It was late evening when the carriage pulled up at the Schottentor and Ludwig walked the short distance to the Mölkerbastei. He had been away for nearly five months. Already he dreaded meeting people again here in Vienna –

even old friends like Breuning and Zmeskall, Schuppanzigh and the Streichers. He would have even worse trouble hearing them than he had before the summer. And the deterioration would continue, he knew that, until he could hear nothing but the dreadful noises. Not even his music. *And if I cannot hear my music . . .*

Melancholy came over him as the servant unlocked the door of his apartment. 'Bring me fresh wine,' he said. 'Now.'

'Too late, sir. I'll get it in the morning.' The servant's voice was like the rasping of a saw on wood.

He went into the bedroom and tossed the contents of his bag on to the bed. He scooped up the clothes and dropped them in a heap in the corner. Then he lifted the folder containing the symphony in F, all but completed. And inside the hard cover, the letter he had written to Antonie.

He did not want to read it and he was about to tear it into a hundred pieces but instead he took out the top left drawer of the desk – the drawer that was shorter than the rest with a gap at the back. Two other documents were there: the manuscript Wolfgang Mozart had given him on his first abortive trip to Vienna, and the Testament he had written in Heiligenstadt. He laid the letter carefully on top of them and replaced the drawer.

Ludwig had known he could not avoid the summons from Archduke Rudolph: 'A matter of great importance,' his note had said. Ludwig had sensed that it was not Rudolph's customary pleading for lessons in composition. More likely, it was to do with the annuity he gave Ludwig, together with Prince Lobkowitz and Prince Kinsky. From the tone of the note though, he knew it could only be bad news. Now he was about to find out the truth.

'Herr Beethoven,' the young Archduke said, dismissing his chamberlain and beckoning Ludwig to a seat, 'we have missed your civilising influence in this city during the summer. You have been away for too long. In Bohemia, I understand. I trust you had a productive and restful stay.'

'Your Imperial Highness, my hearing has deteriorated. You must speak clearly and make allowances if I do not understand what you are saying.'

'And your music? Can you still hear it? Can you still play?'

Ludwig could see the pity in the young man's face. 'Mercifully, yes. If the good Lord takes that away from me . . .'

'Then I am doubly sorry to have to add to your woes. There is bad news. His Excellency Prince Kinsky was thrown from his horse. His neck was broken. He did not survive.'

It took a moment for Ludwig to comprehend fully what he had said. 'Kinsky? Dead?'

The Archduke fingered the silver crucifix he wore round his neck – the symbol of his position as coadjutor to the Archbishop of Olmütz – then crossed himself. 'May the Lord rest his soul and grant him peace. *In nomine Patri, Filii et Spiritu Sanctu.*'

'It was because of his size, imbecile of a man. Too fat. Weight of two men. The horse clearly decided it was too much.'

Rudolph gasped at Ludwig's irreverence, then allowed himself a small smile. 'We should not speak ill of the dead, though I suspect you may have a point. But the unfortunate result of this, as far as you are concerned, Herr Beethoven, is that the Prince's annuity payments cannot resume. You should petition his widow, but I do not hold out hope.'

'He made me a payment in Prague. He said he would instruct his bank here to –'

The Archduke shook his head. 'The bank has frozen his assets while his estate is valued. It would appear he has a great many creditors.'

'Such matters do not concern me. I shall continue to compose.'

'I am afraid there is more news of a similar nature. Prince Lobkowitz's financial situation has not improved – the wretched war has taken such a toll, and not just on the battlefield. He is seriously in debt. It is said he will be declared bankrupt and will have to leave Vienna.'

'Bankrupt? I shall not have his payments either?'

'I regret not. His wife, dear Princess Karolina, is distraught at the turn of affairs. My payments, of course, will continue, but I fear the Exchequer will not allow me to increase the amount.'

Ludwig shrugged his shoulders. 'All war is folly. People always count the cost in lives lost, but there are always other costs too.'

'But at least the war may soon be over. Once and for all,' the Archduke said, injecting optimism into his voice. 'Have you heard about the Corsican's Russian expedition?'

'I knew he had invaded Russia and I predicted then it would be his undoing.'

'Then, sir, you should be a general and not a musician. It has turned into a disaster for him. One from which he will surely not recover.'

'What happened? And speak clearly, sir.'

'The Russian army drew him further and further into their vast country, refusing to engage him other than in skirmishes. Finally the two armies met at Borodino. There was no victor. Then the Russians fell back even further, until he had no choice but to continue to Moscow. He reached Moscow to find the city deserted. Within days those few citizens who had remained put the city to the torch. It burned around Napoleon and his army. He realised he had fallen into a trap, and tried to negotiate with the Tsar, but was refused.'

'Wait. He took Moscow? So he defeated the Russians?'

'No, no, sir. That is the point. Moscow was of no use to him. Once there, what could he do with it? He could not stay because of the onset of winter. His troops would have starved and frozen in the deserted city. So he gave the fatal order to retreat. And on the vast Russian plain, in the freezing winter, his troops were harried and hounded. Only a small number of what had been a huge fighting force survived. And the final disgrace – Napoleon had to leave his few remaining troops and hurry back to Paris to put down a revolt against him.'

Ludwig tried to assimilate what the Archduke had said. So his suspicions had been right. It was a gigantic error, the first the French emperor had made, and it would be his last, without any doubt. 'So Napoleon has finally met his match, and it was not an army but a country. Mother Russia, I have heard it called. I understand it now.'

'It is, indeed, good news for all of us who have suffered at his hands. But unfortunately it will not save the princes of this city whose fortunes have been brought low. I am afraid Prince Lichnowsky too has lost nearly all his wealth. He has been unwell, I believe, and his wife. But I saw him recently. He was asking after you.'

Ludwig let out a sigh. 'He was always too ... I felt ... stifled.'

The Archduke smiled. 'He cares very much for you, you know. He is one of your greatest admirers.'

There was a change in the air in Vienna, and Ludwig sensed it right away. People went about their business with smiles on their faces, streetsellers shouted their wares, strollers once more took to the Bastion promenade and the public parks, and the taverns and coffee-houses were full. Knots of people formed on street corners, discussing the latest events openly.

Even Count Metternich, the iron-fisted foreign minister, was said to have ordered his network of spies to relax their vigilance and the people of Vienna felt as though a weight had been lifted from their shoulders.

There was talk that the European powers that had suffered at Napoleon's hands would capitalise on the failure of his Russian adventure and once more unite to destroy him. This time, they said, victory was assured.

Ludwig's depression was at least partially lifted by the sense of freedom in the city – not least because of the effect it had on his friends.

Ignaz Schuppanzigh was always jovial, but Ludwig had never seen him quite like this. 'Glad you came, Ludwig. If I had to climb those stairs once more, I believe my heart would finally have handed in its resignation!'

Ludwig sat at the round table at the back of the Schwan, for years the meeting-place of the Rhinelanders-in-exile. He drew on the pipe he had purchased at the counter with a small carafe of red wine to add to those already on the table. 'Schuppi, you will have to make your voice sound sweeter than your violin if you expect me to hear what you say. And that goes for you too, young man, whoever you are.' Ludwig gesticulated to a curly-haired young man he had not seen before.

'Moscheles, sir. Ignaz Moscheles, at your service,' he said, his eyes wide with excitement. He was, Ludwig estimated, no more than twenty. With his swarthy skin and mass of dark curls, he reminded Ludwig of Carl Czerny, who was possibly a year or two older. 'Pianist and composer, from Prague.'

'Prague,' Ludwig echoed, wistfully. 'I was there recently. Call yourself a composer, eh? Must say, they're rare. Pianists are commonplace, but not many call themselves composers.' Moscheles had used the one word certain to catch Ludwig's attention. 'How many symphonies, concertos, quartets?'

'Oh, sir, they are a long way off. I have a lot more work to do before I embark on anything of substance. So far, I have just composed studies for the piano. Little more than exercises, really.'

Ludwig was drawn to the young man's modesty. 'Do you know Czerny? Schuppi will introduce you. Same as you, really.

Never known a pianist take such pleasure from exercises. Scales, broken chords, arpeggios. What's he up to, Schuppi?'

'Teaching, mostly. He has a good list of students. He enjoys teaching. It comes naturally to him. Rather different from the great musician who once taught him.' He smiled. Catching Moscheles' quizzical look, he added, 'Herr Beethoven taught Carl. But he is not a kind teacher. Are you, Ludwig?'

Ludwig shuddered. 'Ask me to teach you, young man, and you will receive this carafe of wine over your head!'

Moscheles laughed. 'I must confess I have been in enough trouble already *through* you. I would not wish to be in trouble *with* you as well.'

Ludwig wondered if he had heard the words properly. He looked at Schuppanzigh, eyebrows raised. The violinist smiled, saw that Moscheles, too, was looking at him as if seeking assurance to continue, and nodded.

The young man began hesitantly, 'I studied at the Prague Conservatory under its founder, Professor Weber. He said I should study only the works of Mozart, Clementi and Sebastian Bach –'

'Only?'

'Yes, sir. Only. But one of my colleagues found some of your compositions in the library. We studied them together. I had never seen music like it. I played one work in particular. Your piano sonata in C minor, opus thirteen. It was . . . it was –'

'You were able to play it?'

'Oh, yes, sir. No, I mean I was not able to do it justice, but I was able to play it. It is magnificent, sir. Unfortunately Professor Weber caught me playing it, and he stopped me. He said I would spoil my playing if I continued. He called it eccentric.'

Ludwig saw the horror on Moscheles' face at the realisation of what he had said and laughed. 'Hah! The damn fool professor was right. Eccentric. Hah! A good word. Mind you obey your teacher in future. Isn't that right, Schuppi? Play my music and you will be ruined!'

'I have heard many descriptions of your music, Ludwig, but never "eccentric". Especially not when applied to the Pathétique sonata.'

Ludwig's smile faded. 'No, I mean it. He was right. My music is different. Yet he should not have prevented anyone from playing it. But he is the previous generation. These young musicians are the ones who will carry my music forward. So, did you obey your teacher, Moskolitz?'

'Moscheles, sir. I had no choice. But I made a secret copy of the sonata and carried it everywhere with me so I could learn it. I have it here with me in Vienna.'

'Good, good. One day I will listen to you play it. If I can still hear anything.'

'Ludwig, that's one reason why I brought Moscheles to meet you. To talk about your hearing.'

'I do not want to talk about my hearing. I have a certain deafness, that is all. But, as you can see, I can still converse.'

'Not easily,' Schuppanzigh said. 'You watch our lips as much as our eyes. You lean forward cupping your hands round your ears –'

Ludwig sat back, bringing his hands down on to the table. Schuppanzigh was right, and he had not noticed it. He took his time to relight his pipe, and blew out a thick cloud of smoke.

'I am sorry, Ludwig. I did not mean to offend you, but would you allow me to say something?' Schuppanzigh continued without waiting for an answer. 'Ignaz knows a gentleman who takes a great interest in mechanical contraptions. He has made an instrument that produces music. Also a chronometer, which beats a steady time for musicians –'

'Mechanical music, bah!' Ludwig exclaimed. 'Obviously a charlatan. I do not want to hear any more. And if I do not watch your lips, Schuppi, or put my hands behind my ears, I will not have to.'

Schuppanzigh was not to be put off. 'He says this gentleman, Herr Mälzel from Bavaria, would be able to make an instrument to improve your hearing.'

Ludwig shook his head. 'Tell him he has a far more urgent problem to deal with. Your size. Tell him to make an instrument that will reduce your fatness so you can climb the stairs to my apartment.'

Chapter 5

'Have you seen your brother yet?' Nikolaus Zmeskall asked, as the two mounted the steps of the Rothes Haus.

Ludwig had not.

'The consumption has taken hold.'

Ludwig felt a pang of conscience. 'My damned brothers. If they had stayed in Bonn and never come to Vienna –' he blustered.

'No, no, Ludwig. Do not talk like that. Family is precious.'

Ludwig did not want to quarrel with his old friend. He was grateful to him for accompanying him to see Stephan von Breuning, whom he had not seen since they had argued over that business of Johanna stealing money from Carl. He had intended seeing Breuning – and his new wife Constanze – before leaving for Bohemia, but had not done so.

He looked at Zmeskall as they climbed another flight of stairs. Now in his mid-fifties, his friend had a shock of hair, which had always been white, but which now seemed even more so and he looked down through his thick spectacles to be sure of his footing. 'You're ageing, my friend. You should take a wife to look after you,' Ludwig said.

'No, that blissful state will always be denied to me. I take pleasure in the happiness of my married friends. Stephan and his Constanze . . . Who would have thought, after Julie's tragic death, he would find such happiness?'

'He is an exception. Most marriages are unhappy. My mother called marriage a chain of sorrows.'

Zmeskall pursed his lips. 'There is certainly one to which that description applies. We will talk about it at Stephan's. Josephine Deym, now Stackelberg.'

The woman Ludwig had once loved and wanted to marry – and who had rejected him. How fortunate, he thought, though so painful at the time. If he had married Josephine he would never have known a certain other woman . . .

They stopped outside Breuning's apartment and Zmeskall leaned against the wall to catch his breath. 'It's my knees and ankles,' he said. 'Stiff.'

'You should see Doktor Malfatti. He'll have the solution. "Don't walk." At least your head's not full of dreadful noises.'

The door opened. Breuning was smiling broadly but even so Ludwig was struck by how his face had thinned. The cheeks were less full and the nose seemed sharper. There were dark circles under his eyes. 'Come in, my friends. Stanzi, darling,' he called over his shoulder, 'our friends are here.'

Ludwig walked into the apartment which he had once shared with Breuning. Constanze walked towards them, holding out her hand first to Zmeskall, who raised it to his lips, then to Ludwig, who did likewise. She was a small woman, her dark wavy hair parted in the middle and falling down on either side of her forehead. She had lively eyes and a smile that lifted her cheeks. Ludwig saw immediately the cause of the healthy glow that suffused her skin and gave her face a fleshiness it might not otherwise have had.

'Come, my dear, sit down,' Breuning said. 'I will tell the housekeeper to bring coffee. You must not remain on your feet.'

'Such good news,' Zmeskall commented. 'When shall we all be celebrating?'

'The doctor says August. It will be here before we know it. Well, Ludwig, it has been a while. At last I am able to introduce you to my wife Constanze.'

'Steffen, you know me well enough to know you must shout. More than before. My deafness, quite tolerable before my trip to Bohemia, is now considerably worse.' He turned to Constanze. 'It is a pleasure to meet you and to see my old friend in such good spirits. You know you share a name with the widow of Mozart?'

'Indeed, sir. Stephan told me. He also told me you would be sure to remark on the fact.'

Ludwig struggled to hear the thin voice. 'My dear, you are talking to a deaf musician. You will have to speak with more force.'

Breuning put a cup of coffee in front of Ludwig, which he sipped gratefully.

'Have you met young Moscheles? He told me he knows a man who might be able to help,' Breuning asked.

Ludwig shrugged. 'He can build me new ears, apparently. My

problems will be over. If I am still alive, that is.' He laughed and the others laughed with him. 'To be blunt, Steffen, you don't look yourself. You have lost weight.'

His friend smiled. 'Just pressure of work. Constanze will tell you that it is rare for me to be at home during the hours of daylight, even at the weekend. You know there is talk of war again, after Napoleon's Russian adventure. A new alliance. Such paperwork, so many reports, projections to be drawn up . . . Life would have been easier if I had remained in the Teutonic Order.'

'But in the War Department you are at the centre of events,' Zmeskall said.

'I know. I must be grateful. Also I have a good income and we live comfortably. That is a blessing considering . . .' He gestured towards Constanze.

'Stephan, I was telling Ludwig there is news about Countess Stackelberg. Would now be a good moment to bring him up to date?'

Ludwig saw a cloud cross Breuning's face. Constanze stood up. 'You gentlemen need to talk. I shall join Maria in the kitchen. Do let us know if you want any cake.'

All three men stood as Constanze, supporting herself for a moment on the back of her chair, left the room.

'Ludwig,' Breuning said with a face as long and serious as Ludwig had seen, 'you must prepare yourself for a shock. But before we tell you, let me say that the matter is under control and you need not worry.'

Ludwig was growing accustomed to Breuning's voice, and the coffee, bitter and strong, had dissipated the noises in his ears. He did not know what to expect, but dreaded it none the less.

'She has had a child. It was unexpected and unplanned. According to her sister Therese, Josephine's husband – wretched, wicked man – forced himself on her. The problem is Josephine is saying rather different things. Ludwig, she is saying the child is yours.'

Ludwig took a moment to assimilate the words. Could Steffen really have said that? He turned to Zmeskall, who nodded.

Ludwig did not know how to react. His jaw fell open. And then he began to laugh. The absurdity of it was beyond belief. He looked at his friends, who were both gazing steadily at him, waiting for him to speak. The unasked question was plain on their faces. He took a deep breath, shaking his head as he exhaled.

'No,' he said firmly. 'I did not go to see her before I left for Bohemia. You told me she wanted to see me, Nikola, but we agreed I should not go. And I did not. For which I am now more grateful than I ever imagined.'

He saw the look of relief spread across the two men's faces. 'But why . . . ? Why would she –?'

Zmeskall's voice was sad. 'I am afraid poor Josephine is suffering. Not physically, but in her head. Her family believes she is losing her senses. The doctors can do nothing for her. They say she may end up insane.'

'Her family is looking after her,' Breuning said. 'Therese has taken the child into the country. She and Franz Brunsvik are trying to persuade her to go back to Martonvasar with them. But she is insisting on staying in Vienna to look after her other children – the Deym children. As for Stackelberg, he has taken *his* children back to Estonia. It's possible he's going to have Josephine declared unfit to look after them.'

'There's something else,' Zmeskall said, looking at Breuning and indicating to him to continue.

'The child's name,' Breuning said. 'She is insisting on giving it a certain name. A strange name. I've never heard it before. Minona.'

'Minona? Why Minona?' Ludwig asked.

'She says as far as she is concerned, it is a child with no name. No one must ever know who the father is. At least that is good news. It means she does not intend spreading the untruth.'

'I still don't –'

'Spell it backwards and it is Anonim.'

Ludwig shook his head. 'Poor Josephine. Once she had so much. A sad fate.'

For a while Ludwig considered going to see Josephine. If he confronted her he would surely be able to convince her of the absurdity of her claim. Also, he felt some sympathy for her. He had loved her once; he had pursued her. Had he not also set a song for her, 'An die Hoffnung'?

He thought then of asking Zmeskall to come with him. Between them they would surely be able to put an end to her fantasy. Poor Josephine.

But he decided against it. It would only lead to complications. If she really was unstable, his visit might aggravate her condition. In any case, there was a more important visit he needed to make.

He had been dreading it ever since his return from Bohemia. But he could put it off no longer.

He walked along the wide Graben, bustling now with street-sellers, small carriages, people hurrying this way and that. He was close enough to Taroni's to smell the aroma of coffee that wafted out on to the street. What a transformation in the city! The effects of the Finanz-Patent of two years ago had now been largely absorbed: the people of Vienna had grown accustomed to their new poverty. Since not a single person remained untouched, there was no stigma attached to reduced circumstances and failed businesses, but there was little pity for those it had hurt most: the aristocrats of the empire. The Viennese congratulated themselves on having effected a social revolution – like the French, but without bloodshed.

All the talk in the coffee-houses and taverns was of the impending final defeat of Napoleon Bonaparte. Now the great powers of Europe were plotting a new alliance: Austria, Russia, Prussia, England . . . At last Europe would be rid of the tyrant who had terrorised the continent for so long.

The temptation to enter Taroni's almost got the better of Ludwig, but he turned down the Kärntnerstrasse, then into the Weihburggasse and finally the Rauhensteingasse.

He entered the dark hall of the house on the corner, walked up to a door and knocked loudly. He waited, was about to knock again, when it swung open. There was no light inside – the curtains must be drawn, he thought – and he could barely see his brother's face.

He followed Carl into the room, went to the sideboard and poured himself a glass of wine.

'Take wine from a dying man,' Carl said. The strength of his voice surprised Ludwig.

'Where's your wife?' Thank God, Ludwig thought, that Carl was alone.

'She's taken the boy to the Alservorstadt to see her father. I told her you'd probably come today.'

'Can I open a curtain? It's like a morgue in here.'

'No.' Carl put a hand over his eyes. The theatricality of the gesture annoyed Ludwig and he went to one of the two windows and drew back the curtain anyway. Dim light from the narrow Ballgasse filtered in. 'Kind, caring Ludwig. You drink my wine and abuse my health.'

Carl's voice had acquired a depth it had not had in the

past. It was as if this once energetic, nervous man, with his darting movements and constantly prying eyes, had transferred that strength to his voice. That, and the quiet outside, meant Ludwig had no difficulty in hearing him.

He sipped the wine, looking at his brother over the top of the glass. Carl – to Ludwig's considerable relief – looked better than he had expected. He had lost weight and there was a pallor to his skin, even a certain darkness under his eyes, but they moved with their customary restlessness and the racking cough that Ludwig remembered was absent.

'How is your health?'

'I am dying. It is just a matter of time.'

'What does the doctor say?'

'What does he know? I no longer listen to what he says.'

'Are you still working?'

'I am, and the heartless fools I am responsible to have promoted me and increased my salary by forty florins. Blood money. They do not realise how ill I am.'

'Everyone is always wrong, and you are right! You and Johann, you both know best. Always!' Ludwig flashed angrily.

'You got my letter? You went to see him?'

Ludwig emptied his glass and went back to the sideboard where he refilled it. 'He is a damn fool. He is going to marry the girl. Probably has by now.'

'What's she like?'

'A fat peasant girl who seduced him. And she has a reputation.'

'Couldn't you stop him?'

'I tried. I spoke to the Bishop, the civil authorities, even the police.'

'The police?' Carl asked, with incredulity.

'Did you not do the same when your wife stole money from you?'

Carl was silent for a moment. Then he looked at his brother, moisture glistening in his eyes, which induced in Ludwig a wave of sympathy he could not remember feeling before.

'Ludwig,' he said hoarsely, 'you were right about my wife. You warned me. She is a bad woman.'

Ludwig sighed. 'I knew. I could tell. But you wouldn't listen. Nor Johann.'

'Since I fell ill her attitude has changed. It is as if she expects me to die and is already making plans. She goes out a lot.

Especially in the evening, when she should be at home looking after me.'

'You must talk to her. You are her husband. You must tell her,' Ludwig said.

'She would pay no heed. But, Ludwig, I have made a decision. An important decision, which concerns you. I am going to stipulate in my will that after my death I want the court to appoint you guardian of Karl. You must agree.'

Ludwig was shocked. 'Karl? You want *me* to be his guardian? Over his mother?'

'Yes, Ludwig. I do. You are my brother and I love and trust you. And I admire you for what you have achieved. And I know now you were right about my wife. I cannot let that vile woman bring up my son. If I only knew you were to have him, I would die happy.'

Instinctively, both making the move at the same time, the two men embraced for the first time since they had come to blows by the stream in Heiligenstadt. Ludwig patted Carl's back as he felt his brother's sobs on his shoulder.

Finally, they resumed their seats and Ludwig drained his glass. He felt Carl's eyes on him and expectation in the air between them.

'Does Johanna know?'

'No. I cannot reason with her, she will not listen. This way she will find out after I am gone, and there will be nothing she can do. She can argue and fight and shout and scream, but she will be powerless. It will be in my will. Legally signed and witnessed.'

Ludwig did not know what to say. He wanted time to consider Carl's startling request.

'Ludwig, he is my son. Your nephew. He carries our name. He is a Beethoven.'

Ludwig nodded. The two brothers embraced again.

Chapter 6

The servant said, 'A gentleman called to see you. He left his card.'

Ludwig took it: Prince Lichnowsky. 'What did he want?'

'He said it was nothing important. Just to see you.'

Ludwig remembered the Archduke's words about the prince; he knew he should see him, but it would be just more questions, more concern, more requests to do this or do that. 'If he comes again tell him I am not to be disturbed.'

'Yes, sir. And this letter came for you. From Germany, I believe. It –'

Ludwig snatched the letter from him. 'Leave me. Fill the wine carafe then leave.'

He broke open the seal, kicking the bits of wax as they fell to the floor. He knew immediately who it was from and at the same moment wished she had not written. His hands trembled as he unfolded the single sheet of paper.

My dear Ludwig

The good Lord has seen fit to bless us with a son, whom we have named Karl Josef. He was in poor health to begin with, but I am glad to say he strengthens with every day.

Rejoice with us, dear Ludwig. Franz and I consider ourselves unworthy of the blessings He bestows upon us.

Dear Franz, whose own health will surely suffer if he continues to work so diligently, has asked me to tell you of his fond memories of our stay together in Bohemia.

Yr good friend
Toni Brntno

He tossed it on to the table. Suddenly he felt overwhelmed with pressure. Would no one leave him alone? That mad nonsense with Josephine and her daughter. Carl laying an obligation on his shoulders for which he was grateful but which he knew would weigh heavily on him. Antonie telling him of her joy, yet with her unhappiness almost palpable behind every word.

And on top of all this his annuity had practically collapsed. Only the Archduke's payment remained – all that stood between him and poverty.

He needed to work – but how could he compose here in Vienna, with his mind in such turmoil?

He called the servant. 'I am going away. Baden, probably. I don't know for how long. I don't want anyone to know where I am.'

The smell of burned wood still hung in the air over Baden, though it was almost a year since the disastrous fire that had destroyed much of the town. The sulphur from the waters that bubbled up from underground was slowly reasserting itself, and mingled with the malodorous smell of fresh paint.

Ludwig took a room in the Alter Sauerhof, the old bath-house on the south bank of the Schwechat river, which he knew from previous visits. From here it was only a short walk to the western edge of the town and the Helenenthal valley, with the jagged Rauhenstein ruin standing atop it.

He wanted to compose; he needed to compose. But for the first time he did not know what to compose. Fragmented themes came into his head, but went nowhere. He jotted down ideas that seemed to freeze on the paper – lifeless notes that looked like so many dead insects. He knew there was an old piano in the Sauerhof – hadn't he played the *Andante favori* to Ries and Czerny on it? – but he dared not touch it. His mind was bereft of ideas: what if he sat at it and found that the music did not come?

He walked for hours in the valley, striding as fast as he could, his feet pounding against the earth as he sought inspiration where he had always found it before: in nature. He felt the cold hard stone of the Rauhenstein castle and imagined he was back in his homeland, standing on the Drachenfels.

His head was a jumble of unwanted sounds: one moment unseen waves crashed on the shore, the next he put out his arm to wave away imaginary wasps. All inside his head, the dreadful sounds that shut out the language of music.

One afternoon, sweating from the climb, his clothes sticking to his back, he stood in the Rauhenstein ruin. The broken stone walls surrounded him, seeming to mock him. You're deaf, they taunted him, and you can hear your music no more.

It is all over, he thought. *It is all over*. The roar welled up in him, but when he released it, it was nothing more than a stifled croak, followed by sobs that made his shoulders shake. He sat on a rock, his head in his hands, and the tears flowed through his fingers.

He wanted to take the waters, but he did not have the energy. He knew he needed to change his clothes, but he had not brought any with him. Why could he no longer think straight?

He was no stranger to such confusion, but always in the past it had happened when he was deep in the composition of a new work – the Eroica, for instance, in the vinegar-maker's house in Döbling, or the Fifth Symphony at Troppau. Now he was composing nothing, and it was as if a perfectly proportioned wall filled every crevice in his brain, ensuring that whatever was inside remained trapped.

He needed help, but to whom could he turn? If he returned to Vienna he would have to tell his friends that there was no music in his mind. They would attempt to reassure him, make him see Doktor Malfatti and encourage him to play the piano . . . No, he could not face that.

It was almost with relief that he took the note the clerk handed him. A small smile even stole across his lips as he read the words.

> My dear Ludwig
>   To think Andreas and I are in the same establishment as you, and we did not know it! Will you meet us in the Kaisersaal for coffee at 4 p.m.? We shall be so pleased to see you.
>
>   Your faithful friend
>   Nanette Streicher

Ludwig allowed Nanette to put her arms around him. 'Come, we have taken a table in the corner where we will not be disturbed.'

They went to the back of the room where Andreas stood, beaming broadly. 'Old friend. So good to see you. Here, sit down. Nanette will pour you coffee.'

Ludwig felt none of the irritation such a meeting would normally have provoked. He needed easy companionship. Who better in all Vienna than Nanette and Andreas, both of whom he had known for so many years? Nanette, he knew, would fuss over him, worrying about his appearance and health, whether he was eating properly and sleeping well enough. And with her he would not mind – in fact he would be grateful.

'How are you, Ludwig dear? You look a little tired.'

'Nanette, my head is throbbing, my ears hurt, I hear noises more clearly than your voice, my colic troubles me, my brain is solidifying, I do not have a fresh shirt with me . . . and I dearly wish you were offering me wine instead of coffee.'

Andreas laughed loudly and caught a passing waiter's attention. Nanette glared at him.

'Then it is a very good thing I have found you,' she said to Ludwig. 'I will put things in order for you. How long have you been here?'

'A week. Two weeks. I had to get away. I needed to work, but . . .'

'How's my piano standing up to your abuse?' Andreas asked, a smile permanently on his face.

'Andreas,' Nanette said reprovingly.

'It is terminally ill,' Ludwig said. 'Like its owner.'

'Then you shall have a new one. I wish your health could be restored as easily. You will come to our new showroom, choose one – and admire our latest prized possession.'

Ludwig sipped his wine and looked quizzically at Andreas.

Nanette's voice was infused with enthusiasm, as she said, 'Our new bust. Do you remember Professor Klein took that life mask of you?'

'Hah! He should have lopped my head off. It would have saved me a lot of pain and anguish.'

'He has produced a bust of you in bronze. It is magnificent. It looks so like you. Much more like you than Willi Mähler's portrait.'

A bust in bronze! Ludwig wanted to see it. 'When do you return to Vienna?' he asked.

'Tomorrow at the latest. For the celebrations. All Vienna will be dancing in the street, and there is sure to be a demand for new pianos.'

'I don't understand. Did you say people were dancing?'

Andreas bent forward and spoke clearly. 'Ludwig, have you not heard? No, obviously you haven't. Your head is always full of other things. The English have scored a victory against the French in Spain. At a place called Vittoria, I think. The English commander, Wellington, defeated the French army.'

'Napoleon again?'

'No. His brother Joseph, the so-called King of Spain. No longer. He has been forced to flee. Meanwhile that wretch Napoleon has his own problems nearer here. He has virtually no army left after his Russian escapade. It is said it is only a matter of time before he loses Germany – our homeland – and is then defeated once and for all.'

Ludwig digested Andreas's words. 'I always knew it would happen one day. I can scarcely believe I once admired the man.'

'So come back with us to Vienna, Ludwig,' Nanette said. 'Let me come to your apartment and arrange things for you. And we'll join in the celebrations.'

BOOK THREE

BOOK THREE

Chapter 1

Ludwig looked around the room, bemused, not knowing where to let his gaze fall. It was as if he was standing in a toy factory. He watched as the figure of Johann Nepomuk Mälzel darted from one artefact to another, his half-crouched body and waving arms belying his considerable bulk. '"The Conflagration of Moscow", I call it, Herr Beethoven. And the public have flocked to see it, at five kreuzer a time. I shall recoup my costs, of that there is no doubt. And if interest remains, I shall make a profit,' he said in his lilting Bavarian accent.

Young Moscheles stood to the side, arms folded, a grin on his face. Ludwig glanced at him, then looked back at the inventor.

'Allow me, sir.' Mälzel took his arm. 'See. Here. On this table Napoleon's army, in ranks. He is at the head, on his charger Marengo. Ahead of them, Moscow. The church of St Basil. The Volga. Houses on either side of the river. Now. Watch!'

He ran to another smaller table on which stood a box, holes in its top and a handle on the side. Quickly Mälzel wound the handle. Then he darted back to the large central table and pressed on a pedal. Theatrically he raised his hands to his mouth as if playing a bugle.

Ludwig started as the room was engulfed with sound. The high-pitched call of a bugle reverberated off the walls. A shuddering noise followed and Ludwig watched as Napoleon's army sprang into life, moving forward along grooves in the table.

Mälzel dashed round to the back of the table and bent down, hidden from sight. Ludwig gasped as red and yellow cut-out shapes shot out from the roofs of the houses of Moscow. The city was burning.

Napoleon's army halted. Mälzel wound the handle again. A different sound came from it, deeper, more resonant, rhythmic, a Cossack dance. Napoleon's army swivelled round and began to move back along the grooves. Mälzel dashed back to the large table and threw a lever. Suddenly new figures shot up through the green baize – Cossacks on horseback, tiny sabres glinting in the air. One by one at first, then in groups, Napoleon's soldiers fell over, as the number of Cossacks on the table multiplied.

The music stopped. Of the French army only Napoleon remained, still astride Marengo. A group of Cossacks surrounded him as the music box played a triumphal march. The tricolour, which had stood proudly aloft from his tricorn hat, wilted slowly. The flames of Moscow abated. Napoleon was defeated.

Mälzel came round to the front of the large table, his face flushed and his forehead shiny with perspiration. 'I have a team of helpers when the public is here. The timing is a little better.'

The sounds of the march still rang in Ludwig's ears. He was lost for words. Then he recovered himself. 'How do you make music come from that box?'

Mälzel's face broke into a wide grin. 'Simple. Just a roll with pins. But come with me. There is more I want to show you.'

Ludwig caught a conspiratorial look between Mälzel and Moscheles. He followed them both through a door at the back of the hall into a smaller room. It took a moment for his eyes to adjust to the lack of brightness. Mälzel lit several lamps and Ludwig saw pieces of machinery everywhere. Boxes, rolls, springs, levers, and a long workbench round two walls with all manner of pieces on it.

Mälzel went to the darkest corner and lit more lamps. 'My pride and joy,' he said, removing a cover from a large box. 'My panharmonicon. Soon my name will be known across Europe. This, Herr Beethoven, is a musical instrument that can reproduce an entire orchestra. Not just a bugle or trumpet, like the box you heard, but an entire orchestra.' He pointed to various levers around the box. 'French horns, kettle drums, clarinets, cymbals, great drum, trumpets, bells, oboes, bassoons, triangle, flutes . . . and, sir, strings of the violins, cellos and basses. Never before has that been achieved.'

Ludwig laughed. 'An entire orchestra, eh, Mälzel? Devilish contraption. You will put musicians out of business.'

'It is possible, sir. But you cannot halt the march of science. I have been blessed with a genius which –'

Moscheles interrupted, 'Show Herr Beethoven your chronometer, sir. That will certainly interest him.'

'Indeed I will, sir.' Mälzel walked to the bench on which a long narrow box lay open. 'Would you do me the honour, sir?' He beckoned to Ludwig, who moved forward, took out the instrument and wound it up. 'It is to allow composers to determine the speed at which their music is to be played, and to make the players keep to it.'

Ludwig could just hear the beat the machine made. He reached forward to touch it.

'Careful, sir! It is delicate! This is just a working model. And its name "chronometer" is misleading. It is not a time-keeper, but a provider of a specific time. I have invented a new name, which I will apply to the next model. A metrometer, sir. A machine that gives the meter. A metrometer, or metronome.'

Ludwig had heard enough now: he was tired and Mälzel's infectious enthusiasm was wearing. 'I am not able to hear your voice so well any more, Mälzel. Can we leave this infernal factory and sit down?'

Mälzel was already holding the door open. Ludwig followed him through to a private room and sat gratefully in an easy chair. 'Help me if I do not hear properly, Moscheles.'

'Of course, sir.'

'Now, first something to celebrate our collaboration,' Mälzel said, pouring a thick red liquid into a small glass and handing it to Ludwig. Ludwig allowed Mälzel's words to revolve in his head. Collaboration?

Mälzel pulled a chair close to him, drained his glass with one gulp, wiped his lips and leaned forward.

'You have seen my celebrated "Conflagration of Moscow", sir. To follow on the success of that I will present an entirely new musical work, entitled "Wellington's Victory at Vittoria", to be performed on my panharmonicon. The music to be written by that master of composition, Herr van Beethoven.'

Ludwig looked at Moscheles, who was smiling and nodding. 'It is a good thing I do not hear well, Mälzel, otherwise I might become angry. You are asking me to compose a piece of music for a machine? I hope my ears are deceiving me.'

Mälzel leaped out of his chair. 'Sir,' he said in a deep, ponderous voice, 'I am Mälzel, Johann Nepomuk Mälzel, foremost inventor of the day. Stay where you are, sir. I shall return forthwith.'

Ludwig met Moscheles' eye. 'He is a madman. But the world needs such people.' He smiled. 'I shall reject his idea, of course. My hearing does not allow me to collaborate with anyone. But he is not an easy man to refuse.'

Mälzel was standing before him, holding out a trumpet. But it was not a musical trumpet. There was no mouthpiece or valves, and it curved as it widened. At the narrow end was a semi-circular collar.

'Will you allow me, sir?' Without waiting for an answer, Mälzel went behind Ludwig and placed the collar round Ludwig's neck. Gently he inserted the narrow end of the trumpet in Ludwig's right ear. He took Ludwig's right hand and guided it into place to hold the trumpet. He squatted a short distance from the wide opening, and said, 'Wellington's Victory, sir, at the battle of Vittoria.'

Ludwig gasped. 'I – I heard what you said. Speak some more.'

Smiling, Mälzel reached forward and turned the trumpet towards him. 'It is not a cure, sir. But, as you see, it helps. If you wish, you may keep it.'

'Fill my glass, Mälzel, you devilish magician, and tell me exactly what you have in mind for this absurd piece of music you want me to compose.'

Ludwig enjoyed the walk across the Glacis, the summer sun warm on his back and the curious brass object bouncing reassuringly against his side. So Stephan von Breuning was a father! Ludwig had experienced conflicting emotions since reading his friend's note. The arrival of a baby should be a joyous time, but it had given him cause to reflect.

There was the absurdity of Josephine Deym's fantastic claim. If things had been different, he would have happily been to congratulate her on her new daughter. The birth of Antonie's son had brought him nothing but heartache. Carl's son was now nearly seven – a strange, withdrawn, almost remote child. But with a mother who was a *thief* and a father who was seriously ill, was it any wonder the boy behaved as if he wished he had never been born?

Ludwig found himself longing for the day when the child would be his to look after. That was what Carl wanted. When he was gone, it would only remain to remove the mother's influence.

Breuning's smiling face banished his dismal thoughts. 'Come in, Ludwig. So here I am, at nearly forty, a father. And what a blissful state. I shall go and get Stanzi in a moment and she will bring the baby to show you. But first, a glass. Look, champagne from France. But don't tell anyone of my disloyalty to the empire!'

Ludwig was accustomed to Brenning's voice, but he plunged his hand into his pocket nevertheless and brought out the bulky instrument. Pulling the collar round his neck and putting the end of the trumpet to his right ear, he turned it to his friend and said, 'See? A new man. A man who can hear, even if he looks like the ghost of Hamlet's father.'

Breuning laughed.

'I can hear much better with it, Steffen. It gathers the sound and channels it into my ear. But,' he shrugged his shoulders, 'it is not a cure, and if my hearing continues to worsen it will soon be useless. But for the moment it improves matters considerably.'

'This must be the man Moscheles told me about.'

'An inventor named Mälzel, from Bavaria, a builder of strange machines that destroy armies, set cities on fire and produce music from wooden boxes.'

'I shall make a point of getting to know him. Here, my friend,' Breuning said, handing him a glass, 'I think you need this. But wait, let me get Stanzi and the child and we will drink together.'

Ludwig looked round the room he had once known so well. Those had been difficult days when he had lived here, after his contract had been terminated at the Theater an der Wien.

A minute later, his face suffused with pride, Breuning led in his young wife, his hand at her elbow. In her arms the baby's sleeping face was just visible. A tiny bubble sat on pursed lips.

'Meet Gerhard,' Breuning said, 'my son and heir.'

Ludwig lowered the ear trumpet and looked at the tiny face. It was utterly peaceful. He had never seen a picture of such innocence and contentment. Here was a child loved by its parents, whose lives he had unknowingly enriched, their happiness reflected in his face. How different he is, Ludwig thought, from my own nephew. Karl had looked unhappy from the first, as if the tension that existed between his parents had affected him from the day he was born.

He looked at Constanze, who was gazing lovingly at her child. Instinctively he put his hand forward and lifted the tiny hand that lay bunched on the blanket. He felt the pressure as it grasped his finger.

'He is born of good parents and will be a good man,' Ludwig said, shocked and suddenly embarrassed at his own words.

'Come,' Breuning said quickly, 'let us all raise a glass.' Constanze sat in a chair, cradling the infant. He poured two more glasses, handed one to her. 'To Gerhard,' he said.

All three raised their glasses. Ludwig wished such joy had been visited on his own family. He had never witnessed such a scene in the Beethoven household, *any* Beethoven household, whether in Bonn or at Carl's apartment here in Vienna, and certainly not in Linz.

Suddenly Breuning looked him. 'Ludwig, I have some sad news. Prince Lobkowitz has left Vienna. His debts have overwhelmed him. He was declared bankrupt. Being a Bohemian, he was allowed to leave. He is at his estate and is unlikely to return.'

Ludwig found that, without thinking, he had placed the trumpet to his ear. His excitement at being able to hear so much better had prevented him, for a moment, realising the full import of what Breuning had said. So Archduke Rudolph's dire prediction had come true. There would be no more money from Lobkowitz.

Ludwig sighed deeply. 'Kinsky and Lobkowitz. Both gone. Just the Archduke. I shall have to do some work, Steffen. There is no alternative.'

Ludwig paced up and down the main room of his apartment, singing tunelessly. Occasionally he glanced at the portrait of his grandfather; every now and then he walked to the piano and played a run, or a series of chords, then scribbled down some bars on manuscript paper.

'Rule Britannia' for the British army, 'Marlbrook' for the French. Major key for the vanquishing British, minor for the French. 'God save the King' as a fugue. Drum marches, trumpet flourishes – and the sound of gunfire, cannon on the battlefield. Side drum, bass drum.

It would be in two parts, he decided: the battle itself, then the victory piece. A symphony in two movements. He dashed down more ideas, played more snatches on the piano. He soon had the shape: the two anthems signalling the two armies facing each other, the first shots fired, the battle commences. Slowly 'Rule Britannia' triumphs over 'Marlbrook'. When the last bugle call dies away, the orchestra unites in a stirring depiction of victory.

When he had worked for long enough, he went to the sideboard and cursed to see that the wine carafe was empty.

He opened the door and called to the servant, 'Wine, man, damn you. I have told you, the carafe is never to be empty.'

'I am sorry, sir. I was told you were not to be disturbed.'

'What are you saying? Wait.' He picked up the trumpet and held it to his ear. 'What?'

'There was a gentleman here, sir. He asked to sit in the anteroom and listen to you working. He would not let me announce him. He said you were not to be disturbed. Then he left.'

'What? Someone was here? Who?'

'He left his card, sir.' The servant passed it to Ludwig.

He read the name. Prince Lichnowsky. 'Next time, let him in. D'you hear?'

Chapter 2

Austria was at war with France again and the people of Vienna did not know whether to cheer or weep. But this time there was a frisson of anticipation that the end might be near; that the man who had twice brazenly moved into Schönbrunn Palace and made it his home was about to face final defeat.

The conclave at Teplitz had borne fruit. Austria had formed an alliance with Russia and Prussia. Metternich – the Viennese still uttered his name only with caution and a furtive glance over the shoulder – had offered Napoleon peace terms, but so exacting he knew the French emperor had no choice but to refuse. Metternich, assured of Russian and Prussian support, had declared war.

Weeks of skirmishes followed, but on the morning of 16 October 1813, Napoleon Bonaparte, at the head of fewer than two hundred thousand men, found himself facing almost double that number on the fields outside the city of Leipzig.

There was a spring in the step of the Viennese, but none wore smiles as broad as those on the faces of the Rhinelanders-in-exile. The round table at the back of the Schwan was now the scene of countless nights of celebration. Viennese patrons, who had previously turned their backs to the Rhinelanders, resenting their unusual accents and informal dress, now came over to shake their hands and clap them on the back.

Napoleon had been soundly defeated at Leipzig and the most immediate effect was felt in Germany. Among those who had fought against him were Bavarian troops who had turned against their French officers. King Friedrich of Saxony, who had allied his kingdom with Napoleon, was taken prisoner. King Jerome, who might once have been Beethoven's paymaster, fled from Kassel. The Confederation of the Rhine had come to an end.

Mälzel was in ebullient mood. He approached the table,

carrying a tray loaded with stone mugs, the froth running down the sides, as well as two carafes of red wine. Hands reached up to relieve him of his burden.

'Most generous of you, my new friend,' Stephan von Breuning said.

'We Bavarians have a reputation to live up to. In any case, since Bavarian soldiers single-handedly defeated the man who has been the scourge of Europe —'

There was loud laughter, even from the Viennese who stood close to the table, mugs or glasses in their hands.

'No, no,' said the artist Mähler, who was on one of his frequent visits to Vienna. 'If we had relied on Bavarian soldiers, Napoleon would have added Leipzig to his possessions. Your soldiers would have been found in the nearest tavern, Willi. I say, let us raise a glass to the soldiers of the Rhineland!'

More laughter, and glasses were clinked and raised to lips. Nikolaus Zmeskall sat next to Ignaz Moscheles. He glanced at him, smiled, then said, 'May Ignaz and I consider ourselves honorary Rhinelanders? Maybe Bohemia and Hungary will become part of the German empire, and we will be your subjects!'

'We are delighted to admit you to the honorary society of Rhinelanders-in-exile, aren't we, Ludwig?'

Ludwig put the trumpet to his ear and tried to fasten the collar round his neck. The instrument clattered to the table, almost upsetting several glasses. 'Damn you, Mälzel, you and your infernal contraptions. Take the collar off.'

Swiftly Mälzel pulled a small instrument from his pocket, took the trumpet and bent his head over it. A few moments later he handed it back to Ludwig, who put it to his ear and dropped it again. 'Too heavy. Too big.'

Mälzel picked up his glass. 'Don't worry, I am working on a new model. I think I can achieve the same effect with a smaller trumpet. It helps, doesn't it?'

Ludwig had pointed the trumpet towards Mälzel; now he grinned from ear to ear. 'Yes. I can hear better. But it would be nicer not to look as if I am trumpeter whose instrument has grown, or a trombonist whose instrument has shrunk!'

Breuning said, 'I think we should toast some of our absent friends. Compatriots who have joined us around this table so many times. First, Ferdi Ries, who I believe is now in London.'

A chorus of approval went up and glasses were raised. 'And Ignaz Gleichenstein. And his wife.' Ludwig smiled quietly at the memory of the Malfatti sisters, but said nothing.

'What will happen now?' Moscheles asked. 'Napoleon has been defeated on the battlefield, but he is still Emperor of France.'

Breuning looked round cautiously out of habit, but realised that in the current mood of euphoria it would cause no harm to speak. 'He has fled to Paris. Our forces will regroup and move after him. With the Confederation dissolved there will be no obstacle in their path. He is defeated. He will have to abdicate. Unless he can raise a new army. That is the only threat.'

'He will never be able to do that,' Zmeskall said. 'The French will not let him. They have suffered enough losses, just as we have. So many dead on both sides to satisfy one man's ambitions.'

Mälzel clapped his hands. 'We should do something. Now that we have defeated him, we should do something for all the poor families suffering the loss of a husband or a father. A charity concert.'

Ludwig swung his ear trumpet towards Mälzel. 'I will not play.'

'Wellington's Victory!' Mälzel declared. 'What could be more appropriate? When people hear your famous composition on my panharmonicon, they shout and applaud.'

'Surely you cannot give a proper concert with your machine?' Breuning asked.

'No,' Mälzel responded enthusiastically. 'Herr Beethoven, here is my idea. Orchestrate the Victory piece. We will have a full orchestra. Can you imagine the effect? It will be stupendous. A battle re-created in the concert hall. And you can play another work as well, say a piano concerto. And – and – yes, there will have to be something provided by the incredible magical mind of Johann Nepomuk Mälzel. My Mechanical Trumpeter.'

Ludwig felt all eyes turn towards him. Before he could respond, Moscheles said, 'I would help with the orchestration, sir. If you would permit. So you could concentrate on other things.'

Ludwig tightened his lips. A concert. Yes. But a piano concerto . . . His stomach churned. At the back of his mind was a worry that as yet he had expressed to no one, but which he knew he would have to confront.

He lifted the trumpet from his ear and peered theatrically into the large end. 'What have you stuffed into this infernal machine, Mälzel?' he asked. 'Wool? I didn't hear a single word you said!'

The carriage rumbled through the Stubentor gate, past the hospital, which had for so long received the wounded from one battlefield after another, and into the green leafy Landstrasse suburb. Ludwig alighted at the first stop, pleased that the noise of the iron-rimmed wheels clattering over the cobbles was no longer assaulting his ears.

He walked into the courtyard of the Red Rose, then through the open door and sat in an easy chair in the main room. He saw on a low stool in the corner a black bag, which he knew contained all his shirts, newly washed and pressed by Nanette. He laid his head back against the chair, salivating at the aroma of fresh coffee that wafted across the room. He should have felt calm in this peaceful atmosphere, but he was tense.

'Ludwig, there you are. I was so pleased when I knew you were coming.' Nanette put down a tray and poured coffee. 'Andreas will be here in a moment. Let me look at you. How are you?'

Ludwig sighed. 'Nanette, I am in perfect health. My stomach does not plague me, my digestion is perfect, my hearing is as good as anybody's. I sleep well at night, I eat well, drink little. In fact, I am the perfect embodiment –'

'Now, Ludwig, stop. Don't tease me. How are you? Really?'

'Just my hearing, Nanette. And look.' He pulled the trumpet out of his pocket and held it to his ear. Nanette gasped. 'Now, I am a normal person. I can hear you. You can't tell I'm deaf, can you?' He scowled and tossed the trumpet on to the table, where it rocked from side to side. 'God has been cruel to me, Nanette.' His brow creased and he fought down the emotion that suddenly welled in him.

She knelt before him. 'Oh, Ludwig. Do not be sad. You are the most . . . All of Europe reveres you. There is no musician more respected, more highly regarded, more –'

Ludwig's eye caught movement by the door. Andreas was standing legs astride, untying his leather apron. 'Ludwig! Come to see the pride of our new concert room?'

'Let him finish his coffee, Andreas,' Nanette said, with motherly concern.

Ludwig picked up the trumpet again and flourished it at

Andreas. 'What do you think of my weapon?' He put it to his lips and pretended to play it, then held it to his eye.

'I had heard, Ludwig. And I've heard too that it's effective.'

Ludwig shrugged. 'In company. In the Schwan. Here I don't need it. But if my hearing gets worse . . .' He emptied his cup and followed the Streichers down a corridor to a new set of double doors.

The first thing that struck Ludwig was the room's brightness. High arched windows down one long wall allowed the after-noon sun to flood in. Along the opposite wall stood pianos of different sizes, varying keyboard lengths and inlay decorations. The wood and the ivory keys shone. At the end of the row stood the largest. He moved towards it. The wood was darker than that of the others, the keyboard wider, the legs, he noticed, thicker and sturdier. It was a magnificent instrument, the finest he had set eyes on. He stroked the wood, which felt like silk under his fingers. He touched the keys, but was careful not to push them down. He did not want to know – yet.

He moved to the side of the piano and lifted the lid, propping it carefully on its stand. He looked at the strings, different thicknesses of wire that glinted as the sunlight played over them. The hammers, encased in little pouches of leather, waited to respond to the pianist's touch.

Andreas and Nanette were watching him intently. The moment had come. It was right. He was with two of his oldest, dearest friends. There would be no embarrassment, whatever happened. He took off his jacket, laid it over the piano alongside, and sat on the stool.

He reached forward and played the huge C minor chord that opened the Pathétique sonata, and the dotted semiquaver rhythm that followed. He could hear the sounds! He played the next bars, a repeat of the opening motif higher up the scale. And again higher still.

He played the opening chord again. He needed to be sure. The sound ran through his body – *as his fingers moved forward on to the keys*. He stared at them in horror. The sounds filled his head; the vibration of the notes ran through his body. Yet his fingers were still poised above the keys.

He brought his hands crashing down on the C minor chord. What was he hearing? The continuation, not the chord. He played the chord again, and again, his fingers coming down harder and harder.

He cried, 'Why? Why? *Why?* I can't hear it.' On he played. Slowly the sounds of what he was playing filtered through to his head, clashing with those that were already there. He lifted his hands high, ready to bring them down even harder on the keys.

Then he felt a hand on his shoulder. More sounds, distorted. Voices, he knew. Andreas and Nanette, trying to comfort him. He turned to them, his face a mask of horror. 'I knew,' he said weakly. 'I knew it would be like this. I haven't dared . . . I wanted . . . I knew . . .'

'Come, old friend,' Andreas said soothingly, 'I'm not sure my poor piano can stand much more.'

Ludwig stood up, supporting himself on the side of the instrument. He heard Nanette's voice close to his ear. 'Come over here. Do not play any more for now. Don't worry. Come and see.' He felt them each take an arm and guide him to the far wall of the room.

He turned his head and saw . . . his own face looking straight at him, stern and unyielding. The broad nose, the heavy, determined lips, the mouth turned down at the sides. His hair stood high and wavy, tidier than he had ever known it. Round his neck a cloth was wound several times and tied at the front in a neat knot. The eyebrows were low and the forehead wide and high. The eyes gazed sightlessly forward.

Ludwig reached up and touched the cheek. He let his finger run over the tiny indentation. Then he touched his own face and felt the same blemish – the smallpox scar he had had since childhood. He frowned, imitating the frown of the bust. He turned to the Streichers, his face set in a scowl. He saw the momentary horror on their faces, and grinned. 'See? I am not as fierce as the Professor has made me look. And do you know why? I told you so at the time. The stuff he put on my face. The gypsum. It was heavy. Too heavy. It dragged the corners of my mouth down.'

'Well, Ludwig,' Andreas said, 'you can be fierce. As my piano will testify. I will have to replace several strings.'

Nanette clucked at her husband in admonishment.

A heaviness descended on Ludwig again as he sat in the chair in the living room once more. 'Soon I will not be able to hear what I play at all. I know that. And then what will I do?'

'No, no, Ludwig,' Nanette said. 'I'm sure –'

'Stop, Nanette!' he said sharply. 'I am sorry – but everyone is always saying that, and I know they are wrong. Well, I am not ready to give up yet. Mälzel is organising a charity concert and I am going to direct the orchestra. It will be different with other musicians playing, and so many of them.'

'I heard about the concert,' Andreas said. 'Where is it going to be?'

'In the Grosser Redoutensaal in the Hofburg. Archduke Rudolph has made it available.'

'What are you going to play?' Nanette asked. 'A – a piano concerto?'

Ludwig paused briefly. Then he said, 'That might be a little optimistic. Two works that have not been heard before. My Symphony in A, the seventh. It hasn't been published yet. And another symphony. I have called it Wellington's Victory. I composed it for Mälzel's infernal machine, but Moscheles is going to arrange it for orchestra.'

Nanette clapped. 'Wonderful. But, Ludwig, dear, do let someone else conduct.'

'I shall conduct.'

Chapter 3

Archduke Rudolph hurried over to Ludwig. 'Herr Beethoven, so exciting! I have ordered the doors to the Hofburg to be thrown open. We will not have an empty seat.'

Ludwig made an elaborate display of putting the new, smaller trumpet Mälzel had given him to his ear. 'It will be a strange concert, sir. A true symphony, a Battle Symphony, and a mechanical instrument.'

'A noble gesture of yours and Mälzel's to give a charity concert for the war wounded. It is much appreciated.'

'Mälzel's idea. He is a madman, obsessed with his machinery.'

'I must admit, Herr Beethoven, my obsession is more with the music than the machinery. And I must confess myself somewhat surprised that you agreed to compose a piece for Mälzel's machine.'

'Moscheles orchestrated it. It will rouse the audience. Future generations will not know it but they will know my Seventh. That is why I insisted on performing it as well.'

'The symphony?'

'In A. I composed it before I went to Bohemia. Almost immediately I began another symphony. In F. A and F. Two bright keys. Sharps. I needed to. The Eighth has not been heard either. But tonight it is the turn of the Seventh.'

'And you will conduct?'

'Do not try to dissuade me.'

The Archduke smiled. 'Certainly not, sir. It is your symphony. And I understand the orchestra will contain some distinguished musicians.'

'Indeed it will, Your Imperial Highness,' said Moscheles, who had joined them. 'Herr Hummel will sound the cannonade on the English side, Herr Meyerbeer on the French. I shall beat the cymbals. And to direct the cannonade, none other than Oberkapellmeister His Excellency Signor Salieri.'

'What?' Ludwig thrust his ear trumpet towards Moscheles. 'Salieri? I knew nothing of this.'

'He has heard of the great popularity of the Battle Symphony and asked to be involved. I knew you would be pleased to accept.'

'Indeed,' the Archduke said quickly, 'it is an honour, a recognition of the unique position you hold in this city, Herr Beethoven.'

Moscheles was becoming restive. 'The musicians are assembling, sir, and the audience. Are you ready?'

'Yes, yes. Come on. Do you have the score?'

'It is on the stand, sir. Would you like me to turn?'

Ludwig was enjoying the young man's discomfort: it reminded him of Ferdinand Ries. 'Take the score away. I don't need it.'

He walked to the music stand and nodded to Franz Clement. It was comforting to see the competent violinist in the leader's chair. Ignaz Seyfried, with Clement, had rehearsed the orchestra and the reports were good. There had been the usual complaints: the woodwind, as always, had urged him to simplify passages, but as always he had refused. And there had been voices of discontent when he had made it known that he would conduct.

But this is my symphony. *And I need to know that I can hear my music.* It was a large work, with a huge first movement, different in every aspect from the Pastoral Symphony that had preceded it – and different, also, from the Eighth that came after. It was the outer movements, the first and fourth, that had vexed the players. The first, with its huge staccato runs so near the opening, its bouncing semiquaver rhythms, and the unexpected holds, which made it all the more difficult for the instruments to begin in unison again. The fourth, with an opening which, the horn player complained, Ludwig had scored so that it was impossible to play – semiquaver chord on the strings answered immediately in the wind, when a unison chord would have been so much easier – leading straight into a furious swirling passage that demanded virtuoso skills from the strings that perhaps only Clement was capable of playing.

Ludwig heard what he knew was applause. He glanced over his shoulder to see Archduke Rudolph acknowledge the ovation and waited for him to take his seat in the front row. His eyes skimmed over the hall, the largest and most ornate in the Hofburg Palace. A bust of Emperor Franz stood in one corner, its shoulders draped in the red and white imperial sash.

Vast windows reaching from floor to ceiling gave out on to Josefsplatz. He saw familiar faces – the Streichers were sitting about half-way back, and there was Stephan von Breuning, with Zmeskall and Schuppanzigh. His brother Carl, he knew, was too unwell to attend, and with relief he saw that Johanna was not there.

He turned back to the orchestra and raised his arms. He waited until Clement, looking around the players, nodded, and brought down his arms. The staccato chord reached him a moment after it was played. He winced as it reverberated in his head. The oboe solo – sedate minims leading to another staccato chord – was thin and piercing, and hurt his ears.

He wondered how he could go on, but slowly, very slowly, the sounds began to unravel and he could hear the harmonies, *his* harmonies. Dynamics, dynamics. The chords must be *forte*, the oboe *piano*. He crouched low to indicate the soft passages, leaping up for the loud – those staccato semiquaver runs that had so upset the musicians.

Introduction, treat this as an introduction, he wanted to shout at the players. Tension, build up expectation. A turning phrase, brief, encapsulating the idea that is to come.

When the first main development section came, brought in by the flutes and oboes, he allowed himself a smile of satisfaction. A singing theme in the flute. The player was ignoring the grace notes but, then, Ludwig knew he would. It robbed the theme of an essential quality – a jauntiness almost – but nothing could be done about that. At least the symphony was progressing and as far as his wretched ears could tell there was no more than a smattering of wrong notes.

He drove the orchestra on, noting with satisfaction that Clement's head was moving in time, taking the orchestra with him.

Once Ludwig was aware that he was shouting, his voice matching the horns.

Pause. After a long passage, the theme in the first violins, punctuated by chords in the wind, the orchestra *must* pause on a unison chord. He held up his arms high, palms outward. Wait . . . wait . . . He brought his arms down again to indicate the resumed dotted rhythm, but the musicians were not following him. They were not playing. *Not playing.* He looked at Clement, who held his violin high, gesturing to the other players to pause again. Pause again!

Of course, the second pause! He let out an audible gasp of relief. He had forgotten the second pause, a bar after the first. He hurriedly corrected himself, crouching low again to indicate the *pianissimo* passage that led to the *crescendo*, slowly lifting his body and jumping clear of the ground at the *fortissimo* entry.

Why a funeral march for the second movement? several of the players had asked. It is not a funeral march, others had replied, it represents the trudging of the French soldiers on their retreat from Moscow. No, yet others had said with a shrewd smile, it is the forlorn pleadings of a lover . . .

Allegretto, Ludwig had replied. Obey my marking. And *piano*. It is music. Pure music. Do not try to put images to it. Just play it as I have written it. He set a brisk beat, exactly the opposite of what the music seemed to require, and smiled. 'Sing!' he called, as the wind began the second section, the modulation to the major. And at the close of the movement, almost a dropping away, similar to the effect he had used at the end of the funeral march in the Eroica. *Pianissimo, pianissimo.* A sudden *forte*, before a *diminuendo* to *pianissimo* again. So unexpected!

He paused to wipe his brow and nodded to Clement, who turned to the musicians and gave an A for the instruments to tune to. In the moments before the third movement, the Presto, Ludwig allowed the sounds he had created to swirl around in his head. The symphony, he thought, developed by Mozart and Haydn. But I have taken it forward, to realms they never dreamed of exploring. Scherzos, funeral marches, birdcalls, thunderstorms, sudden changes from loud to soft, unexpected key modulations.

And I have composed just eight. Mozart more than forty; Haydn more than a hundred. *But what is the use if you are composing the same music over and over again?* In that moment he resolved not to touch the symphonic form again until he had something new to say. *And if it means I shall reach the end of my life having composed no more than, say, ten symphonies, so be it. They will be ten symphonies, each one different from the one that went before.*

As soon as he gave the beat for the Presto he knew it was too fast – not for his music but for the musicians. He slowed a fraction and could feel the relief that swept over them. This time the strings ignored the grace notes, even Clement.

He opened his arms to indicate the expansiveness of the central trio, long sustained minims in the strings, the theme carried by the horns. The sounds were now clear in his ears and they were good enough. And relief again at the resumption of the Presto, which was quick enough to disguise any occasional wrong note. Ludwig brought his arms down emphatically five times to indicate the chords that closed the movement. Unison. Good.

Barely a pause, and into the whirlwind of the final movement, the violin bows flying across the strings. Ludwig saw that only Clement and one or two other violinists were using the full length of the bow, the others incapable of playing the turning semiquaver phrases in anything other than a blur. But Clement's playing was strong enough for the theme to be heard.

Ludwig drove the instruments on, gesturing to the timpanist, eyebrows raised. He had scored a huge role for the timpani, using the drums in almost every beat of the long movement. It was essential the man did not allow the momentum to slack. Whatever Ludwig did, however swiftly he beat the tempo, if the timpanist began to slow down, the orchestra would slow down with him, and that must not happen.

But the timpanist relished it, gratified to be brought out of the shadows to which he was usually confined.

Ludwig allowed him to carry the beat. He half closed his eyes and let the music he had composed wash over him, his ears now adjusted to it. The music rushed headlong, causing Ludwig to breathe in small gasps in time to it. He crouched, trying to indicate the difficult little dotted rhythm passages which he had written *piano* on the first beat, then *forte* on the second and last beat. Almost impossible to play properly, he knew that. But maybe, one day, musicians would be competent enough . . .

More dotted rhythms, swirling semiquavers in the strings, double bowing . . . He had never composed anything so furious, yet so controlled. The timpanist played perfectly, taking the orchestra with him.

In the final bars the timpanist played his A and E drums alternately, his sticks almost invisible to the eye, and he timed his semiquavers perfectly to end the symphony.

Ludwig allowed the sounds to reverberate in his head and die slowly away. Then he stepped out from behind the stand and strode across to the timpanist, arms outstretched. He embraced the startled musician, then took the man's right hand in both his and pumped it up and down. 'Bravo, Herr Timpanist. Bravo!'

He walked back to the stand. This time he made Franz Clement get up and gestured to the whole orchestra to do likewise. Finally he stood before the audience and acknowledged their applause. Archduke Rudolph was walking towards him.

Instinctively he put his hands to his ears, looking round for the ear trumpet but the young man simply shook his hand and clapped him on the shoulder, mercifully saying nothing.

Suddenly Moscheles appeared. 'Come, sir,' he said. 'Follow me.' Swiftly the young man moved to the side of the hall and into an anteroom. Ludwig saw the Archduke close the door behind him. Then he and Moscheles stood looking at him, their faces wreathed in smiles. Neither spoke.

Rudolph went to a sideboard, lifted a jug and a moment later returned to hand Ludwig a glass of chilled water. Then he went to a cabinet, poured a glass of rich red wine and exchanged it with Ludwig for the empty water glass.

Ludwig felt the wine flow through him, giving him strength. *I heard my music. I heard my music.* He would not yet give up all hope of playing the piano in public again. *Maybe, maybe . . .*

'You can speak to me now,' he said. 'The wine, the best medicine known to man, has cured me of all ills.'

'Congratulations, Herr Beethoven,' the Archduke said. 'A symphony that will be marvelled at a century from now.'

'Congratulations, sir,' Moscheles said. 'I wish Herr Haydn could have been here.'

Ludwig heard a strange sound. 'What is that noise? Where is my damned trumpet?'

Moscheles handed him the trumpet. 'Herr Mälzel is playing a march on his Mechanical Trumpet, sir,' he said, his mouth close to the end of the ear trumpet. 'Do you wish to go back into the hall?'

'Why? To watch an infernal machine? You cannot make music from a machine.'

'Mälzel has captured the public mood, Herr Beethoven,' the Archduke said. 'And so, may I say, have you, with your Battle Symphony.'

'It will soon be forgotten. And I will not mind. But the symphony must not be forgotten.'

Ludwig listened to the strange, strangulated sound from the hall, and knew his ears were not entirely to blame. He rather wished he had not acceded to Mälzel's request to compose the Battle piece. But the man had been kind to him, and his work on that other instrument – the metronome – would, Ludwig was sure, one day be of use to composers and players alike.

The applause was rapturous and sustained. Ludwig chuckled. 'No musician ever became poor giving the public what they wanted to hear. Come. I shall direct two armies in combat in the Redoutensaal.'

The musicians were assembling; the audience was sitting expectantly. Kapellmeister Salieri, a tall, thin figure with a long, sallow, unsmiling face, nodded to Ludwig, muttered a few words which he did not catch and took his place at the front of the hall and off to the side.

Ludwig stood in the conductor's position in front of the musicians, all of whom were standing. He turned and saw Archduke Rudolph nod to him. The buzz of conversation suddenly died, as if at an invisible cue.

Ludwig nodded to the musicians, who moved in a wave to the extreme front of the hall. There they split into two and moved in opposite directions down two short corridors that led off the hall to further rooms, like the crossbar of a letter T. Within moments, not a musician could be seen. There was an audible gasp from the audience.

Ludwig raised his arms, paused, and lowered them. From the left, hidden by the corridor, a drum beat sounded, slowly at first, then gradually louder, culminating in an extended roll. The trumpeter played the fanfare, all on a single note with just one lift to a higher one.

Slowly, marching, but lifting their knees so the steps could be short, the left-hand section of the orchestra, representing the English army, walked out of the corridor into view of the audience. As they came, they played, *piano*, 'Rule Britannia', wind instruments only, and walked slowly to the centre of the room. There, the string players sat down but the wind players stayed standing. The players brought the single verse of the anthem to a dignified close.

Ludwig was crouching, his eyes wide open and his lips pursed forward to indicate the softness of the playing required. Suddenly he leaped up and indicated to the drummer in the right-hand corridor to begin. Another drum roll, and another fanfare, this time the French. Then, to the gentle sound of the French marching song, piccolo taking the tune, 'Marlbrook s'en va-t-en guerre', the right-hand orchestral section walked to the centre of the room. There, the string players joined the wind and the verse was completed with a rising flourish.

Another French fanfare, answered by the British – Ludwig

swivelling from one side to the other – and the battle commenced.

Unnoticed by the audience, as the two orchestral sections moved towards the centre, their places had been taken by the big Turkish drums and cymbals, brought on by Hummel and Meyerbeer. Salieri stood in front of them, Hummel to his left, Meyerbeer to his right. At his down beat they sprang to life, Hummel, his ring-encrusted fingers flashing in the light, firing the English cannon, Meyerbeer the French. As the orchestra played a rising sequence, drawing up to a climax, cannon and musket fired barrage after barrage at each other. Moscheles beat the cymbal; the side drummer cracked his sticks against the taut skin of his drum. The firing continued; the orchestra played on.

All around the gunshots clattered – so realistic, Ludwig thought – and the orchestral sounds swirled as trumpeters on both sides urged their troops onward.

Leaning forward from the waist, reaching with his arms, Ludwig indicated to the players to enter the driving section, the charge. A chromatic sequence rose, *crescendo*, to a climax. The cannon crashed, Salieri's arms marking the beat for them.

The English guns firing. Emerging gradually from underneath them, the English trumpeter sounded 'Rule Britannia, rule Britannia'. Then the orchestra, quieter, ever quieter, *diminuendo*, until there was practically no sound left. A single shot. Another single shot.

From the right, the opening bars of 'Marlbrook' in the minor now, struggling to be heard, a pleading, broken sound. No longer a triumphant march but a funeral march. Another single shot. The dying notes of the French anthem. A final, fatal shot.

Ludwig held up his arms for silence. There must be complete silence before the second part of the work, the Victory Symphony. A Victory Symphony to end the piece.

But in the silence that followed the battle, the sounds of the cannon and muskets reverberated in Ludwig's head, crashing, banging, hurting. Why were they still beating the drums? Why was Moscheles smashing the cymbals? But he knew they were not playing. What should he do? Would he hear the players? How could he give them the beat? Slowly, eyes still closed, he raised his arms. But even as he did so, he heard the chord that began the Victory Symphony and the rising, triumphant chords, trumpet sounding the top note, that followed.

He lowered his arms and looked over his right shoulder. Kapellmeister Salieri, smiling at him and nodding, was directing the orchestra. Ludwig stepped gratefully from the platform and Salieri moved into his place. Ludwig sat in a chair against the wall, closed his eyes and listened to the sounds he had created.

This, the Victory Symphony, was the real Beethoven, he thought. After the pyrotechnics of the battlefield, this was the music that mattered. The sudden halt – unexpected, make them listen – and the sounding of the British national anthem, 'God Save the King'. Slow, dignified, an unexpected key change. Then back to the swirl of the Victory Symphony. The wind hint at the national anthem again, interrupted by trilling strings. More trills, answered by the horns. *Piano, pianissimo*. And the strings lead off the full orchestra into the finale. A *fugato*. A *fugato*! Who, at this point, would have expected a *fugato*!

Crescendo. Yes, drive them on, Salieri, thought Ludwig. The sounds swept over the room towards him, and he could hear them clearly. My sounds, created by me. Perfect unison for the closing chords. Movements to his left. The audience standing, applauding, led by Archduke Rudolph. Heads turned to him. He allowed a small smile to creep across his face.

It is what the audience wanted, he thought.

Chapter 4

Not long after the successful concert in the Hofburg, Archduke Rudolph again made the Grosser Redoutensaal available to Ludwig for the first public performance of his Symphony in F, the eighth. Again Ludwig conducted, confident that the work would be equally well received. But applause was lukewarm, heads shaking at the audacity of the composer. There was much argument about the discords in the wind in the third movement, just before the trio. Were they intentional, or had the musicians simply had a bad evening? Ludwig refused to settle the matter – and even he wished the cellos had not tried to play every note in the trio itself, thereby slowing the pace and destroying the beautiful melodic line he had given to the horns.

But the depression brought on by the failure of the symphony was soon dissipated by a development so sudden and unexpected that it brought about a complete transformation in his mood.

There had been yet another change in the administration of the Court Theatres. The new director, Count Ferdinand Palffy, anxious to provide entertainment to match the mood of optimism over Napoleon Bonaparte's impending final defeat, decided that the Kärntnertor theatre should stage an appropriate work. He summoned his stage managers to a meeting, and it was Carl Friedrich Weinmüller, who was also an established bass singer, who brought up Beethoven's name. 'At the moment there is no composer in the city more popular than he. His concerts draw full houses and his pieces are talked about.'

'Not always with total enthusiasm,' Palffy commented. 'The new symphony was hardly a *succès fou*.'

'But, as Weinmüller says,' Johann Vogl added, 'he can fill a concert hall.'

'He is unpredictable. Often he is late delivering scores. My esteemed predecessors, Barons Braun and Hartl, told me they despaired of him.'

'Then who else is there?' Weinmüller asked.

Palffy said sternly, 'My budget is limited. It costs more to provide entertainment than to wage war. I cannot afford to commission a new piece. Something we have staged before which –'

'Which expresses the triumph of good over evil, of freedom over oppression, of Austria over the French.'

Palffy's eyebrows shot into his hairline. 'You have something in mind, Weinmüller?'

'Beethoven's *Leonore*. It is perfect. Not only is the plot ideal but, if I remember correctly, when it was first performed the French officers in the audience got up and walked out.'

'But it was flawed,' Vogl said. 'He revised it and it still failed.'

'No, no. It was a success. But he withdrew it again. He had a quarrel with Baron Braun.'

'Weinmüller is right. It did succeed, but for some reason Beethoven did not want it performed again.'

'If I may suggest, Count,' Weinmüller said, 'you should ask him for permission to restage it. It is a fine work. I remember it well. In fact, at the time I rather wished I had been asked to sing the part of Rocco, the gaoler.'

Ludwig sat at the piano, sending his fingers in deliberately unexpected directions. No particular theme was emerging, more what an observer would hear as casual improvisation.

But Ludwig was concentrating hard. Each note, each chord, was carefully chosen. At first the sounds jangled in his ears, jostling with each other and clashing. But slowly they became clearer. He played loudly; he played softly. At times he was not sure whether he could hear what he was playing, or whether the vibrations that ran up his arms and into his frame translated into notes in his head.

No matter. He was understanding what he was playing. It was not like it had been when he had played in the Streichers' piano showroom. He was learning – relearning – to play, despite his deafness. For if he could no longer play the piano, how could he possibly rewrite his opera *Leonore* for the Kärntnertor theatre?

'Come in, Treitschke,' Ludwig said, ushering the man to a chair. 'Wine, Holz!' he called to the servant. 'Two glasses.'

He gazed at Treitschke, hands on hips. He remembered

now the lively face of the Kärntnertor's resident dramatist. He remembered, too, how he had agreed with what Treitschke had said about the opera at that fateful meeting at Prince Lichnowsky's apartment after the disastrous performance in front of French officers. Structure, Treitschke had said. That was what was at fault. Not the music, the structure. And so the opera had been restaged, reduced to two acts. But Ludwig had not been satisfied: the structure was still not right and that was why he had withdrawn it after a furious row about receipts with Braun.

'It has been a few years, Treitschke, and you will notice a change in me.' He flourished the ear trumpet. 'Speak into this clearly and I will have a chance of hearing what you say.'

The servant brought in the wine and poured two glasses. Ludwig took a sip; Treitschke put his on a small table.

Ludwig waited for the other man to speak. Finally he said, 'Your opera, sir. *Leonore*. I understand –'

'Yes, yes. Palffy wants to stage it at the Kärntnertor. I told him it would have to be rewritten. I will not let it be performed as it is.'

Ludwig noted that the other's eyes suddenly sparkled. 'I agree, Herr Beethoven. And I told Palffy so. But Herr Breuning's text, though I do not wish to criticise –'

'No, no. He is not a poet or playwright. He did his best. Will you rewrite the libretto, Treitschke?'

'I have many onerous duties at the Kärntnertor, Herr Beethoven, but it would be a great honour, sir, to be associated with Vienna's greatest composer. Will you let me have your ideas, sir, to guide me?'

Ludwig put down his trumpet, emptied his glass, and spoke forcefully. 'Too much dialogue. An opera should be about singing, not talking. Cut as much as you can. Still two acts, but there is a problem at the end of Act One. The prisoners must return to their cells. I have always thought that. And the two main arias – Leonore's and Florestan's – have to be improved. That is for me.'

'I felt it was still too long, sir. Will you allow me to cut pieces?'

'Damn you, Treitschke. Yes. But let me know which pieces, and remember, with less dialogue you won't have to cut so much. But you are right, it was too long, too –'

'Serious. Gloomy,' Treitschke interjected. 'The whole of Act Two is in the dungeon.'

This gave Ludwig the opening he had been hoping for. 'The Gold aria – Rocco's gold aria – goes back in. D'you understand, Treitschke?' They had made him take it out before and now was his opportunity to put it back. It meant so much to him.

'I do, sir. And I agree with the decision. I will get to work at once.'

Ludwig walked to the sideboard and poured himself more wine. Then he sat at the piano and played for a full hour – snatches from the opera, his opera, which he knew at last would be right. How many years had it been? Eight, at least. This time he would write it his way, in collaboration with Treitschke who, he knew, was an able playwright. Those who could remember the previous attempt would hardly recognise the new version. Yes, he thought, hitting chords on the piano, I will even give it the name I always wanted, and no one will stop me this time. *Fidelio*.

Prince Karl Lichnowsky and Nikolaus Zmeskall walked slowly along the Herrengasse towards the Mölkerbastei.

'My poor limbs,' Lichnowsky said. 'Even walking is now difficult. I dread what four flights of stairs will do to me.'

'I am sorry to hear that,' Zmeskall said sympathetically. 'Mind you, it is some comfort to me to know I am not alone, if you will forgive my impertinence.'

Lichnowsky grunted. 'Forgiven, young man. I have infinite sympathy for you, since you are so much younger than I.'

'A full two years, or maybe three. Still, when it comes to eyesight, mine is not only worse than yours, I probably wear the thickest spectacles in all Vienna.'

'If we were a little younger, people might mistake us for war veterans. The walking wounded. Talking of the war, what is the news from Paris?'

'Napoleon surrendered rather than see his capital city destroyed by the allies. He said he could not bear to see Paris suffer the same fate as Moscow. Tsar Alexander insisted on an unconditional abdication. Now he is to be banished from France.'

Lichnowsky nodded sagely. 'I had heard that, but I did not believe it. He will never go.'

'He has no choice. He is to be taken under military escort to a small island in the Mediterranean where he will be under constant armed guard. It is the end of Napoleon.'

The two men entered the building owned by Baron Pasqualati

on the Mölkerbastei. 'Wait,' Lichnowsky said. 'Let me get my breath before we climb. I do not know how our friend manages these stairs all the time. He must have lungs like an ox.'

'May I ask, sir? Forgive my impertinence, but how is Princess Christiane?'

A look of deep sadness settled on Lichnowsky's face. 'She has never been the same since the surgeons . . . practised on her.'

'I'm sorry. I didn't mean –'

'No, no, Zmeskall. Her mind has become unbalanced. She imagines things. It is difficult. I have to spend much of the time with her. It has been worse since . . . We fared badly during the war. We lost a lot, but I don't resent it. It was for the Empire. But Christiane did not take it well. She never wanted to move into the city, yet we had no choice.'

Both men were panting as they climbed the stairs. Lichnowsky went on, 'You know, I shouldn't say this but she is on the point of losing her mind completely and in a way it will make my life easier. I miss seeing my friends, my colleagues.'

Zmeskall gestured to the top of the stairs. 'There. Do you hear? Our friend is hard at work.'

'I hear he is revising his opera.' Lichnowsky took a deep breath. 'It caused a lot of pain between us. We worked so hard to persuade him to revise it after it failed. My dear wife was the main force. He improved it so much, but then he withdrew it.'

Lichnowsky and Zmeskall entered the apartment. The door into the main room was open slightly, so that they could glimpse Ludwig at the piano.

'He has been refusing to see me,' Lichnowsky said quietly to Zmeskall. 'But I don't mind. He is always so preoccupied in what he is doing. It will be nice to talk to him at last.'

He handed his card to the servant, who took it into the main room. Both men smiled at the sudden torrent of words that poured through the door.

A moment later the servant reappeared. 'I am sorry, gentlemen. Herr Beethoven says he is not to be disturbed.'

'But,' Zmeskall pleaded, 'we are two of his oldest friends.'

Lichnowsky laid a restraining hand on his arm. 'It's all right,' he said, to the servant. 'We understand. Allow us to sit here for just a few moments and listen to him. That in itself is honour enough.'

Then the music stopped and they heard a heavy tread cross the room. Lichnowsky's face brightened and he half raised himself from the chair. There was an audible click as Ludwig turned the key in the lock. Desolation was stamped across Lichnowsky's face. 'Come,' he said to Zmeskall, 'I think we should leave.'

Chapter 5

The Hotel Römischer Kaiser, the Roman Emperor, stood tall and imperious, as befitted its name, where the Renngasse joined the wide triangular space known as the Freyung. Facing it, faded and dilapidated since the death of its owner, was Prince Kinsky's palace; alongside it the Schottenkirche, the Scottish church, and its convent, which centuries before had given refuge to thieves and foreigners.

In an office off the ornate hall, with its double-width staircase and chandeliers, the hotel proprietor was discussing an idea with Ignaz Schuppanzigh. 'A small concert, my dear Schuppanzigh, for the benefit of the families of those gallant Austrians who fell in the campaign against the monster Napoleon. Nothing too grand, a recital rather than a concert. In the main foyer. A small ensemble.'

Schuppanzigh nodded enthusiastically. 'The Razumovsky string quartet, which I am privileged to lead. Would that be suitable?'

'Certainly, sir.'

'Do you have a date in mind?'

'The eleventh of April, Monday, a little under a month from now. I have a distinguished guest list who will be attending a conference here the weekend before. Diplomats, discussing the future of our continent now it is rid of that odious Frenchman. There will be a farewell banquet on the Monday. My idea was to offer this entertainment before they enter the dining salon, and to ask them to make a charitable donation, all proceeds to the Military Widows and Orphans Fund.' He added quickly, 'After deduction of suitable fees for your ensemble, of course, though I would ask you to bear in mind the charitable nature of the event.'

Schuppanzigh nodded. 'Do you have any particular music in mind?'

'No, sir. But I was struck at the success of the charity concerts given by Herr . . .' he looked down at a piece of paper '. . . Bethoffen, I believe, is his name. I am not very knowledgeable about musical matters. But I understand his music has gained a certain popularity.'

Schuppanzigh went straight to see Carl Czerny, who was establishing himself as one of the city's foremost players of the music of his former teacher. His performance of the Emperor Concerto at Prince Razumovsky's grand new palace three years before had won him a place alongside already established pianists such as Hummel, Cramer and Wölffl, and his comparative youth presaged an impressive career.

An idea had been forming in Schuppanzigh's head and he wanted to talk it over with Czerny. 'Tell me, you know intimately the music of our esteemed friend Beethoven. Did he not compose a Piano Trio not so many years ago which he dedicated to Archduke Rudolph? A lengthy work. I remember asking him to let me see it, but he refused. But Zmeskall showed me some sheets and I remember thinking how remarkable it was.'

Czerny crossed to a table on which separate piles of manuscript paper lay. He searched through one of these and extracted a thick set of papers, held together by cord through holes in the margin. '"Grand Trio in B flat, dedicated to His Imperial Highness Archduke Rudolph",' he read. 'Due to be published by Steiner. He gave it to me for corrections. In fact, I will need to talk to Herr Beethoven about it sooner or later.'

He crossed to the small upright piano in the corner of the room and played a broad, expansive theme, descending first then ascending, ending four bars later in rising trills. 'Beautiful, isn't it? And I believe the *Andante cantabile* is one of the most serene pieces he has ever composed.' He played the opening of the third movement, a lyrical yet noble theme that lasted no more than four bars.

Schuppanzigh moved his head slightly from side to side. 'Extraordinary, isn't it, that someone with such a tempestuous character, who often finds it so difficult to articulate, can write music like that? Music that touches the soul.'

'Music is his language. Notes are his words. He cannot express himself any other way. Unfortunately there are few people who can converse with him like that. Mozart would have been able to. Bach, of course. Even our late Haydn. We are mere interpreters.

That is why we must always be tolerant of him. It is the price of genius.'

'Nicely put, Czerny. Better to have only a mediocre talent and be fat and happy, like me.' Then Schuppanzigh explained about the plan for a small concert at the Römischer Kaiser. 'I suggested a quartet, but then I remembered this trio. I am going to suggest to Beethoven that we play it, with him on the piano – that will please the proprietor – me and Linke on strings. We could also play the Trio in D, the one known as the Ghost. Two pieces. Perfect.'

'Yes,' Czerny said, laughing. 'The ominous rumblings in the second movement. There's no problem with that one. Breitkopf published it some years ago. But he will have to help me with corrections to the Archduke Trio, though that should be straightforward. And you will have to play from manuscript. Do you think Herr Beethoven will be able . . . ? I know his hearing is not improving.'

'Zmeskall told me he is playing again. I'll ask him.'

'Let me know what he says. If you wish, I will happily play for you.'

Ludwig felt a bolt of elation when he read Carl's note inviting him to lunch at the Schwarzen Kameel on the Bognergasse. For some weeks a cloud of guilt had hung over him that he had not been to see his sick brother. But the thought of going to that dark corner house, watching his brother's laborious efforts to breathe, a handkerchief to his mouth, was too much to contemplate. Also, he could not bear the thought of confronting Johanna. Only the prospect of seeing Karl, now in his eighth year, tempted him to go the Rauhensteingasse. The boy was thin with a sensitive face, utterly unlike his father, though he had the same darting and inquisitive eyes. He was, Ludwig had to admit, much more like his mother. How could his brother possibly be well enough to sit in a restaurant and eat? The question was only partially answered by Carl's words in his note. 'I have recovered from my illness and my health is restored.'

Carl held his arms out expansively. 'D'you see, Ludwig? I am better. The fever has left me. I never had consumption. I knew it all along. I remember Mother, how she suffered. I was never like that.'

Ludwig did not know what to think. When he had seen Carl

sitting in the corner of the dark room clutching the handkerchief, he could think only of their mother. The image seemed as similar as it was possible to be. Even, Ludwig had noticed in the gloom, the same pink flush in the upper cheeks that was the inevitable sign of the dreaded disease. Looking at his brother now, he was struck by the pallor of his skin, which seemed stretched and parched, like light-coloured leather. His eyes still darted this way and that, but more slowly as if mired in the dull whiteness that surrounded them. But here he was, sitting in a busy restaurant, clearly stronger than he had been for many months, relishing the meal he was about to eat.

'I am back at work, which has not pleased certain people, namely those who assumed I would never return and who expected advancement as a result. I cannot say it is not tiring, but with each day I feel a little stronger. And I hear things are not going badly for you, my illustrious brother.'

It occurred to Ludwig as his brother spoke that although he was holding his ear trumpet it was not to his ear. Yet he could hear Carl's words! Not perfectly, but well enough to understand them. He felt a surge of joy. 'The Kärntnertor wants to stage my opera,' he said. 'I am working on a new version. And I am going to perform in two of my trios at the Römischer Kaiser. One I am rewriting.'

'Ah, brother, you need me to advise you again. Do not rewrite. Always rewriting, always dissatisfied. That way you upset publishers and earn less money. Feed their appetite for new works.'

Ludwig felt the familiar irritation towards his brother. Always interfering, always claiming to know better. But Carl's next words dissipated it.

'Do not worry, Ludwig. I will not intrude in your affairs. My musical days are far behind me. Let us talk of family matters.' He poured wine for them both, broke some bread and pushed a large piece into his mouth. 'Have you heard from brother Johann?'

But Ludwig did not want to talk about their family. His head was full of music; the opera constantly revolved in it. Treitschke had begun to supply him with a new libretto and he had known immediately it would be right.

He pulled himself together. 'He is a fool. He will ruin his life with that woman.'

'I rather fear you are right.'

Ludwig's head snapped up. 'Why? What has happened? Have you heard from him?'

'I received a letter. He married the woman after you left, as you predicted. But since then he has had nothing but misery. He said her character changed once they were married. He describes her as stupid and wilful.'

'Do they have children?' Ludwig asked, concern in his voice.

'She has told him she cannot have any more. He does not know why this is so, only that it is and he will therefore have no son.'

Ludwig could not help his sigh of relief. 'It is a blessing. We do not want any more children born of evil women carrying the name of Beethoven.' Realising suddenly the import of what he had said, he looked up at Carl, who held up his hand.

'I have told you before you were right about my . . . about Johanna. She has something dark about her. All I thank God for is that Karl has not inherited it and I am now well enough to take charge of his upbringing again.'

For some minutes the two brothers ate in silence. The wine had induced a lightness in Ludwig's head, an optimism that he wished would last after it had worn off. But he knew it was an illusion.

Carl spoke again. With a twist of despair, Ludwig realised his words were no longer as clear. Carl was speaking urgently, but as quietly as he could, leaning across the table. 'Have you heard about Lichnowsky?'

Ludwig motioned to Carl to speak more slowly. His head was spinning. Something about his brother's expression told him that he would understand better by looking directly at him. 'Prince Lichnowsky. You know his wife has been unwell. Ill, for some time. Ruined by the surgeons. It was rumoured they removed her breasts. Her mind too.' He tapped the side of his head with his finger. 'Mad, it seems. Lichnowsky was at the Blauen Säbel in the Walfischgasse. You know what I mean?' Carl pushed his forefinger through the looped thumb and forefinger of his other hand. 'This woman came up to him, a mask in front of her face, and he reached forward to touch her. Suddenly she pulled down the top of her dress and she had no breasts. Everyone screamed. Even in the candlelight they could see. He rushed out with his face covered but within days the whole city knew. I'm surprised you hadn't heard. He hasn't been out of his apartment since.'

Chapter 6

Carl was wrong: the Archduke Trio needed revision. Ludwig pushed away the pile of manuscript papers, and looked at another pile, Treitschke's new libretto for *Fidelio*. So much work to do on it! But Treitschke, Ludwig knew, had written the definitive version. The plot was tighter, the characters better defined and expressing themselves in song rather than dialogue. The prisoners now returned to their cells at the end of Act One, after a furious Pizarro discovers Rocco has let them out; the finale to the opera now took place in the town square, with the joyous townsfolk celebrating Florestan's release.

He poured himself some of the coffee his servant had brought in, broke a piece of bread, dipped it in the cup and sucked it noisily. Let Palffy curse, he thought, let Treitschke worry. He picked up the score of the Archduke Trio and went to the piano.

He played the broad opening theme and smiled with satisfaction as the sounds wafted into his head. But he dreaded the moment he would lift his fingers from the keys. The sounds, he knew, would become distorted, replaced by a whistle, or a whoosh, or that throbbing pain in his head.

As he played, he thought about the composition and the work he would do. First, reorder the movements. The Scherzo as second movement rather than the third! Then more variations of the theme that opened the third movement, the Andante Cantabile. His fingers played the chords that opened that theme. Had he ever composed a more noble theme? Yet it was really quite simple – but with so much potential, so much to explore. Yes, more variations. And the final movement, so different in character from the preceding three. Jaunty, almost light.

Quickly he returned to the table and began to write. He worked quickly, as if in defiance of the pain that he knew lurked only a moment away. But the sounds of the notes he was writing remained as clear as if he was still sitting at the piano.

On he scribbled, singing as he did so, relishing the complaints that would come from Schlemmer, the copyist, and Schuppanzigh and Linke that he was making them learn whole new sections with the performance only days away.

But by the time I have finished with it, the Trio will be right, he thought. Right for posterity, for generations to come. With a sudden flush of exuberance he swept his arm across the table, sending the already battered ear trumpet clattering to the floor.

Damn my stomach, he thought. Damn my bowels. 'Coffee and wine!' he shouted through the door to the servant. 'Hurry.' The rehearsals with Schuppanzigh and Linke had gone well, but the piano in the Römischer Kaiser was badly out of tune. The proprietor had promised to rectify this before the performance.

But it was not this that worried Ludwig, it was the fact that Schuppanzigh had had to tell him it was out of tune. As soon as he had returned to his apartment Ludwig had sat at the piano for several hours, playing randomly to test his hearing. He needed to be sure. Was he hearing what he was playing, or what he imagined he was playing?

By the time he had finished he was convinced he could hear his music. But then his stomach had begun to trouble him, just as it had in the past before a concert.

He summoned Doktor Malfatti, knowing even as he did so that the lugubrious face would do no more than intone that his digestion was a reflection of the way he lived. He would remind the Italian doctor that he himself had encouraged Ludwig to drink wine if it relaxed him; Malfatti would reply that he had not encouraged it, merely acquiesced to it, and that that was some time ago, since when Ludwig's health had clearly worsened. And then finally, as if dispensing gold dust, he would give Ludwig a jar of thick white liquid which – as he would stress – would relieve the symptoms but not cure them.

Later, Ludwig grimaced as he swallowed the sickly sweet liquid, then reached for wine to wash it down. Damn Malfatti, damn Palffy, damn Treitschke, damn my brothers, damn my health – damn everyone and everything.

He reached up, plucked the top hat from the hook by the door and pushed it down on to the back of his head. He was satisfied that the revised trio was now right. It was his most substantial work for piano trio. He had wanted to play first the Trio in D, the one that some damn fool had christened the Ghost, and finish with the B flat, to which Schuppanzigh referred constantly as the Archduke. But Schuppanzigh had said no, it was much better to begin with the Archduke. Diplomats, he said, had limited attention spans – better to catch their attention right at the start.

They give my music names, they tell me what order to play it in . . . He strode along the Schottengasse, almost collided with a street urchin and reached out to push the boy aside. But his hand missed the small shoulder as the boy darted away, instantly replaced by another. Then there were at least four or five boys, skipping this way and that on dirty feet, squealing with laughter. One, the ringleader, marched ahead, lifting his knees high and blowing on an imaginary trumpet.

Ludwig knew they wanted to rile him, watch his notorious anger explode. But the effect they had on him was unexpected: he envied them – carefree, beholden to no one, devoid of commitments. *Normal.* He smiled at them, pushed his hat further down on the back of his head and lengthened his stride. Disappointed, the boys danced away.

Ludwig's heart sank at the sight of the liveried carriages drawn up outside the Römischer Kaiser. He pulled up the collar of his coat and, keeping his face lowered, threaded his way through the milling throng into the hotel. He patted the coat pocket for reassurance and felt a shaft of panic. He had left his ear trumpet at the apartment. But what did it matter? If he could not converse, so much the better, and the trumpet would be of no use to him once he started playing.

Schuppanzigh was bustling over to him, bearing his bulk with surprising ease, his jowls quivering. 'We were worried about you. You said you would be here earlier to test the piano,' he said urgently, close to Ludwig's ear.

Ludwig heard him as if through a thick curtain. Pain knifed through his bowels and perspiration broke out on his forehead. 'What?' he asked aimlessly, though he had understood.

'I tested it for you,' Schuppanzigh continued. 'It's not too bad. You won't have to transpose. Anyway, these are not experts here. Just diplomats.'

Ludwig glanced around. Only one familiar face. Count Razumovsky hurried over. 'My dear Beethoven, such an honour. May I introduce the Tsar's negotiating team after the performance? And will you promise to come and perform at my palace again soon?'

Ludwig managed a weak smile. Razumovsky had been a constant champion of his music but he was grateful that the Count hurried away without waiting for a response.

Schuppanzigh was speaking again. 'Ludwig, you look pale. Are you feeling well? Why do you not let young Czerny play in your place?'

'No! Come on.' Ludwig rushed to the back of the room, to the piano and music stands, and tossed his hat into the corner. He played some notes, which jangled in his ears. He played some more, then chords, then a few runs. Slowly, the sounds he wanted to hear filtered through into his head. It would be all right. He could hear. He looked towards Schuppanzigh, who was surveying the audience. Joseph Linke was sitting impassively in his chair, running his fingers up and down the fingerboard of his cello, his head moving in time to his silent playing. The proprietor came over and talked to Schuppanzigh, who glanced round at Ludwig and Linke and nodded, then came up to Ludwig. 'He says five minutes more, to give latecomers time to arrive, then he will ask them to take their seats.'

Ludwig tried to steady his breathing, but the tension in his chest welled up in his throat. It was only a matter of time before the throbbing began in his head. No matter, he thought. I can bear any amount of pain *as long as I can hear my music*.

Schuppanzigh was talking to him again, but he could not make out the words: his head was prepared to hear music and nothing more. Words were an intruder. Carl Czerny walked up to Schuppanzigh, who shook his head almost imperceptibly. Ludwig knew what had passed between them. *No*, he thought. *No. It is my music and I will play it*.

A sharp noise hurt his ears. The hotel proprietor was clapping to attract everyone's attention. Ludwig sat at the piano and kept his eyes on Schuppanzigh. He would take his lead from him now, but once the music started the two string players would follow him. That was what they had discussed in rehearsal.

Ludwig screwed up his eyes as a distant whistle grew louder. It could not be coming from inside his head. He looked towards Schuppanzigh, who was arranging his music on the stand. If someone *had* whistled, neither Schuppanzigh nor Linke seemed concerned at it.

Schuppanzigh looked at Ludwig and nodded. Ludwig nodded

in reply. *I must play*, he thought. *That is the only way to stop the noises. With my music.*

He stretched his hands forward over the keys and looked at Schuppanzigh, who was settling his violin under his chin, his bow poised in the air. Ludwig waited for the nod then played the solo opening bars of the Trio in B flat, the Archduke. Ah, how sweet it sounded. At last, music, just music, in my head. It flowed out from under his fingers, and on the last beat of the sixth bar he listened for Schuppanzigh's accompanying entry and Linke's, which followed it a bar later.

He jumped as he felt a hand on his shoulder. Schuppanzigh looked down at him, eyes wide and frightened. He whispered harshly into Ludwig's ear, 'You lost the beat, Ludwig. You must watch me. We must stay in time with each other. We have to start again.'

We have to start again. Had Schuppanzigh really said that? Ludwig glanced at the audience. Hands were raised to mouths as whispers ran round the room. *What was I hearing? If I lost the beat, what was I hearing?*

Consternation flowed through him, then dread. His fingers curved just above the keys. He looked at Schuppanzigh, who nodded back at him, his face still wreathed in anxiety. Louder, thought Ludwig. *I will play louder. They will hear me and follow my beat.*

He began again. The sounds flowed into his head and he closed his eyes. The notes were like a soothing balm, quietening his ears and steadying his breathing. He heard the violin entry, then the cello. He threw back his head. *Listen to my language*, he wanted to shout, *and you will understand me.*

He did not jump this time; his body just sagged. His shoulders slumped and his fingers collapsed on the keys as he felt Schuppanzigh's hand again. He gritted his teeth and looked up at Schuppanzigh, whose eyes were now moist. 'Come, my old friend,' he said, close to Ludwig's ear. Ludwig allowed himself to be led to a chair that stood empty by a door in the side wall. He knew that all faces were turned towards him. He had tried to speak to them but had failed.

The total despair that he had expected to overwhelm him did not materialise. Instead, he braced his shoulders. The audience was looking once more to the front. Carl Czerny was sitting at the piano. He began to play, Schuppanzigh followed and then Linke.

To Ludwig's surprise, the sounds floated over the heads of the audience towards him. He could hear them and they pleased him. *Not too fast, Czerny*. Remember it is *allegro moderato*. Do not forget the *moderato*. The three musicians were playing in perfect harmony, feeding off each other, alternating the melody, leaning one moment towards each other, the next away. *They are playing my music just as I intended.*

He allowed his head to rest against the wall, as a thought swept over him. A thought that should have caused him pain, but did not. *From now on, let no one ask me to perform for them. I am Ludwig van Beethoven, composer.*

Chapter 7

The servant handed Ludwig an envelope embossed with Prince Lichnowsky's seal. His heart sank. He remembered the extraordinary story Carl had told him. The Prince had doubtless come to inform Ludwig of his latest problems; he would want sympathy. He remembered, too, how the Prince had frequently come to the apartment and that he had refused to admit him. But now guilt overtook him. 'Show him in,' he shouted after the servant. He pushed the dozens of sheets of manuscript paper to clear a space on the table, crossed to the piano and closed the lid purposefully. The Prince will have heard of the disaster at the Römischer Kaiser and want to talk about it. I do not.

'Send him in!' he shouted again. Nanette Streicher had been among the first to visit him to sympathise, sweeping through the apartment bundling up the clothes that needed cleaning. Stephan von Breuning had reminded his old friend that he would always be on hand should he require company. Zmeskall had tried to persuade him to indulge in the comforts of the Walfischgasse by the Bastion, but Ludwig no longer sought his pleasures in that way.

And he had written to Antonie Brentano. How many drafts of the letter had he composed? In the end it had been short and almost business-like – not what he had originally intended at all. He enquired after the health of Antonie and Franz, and their children; and he expressed the hope that they would return soon to Vienna.

Since that dreadful evening at the Römischer Kaiser Ludwig had more or less discarded the ear trumpet. For some time he had suspected that its efficacy was waning and had thought of asking Mälzel to make him a new model with a wider bell, but the man had left on a prolonged tour of Europe. What was the point, anyway? In only a few more months he would need an even larger one.

Damn Lichnowsky, where was he? He picked up the envelope and only then noticed that it had a black border. He broke the seal. He remembered the Princess's radical surgery. Had she . . . ? God, poor woman, he thought. His eyes flew over the ornate Gothic script.

> Her Imperial Grace the Princess Lichnowsky, née Thun, deeply regrets to inform you of the sad and untimely demise of His Imperial Grace and Most Exalted Excellency the Prince Lichnowsky. Details of the obsequies will be communicated to you.

Count Palffy let it be known that he would allow Ludwig several performances of *Fidelio* in the Kärntnertor theatre, and that if they were successful he would give him a benefit performance in July. Ludwig worked hard on the opera, as if occupying his mind fully would leave no space for worrying about his ears – or the death of his former patron, with whom he had such a long, testing relationship. Or the apparent shambles of both Johann's and Carl's marriages. Or his own financial problems caused by the death of Kinsky and the exile of Lobkowitz – at least the benefit performance, if it ever happened, should relieve that problem somewhat.

He was finding it difficult to revise the opera. Once he had started, he found he could not stop: a change here meant a subsequent change there, which led to another somewhere else. He wrote impatiently to Treitschke:

> I assure you, dear T, that this opera will win for me a martyr's crown. Had you not taken so much trouble with it and revised everything so satisfactorily, I would scarcely have been able to bring myself to it – but by your work you have salvaged a few good bits of a ship that was wrecked and stranded.

And a few days later:

> Let me add that this whole opera business is the most tiresome affair in the world, for I am dissatisfied with most of it – and – there is hardly a number in it which *my present dissatisfaction would not have to patch up here and there with some satisfaction* – And that is very different from being able to indulge in free contemplation or inspiration –

It was not that he was new to revision: he frequently rewrote or revised, but this was to order. Of the two previous versions of the opera, one had failed and the other was unsatisfactory. Now a third, with singers to satisfy, as well as a stage director, designer . . . not to mention musicians.

There were good reports, though, of the singers. Madame Hönig, the Kärntnertor's resident soprano, had declared the new aria for Leonore impossible to sing, but yielded at the last moment to Anna Milder, who had made a success of the role at the Theater an der Wien and whose old quarrel with Ludwig had been forgotten. Weinmüller achieved his desire to sing Rocco. Johann Vogl had the necessary characteristics to play the evil Don Pizarro, and the Italian tenor Signor Radicci was a worthy replacement as Florestan for the excellent Joseph Röckel, who was sadly no longer in Vienna.

The first performances, beginning in late May and conducted by the Kärntnertor's resident Kapellmeister, Michael Umlauf, were a success. Ludwig insisted on composing an entirely new overture in time for the second performance – the fourth in the history of the opera! – and it was encored each time it was played. The return of the prisoners to their cells at the end of Act One and the final act in the sunlit town square solved the structural problems.

Florestan's aria at the opening of Act Two had been given a new lyrical coda by Treitschke – after the despair, the longing of a condemned man for his wife – Ludwig had set it and was pleased with it. He was still unhappy with Leonore's great aria, 'Komm Hoffnung', though. It needed yet more work. And Ludwig had withdrawn Rocco's Gold aria.

Nevertheless, Count Palffy confirmed the news Ludwig had been waiting to hear. The performance of *Fidelio* for Ludwig's benefit was to be held in the Kärntnertor theatre on 18 July. Michael Umlauf would conduct.

Ludwig dashed off an angry note to Palffy.

COUNT – Tell your Kapellmeister his services will not be required. I have not laboured this long and hard to yield the podium to another. I will direct my opera Fidelio myself.

Carl Friedrich Weinmüller came to see Ludwig – a tall, thin man, whose jacket sleeves were too short, with a doleful but innately honest face. Rocco the gaoler, thought Ludwig; a man of principle, who had to allow himself to be corrupted for the sake of his family, but who in the end would help to see justice prevail. Ludwig noticed the sparkle in Weinmüller's eyes – another characteristic Rocco must have, lugubriousness touched with humour.

'Herr Beethoven,' he said, in a deep, sonorous voice. 'Forgive my intrusion.' He coughed nervously into his cupped hand, turned away and dug deep into his pockets.

Ludwig wondered what he wanted. All the singers, it seemed, had asked him to alter this or that, adapt this or that, simplify this or that. For Weinmüller it would be the top D entry in the First Act quartet that Rothe had made such a hash of.

Weinmüller turned back, his shoulders now hunched, his hands held out in front of him, large gold coins in his broad palms. His eyes were wide and bulging.

> *Hat man nicht auch Gold beineben*
> *Kann man nicht ganz glücklich sein . . .*

The 'Gold' aria wafted towards Ludwig. For a moment he considered going to the piano and accompanying Weinmüller, but he dared not.

And how well he was performing it. Just the right amount of humour – not trying to draw laughter from the audience, but showing a man who cared for his daughter and wanted her to know that only with money could one lead a happy life – and with just the right smidgen of guilt at the ignoble idea.

> But when in your pockets it jingles about,
> You'll hold fate in your hands with never a doubt,
> All the power and love in the world will be yours,
> No more longing and yearning, it'll open all doors.

Ludwig watched Weinmüller slowly draw his body up and shoulders back as he approached the end of the aria, to declaim boldly and shamelessly his creed.

> Luck is nothing: it's just bought and sold,
> But there's nothing as mighty in life as Gold. As Gold.

He remembered again the importance of the aria. It was not

just a comic interlude: it laid the foundation for Rocco's acceptance of the blood money from Don Pizarro to make possible
Florestan's murder. Weinmüller had expressed that perfectly.

'All right, Weinmüller, or should I call you Rocco? You shall
have your "Gold" aria. I will reinstate it.'

With only a week to go before the benefit performance, Ludwig
succumbed to a fever. He had been fighting it for days, but
the familiar strains of preparing for an important occasion were
taking their usual toll. At first the wine he sent the servant out for
helped. But then the throbbing in his head increased in intensity
and he called in Doktor Malfatti.

Wordlessly the grim-faced Italian probed Ludwig's torso,
holding a trumpet first to his stomach then to his back. 'Breathe
deeply,' he said firmly. 'Nothing wrong with your lungs, and
that's all that matters. Must watch out for consumption. Runs
in the family. Just a fever. Rest. Stay indoors. Do nothing
strenuous.'

Ludwig looked at him contemptuously. 'I conduct my opera
at the Kärntnertor on Monday. How can I rest?'

'Doctors are here to give advice. If you choose to ignore
it, that is your right. But do not complain if you do not
recover.'

'Will you not give me some powders to take?'

'If you wish. It will only be a temporary solution. I notice you
do not use your ear trumpet any more.'

'I can still hear – in the right conditions. The trumpet was
doing no good. It made people stare.'

'Be grateful you are not ill like your brother.'

Ludwig looked up sharply, unsure whether he had heard
properly. 'My brother, did you say? He is better. He told me
so himself.'

Doktor Malfatti jutted out his chin. 'My colleague Bertolini
fears the consumption will return. Once it inhabits the body it
never fully leaves. But who is to say how long?'

Anna Milder was being temperamental. The new introduction
to 'Komm Hoffnung' was causing her problems. Ludwig had
always felt that the original introduction, which consisted of a
lengthy piece of dialogue followed by a short recitative, was
unsuitable, that something much more dramatic was needed,
and Treitschke had provided him with a perfect text: venom

towards the evil Pizarro, mixed with defiance and resolve, and a determination to rescue her husband. 'But the orchestra plays a top C, and I am expected to enter on E flat. How will I be able to do that? And only four bars later I have to descend to low E flat. That is too low for a soprano. It is for a contralto's voice.'

Ludwig remembered how she had withdrawn from the concert on that icy December evening nearly six years ago; she had complained of too little rehearsal. Now he went out of his way to rehearse her, both at the piano and in front of the orchestra. He knew that her voice was equal to the task; it was just a question of smoothing her feathers.

'Herr Haydn was right,' he said. 'You have a big voice. It is bigger now. It has grown as you have grown.'

Anna Milder folded her arms across her imperious bosom. 'I am not sure that is a very good choice of words, Herr Beethoven.'

But Ludwig was already steering her towards the two young men, Ignaz Moscheles and Carl Czerny, he had brought in to help. They fussed and fawned over her, complimenting her in extravagant terms that did not fail, Ludwig noticed, to bring a smile to her face and an upward tilt to her head.

On the day of the concert – Monday 18 July 1814, a day for which Ludwig had waited almost nine years, since the first failed performance of *Leonore* – he awoke to find that the stomach pains had gone and his head was quiet. The pains, he knew, would not return but the dullness in his head, and the noises that accompanied it, would begin at any moment. He must not let them overcome him.

He poured himself a cup of thick black coffee, but his eyes went to the wine on the table near the window, the early-morning light making it an even deeper crimson. But he knew he dare not yield to temptation.

He saw a white envelope wriggle its way under the door. He had told the servant, after he had brought in the breakfast, not to disturb him again. Letters often brought him news he did not want to hear so he considered leaving it there. But even from where he was sitting he could see the embossed Imperial crest.

Herr Beethoven
    I wish you success tonight with your opera, Fidelio. It cannot fail to triumph, as it so justly deserves, confirming your place

at the head of the Empire's musical artists. There is surely no greater composer than you in the whole of Europe. Vienna will applaud you tonight, as the continent of Europe will applaud you tomorrow.

Your devoted admirer and student in music

Rudolph

Chapter 8

From the fifth bar of the overture Ludwig knew that his opera was finally going to succeed. In this entirely new overture, which unlike its three predecessors did not contain a single theme from the opera and was considerably the shortest, he had given the two horns a difficult entry after only four bars. Following a staccato rising opening from the strings, the horns had to play four *piano* semibreve chords in the upper register in perfect unison.

How the two players had complained! But now, as the sound penetrated his head a second after it was played, he could tell it was perfect. These two horn players alone had set the tone for what was to follow.

Ludwig drove the orchestra forward in the overture, so that the strings, who had to play bar after bar of swiftly moving semiquavers, seemed to be sawing the air with their bows. The *sforzando* end to the overture, though, sharp and abrupt, left a void in his head.

The curtain rose and he felt a blast of cool air sweep off the stage. In his head the final chord still jangled. It was a unison E, the bright home key of the overture. But as it revolved behind his ears it wavered and clashed, as if different instruments were playing a semitone off-pitch.

He steadied himself on the rail. There was a problem. The opening to the first scene of the first act was *piano*, the strings playing a skittish series of semiquavers, over which Jaquino tries to woo the resisting Marzelline. How would he be able to set the tempo if his ears could not hear the music? He lifted his arms and gave a weak beat. He saw the second violins and violas play. The sounds reached him in a jumble. He heard a voice. Jaquino was singing; Marzelline was singing. But they were tuneless sounds, grating with a sharp edge.

My damned ears. He saw that the musicians were playing, looking up at him for the beat. The singers continued, glancing towards him every so often. With a sense of relief he realised that whatever tricks his ears were playing him, the opera was progressing unscathed.

It must not lag. He increased the tempo. The cellos and basses ended the duet and Ludwig lowered his arms for the short dialogue that followed. It was Marzelline's aria next – *but how will I hear her voice?*

He gave the beat; Marzelline held out her arms and began singing. She had a light, high voice with a rapid vibrato. Ludwig could hear it, but he was aware that the sounds reaching his ears did not coincide with the movements of her mouth. *Why is she not looking at me?* Each time she glanced towards him he noticed that her eyes did not meet his, as if she was looking over his shoulder. No matter, she was singing and the orchestra was playing.

More dialogue, with Rocco and Leonore making their first appearance on stage, and then the quartet, so essential, he had always thought: it is the quartet that brings the different elements of the opening together. Marzelline expressing her love for Fidelio, unaware that he is really Leonore in disguise; Rocco his hopes for his daughter's happiness with Fidelio; Jaquino his sadness at Marzelline's obvious love for Fidelio; and Leonore herself, in disguise, aware that Marzelline's misguided love for her is putting her plan to rescue her husband at risk.

He held out his arms, marking each singer's entry in the canon opening. In his head he heard the harmonies perfectly. He closed his eyes. He was still beating the *piano* section near the end when he heard the *fortissimo* unison that ended the quartet. He opened his eyes in horror, but none of the singers or the musicians were looking at him. *Good, good.*

The Gold aria. Rocco's moment. Weinmüller's strong bass voice entered Ludwig's head as clearly as it had in his apartment. He barely gave the beat. Rocco was acting out his movements perfectly and the orchestra following him.

Ludwig prepared himself for the trio that followed. This was the first moment of pure dramatic intensity. The domestic sub-plot was over: from now on the drama of life and death, freedom and oppression, love and loyalty would unfold.

The singers seemed to be looking past him again, singing to the audience. Good, that was how it should be. Marzelline's high-pitched voice was lost to him. He waved his arms, knowing he was off the beat, but seeing from the violins that they were playing as if nothing was wrong.

The *fortissimo* unison ending, but a sudden *piano* from the strings. He crouched low, arms above his head, hands barely moving. He could not hear the players, but he sensed they were following him.

Even before he had stood up again he felt the vibrations pass through him as the timpanist struck the opening notes of the march, the crucial march that heralded the entry of the evil Don Pizarro. *Why did he not wait for me?* No matter, the orchestra was playing as the scenery at the back of the stage revolved.

More vibrations as the soldiers marched on to the stage. He knew without turning that the strange sound coming from behind him was hissing, to greet the villain of the piece. On came the governor, striding imperiously, eyes darting this way and that, like a hunted animal watching out for a predator. His eyes opened in fear as he read a dispatch saying the district commissioner was on his way to inspect the prison. The one man who must never know of his plan to murder Florestan. Ludwig waited to hear Pizarro's dramatic entry, an unexpected C sharp as his second note – in the key of F! Yes, there it was. Perfect. But Pizarro's lips were mouthing other words.

The performance moved on towards the end of the first Act. Anna Milder sang her aria, eyes wide, perfectly holding the final notes until it seemed she had no breath left.

They had reached the Prisoners' Chorus. Ludwig was tired and clenched his teeth. *Pianissimo.* It began with a series of rising minims played by the strings alone. He raised his arms for the orchestral introduction. *Why do they not begin playing?*

The violinists lifted their instruments and began to play while his arms were still at his sides. He saw their bows pass across the strings but no sound came forth. Slowly, slowly, the sound came into his ears. And the breath of cool air that washed over his face told him that the prisoners were coming on to the stage for their brief moment of liberty. Ludwig found he was singing with them in this, their great hymn to freedom.

No wonder the French soldiers had been so angry; no wonder they had walked out of the Wien all those years ago. Let no one misunderstand, he thought, what this moment represents. The Prisoners' Chorus is for all people who are oppressed by tyranny, not just now but for all time, for centuries to come. Let them hear this and take heart. And let all oppressive regimes, who imprison people for no cause, who commit murder, who rule through terror and who forbid freedom of thought . . . let them tremble. But now the prisoners have to return. There is no choice for now, but in the end, justice will prevail.

The raucous noise behind him cut into his head. 'Bravo! Bravo! Beethoven! Bravo!' A hand touched his shoulder and he turned to see Kapellmeister Umlauf, a baton sticking out at an angle from his closed fist.

Ludwig looked at the audience, every face turned to him, mouths open, cheers and applause coming, it seemed, from every seat.

He leaned on Umlauf for support, then stepped down into the orchestra pit and warmly shook the leader's hand. All the musicians stood, bowing to him, the string players tapping their music stands with their bows. Another roar went up from the audience as the singers came out from the closed curtain on to the stage.

In the interval Ludwig allowed a courtier to lead him to the royal box, where Archduke Rudolph stood waiting for him. With a fatigue that he thought would consume him, he watched the musicians resuming their places. He made no attempt to rise from the deep, comfortable chair as Michael Umlauf took the conductor's podium. He should have realised it all along.

I can no longer perform in public and soon I will no longer be able to conduct my music. But I can compose. However bad my hearing becomes, I will always be able to compose. That much I know now with certainty.

Florestan's despairing cry rang out across the auditorium. '*Gott! Welch' Dunkel hier!* God! What endless night!'

Sitting in the box on the side of the auditorium, Ludwig found the music more easily comprehensible but it was muffled.

He allowed his eyes to wander over the audience. How rapt their attention was! The sympathy they felt for the doomed Florestan was almost palpable. Yet they knew that ultimately he would be saved. Probably every single person in the auditorium knew the plot.

'*Ein Engel, Leoneren, Der Gattin, so gleich.* An angel who is none other than Leonore, the wife I adore.'

A face floated into his mind, a soft, gentle face, and a voice that soothed every vestige of his pain. Tumbling auburn curls and deep, wide-set eyes. The woman he had adored.

Ludwig watched Leonore approach the starving prisoner, love exuding from her face as she offered him a few drops of wine to drink. He felt tears prick behind his eyes. Love, true love. *I have known it, but will never know what it is like to live with it. To live with someone who loves me and would be prepared to sacrifice herself for me. Like Leonore . . . Like Antonie. I am destined to be without love.*

'*O namenlose Freude!* Oh joy beyond words!' the lovers sang, as the evil Pizarro, his murderous plot foiled, is led off the stage.

My hymn to love, Ludwig thought. In his head the voices of Florestan and Leonore mingled with the chorus of townsfolk, celebrating the rescue of Florestan by his wife – and then with the applause and cheers. He looked at the singers lined up on stage, bowing to the audience, and the musicians with Umlauf at their head.

But the applause seemed to be coming straight towards him. He looked at the audience and saw that they were standing and applauding *him*. Gripping the sides of the chair he stood up and nodded to them, then motioned to them to be seated and pointed at the stage.

At last. At last, I have given my opera Fidelio to the world.

BOOK FOUR

Chapter 1

Vienna revelled in being chosen as the site for the Congress that would reshape Europe in the wake of Napoleon Bonaparte's defeat. On the opening day in the Prater, four thousand veterans of the Austrian army marched past the crowned heads of Europe. Huge tents contained food and drink, and sports and entertainments lasted all day.

Crowds gathered in the Augarten to see the aviator Kraskowitz ascend gracefully in his huge inflated balloon, his small figure on tiptoe in the basket suspended beneath, waving the flags of every nation represented at the Congress.

The city was a whirl of activity. Balls, soirées, banquets, picnics, wild-boar hunts, sleigh-riding expeditions to the green snowless slopes of the Vienna Woods: no expense had been spared by Emperor Franz to entertain the assembled heads of state. The festivities permeated down to the ordinary people of Vienna who, having lived for so long in the shadow of the all-conquering French army and seen their families decimated in futile attempts to triumph on the battlefield, threw themselves into the celebrations of Bonaparte's final defeat.

Gossip and intrigue were rife, as if the removal of the common enemy, France, had allowed the citizenry to revert to its natural predilection for secrecy and scandal.

On Monday 26 September, in the presence of the King of Württemberg, the King of Denmark, the King of Prussia, Tsar Alexander of Russia and Emperor Franz – along with the lesser personages of Prince Metternich, Prince Talleyrand and Viscount Castlereagh – the new opera *Fidelio*, by Ludwig van Beethoven, was performed at the Kärntnertor theatre. Two more performances followed in as many weeks.

Archduke Rudolph wrote to Ludwig:

Most esteemed composer and artist

Your glorious work Fidelio, after a long and difficult labour, is now safely delivered to the world, and all who hear it, in whatever country and of whatever generation, will revere your name.

Yr humble servant
Rudolph

'Come in, Count. My wine is from the Schwan in the Neuer Markt, not some château in Bordeaux, but if you can bear to drink it, you will find it as good a medicine as any.'

Count Razumovsky held up his hands, palms outward. 'Put like that, I am tempted. Medicine is what I need, but I fear my doctor would not be too pleased if I sought it in your carafe.'

'Remember to speak clearly, Count, and close to my ear.'

'Do you not have an ear trumpet?'

'Pfft! Manic contraption made by a maniac. If my ears heard nothing, all it did was amplify the nothingness. I heard nothing more loudly than I heard it before! You do not look well, Count.'

Razumovsky sighed. 'I fear this wretched Congress is taking its toll. I have never worked so hard or for such long hours. At my stage in life – I am over sixty now, you know – one should not expect such a sudden burst of activity. The late nights, poring over countless documents by candlelight, have affected my sight. I fear it is failing. Soon these spectacles will be of no more use to me than your trumpet is to you.'

'Hah! Me deaf and you blind. We will walk in the street together and give the urchins something to laugh at.'

Razumovsky smiled weakly. 'Now, Herr Beethoven, I know how busy you always are. But I have come on an important mission. His Imperial Majesty the Tsar of all the Russias wishes to meet you. Your reputation in Moscow and St Petersburg is unsurpassed.' His smile broadened. 'Even the quartets you wrote for me are now played with relish!'

Ludwig poured some wine and sat opposite Razumovsky. 'The Tsar, did you say? Wants to see me?'

'Indeed he does, sir. Would you do him the honour?'

Ludwig looked into the glass, swilling the wine round until small bubbles broke the deep red surface.

'Will you send a carriage to bring me to your sumptuous new palace? I do so hate using public carriages. People stare.'

'The meeting can take place nearer than that,' Razumovsky said. 'I bring you an invitation from His Imperial Highness the Archduke. He is holding a reception in the Amalienhof for His Majesty, and he very much hopes you will attend. Tomorrow at six. Can I tell him you will be there? His Majesty, I should say, is an accomplished musician. You will have plenty to talk about.'

'As long as he has a strong voice.'

'And, my friend,' a kindly smile settled on Razumovsky's countenance, 'I do so want you to come to my palace. I shall be holding a ball in honour of His Majesty at the end of December. Before he returns to Moscow. I would be delighted –'

'One reception is enough for the year, Count. I shall come to the Amalienhof.'

Ludwig had sent an urgent note to Moscheles, telling him to come to his apartment the next afternoon 'for a reason of great importance and secrecy', and was surprised when Carl Czerny appeared.

'Hah, Czerny. Do not expect a lesson. I do not have time.'

'No, sir. I come in place of Moscheles. He has left the city for Budapest, where he is giving recitals. I am looking after his affairs.'

Ludwig motioned to Czerny to sit down. 'And you, Czerny? You are a capable pianist. Not inspired, but capable. Are you performing too, feeding the insatiable public?'

Czerny smiled. 'I teach, sir. That is what I enjoy doing most. I have composed a series of exercises exploring the keys. Chords, arpeggios, chromatic runs, but incorporated into small pieces to make them more interesting for the student.'

'That is not composing, Czerny. That is writing.'

Czerny shrugged and Ludwig smiled. He liked Czerny; he always had, ever since he had been brought to him as a child to play. He remembered, without bitterness, that it had been Czerny's innocent remark that had first made him confront his developing deafness.

'Do you wish to meet the Tsar of all the Russias? And His Imperial Highness the Archduke?'

Czerny's cheeks coloured and he stammered. 'Sir, I – I would not –'

'At six. An hour from now. I need you to accompany me. You must be my ears. You'll come, won't you?'

Czerny stood hurriedly. 'Sir, will you allow me to hurry home and change my clothes? I shall return immediately.'

'If you must. But be back here within the hour. I shall not be changing.'

The Archduke's carriage was waiting outside on the Mölkerbastei, and a servant in a wig and frock-coat held the door open.

'Teaching will not get you this,' Ludwig said to Czerny with a glint in his eye, as the carriage rattled on the cobbles of the Herrengasse. People tried to see through the curtained windows. Men doffed their hats; women curtsied. 'You must not leave my side. There'll be the Archduke, the Tsar and Count Razumovsky. Just the three. No doubt the Tsar will ask me to play the piano and I will refuse. If necessary, you will argue for me.' He fluttered his fingers. 'My deafness, the unfamiliar piano, whatever you like, but I will not play. I will talk to them about my opera, my symphonies, my piano sonatas – new compositions, if they wish. But if they ask me to play . . .' He leaned towards Czerny. 'You see, young man, my deafness . . . You understand, don't you?'

'Do not worry, sir. I shall look after you.'

The carriage rumbled across Michaelerplatz, through the great arched entrance of the Hofburg palace, and across the courtyard to the Archduke's private wing. A courtier stood waiting for them at the bottom of the steps of the Amalienhof. They followed him wordlessly up to the large double doors that opened into the salon. The Archduke was standing with Count Razumovsky. 'So good of you to come, sir. Such an honour.' He clasped Ludwig's hand warmly, then turned to Czerny. 'And you, Herr Czerny. Good of you to give your time.'

Ludwig's eyes swept round the otherwise empty room and he felt a spasm of disappointment.

'I shall not delay you, sir,' he heard the Archduke say, close to his ear. 'Our guest, His Majesty the Tsar, awaits us in the audience chamber. The Emperor's audience chamber.'

Ludwig caught Razumovsky's encouraging nod and followed him and the Archduke through another set of double doors, along a short corridor and into a large room, lined with mirrors and full-length portraits. At the far end, where chairs and sofas were arranged, Ludwig saw about half a dozen men in formal military uniform. Set a little apart from them were two women, in billowing white dresses encrusted with jewellery, hands folded demurely on their laps.

The Archduke approached the group, coughing delicately into his hand. One of the women stood up and approached him. He took her hand and kissed it. Then a tall thin man with erect bearing came over, his hands behind his back. The Archduke bowed his head and the tall man nodded curtly in response.

Czerny whispered into Ludwig's ear, 'Their Majesties the Emperor and Empress.'

Ludwig tensed as the woman hurried towards him, arm outstretched. But this was not the Empress he had snubbed in Teplitz: the Emperor had remarried recently after the untimely death of his second wife. There had been rumours that the new Empress was austere and withdrawn: the broad smile on her face showed otherwise.

'Herr Beethoven, such an honour to meet you. Franz, this is the musician they talk so much about.'

Emperor Franz brought his heels sharply together and bowed stiffly from the waist. Unsmilingly he said, 'An honour, sir. Heard about you from my brother.' He tossed his head in the Archduke's direction. 'Introduce you, sir. Distinguished company.'

Czerny continued to whisper into Ludwig's ear as the Emperor indicated his guests: 'His Majesty the King of Prussia, sir. His Majesty the King of Denmark. His Majesty the King of Bavaria. Most honoured guest His Majesty Tsar Alexander and Her Majesty Tsarina Elizabeth.'

Czerny's voice faltered as he repeated the litany of names, and Ludwig felt him shrink behind his shoulder. Ludwig looked at each monarch in turn: the King of Prussia, back ramrod straight, curled moustache, eyelids half closed over bulging eyes; the King of Denmark, blond hair combed forward, intense blue eyes, a courteous smile; the King of Bavaria, an untrimmed moustache trailing down at the ends, colliding with side-whiskers, a broad grin on a florid face, one leg cocked out, knee bent, hand on hip. But his attention was caught by a small man with thinning hair and a boyish smile, who was walking towards him. He was dressed in a high-collared tunic with gold braid and over-large epaulettes. A broad red sash passed across his chest and a gold cross hung from an elaborate brooch, above which was a line of medals. The whole ensemble seemed too heavy for his slight body.

'Herr Beethoven, sir. Alexander. An honour, sir. And may I present the Tsarina.' Elizabeth was small, too, verging on plump, but her eyes, like her husband's, were lively and alert.

Ludwig nodded to both of them, not knowing what to say. But the moment was saved by Archduke Rudolph. 'Their Majesties have all attended *Fidelio*, sir, and I believe were all most impressively entertained.' Ludwig could hear him clearly but he allowed Czerny to repeat the words in his ear. They would make allowances for him, he was sure, obviating the need for him to make conversation.

'Hope you'll compose something in honour of my guests, sir,' Emperor Franz said, raising his eyebrows languidly. 'Be most obliged.'

At this Ludwig felt a frisson of antipathy but allowed it to pass. He took a glass of wine from a silver salver held towards him by a servant, grimacing as the unexpected sweetness of the thick golden liquid burst in his mouth.

He sat in a chair, Czerny crouching at his shoulder.

'I must say, Herr Beethoven,' the Tsar said, 'how much the Tsarina enjoyed your opera. I understand the French soldiers had different views when they saw it here.'

'Damn French,' the King of Bavaria said, his voice booming, albeit muffled by the copious hair surrounding his mouth. 'Taught them a lesson at Leipzig. Won't have any more nonsense from that Corsican.'

'I would have felt a little safer,' the Danish King said, in a measured voice, 'if he had been exiled a little further away. The Mediterranean is rather too close for comfort.'

'One move out of him and Prussia will crush him.' King Friedrich's tone was cold.

'The men, always talking of war.' Tsarina Elizabeth moved to take a seat close to Ludwig. 'Will you come and visit us in the chilly north some day, Herr Beethoven? I can assure you of a welcome warm enough to melt the snow we have to live with for much of the year in St Petersburg.'

Ludwig waited for Czerny's repetition, then smiled and nodded in appreciation. He sipped the wine again, aware of a lull in the conversation.

Count Razumovsky spoke. 'Their Majesties greatly admired your quartets, Herr Beethoven.'

'Once our ignorant musicians were persuaded of their merit,' the Tsar added, smiling.

'I am asking Herr Schuppanzigh to play them at the reception I am giving for Their Majesties at my palace – the Russian embassy,' Razumovsky said.

'Hah!' the Tsar exclaimed, leaping on the Count's words. 'I think your first choice was more accurate. I do believe the Russian embassy in Vienna is the most costly and ornate mission in the civilised world. Our exchequer has barely survived the strain.'

There was general laughter, and Ludwig saw Razumovsky flush.

'Meant what I said, Beethoven,' the Emperor said, with a touch of ice to his voice. 'Expect you to compose something to honour my guests. Most distinguished gathering in Europe. Celebration dinner in the Redoutensaal. End of the month. Liaise with my brother.' He turned his back and began to talk to King Friedrich. The Archduke understood the movement and stood up. 'Their Majesties do not wish to detain you any longer,' he said, diplomatically. 'Let us return to the Amalienhof.'

Ludwig drained his glass, watched Czerny bow and followed the Archduke back in the direction they had come.

In the salon of the Amalienhof, he slumped tiredly into a chair. The Archduke handed him a glass of red wine and pulled a chair close to him. Ludwig took a sip. 'What was that wine I was given?'

'That,' said the Archduke, 'was the Emperor's favourite. It comes from a château near Bordeaux. Yquem, I think. Supplies were interrupted because of the war. Now, with Napoleon out of the way, he is receiving it again. It is said,' he moved forward conspiratorially, indicating to young Czerny that what he was about to say should not be repeated outside the room, 'that the Empire is governed better now the Emperor has his Château Yquem!'

'It improved, I must admit,' Ludwig said. 'Good thing I took to it, or I might have given him an insolent answer to his demand to compose a piece of music.'

The Archduke sucked in his cheeks. 'I am sorry. I did not expect him to be so direct. He asked me for advice. I advised against it, but cautioned him to ask politely. I assured him of your standing, your reputation.'

'What does he want?'

'Just something simple. An anthem, even. He is proud that Vienna was chosen to host the Congress to redraw the map of

Europe. He would like something patriotic. But do not concern yourself, Herr Beethoven, I am sure Herr Hummel –'

Ludwig got up and walked to the piano in the corner. Without stopping to think, he played a series of rising chords. 'Vienna, Vienna!' he sang tunelessly. 'Vienna, Vienna!' He turned to the Archduke and said, 'The English name Vienna is easier to set to music. What use is Wien? Find someone to provide me with a text.'

Chapter 2

Ludwig had not been before to the tavern Zur Rose in the Wollzeile, a long narrow street just above St Stephansdom named for the wool market that had stood there in the Middle Ages. It was a large open room crammed with small round tables, each one occupied with a group of men arguing, it seemed, about the future of Europe, shouting to emphasise a point or simply to make themselves heard. Between the tables other groups stood, talking and gesticulating just as volubly.

He wished he had not agreed to meet Alois Weissenbach. He was sure he would not like the man. A surgeon from Salzburg who wrote poetry and drama, recommended to Ludwig by – of all people! – the dour Doktor Malfatti, of whom Ludwig had found it hard to believe that he had ever read any poetry in his life. But nothing could be worse than the text the Archduke had given him, by a poet whose name he had already forgotten.

He forced a smile as he saw a corpulent figure rise. He knew immediately it was Weissenbach, if for no other reason than that the table he stood at was the only one with just a single occupant. He was in his late forties, Ludwig estimated, with a bald head framed by unruly curls, thinly wired spectacles set forward on his nose, dressed in the green serge of the Tyrol from where he originated. A full stomach strained at his waistcoat, and his face was broad and fleshy, indicating a certain satisfaction with life.

'My dear Herr Beethoven,' he said loudly, taking Ludwig's arm. 'Come. I have made arrangements. We invalids must be looked after.'

Ludwig followed Weissenbach past several tables and through a door into a small back room. 'Good. Excellent,' he boomed. 'Be seated, sir. Alois Weissenbach, physician and poet, at your service. Here, some wine.' He poured two glasses and handed one to Ludwig. '*Deaf* physician and poet, sir.'

Ludwig's jaw dropped, thinking at first that the man was poking fun at him.

'Deaf?' he echoed feebly.

'Deaf, sir. Something I understand we have in common, as well as being artists. So I shall shout at you and you can shout at me! I had typhus as a young man. Nearly died. When I recovered my hearing had almost gone and it has been the same since. Both ears.'

'Mine began after an illness too, but it's been gradual. The doctors expected it to improve, or at least stop getting worse. But I always knew.'

'Hah! What do doctors know? The most popular doctors are those who tell the patients what they want to hear. Believe me, sir, if it is gradual, it will continue getting worse until you hear nothing at all. And how will you compose your music then, sir?' Weissenbach asked, his face close to Ludwig's.

'I can hear the music in my head, feel it in my body. I don't need my ears.'

Weissenbach nodded slowly. 'So I had heard. And I have heard the music to prove it. My deafness, although worse now, at least allowed me that. Your symphony in C minor, sir, is the most remarkable piece of music I have ever heard.' He thumped his fist on the table – three short blows and a fourth, holding his fist down after the fourth. 'Do you know, sir, all the anger and frustration I have felt for so many years about *my deafness* . . . When I *heard* your music it gave me new strength, new resolve, new determination. I composed a verse on it, but I shall not force you to listen to it. You would plead deafness!' He broke into a peal of laughter.

Ludwig felt in his pocket. He pulled out a sheaf of crumpled papers. 'You talk of poetry, Weissenberg. I shall read some for you.' He put the top sheet on the table and smoothed it out with the edge of his hand. He drained his glass, noting that Weissenbach immediately refilled it, and stood, one hand dramatically over his heart.

> 'Hear ye the clang of captives' chains?
> Hear ye the sighs of the river's flood?
> See ye the Danube red with blood?
> Who shall we beg to relieve our pains?'

Ludwig sat down heavily. 'I am supposed to set this – this – rotting sewage to music. I cannot and I will not.'

'Will you allow me to write a poem for you? An epic poem?'

'Do you know what is required?'

'I spoke to the Archduke's chamberlain. There is a reception at the Hofburg for the royal guests. The Emperor – His Imperial Majesty – wants a piece to honour them, with the city of Vienna portrayed as host.' He took a piece of paper from his inside pocket. 'I am only in Vienna for a short time, so I made some notes right away. Vienna, soprano. Then three other solo voices to represent . . . He didn't say, but I have some ideas. A chorus representing the people. And orchestra, of course.'

Ludwig leaned back. 'A cantata. I shall regard it as a *divertimento*. Let me have the words as soon as you can, Weissenberg.'

The Grosser Redoutensaal, where Ludwig had earlier conducted his Seventh Symphony and the Battle Symphony, was decked out as it had never been before. Bunting and streamers crisscrossed the huge hall; bunches of balloons were suspended like overripe grapes from the balcony that ran round the walls, the flags of the nations of Europe clustered above the proceedings below.

A grand rectangular table took up most of the hall, seating at least a hundred guests. All the delegations to the Congress of Vienna were there. At Ludwig's shoulder, Archduke Rudolph pointed out the tall, thin, ascetic Viscount Castlereagh, head of the British delegation; Prince Talleyrand, gesticulating and arguing as if it was his country, France, that had won the war; Prince Metternich, his face cold, alert and scheming, knowing that at last Austria was in control of the momentous events reshaping the continent.

The Archduke pointed to a number of empty chairs. 'Waiting to be filled, Herr Beethoven, at the appropriate cue from your music. Now, if you'll excuse me, I should resume my place at the table.'

Such an absurd piece of music! Ludwig mused. Why had he done it? Even young Czerny, who had assisted him with the orchestration, had suggested timidly that it was 'different' from anything else he had composed. Weissenbach's text had amused him: florid, colourful, melodramatic, and entitled 'Der Glorreiche Augenblick', The Glorious Moment, exactly what was required. Ludwig had swiftly and easily set it to music.

At the front of the great hall, to which led the two corridors he had used to such effect for the Battle Symphony, a thick deep blue velvet curtain hung. Now the musicians and singers were filing through it, taking their places for the performance. Ludwig had decided not to try to conduct: he wanted to sit in the hall and watch the spectacle. Ignaz Seyfried, Kapellmeister at the Theater an der Wien, had taken rehearsals and was going to direct. He moved his chair a little away from the table so that he could have a clear view.

Europe steht! Europe stands alone! the chorus sang, voices and orchestra sounding *fortissimo*. Ludwig found himself beating gently in time. He wanted to tell them, quietly now, a slow *crescendo*, so that Weissenbach's words could be heard in all their inflated glory.

> The people enraptured call out in their millions,
> To the one noble figure adorned with a crown
> And encircled with light.

Ludwig looked around the hall and saw that every face was turned to the music, fingers and toes tapping. So easy, he thought, to please you all. And yet you do not realise that this music, that you believe will for ever glorify the Congress of Vienna, will be forgotten as quickly as the Congress itself. You believe you are altering the shape of a continent. *Do you not understand that what you are doing will not endure? Nothing endures, except art.*

A frisson of excitement ran round the hall. From out of the curtain there emerged a statuesque woman, dressed in a deep red frock that swept the floor. A silver-spangled cloak covered her shoulders. A large diadem, whose stones reflected the candlelight from the chandeliers, sat atop her hair, itself enclosed in a golden net. Her arms were flung wide, and in her right hand she carried a long silver wand with a bright star at the end. Vienna!

A spontaneous burst of applause erupted from the table.

The chorus sang out, using the English name for the city, as Ludwig had stipulated.

> Vienna! Vienna! Adorned with crowns, belov'd of
> the gods, Hostess now to your majestic guests.

'Vienna' stepped forward, arms still outstretched, ready for her all-important recitative and aria, the high point of 'Der Glorreiche Augenblick'.

The violins trilled their gentle opening. 'Vienna' drew breath and her chest expanded to alarming proportions.

> Oh, Heaven! What rapture! What joy!
> Before my eyes is about to enfold!

The guests were entranced, and sadness coursed through Ludwig at the effect this ridiculous spectacle had wrought on them.

> My bosom throbs! Oh, stammer my tongue!

He saw the curtain twitch, as 'Vienna' declaimed she was no longer a mere city, but the essence of Europe itself. The first critical moment had arrived.

> The Hero who bestrides the clouds,
> One foot at either end
> Of the ancient Caucasus,
> His blessings doth he send
> From Memel to the Arctic Sea.

Now the fanfare. The drum gave the beat, the orchestra played the dotted rhythm. The curtains were folded back and a nervous balding man, resplendent in military uniform, stepped forward. The Tsar of All The Russias.

The entire room rose to its feet and applauded, smothering the music. The Tsar bowed quickly and walked as swiftly as he could to his seat.

> The Ruler who bestrides the Spree,
> Whose land was cruelly taken,
> Yet from this a kingdom made,
> His people ne'er forsaken.

The curtain folded back again and the King of Prussia, exuding all the authority the Tsar had failed to muster, stood rigidly to attention. Waiting for the applause to subside, he brought his heels smartly together and strode off, one arm held close to his side, the other crooked around a feathered helmet.

Ludwig could not help smiling as he watched the King of Denmark and the King of Bavaria receive similarly exaggerated accolades. Every member of the audience was rapt with attention: they knew what was coming next.

> And the crownèd head who strives and toils
> With th'ardour of his illustrious line
> Has built a paradise, no less,
> Germania! Germania mine!

Emperor Franz stepped forward, his dour face showing not the slightest trace of pleasure. The audience clapped vigorously but his eyes were fixed somewhere on the balcony.

Seyfried held his arms suspended in the air. The music could not continue over the applause. As if at some unspoken order it suddenly transformed into a steady unison beat, and to that the Emperor marched to his seat.

Seyfried made sure he had the orchestra and singers' attention and the music resumed. The hum of conversation drowned the thin violin solo that Ludwig had perversely scored to follow the Emperor's appearance. Then it was the turn of the chorus: the people.

> Hail Vienna! Hail to Thee!
> Hail Vienna! Hail to Thee!

Ludwig looked across the room and saw Alois Weissenbach, listening intently, his hands cupped behind both ears. He stood up, mindless of the scraping noise his chair made, and walked over to him.

'Weissenbach!' he whispered loudly into the man's ear, making him jump with fright. 'Come. Enough of this. To the Wollzeile!'

He recoiled at the look of horror on Weissenbach's face. The man was clearly enraptured by what he was witnessing: his poetry being declaimed before the crowned heads of Europe. In the company of His Imperial Majesty the Emperor!

'Bah! You're no better than anyone else,' Ludwig muttered, knowing his words were unheard. He reached forward to the table, grasped a half-full carafe of wine and returned to his chair.

Chapter 3

Vienna was reeling from two events that followed each other within a matter of weeks. On the last day of 1814, in the small hours of the morning and mercifully after all the guests had left, a flue carrying heat into the wooden structure built on to Count Razumovsky's palace caught fire. The structure was destroyed within minutes and the flames spread to the palace itself.

The Count, ordering that the Tsar and Tsarina in the far wing should not be disturbed, battled with his staff to douse the flames, but for twelve hours the fire raged, demolishing a large part of the palace, along with priceless paintings and sculptures. The room that the Count had devoted to the Italian sculptor Canova was destroyed, along with every sculpture.

Days later he was found wandering in the ruins, a bandage around his head. He was mumbling that he could not see, that the smoke from the fire had ruined his already failing sight. Doctors assured him his eyes would improve but they could not ease his anguish at the destruction of all he held dear.

The Tsar, now back in St Petersburg, agreed to loan him the enormous sum of four hundred thousand roubles and promoted him from Count to Prince. Razumovsky knew not only that he would never be able to repay him but also that at least double the sum was required to rebuild the palace. After a period of soul-searching he made a series of decisions. He would retire from the Russian diplomatic service, disband the quartet led by Schuppanzigh, which had been his especial joy, and sell his ruined palace. When he announced his departure from Vienna, all his friends and colleagues came to bid him farewell. Instead of leaving, though, he took an apartment in an unfashionable part of the city and became a recluse.

The second event soon eclipsed the fate of Prince Razumovsky. On 1 March 1815 Napoleon Bonaparte escaped from the island of Elba, marched through France gathering an army around him, and once more threatened the safety of Europe.

The Congress of Vienna, of which the city had been so proud, was rendered worthless, except that it cemented the alliance against France, which suddenly bore fruit. At the head of his army, Napoleon found himself facing the English army under Wellington, reinforced by the Prussian army under Blücher, near the Belgian town of Waterloo.

When word reached Vienna that the French Emperor had been defeated, taken prisoner and transported to a small island in the South Atlantic Ocean where he would remain for the rest of his life, no one believed it.

While Europe trembled, then rejoiced, Ludwig had time to reflect on his new-found status. He had been fêted by the Emperor and he had shaken hands with kings. No other composer or musician had enjoyed such renown.

And he could compose. He wrote an overture, 'Namensfeier', in honour of the Emperor's birthday; incidental music to the play *Leonore Prohaska*; and attempted to rekindle his friendship with Wolfgang Goethe by setting two of his poems – 'Meerestille' and 'Glückliche Fahrt', Calm Sea and Prosperous Voyage – to music. He dedicated them to their author and sent them to him.

Now Ludwig felt himself Goethe's equal. He may not have had his upbringing or breeding, but had Goethe conversed with royalty? Yet after months had gone by and Goethe had not responded, Ludwig was unruffled: the man clearly still considered himself superior to a mere musician.

He had other inducements: the ever-faithful Ferdinand Ries, now making his way in the musical circles of London, had persuaded the Philharmonic Society of London to commission a set of three overtures, for a fee of seventy-five guineas. With Czerny's help, Ludwig obtained the scores for two overtures he had written some years before and sent them – with 'Namensfeier' – to London.

He began a new piano concerto, but he could not make it work. Time and time again he returned to the manuscript. He pounded the piano keys in frustration, and Andreas Streicher had to make frequent visits to repair broken strings. Why the sudden block? He could not tell. If he could not hear the notes clearly, he could, at least, feel them, and in any case he knew exactly what sound they would make.

Willibrord Mähler, in Vienna briefly, asked if he could paint a new portrait. Ludwig agreed, hoping it would take his mind off the concerts. He sat in the chair, lips pressed together, eyes blazing. He refused to take up any pose – as he had with the lyre for the earlier portrait – and instructed Mähler to paint only his head and shoulders.

When he looked at the completed work, he hardly recognised himself. Mähler had painted a man in the prime of his life, in flamboyant collar and cravat, but whose face betrayed impending failure. No, he thought. It cannot be. At the height of his powers, receiving commissions . . .

On a sudden whim he gave notice on the apartment in Baron Pasqualati's house that had served him so well and moved right across the city, so that he now looked east to Hungary and the Carpathian mountains. Still inspiration would not come. In solitary moments, drinking wine and gazing across the Bastion wall, he knew what the problem was but could not bring himself to admit it. It was what he had quietly dreaded for two years and, sooner or later, would have to resolve. His brother Carl was ailing again, and if he died, what would happen to his son Karl, the sole Beethoven of the next generation?

In the event, he was precipitated into action by a visit from Stephan von Breuning, who looked round the apartment disdainfully. 'Why have you moved here? Your other apartment was more comfortable.'

'Shout, damn you, Steffen. You know I can't hear.'

'Baron Pasqualati is sad. He was proud to have you as his tenant and expected you to stay.'

'Must I live my life the way other people want me to live it? Can I not make my own decisions?'

'When people give you advice, Ludwig, they do it for your sake. To help you.'

'I do not ask for it.'

'But you could not do without it. You have friends, Ludwig. And you also have a family.'

Ludwig's stomach twinged. He said nothing.

'While you have been moving in circles the rest of us only dream of, your brother Carl has been languishing with consumption.'

'He was better. He told me so himself.' Ludwig had reminded himself of this many times.

'How long ago did he say that?'

Ludwig did not reply.

Stephan sighed. 'He had a relapse some months ago. He is very ill.' He looked straight at Ludwig. 'He is dying, Ludwig. And you have done nothing.'

Ludwig thumped the arm of the chair. 'What can I do, Steffen? He does not want me there. And that – that – woman!'

'Stop! Do not talk like that. Johanna is losing her husband, and will be left alone with a child to bring up.'

'No! She must not be allowed to. Karl is a Beethoven. *I* will bring him up. My brother wishes it. We have talked about it before.'

'What do you mean?' Stephan's tone betrayed his bewilderment and shock.

For the first time in the fraught conversation Ludwig felt he had the upper hand. 'Nothing. It is between Carl and me.'

'So be it. So many times I have tried to help you Beethoven brothers, and always I am rejected. I will not put myself between you any more. Do what you want, Ludwig, but I urge you, for your dead parents' sake, to be compassionate. Remember, Carl's death will be a tragedy. Barely forty years old, and leaving a widow and a fatherless son.'

'I am not as ill as people say,' Carl said, lifting his head with difficulty from the pile of pillows propped up against the iron bedhead. 'The doctors have tried to kill me off before, but I won't let them.'

'What do you mean?' Ludwig asked, moving closer to his brother to be sure of hearing him, although every fibre in his body willed him to move back.

Carl struggled to sit up, the effort bringing out beads of perspiration on his forehead. 'Here, help. Put your arm behind my shoulder.'

As Ludwig unavoidably put his head closer to his brother's face, he heard him say, 'They're poisoning me. I have powerful enemies.'

Ludwig was appalled. 'Do you mean that?'

'Of course I do. Why else would I be ill, then recover, then fall ill again? No illness does that. Remember Mother? It was not like that with her.'

The effort of speaking made him cough. Ludwig stepped back. The spasm ended with a rasping noise in his brother's throat, and he brought up mucus into a handkerchief he held to his mouth.

He folded it quickly and pushed it under the pillow. 'Even my office is conspiring to kill me,' he said weakly, 'I applied for sick leave last month and they refused me. It's a conspiracy.'

'I will have something to say about that,' Ludwig said angrily. 'I will speak to the Archduke. I have friends in high –'

Carl interrupted, 'Too late now. They could not stop me staying at home this time. Anyway, anyway . . .' he wiped his mouth with a fresh handkerchief '. . . I cannot ignore what that charlatan Bertolini says. He says I am dying. I'm not, of course. But what if I were? I have to consider my options.'

'What do you mean?'

'I have to consider Karl. Ludwig, you remember we spoke about you becoming his guardian in the event of my death? That was last time the doctors told me I was dying. They were wrong then and they are wrong now. But I want to formalise it. In my will.'

'Of course I will look after him.'

'My wife. Johanna. I don't want –' The cough erupted again, but subsided more quickly this time. 'I cannot stop her having contact with the boy. But I do not want her to be responsible for his upbringing.'

'Why should she see him?' Ludwig snapped. 'She is immoral, you told me so yourself.'

'She is more immoral than even I believed. I know she has taken . . .' he paused, as if he could barely bring himself to say the word '. . . lovers. I know because I have spies who have told me.'

Ludwig gasped, 'Impossible! She could not do that while you lie sick in bed.'

'It would not surprise me if Karl were to have a half-brother or sister before long.'

'Then you must not allow her near the boy. You must not!'

Carl sighed. 'She is his mother. I cannot stop it. But you must take care of his moral welfare. Go to that drawer over there. Bring me the folder in it.'

Ludwig did as he asked. 'It is my will. I would like you to read it,' Carl said. 'With most of it you need not be concerned. But read aloud paragraph five.'

Ludwig put on a pair of spectacles. '"Along with my wife I appoint my brother, Ludwig van Beethoven, co-guardian of my only child, my son Karl. Inasmuch as my deeply beloved brother has often aided me with true brotherly love in the most magnanimous and noblest manner, I ask, in full confidence and trust in his noble heart, that he shall bestow the love and friendship which he often showed to me upon my son Karl, and do all that is possible to promote the intellectual well-being and further welfare of my son. I know that he will not deny me this, my request."'

Ludwig felt tears start in his eyes. He looked at his brother, the emaciated face, hollow yet flushed, the pale watery eyes, the hair now dusty and lifeless. Suddenly all the resentment he had harboured against him dissolved, his meddling with publishers, his attempts to pass off his own worthless music as Ludwig's own now forgotten.

'Of course I will do that,' he said, a catch in his voice. 'But,' the anger welled up in him, 'you must take that woman out of this.' He waved the document in front of Carl's face.

'She is his mother.'

'You must, do you hear? If you do not, I – The boy must not –' Ludwig could scarcely contain himself. A mixture of anger and anxiety consumed him. Karl van Beethoven, bearing the family name, in the hands of such a woman. 'Delete those words,' he said, stabbing the paper with his finger. '"Along with my wife". And "co-". That is all it will take. You must cross them out.'

Carl wiped his mouth again. His eyelids half closed. He nodded weakly. 'Pass me the pen.' He did as Ludwig had asked, then laid his head on the pillows and spoke quietly. Ludwig moved nearer to be sure he could hear. 'They will come tonight to witness it. Neighbours and Johanna. I have to sign it in their presence . . .' His words trailed away.

'You must be strong, Carl. You must resist her. You must not change it back. The welfare of your son depends on it. I will nurture him as if he were my own son. That way the name of Beethoven will be preserved and respected. That is what you want, isn't it? That is how it must be. Tell me you understand.'

Carl gave the smallest nod, then allowed his eyes to close.

Chapter 4

On 15 November 1815, Carl van Beethoven died. To his fury Ludwig was not notified of his brother's death until four days later, in a letter that sent him into a paroxysm of rage. It was from Doktor Schönauer, a lawyer whom Carl had appointed executor of his will.

> Herr Beethoven
>
> It is my sad duty to inform you of the sudden death of Herr Carl, your brother. Under the terms of his will, signed and witnessed in my presence and delivered under seal to the Imperial and Royal Landrecht of the province of Lower Austria, you are appointed co-guardian of your nephew Karl, along with the aforesaid's mother.
>
> The necessary documents, requiring your signature, are currently being drawn up and will be available in my office in one week from now.
>
> > Schönauer, Doktor of Law

So Johanna was co-guardian of Karl. Slowly everything dropped into place in Ludwig's mind. Carl had been right: he had not had consumption, he had been poisoned. Why else would the lawyer refer to his 'sudden death'?

What could he do? Suddenly it was obvious. All he needed was proof that Carl had been poisoned: then any changes he had been forced to make to his will could be declared invalid. Ludwig pulled his overcoat from the hook behind the door, picked up his top hat and clapped it on his head.

Ten minutes later he stepped out of the carriage and strode, head down, into the hospital at the entrance to the Landstrasse suburb, where once he had stood with Nanette Streicher watching the wounded being carried in after another battle against the French. He went straight to the office of Doktor Andreas Bertolini at the end of a long white corridor and strode straight in.

A nurse looked up, horrified. 'Sir, the doctor is examining a patient. You must remain in the waiting room.'

'I need to see Bertolini. *Now!*' He stared at her, eyes bulging. She took a few small steps backwards and disappeared behind a curtain.

Moments later Doktor Bertolini emerged, wearing a soothing smile. 'Herr Beethoven. My condolences, sir. You have lost a fine brother.'

'I can't hear you, Bertolini, I am deaf. My brother was poisoned and I want you to prove it.'

Bertolini gestured him to a chair but Ludwig remained standing.

Bertolini regarded him over his spectacles for a moment. 'Carl said the same thing to me. I can assure you, sir, there is no truth in it. Your poor brother was suffering from consumption, as your late mother did. It is the curse of our age.'

'Bertolini, as my brother's next-of-kin I am entitled to demand a post-mortem examination.'

'I regret, sir, you are not his next-of-kin. That honour falls to his widow. However . . .' He stopped, as if weighing up whether to continue. 'However, as his eldest blood relative you are entitled to make such a demand. But I assure you there is no need.'

'I demand it. Have the papers prepared for my signature. If my brother was poisoned, certain people will be made to regret it.'

Ludwig walked into the offices of the lawyer Leopold von Schmerling, whose name Zmeskall had given him.

'I can't hear, Schmerling, so speak up. And if you do not say what I want to hear, I will instantly become more deaf.'

Schmerling glanced once more at the papers in front of him before speaking. 'May I say, first of all, Herr Beethoven, how honoured I am to meet you. I have always admired your music. I am a pianist of sorts myself, though with no pretensions.'

Ludwig waved his right hand impatiently to force the conversation on, which flustered Schmerling. 'Yes, well, I have made a thorough study of all the documentation, and it seems to me you have a *prima facie* case. The codicil to your brother's will, reinstating your sister-in-law, was clearly added without your knowledge or consent.'

'So I can have the boy?'

'It is not as straightforward as that. Nothing to do with the law ever is. Your late brother's will has been deposited with the upper court, the Landrecht. You will have to petition the court to annul the codicil.'

'How do I do that?'

'I will draw up a document for you.'

'And what if Carl was poisoned? That would alter everything, wouldn't it?'

'I understand the medical authorities are investigating. We await the outcome, but in the meantime –'

'You must tell them what an immoral woman the widow is. That she poisoned my brother. That she was tried for embezzlement and sentenced to house arrest. I also know she consorted with other men while my brother lay dying.'

'For the moment, just a straightforward petition, I think, is all that will be required. Good day, Herr Beethoven.'

The Landrecht summoned Ludwig, with his lawyer, to appear before it on 2 December. Frau van Beethoven and her lawyer were likewise called.

Ludwig shuddered as he entered the tall building on the Herrengasse with Schmerling. Men dressed in black cloaks and high white collars walked silently along corridors, clutching piles of papers. It was an alien world. Schmerling led him into a wood-panelled room, dominated by a high, leather-backed chair, two smaller chairs to either side of it. He sat on a hard bench next to Schmerling. Across the courtroom, next to her lawyer, was Johanna, dressed in black, a veil covering her face.

Five men filed into the room from a door at the back and sat down. Ludwig strained to hear what the man in the middle chair said. He was reading from a document, but his words were jumbled. Johanna's head was moving up and down as sobs convulsed her.

Suddenly the men stood up and filed out. A wave of joy swept over Ludwig. 'Do I have the boy now?' he whispered urgently into Schmerling's ear.

Schmerling led him out into smaller room a little way down the corridor. 'They have deferred judgement. We are to come here again on the fifteenth. There is no cause for concern. Nothing in the law ever happens quickly.'

Doktor Bertolini sat across a table from Ludwig in a meeting room at the hospital. 'I have conducted a post-mortem on your brother, Herr Beethoven, as you requested. I established beyond doubt that the cause of death was consumption, brought about by excessive fluid on the lungs which, ultimately, we were unable to drain. There are no suspicious circumstances, and I have filed the report accordingly.'

'She is still an immoral woman, Schmerling. She is a convicted embezzler. It is enough for the court to give the boy to me.'

'At the hearing on the fifteenth, Herr Beethoven, I think it would be effective if you were to address the tribunal and state your case. I will draw up a document for you and all you will have to do is read it. It will sound much better coming from you than if I were to do it. Of course, the other side will have the right to reply, but they cannot deny the facts we will put to the court.'

To Ludwig's relief Johanna was not in the courtroom on the fifteenth, but the satisfaction he felt was dispelled by Schmerling. 'It is a tactic by the other side. The tribunal will not be able to make a judgement. It will mean another deferral. I hope, though, we will be able to state our case.'

There was a knot in Ludwig's stomach as Schmerling made some preliminary remarks to the tribunal. Why was it necessary to go through such a ridiculous procedure? Carl's wish was clear: the codicil to his will had been forced out of him on his deathbed; his widow was a woman of loose morals who had been convicted of –

He felt Schmerling's hand under his elbow, guiding him once again out of the courtroom. Bewildered, and growing angry, he sat across from Schmerling in the small anteroom.

'As I suspected,' Schmerling explained, 'they said they could not allow you to make your statement without the other side being present.' Ludwig protested but Schmerling said, 'Do not worry, Herr Beethoven, they have given us three days to present our case, and we can do it in written form. We will not need to return to the court.'

That same day Schmerling penned a letter in Ludwig's name to the chief magistrate of Vienna, asking for documentary proof of the charge against Johanna of embezzlement four years before. The magistrate refused this, but after pressure from Schmerling agreed to forward the papers to the Landrecht. Schmerling then drafted a long statement on Ludwig's behalf, detailing how Carl van Beethoven's will was changed under duress, and drawing the tribunal's attention to the documentation provided by the chief magistrate.

On 9 January 1816 the tribunal delivered its judgement. Ludwig van Beethoven was appointed sole guardian of his nephew Karl.

Ten days later, his lawyer at his side, he appeared in court once more and swore on the Bible to provide for his nephew's welfare, education and moral upbringing until the boy achieved adulthood.

BOOK FIVE

Chapter 1

The notes would not come. Ludwig pounded the side of the piano in frustration. 'No, no, no!' he shouted, snatched up the manuscript and scratched out the words on the title page. 'No more piano concertos. If I cannot perform them in public, there is no point.'

He threw himself into a chair. 'Damn! Damn everyone. Everything.' Despair overwhelmed him. Such a short time ago it had seemed he had all he wanted. He was composing, receiving adulation from all quarters, meeting royalty. Then Carl had died. And Carl, the brother who had blighted his life for as long as he could remember, was still blighting it now. Was he the only one who could see how important it was to keep his nephew away from his mother? Stephan von Breuning had tried to argue with him; Nanette Streicher had begged him not to go through the courts . . . Karl was a Beethoven, guardian of the name. He must not be corrupted. *He must not.*

Ludwig had placed Karl in a boarding-school in the Landstrasse suburb, not many streets away from the Streichers' piano factory. The owner of the school, a man of Spanish extraction, who habitually rubbed his hands as if determined not to let any dirt sully them, had declared himself fully in support of Ludwig in the battle against Johanna, promising she would be allowed to visit her son no more than once a month, as the court had stipulated.

But things were not going well. Karl was frail. He was reluctant to join in games with other boys and was becoming withdrawn. His work was poor and he was making no effort to learn. Ludwig considered taking the boy out of the school and employing a tutor. But he knew that was not practical. The boy had to be made to learn.

There was one course of action Ludwig could take, and he did so immediately: he ordered Carl Czerny to give Karl piano lessons, and was gratified to hear that the boy was talented, gifted, even. Czerny had remarked that maybe one day he would become a musician like his uncle.

Ludwig remembered what Czerny had said whenever concern for his nephew threatened to overwhelm him. But it was as if that anxiety was affecting his whole life. First Ferdinand Ries had written to him from London saying that one of the members of the Philharmonic Society had discovered that the three overtures Ludwig had sent had already been performed in Vienna. They had considered asking him to return the seventy-five guineas, but Ries had prevented that. The landlord of his new apartment had said that other residents were complaining about his playing the piano late at night. And Baron Pasqualati had let his old apartment.

But the worst problem of all was that he could not compose.

It was Johanna's fault, he thought angrily. All Johanna's fault.

The servant walked into the room. 'The widow Beethoven, sir. Shall I show her in?'

Ludwig was puzzled, but before he could reply Johanna, clothed from head to toe in black, stood before him.

'What do you want? I am busy. I am in the middle of –'

'Why have you done this to me, Ludwig?'

To his chagrin, Ludwig could hear her clearly. She was making sure of that.

'I have only obeyed my late brother's wishes.'

'Carl was mortally ill. He did not know what he was saying.'

'Hah! You are wrong. Long before he was dying, more than two years ago, he told me he wanted me to be guardian of his son.' Ludwig was gratified to see her shock, even through the thick veil.

She recovered her composure. 'My son too, Ludwig. I am his mother.'

But Ludwig had gained the initiative and would not let it go. 'My brother was perfectly clear in his wishes. He wanted me to be sole guardian of Karl. He talked a lot to me about you. I will not hurt you by revealing his words. But he knew . . . I know . . . you are not a fit person to be a mother, and Karl must be assured of a proper moral upbringing. You are not capable of giving him that.'

Johanna opened a small black bag that hung from her wrist and took out a handkerchief. Its whiteness stood out starkly against her black glove. She lifted the veil and Ludwig caught a glimpse of pure white skin, flecks of powder falling away, as she reached up and dabbed her nose, then patted her eyes.

'You must go now. There is nothing more to be said. I will take care of the boy. You may see him once a month. You are entitled to that.'

There was unexpected strength in her voice when Johanna said, 'He is ill, Ludwig. Did you know that? You did not, did you? Of course not. But I am his mother and, try as you might, you will not keep me away from him.'

Ludwig cursed as he realised he had missed the carriage. He had no alternative but to walk to the Landstrasse. It was not far, and it was a walk he had frequently taken out of choice when he went to see the Streichers, but now he just wanted to get there as quickly as possible.

There was a damp film on his brow and he was breathing heavily as he strode through the gate into the school grounds.

'Herr Beethoven, I am so glad you came. You must have received my letter,' Giannatasio del Rio, the principal, said, wringing his hands even more furiously than usual.

Ludwig's head pounded with the effort of the walk and his ears whistled. 'Is my nephew ill? Speak slowly and clearly – I can never understand that dreadful accent of yours.'

'Sir, Herr Beethoven, Master Karl has been taken unwell, but he is in good hands. I –'

'Why did you not tell me? Why did I have to – My sister-in-law knew before I did.'

Giannatasio threw up his hands in a gesture of despair. 'That woman, sir!' He rolled his eyes. 'It is very difficult. She is very determined.'

'What are you saying?' Ludwig roared.

'She is a very determined lady. She comes to the school very often. My staff have orders. They know what is allowed. But sometimes . . . I have been told she once disguised herself as a man to see her son.'

'I will apply to the court,' Ludwig bellowed. 'I will speak to my lawyer. She must be stopped! The court has made a ruling. She must not disobey it.'

Giannatasio nodded. 'Once a month. That is most clear.'

Ludwig looked round the book-lined room, wondering if the Spaniard had a carafe of wine on any of the shelves. He needed the fortitude that wine would give him. He was scared of what he was about to hear.

Giannatasio's hands flapped at his sides. 'I regret to tell you, Herr Beethoven, there is a physical problem, an abnormality that has developed. Your nephew complained of a severe pain in his groin.' He gestured towards his thighs. 'I called in the doctor, of course, and he diagnosed what is called a hernia. He will need surgery to correct it.'

'*Surgery?*' Ludwig almost shrieked. 'I will not allow it. I will *not* allow a – a – *surgeon* to go anywhere near my nephew. Is that understood?'

'Sir, I regret to tell you that there is no alternative. The boy is unable to participate in school activities of any kind. His studies are interrupted. I have had to stop Herr Czerny coming to give him piano lessons. He is in too much pain, sir. But it will soon be resolved. The surgeon has spoken to the boy's mother, who is his next-of-kin, whatever the court has ruled regarding his welfare. She has to give her permission – and she has done so. But, Herr Beethoven,' he said, in a mollifying tone, 'you do not have cause for concern. The operation, according to Doktor Smetana, is straightforward. All that will be required afterwards is rest.'

'He will recuperate with me,' Ludwig said suddenly, and vehemently. 'I will take a room in Baden. He will come there immediately afterwards and rest with me.'

'Ludwig! Come in. I am so glad you came. I must admit I did not expect it.'

'I will not stay, Steffen. Give me some wine, tell me what you have to tell me, then I will leave.'

He took the glass gratefully from his old friend, blinked as the sharpness bit against his throat. He looked at Breuning's smiling face. 'Always so happy, Steffen. Where are your wife and child? Let me see the happy group.'

His words caused his friend to wince. He had not wanted to speak as he had, but there had always been something about Steffen . . . A certain smugness, a way of always seeing the good in any person, any situation. Commendable, Ludwig knew, but infuriating. No wonder he had fallen out with him when they had shared this apartment. It had been like living with a saint.

'Not now, Ludwig. That tone disturbs me. Stanzi will be out with Gerhard in a moment.'

'What is your news, Steffen? If it's bad, I'll just close my ears to it. There are advantages to being deaf.'

Breuning turned, wearily resigned, to him. 'You remember Ferdinand Ries?'

'Ries? Of course I remember him.'

'Well, he has married. His wife is English.'

'*Good* news?' Ludwig barked 'I shall write him a letter of commiseration.'

'Enough!' Breuning said in a voice Ludwig had not heard before. 'You are being cruel, Ludwig – again.'

'What do you mean, Steffen?'

'I am sorry, Ludwig, but I do not regard it as acceptable behaviour to take a child away from his mother.'

All the fury and frustration of the last months welled up in Ludwig. He banged his clenched fist on the arm of the chair, spilling his wine over his trousers. 'Damn you, Steffen! You are not a Beethoven. You do not know what passed between my brother and me!'

'I am a human being, Ludwig. And a compassionate one. And what you did was wrong.'

Ludwig stared at him, momentarily lost for words. Then the most powerful argument of all came to him. 'It was not me, Steffen. It was the law. The Landrecht, the highest court, decreed it.'

Breuning took a deep breath. 'It is better we do not argue. I will go and get Stanzi and Gerhard.'

Ludwig's heart was pounding and he walked to the sideboard to pour himself more wine. Damn Steffen and his righteous pontificating. Always so reasonable, so conciliatory. How many times had he been through the arguments in his head? *But the court ruled in my favour. All I was doing was carrying out the wishes of my dead brother.*

Then he softened. Poor Steffen. What did the future hold for him? He had a mundane position in the War Department at the Hofburg, with no hope of advancement. His salary could not be large, yet he had a wife and child to keep. Poor Ries. How much could he earn in London from piano lessons? Yet he, too, was now married, with no doubt a child to bring up before long. Poor Johanna, even. Yes, poor Johanna, a widow already, barely thirty, and condemned by her husband so that she must lose her child.

A face floated before him – a sweet, pure face, soft and gentle, framed by auburn ringlets – and self-pity flooded over him.

His eyes fell on a folder that lay on the sideboard. He opened it and a couple of pages fell out. He gathered them up quickly, and as he did so his eyes fell on the neat writing that filled the first page. It was a poem, entitled '*An die Ferne Geliebte*'. To the Distant Beloved. He read the first two verses.

> On the hillside sit I gazing
> In the blue and foggy mist,
> To the distant pastures grazing
> Where first, my love, we kissed.
>
> Mountains, valleys, separate us,
> Yet I long for you each day.
> No joy and comfort there to sate us
> Oh, why are you so far away?

Oh, why are you so far away? The words so perfectly expressed what he felt about Antonie, far away with her husband and children in Frankfurt.

'They are fine words, aren't they?' he heard Steffen say, close to his ear. 'Written by a young man I know. Alois Jeitteles, a physician at the General Hospital.'

Ludwig nodded slowly. 'They would set well to music. I would like to set them. Would you permit me?'

'Take them, Ludwig. No, wait,' Stephan added, 'here are Stanzi and Gerhard. While you are speaking to them, I will write a copy for you. Then you can keep it, mark it, do what you wish to it.'

Ludwig beamed with delight when Constanze and the little boy came in. Her face was radiant, her pleasure at seeing him clearly genuine. Young Gerhard, barely three years old, stood beside her, holding her hand. His face was round and cherubic, framed by lustrous wavy golden hair.

Gerhard looked up at his mother expectantly, loosened his hand and ran over to Ludwig. Holding his arms to his side, he bowed from the waist. 'Good day, sir. My papa tells me you are a great man.'

Ludwig did not hear the child's words clearly but he saw the parents laugh easily. Ludwig bent down to him. 'So, young Breuning, it is a pleasure to meet you. But I am just a deaf old composer, and you will have to speak loudly to me. In here.' He pointed to his left ear.

'You speak like my papa,' Gerhard said.

Ludwig sat down and beckoned the little boy to come to him. Unhesitatingly Gerhard ran forward and, with no trace of shyness, stood by the chair and leaned towards Ludwig's ear. 'My papa has told me about you. You are a very famous man.'

Ludwig laughed. 'Your father and I have known each other since we were boys. He comes from a fine family. Tell me, young man, can you play the piano?'

Without answering, Gerhard ran to the small piano that stood against the wall and brought his flat palms down on the keys. Ludwig clapped his hands to his ears.

'Enough, Gerhard,' his father said. The little boy ran back to Ludwig, with a mischievous giggle.

'What will you be when you grow up?' Ludwig asked. 'Have you decided yet?'

Breuning laughed. 'As a matter of fact, Ludwig, he has. He wants to be a physician, don't you, Gerhard?'

The child's eyes blazed with an intensity beyond his years. 'Yes. I want to make sick people well. I want to cure them.'

'Very noble,' Ludwig said. 'I hope you become a better doctor than the fools I have to deal with.' He noticed that the top button of Gerhard's trousers was unfastened. 'Come here, boy. There. Now you can run around without losing your breeches. From now on I will call you Hosenknopf. Trouser Button. Do you like your new name?'

Chapter 2

In Baden Ludwig took a large house, owned by a Polish count, on the banks of the Schwechat. There was a music room and a permanent staff of cook and servant. He gave orders that none of the other rooms were to be let. He wanted privacy to work and for Karl to recover from the operation.

He moved there in advance of the boy to make sure that all was in order – and to work. He had already begun setting the poems by Jeitteles – six in all – to music, and was also working on a new piano sonata. But this unexpected burst of creativity did little to lighten his mood. The poems, which emphasised his loneliness, magnified the depression that had settled on him. The music he composed was wistful, redolent of a heartfelt longing.

The sonata, too, matched his mood. Above the opening of the first movement, which he had marked *piano*, he wrote on the manuscript paper *'etwas lebhaft und mit der innigsten Empfindung'* – rather briskly and with the deepest feeling. The first bars – a rising gentle phrase – were like a delicate question in the middle of a quiet conversation.

The songs and the sonata were composed with a mounting sense of frustration, as if he knew there was still a vast well of music within him but that he was unable to bring to the surface. Both compositions contained sudden outbursts: he invested the words *innere pein*, inner pain, with a dissonance that shattered the serene calm of the second poem of the set.

He considered returning to Vienna to be with his nephew in the days leading up to the operation, but decided against it. Should he allow Johanna to visit Karl? Steffen, Nanette and the others would say that he should. Let events take their course. And if she went, at least he would not be criticised for stopping her.

The house was big and empty, the dying heat of late summer failing to penetrate its thick walls, which were already chill with approaching autumn. He took the waters at the

Johannesbad, but nothing, it seemed, would lift his depression.

He looked at the wide moist eyes, their pupils black as coal. 'Josephine!'

'Ludwig. I heard you were in Baden. May I come in?'

When he first saw her, he was thrown into confusion. Zmeskall had called her emotionally unstable, and he remembered the claim she had made of her baby. Oh, God, he thought, what trouble had she brought with her? But he was curiously drawn towards her. There was a certain vulnerability about the slight figure, which seemed as if it would buckle at the smallest pressure, that attracted him now as it had before.

They sat together in the large drawing room sipping coffee and eating cakes that the servant had brought.

'Josephine, I am deaf.'

Instantly she moved her chair close to him. 'There, Ludwig. Can you hear me? I know about your ears. Nikolaus Zmeskall told me. You poor, dear man.'

Instinct told him to move back, but he could not. She was in the room with him; they were going to talk. If she did not sit near to him, he would not hear her.

'How is your health, Josephine?'

'Will you not call me Pepi, as my family do? It would make me so happy.'

Ludwig did not reply.

'I have had more than my fair share of woes, Ludwig. Stackelberg took my children.' She pulled a lace handkerchief from the small bag she held on her lap and dabbed her eyes. 'I have only my Minona.' She looked up at him quickly, then cast her eyes down again. 'Therese, my sister, has taken her to our mother in Hungary so I am alone.'

'He is a scoundrel. You should take him to court. Win your children back. The court will understand.'

Josephine smiled ruefully. 'I do not have your influence, Ludwig. And I am Hungarian, my husband Estonian; they would not listen to me. No, I am doomed to spend the rest of my life in misery.'

'You must not say that. Something good always comes of sadness.'

'Do you really believe that, Ludwig? Do you say that to yourself when you are sad?'

Ludwig realised she had caught him out – exposed the platitude he had unthinkingly uttered.

'How long are you staying in Baden?' she asked.

'It depends on my nephew. He is coming here to recuperate from an operation. Maybe another month, maybe less.'

'I am staying in an apartment in the Wassergasse, across the river. Will you come and see me there? I am alone.'

He saw the fire in her eyes and a curious sensation swept over him. His breath quickened. Angry with himself, he picked up the coffee cup and drained it.

'Will you, Ludwig? Please say you will.' He nodded quickly. 'Oh, I shall so look forward to it. You will not forget, will you? Now, I will not detain you. I remember how you like to be alone to work.'

She placed her hand fleetingly on his shoulder, then turned and left.

Ludwig wanted to move towards Karl, but the boy took a pace backwards.

'Karl, come here,' Ludwig said, with a sharpness he had not intended.

Giannatasio whispered into the boy's ear and he took a hesitant step forward.

'He must not stand for long, Herr Beethoven,' Giannatasio said. Ludwig looked at the boy and saw that his lower body was swollen. 'He must wear the truss for one month. For a week he must walk as little as possible, and then only short walks to exercise his legs. That is what Doktor Smetana has ordered.'

Ludwig went to Karl and patted his head. The boy tensed. 'Come, Karl. Come and sit down. I will play the piano for you.'

'Sir,' Giannatasio said, 'I trust you received my letter and that our room is in order.'

'What?' The man irritated him. He wanted to be alone with Karl, to talk to him, comfort him, try to get to know him better. 'What are you talking about? What letter?'

Giannatasio cast his eyes upwards. 'I told my secretary to check the address. Stupid man. We cannot return to Vienna tonight. It is too late. My daughter and I, that is. Fanny. We shall stay tonight and, with your permission, tomorrow as well. That will give us a whole day in this delightful place.'

A young woman of about twenty-five, with a lively, smiling

face, came into the room, carrying two bags, which she deposited on the floor.

'Ah, Fanny. Herr Beethoven. You will curtsy to him and be very polite. He is an important man.'

Ludwig saw the young woman's look of exasperation at being treated like a child. He returned her smile, and nodded as she curtsied. It occurred to him immediately that a female presence would be of benefit to Karl, who was looking at her longingly.

Fanny went over to the boy, bent down, and said, 'Now, Karl, let me take you to your room so you can rest.'

Dinner that night was stilted. Karl remained in bed, refusing food. Ludwig found it difficult to hear what either of the Giannatasios said, relishing instead the wine, which immediately made him sleepy. He agreed to Fanny's suggestion that in the morning they should all take a walk in the Helenenthal, bringing with them a picnic that she would prepare.

'Why do you not come with us? It will do you good,' Ludwig said. But Karl allowed his unmoving eyes to answer for him. The beguiling image of little Gerhard von Breuning floated into Ludwig's mind, and he felt a sudden surge of annoyance. As if he did not have enough problems without a sick nephew. He reached down to pull the sheet off the boy.

In a move as quick as any angry cat's, Karl's hand shot up and his nails sliced across Ludwig's cheek. Ludwig leaped back, his fingers at his face. He felt the torn flesh, the warmth of blood; he raised his hand to hit the boy then saw the sudden look of fear on his nephew's face and lowered his hand. 'Water!' he shouted down to the stairs to the servant. 'Cold water. Be quick!'

He bathed the wound, which was shallow, then tore off a piece of wool from the roll that lay on the dresser and pressed it to his face. Then he went downstairs to where Giannatasio and Fanny were making last-minute preparations to the hamper.

'Oh, sir,' Fanny said, alarmed. 'What happened to your face?'

'Servant. Damn insolent fool. His temper has lost him his job. Come. I need to walk.'

They took a carriage along the Weilburggasse, which followed the Schwechat, out of the western end of the town and into the beginning of the Helenenthal. Before them the valley stretched, bisected by the river, which rose way off in the hills of the Wienerwald and gathered strength as it descended towards Baden, through the town towards the Danube into which it flowed. Under a tree to the right of them a small number of cows grazed.

The driver heaved the hamper off the carriage and walked with it to a flat piece of ground near the riverbank. He touched his cap as he took a coin Giannatasio held out to him. Fanny busied herself laying a blanket on the grass, then spreading out the plates, cold chicken, ham, bread and fruit. Giannatasio opened a bottle of white wine, poured two full glasses and a half for his daughter.

Ludwig applied himself to the food and drink with gusto, making no attempt at conversation and ignoring any remark that might have been directed at him. Soon he noticed that father and daughter were chatting happily together, leaving him to his meal.

'Come on,' he said, 'I need to walk.' Without waiting for the others, he set off into the valley. Ahead, the water dropped a level, crashing over a ridge of rocks. Ludwig liked the sound of water: he could not tell what was coming from outside his head and what from within. It allowed him to pretend his affliction was less bad than it was.

He looked ahead and up to the right. Stretching up through the thick woods were the broken towers of the Rauhenstein ruin. The Giannatasios were close behind him. Without saying anything, he turned up and began to climb.

'No. Please!' Fanny hurried ahead of him. 'It is so gloomy up there. Can we not walk along the river? It is so much nicer.'

Ludwig looked down at the fresh young face. The breeze was lifting Fanny's golden hair clear of her face; her starched linen blouse stretched tightly across her chest, rising and falling with her breath. Her hands were on her hips, which gave her an air of determination, and her long skirt flapped against her legs, emphasising the shape of her thighs.

Ludwig smiled at the wholesome sight of her, and the knowledge that with a simple nod he could make her happy. 'Come on then, young lady, if it is the river you prefer.'

Fanny gave a skip of delight and ran back down the slope to the river. Ludwig's eyes followed her, as her skirt danced around her legs. He was distracted – and somewhat annoyed – by the sound of Giannatasio's voice. He wondered if he could dismiss conversation by claiming his ears were worse here in the open air. But the wretched man was close to him and speaking emphatically. To complain would only make him redouble his efforts.

'Forgive my impertinence, Herr Beethoven, but have you considered taking a wife?'

Ludwig was dumbfounded and considered ignoring the question, but again he knew that Giannatasio would only persist.

'I am unhappy in love,' he said, loudly. He knew that Fanny was close enough to hear, and he felt excited to be talking of women within her earshot. 'I have loved, but in vain.'

'But you shall surely love again, sir?'

'There is no man who admires women and their beauty more than I. I relish every aspect of them, from the way they look, to the gentleness of their voice and the warmth of their skin.' He noticed that Fanny slackened her pace slightly, so that she was even closer. But she continued to walk ahead, without turning her head.

'Indeed, sir,' Giannatasio said, somewhat surprised.

'There was a woman once. I loved her and she returned my love. She was the greatest love of my life. A union with her would have made me happy for ever, but, alas, it was not to be.'

'Oh, poor, poor Herr Beethoven,' Fanny said, turning now and looking at Ludwig as she walked. Her face was flushed. 'But surely, sir, as my father says, there will be another who will love you?'

'I have a wife, young lady. A wife, lover, mistress. But she is demanding. She does not always treat me kindly. Right now, she is even treating me cruelly.'

'My dear sir, that is abominable,' Giannatasio said, indignantly. 'Shall you not talk to her?'

'Oh, Papa, Herr Beethoven is talking of his music. You are, sir, aren't you?'

Ludwig gave a little bow.

The conversation died away, and they retraced their steps to the picnic site, where the driver was waiting with freshly brewed coffee. Giannatasio turned to Ludwig. 'You will treat your nephew gently, won't you, sir?'

Ludwig's hand flew involuntarily to his cheek, but he just nodded.

Chapter 3

Heat flowed through his body as he crossed the wooden bridge over the Schwechat, his footsteps echoing in the still evening air. His head was pounding, but he felt no pain. He saw how the few people making their way home had scarves tied tightly round their necks, their breath visible against the dusk. His coat was open and the air that penetrated his shirt felt good. He increased his stride. Soon he felt his shirt stick to his skin as the wind blew it against him. He swung his arms high, bathing his hot hands in the air.

He climbed the outside steps of the building in the Wassergasse and knocked at the door on the first floor. No one answered and Ludwig felt a dull ache of disappointment. Then, suddenly, he was looking into Josephine's expectant face.

She beckoned him in and slipped his coat off his shoulders. Swiftly she poured a glass of wine and handed it to him. Neither of them had spoken. He took the glass and sat down, staring at a point on the floor in front of him. His mind was in turmoil. Josephine, he knew, was a deeply unhappy – and wronged – woman. Her two marriages had left her badly scarred. She was prone – as Zmeskall had told him – to sudden mood changes and irrational behaviour.

He gripped the arms of the chair. It was as clear as crystal. He should not be here. He had to leave.

He looked up to see her standing before him. She was wearing a dressing gown, which was open to reveal bare skin underneath. He could see the pale flesh of her stomach, the hint of heavy breasts, with which she had fed seven children and which belied the slight body from which they hung. The dark shadow at the tops of her legs was almost hidden by a fold of the robe.

His chest was tight and his breathing rapid. Carefully he put down the wine glass. 'Josephine,' he said hoarsely, 'this cannot be. This *must* not be.'

She reached down and took his hand. He allowed her to lead him into the bedroom, where a single candle flickered on the wall. There was a strong smell of scent and the bed was covered with a heavy velvet blanket. He felt the stiffening in his loins.

She stood facing him, slid the dressing gown off one shoulder, then the other. She stepped clear of it as it settled on the floor.

'Josephine. Wait. You must understand. You must realise . . .' She untied the lace that held his shirt closed, pushed in her hands, rubbed them over his chest and up to his shoulders. Her lips were parted and he could feel the heat of her breath on his face.

'Josephine!' he said, sharply. 'You know that it will mean nothing. That there can be no more.'

She began to kiss his face, cheeks first, then his neck, then his lips. He returned her kisses. Why not? he thought. I am being honest. *I must be honest.* Grasping her shoulders, he pushed her a little away from him. He opened his mouth to speak, but she put her forefinger against his lips. Her eyes closed, she leaned towards his left ear. He felt her lips against it. 'Shhh. Do not say anything. I understand. Just this once. Then we return to our other lives.'

She led him to the bed. She was untying his trousers, which fell to the ground, then pushing off his shirt.

'Now, Ludwig. At last. Now.' She climbed on to the bed, pulling him after her. Expertly she guided him into her and instinctively he thrust deeper. He seized her hair and felt her nails in his back. Her cries intensified.

The pressure in him mounted until he could take it no longer and, with a long growl, he exploded into her. Without opening his eyes he allowed his head to collapse on the pillow next to her, as he relaxed.

Then he realised she was pushing at him. He opened his eyes.

Her face was contorted. 'Off. Now. Off. I want you off me. Off me, or I will call for help.' She was staring wildly in front of her. Her eyes seemed to be covered in a grey film. 'What do you think you are doing? You think you can treat me like that? You abuse me, steal from me. My children, oh, my dear children. Where are they? Where have you taken them? Off! Get off!' She pushed harder against Ludwig's shoulders. Swiftly he pulled himself clear of her. He had to talk to her, reason with her . . . But she was still staring into the distance. She was half sitting now, supporting herself on one arm and turned away from him. 'Beast! Beast!' she said, and sobs convulsed her.

Hurriedly Ludwig pulled on his clothes. Walking towards the door, he looked back once more. Josephine's head was buried in the pillow, her small fist pounding it. He closed the door behind him and walked as fast as he could across the Schwechat to the Braitnerstrasse.

'The doctor said you should walk. Why are you being so defiant? Eh, boy? Speak up! What are you trying to say?'

'It's raining.'

'Yes, it's raining. So much the better. The rain brings out all the smells of nature. Come. We will walk in the valley and you can exercise your legs.'

Ludwig strode from the house and got into the carriage. He felt a quiver of satisfaction as the carriage shook under Karl's weight. There were no words between them as it moved west through the town and dropped them at the entry to the valley.

'Wait. We'll be an hour,' Ludwig said to the coachman. 'Come, Karl, let me teach you how to walk in nature's surroundings.' He took the boy's hand but after a few paces it was wrested away.

'Slower, Uncle. Please.'

'Come on, boy. You need to put strength back into your muscles.'

After a while Ludwig realised Karl was no longer with him and looked round to see him sheltering under a tree. 'Damn you, boy. Here, have my coat.' Ludwig took it off and threw it around him. He moved Karl firmly away from the tree. 'See? I do not mind the rain. Walking in the rain is best. There is no one else. You are alone with nature. Come. We will climb to the castle.'

Ludwig strode up the winding path that led to the Rauhenstein ruin. Frequently he checked that Karl was coming and although the boy fell further and further behind, he was following. The trees were all around, their high leafless branches forming a makeshift roof and lightening the rain, if not completely shielding them from it.

'Come on!' he called. 'We are nearly there.' His breathing eased as he reached the top of the winding path and came on to the level ground on which the ruined castle stood. The stone towers loomed above him, the jagged walls of the old rooms around him. He strode from one to another. Huge drops of water plunged down from the rafters, splashing on to the ground.

He looked for Karl but could not see him. He walked through the ruin on to a ledge at the same level as the tops of the fir trees, which dropped away down the valley to the river, their needles looking like a lush green carpet stretching into the distance. He turned his face up and allowed the rain to run down it along his neck and on to his shirt.

He shook his head and saw the drops fly off his tousled hair. He cursed under his breath at the thought of Josephine and what had happened. He had not seen or heard from her since. He presumed she had returned to Vienna. What a fool he had been. So weak! Yet he felt no remorse. It was she who had initiated it, she who had refused to let him go.

And afterwards? Had she really thought he was Stackelberg? Or Deym, even? What did it matter? Another man's pride might have been hurt, but not Ludwig's. He had been relieved. No one need ever know. And if she spoke about it, who would believe her?

He turned. Still no sign of Karl. He walked through the castle again. A flutter of panic ran through him as he still could not see his nephew. 'Karl?' he called. 'Karl!'

He retraced his steps. Where was the damned boy? What if the walk had damaged him? What if his wound had reopened? He started down the winding slope – and saw the boy half-way along it, walking easily towards the river, Ludwig's coat held high over his head against the rain.

The boy is defiant, Ludwig thought proudly. A Beethoven family trait.

Chapter 4

The fever began with the usual soreness at the back of his throat. He woke in the night unable to swallow. The next day his head was heavy and throbbing with pain, his nose streamed and his eyes filled with tears every time he looked at the daylight. He tried to drink wine to relieve the pain, but it burned at the back of his throat so intensely that he could not bear to swallow it. By the end of the day every muscle ached and he resigned himself to yet another spell of illness.

Nanette Streicher came to see him and insisted on calling in Doktor Malfatti, who examined Ludwig and then took Nanette into another room to confer with her.

She came back and tried to talk to him but her words were mangled and made no sense. He looked at her despairingly. She found some paper, a pencil, and scribbled quickly.

> The doctor says there is nothing to be done until the fever abates. Then he will prescribe powders. I will come regularly to give you food and change your bed linen.

Ludwig snatched the pencil from her and wrote:

> He is a charlatan, imbecile. Not see him again. Get another doctor.

Nanette wiped his brow with a handkerchief and left.

The fever would not go. It abated, then returned with renewed force. Ludwig stayed in bed, sweating heavily. The nightshirt that Nanette kept replacing for him felt like sackcloth rubbing on his sore skin.

She came frequently, with chicken broth, and replenished the water jug that stood by his bed. She also brought news of Karl: the boy had recovered fully from his operation now and Giannatasio was pleased with his progress. Carl Czerny had resumed the piano lessons and he was coming along well. She also informed him – skirting over the matter swiftly – that Johanna was not trying to see her son more than once a month.

One day in late December Nanette could not disguise the sadness on her face when she told Ludwig that his old benefactor, the unfortunate Prince Lobkowitz, had died at his estate in Bohemia, without having been able to discharge his bankruptcy.

The winter of 1816 was fierce and became colder still in the new year. Ludwig had not left his lodgings for several months, and Doktor Malfatti was insistent that he should not do so for some time to come. The fever had gone but it had left Ludwig with a weakness that he had never experienced before. And he knew beyond any doubt that his hearing was considerably worse. His head still throbbed with pain and the noises were louder. Several times he went to the piano and played short passages but the sounds jarred in his head. He looked at the pile of manuscript paper that stood on a small table by the piano. Empty, it stared back at him.

What did the future hold? He could drink wine again, in small quantities, but it only served to depress him all the more. *What if I can no longer hear my music? What if there is no music left in me to compose?*

Nanette came almost daily and Ludwig looked forward to her visits, then longed for them. She was always smiling, always encouraging, always with news of Karl, or Stephan von Breuning, or little Gerhard, who, she said, now had a baby sister.

'Nanette, I must get out of this place. I cannot look at these walls any longer.'

'It is still too cold, Ludwig. You must stay indoors. Doktor Malfatti will be angry if you disobey him.'

'He can go to hell! What has he done to help me? Nothing. Just powder after powder. Six different types. Always changing. And still I am ill. All I am doing is making the apothecaries rich. No wonder my brother Johann is well off.'

On one late winter's day, as the sun did its best to pierce the gloom, Nanette tied Ludwig's coat tightly around him, made him wear his hat and gloves, and walked with him on the Glacis. The air felt good on his skin, and he enjoyed feeling

Nanette put her arm through his. Was any friend so loyal? My God, he thought, how I envy Andreas.

Twenty-four hours later the fever struck again: he shivered uncontrollably, yet his skin was burning. Nanette was mortified: it was the sudden exposure to the cold air that had brought it on.

One day when she arrived, he knew instantly that something was wrong. 'What is it, Nanette? Has the Italian told you I will never be well?'

'Of course not, Ludwig dear. It is just . . . I was not going to tell you, but I can't hide it. Our dear old friend Wenzel Krumpholz has died. He was walking on the Glacis with his wife when he clutched his hands to his head and fell in a faint. He died before they could do anything.'

Ludwig sighed. Old Krumpholz the mandolin player, who, all those years ago, had first brought the young Czerny to play for him. He had composed music for him. He had been such a kind, gentle man, who had not yet reached his seventieth year.

Lobkowitz, Krumpholz . . . *and me.* Ludwig was approaching fifty, and suddenly he was struck by intimations of his own mortality. He had been unable to shake off the illness, which had returned with added ferocity each time he had thought it spent. His hearing was deteriorating fast. His music was trapped within him.

Doktor Malfatti came to see him, but he was in no mood to receive him.

'Where have you been, Malfatti? How long is it since you came to see me? Eh? Just quack powders, that is all you give me. Get out. I do not want to see you again.'

Malfatti took the ear trumpet from his bag.

'I said you should leave, Malfatti, or are you more deaf than I? That would be impossible. If you speak to me now I will not hear you. So do not waste your breath. You are a quack and a charlatan, Malfatti. No better than any of the others.'

'Remove your shirt.'

'Go, Malfatti. It is all over. My work is done. Leave now, before I order the servant to eject you.' Ludwig flung back the sheets and staggered to the door. He held it open, breathing heavily. 'Now, Malfatti, and do not ever return.'

It was not long before Nanette came again, as he knew she would. He had expected Malfatti to inform her of his condition and he was prepared for what he knew she would say.

'It is enough, Nanette. My time has come.'

'Oh, Ludwig,' Nanette said enthusiastically, 'I have so much to tell you. Such good news. Karl has passed his first music examination. Czerny says he is progressing so well. And I have found you new lodgings in the Landstrasse, near to Señor Giannatasio's school so you can see Karl more readily, and near to Andreas and me as well so I can look after you.'

Ludwig gazed at her. He could hear her words. His head was no longer pounding and although the heaviness was greater than before his illness, *he could make out her words*. But he said, 'My hearing is worse, Nanette. Worse than it has ever been, and it will continue getting worse until I can hear nothing at all.'

'But you heard what I said, didn't you, Ludwig? I have found you such a nice apartment and we will be neighbours. Away from the centre of the city and the dreadful wall. And isn't it exciting about Karl?'

Ludwig kissed her lightly. 'You are so good to me, Nanette.'

In early May, Ludwig heard from his lawyer Schmerling that Johanna van Beethoven wanted to use her inheritance from her late husband to contribute to the education of Karl. She was prepared to make an immediate deposit of two thousand florins, and half her pension each quarter.

Ludwig's suspicions were immediately aroused, but Schmerling assured him she had made no demands – nor would she have been granted any if she had.

Chapter 5

Ludwig liked his new lodgings in the building named Zum Grünen Kranz – At the Green Garland. No longer did he look out over the Bastion wall to the empty plains beyond. Instead, his apartment, on the second floor, was at the same level as the tops of the linden trees that lined the broad Landstrasse avenue, leading south-east out of the city, following the line of the canal called the Danube Arm to the wide fields beyond.

Directly across the Landstrasse from the Grünen Kranz was a tavern called Zurr Goldenen Birne, At the Golden Pear, of which he soon became a regular patron. He walked always to the small round table at the back of the dimly lit room, at which there was only a single chair. Before long, other patrons had ceased to stare at him as he walked in, head down, a frown creasing his forehead, frequently muttering to himself. It soon became generally known that this was Europe's most famous composer, who liked at all times to be left alone.

In the corner of the room overlooking the Landstrasse was Ludwig's piano. Hesitantly, at first, Ludwig played on it again, allowing his fingers to roam aimlessly. It no longer surprised him that he could barely hear the notes and sometimes not at all. He experimented, sometimes playing loudly, sometimes softly, sometimes chords, sometimes chromatic runs. He sat with his head back, then forward, first one ear over the notes, then the other.

One day he played a huge series of major chords, prefaced with a single quaver deep in the bass. He heard them clearly in his head moments before he played them. As he struck the last chord he felt the keys go slack under his fingers. He got up and looked inside the piano; several wires curled upwards, still vibrating from the force that had snapped them.

Stephan von Breuning brought Ludwig a long letter from

Ferdinand Ries in London. 'He wasn't sure of your address, so he sent it via me.'

Ludwig snatched it from him. It was several pages long. 'I cannot read this. What does he want?'

Breuning smiled. 'It is complicated. Can you hear me if I shout? Would you like me to write it down?'

'No, no,' Ludwig said impatiently. 'Into my left ear. Loud.'

'The Philharmonic Society of London invites you to come to London next January.'

'Louder, Steffen.'

'They ask you to compose two grand symphonies, for which they are offering you three hundred guineas, and they invite you to direct the first performances in London.'

'*Two* symphonies, did you say?'

'Two. Three hundred guineas.'

'London,' Ludwig said, more to himself than to his friend. 'London.' He glanced at Breuning. 'If Ries knows I'm deaf, the Philharmonic Society must know?'

'Of course, and Ferdi will look after you.'

After Breuning had left, Ludwig was overcome with apprehension. Two symphonies? It was impossible. It was so long since he had composed anything substantial. He could not do it.

Nikolaus Zmeskall, his shock of hair whiter than ever and his shoulders even more stooped than Ludwig remembered, came to see him and immediately suggested they cross the road and drink wine in the Goldene Birne. 'I'll come straight to the point,' he said, after Ludwig had had a glass. 'Would you see Johanna?'

'You are speaking into my deaf ear, Nikola. I cannot hear you.'

Zmeskall leaned forward. 'The schoolteacher with the Spanish name won't let Johanna come to the school.'

'I instructed him.'

'She says she is prepared to come to your apartment to see her son. That way you need not be suspicious. Would you agree, Ludwig?'

Ludwig thought for a moment. 'Will you be there too, Nikola? Then you can see for yourself what an evil woman she is.'

'If you wish.'

Ludwig jotted some sketches for the first of the two symphonies for the Philharmonic Society of London. He tried to play them on the piano, but it was useless. He heard the sounds more clearly in his head than from the broken instrument.

When he reached the Streichers' piano factory, he found Andreas in tense mood. 'Nanette has broken her wrist and I am taking her to Baden for a short rest.'

She was sitting in an easy chair, her arm, the lower half wrapped in plaster to the first joint of her fingers, resting on the side. 'Hello, Ludwig, I am glad to see you. Andreas wanted to tell you, but I wouldn't let him. I know how you dislike being disturbed.'

'Take warm baths, Nanette. They are the cure for everything. Except deafness.'

Nanette regarded him fondly. 'I have your laundry, Ludwig. Over there in the bag. I will tell the housekeeper to come and collect it while we are in Baden so you will not have to worry about it.'

Ludwig could barely hear her but he understood what she was saying. He turned to her husband. 'Andreas, I need a stronger piano. Will you build me one?'

Andreas's eyes lit up. 'I am glad you mentioned that, Ludwig. I have some news which may interest you.' He picked up a sheet of paper. 'Have you heard of the firm of Broadwood and Sons?'

As he spoke, a low whistle, which had been lying like a serpent in Ludwig's ears, rose in intensity. It pierced his head and he screwed up his eyes in pain. It passed almost as quickly as it had begun. He saw Nanette's consternation. 'I am sorry. It often happens like that. What were you saying, Andreas?'

'Broadwood and Sons. Of London. Piano-makers. One of the best in Europe. Thomas Broadwood, one of the sons, is coming to Vienna. You should meet him. English pianos have a different movement. Heavier. It might suit you.'

Ludwig thought for a moment. 'I have been invited to London, but I am not going. They want two symphonies. I will meet this Broadwood here, in Vienna. He can take the message back to them.'

Carl Czerny brought Karl to Ludwig's apartment. The boy – thin and tall for his age – stood, head lowered, hands clasped in front of him, clearly uncomfortable in the company of adults, yet giving the impression that he would be equally ill at ease with children of his own age. He had none of the boisterousness or mischief of a boy soon to enter his teen-age years.

'Karl, my boy!' Ludwig called to him. 'Is he practising, Czerny? Are you practising, my boy? Practise, Karl. You must practise, if you are to be a great musician.'

'If I may say so, sir,' Czerny said, 'he is a little nervous. He was reluctant to leave school, weren't you, Karl?'

The boy nodded almost imperceptibly. 'Are you enjoying your school?' Ludwig asked and turned to Nikolaus Zmeskall. 'Fine boy, isn't he, Nikola? True Beethoven. Your father would be proud to see you, boy.' Ludwig slapped him on the shoulder. Karl flinched. 'You'll have to speak loudly or I won't hear you. Understand? Here. Shout. Try it.' Ludwig bent his left ear to Karl's face, but the boy said nothing. 'Good. You don't want to hurt your poor uncle's ears.'

Ludwig straightened as Johanna walked into the room. Her appearance took him by surprise. Although he had had frequent contact with her about Karl, he had rarely seen her since the court action, and in the past months he had found it difficult to bring her face to mind. Looking at it now, he was struck, as he had been in the past, by its strength. Her eyes shone with intensity and her lips were compressed. Her hair, darker than he remembered, was pulled straight back and tied in a knot, a style favoured by lower-class women for its simplicity but which gave her an added impression of determination.

The thought ran through Ludwig's mind that Karl had inherited neither his mother's strength nor his father's wiles.

'Good,' Ludwig said expansively. 'You may greet your son.' Ludwig watched Karl turn to his mother and his lips curve expectantly. She went to him, glanced at the three men watching her, then planted a kiss on the boy's forehead.

Ludwig saw that Johanna was speaking to her son but he could not hear the words. Intermittently Karl nodded.

'What are you saying? Mmh?' He felt Zmeskall's restraining hand on his arm. 'She's not allowed to do this. I made it clear –' Zmeskall tightened his grip.

Johanna was adjusting her son's scarf, talking easily to him. She put a hand to his cheek and stroked it. Karl's eyes were moist. Suddenly he nodded vigorously and his shoulders began to shake. Johanna reached into her bag and pulled out a handkerchief, dabbed his eyes and nose, making comforting sounds to him.

It was the moment Ludwig had anticipated. She had made

Karl cry. The boy had been perfectly content, albeit a little nervous, yet his mother, deliberately, blatantly, uncaringly, had distressed him.

'Stop, woman!' Ludwig said abruptly. 'You must stop now. Czerny, make sure Karl is all right. Johanna, sit over there. Karl? You must not cry. Be strong.'

Ludwig got to his feet and looked around him, first, at Johanna, who returned his gaze coldly. Zmeskall and Czerny, on opposite sides of her, wore conciliatory expressions. Karl was gazing at the floor.

'Karl does not like his school, do you, Karl?' Johanna said, turning to her son. Her voice was firm and strong, as if forestalling Ludwig's reluctance to hear her words.

Ludwig looked at his nephew. 'That's not true, is it, Karl? Señor Giannatasio is good to you, isn't he?'

Karl turned his face towards his uncle. At first Ludwig thought he was about to cry again. But his eyes were filled with an intensity Ludwig had not seen before. *'I hate it!'* Karl said. Then, quieter, 'I want to go home.' He clenched and unclenched his fists, staring straight in front of him. Ludwig looked at Johanna, expecting her to move instinctively to her child. But she stood stock still, unmistakably triumphant.

Chapter 6

'I am taking the boy out of the Spaniard's institution, Steffen. He is going to live with me.'

'Ludwig, that is not wise. You must permit me to reason with you.'

'I don't want you to reason with me, Steffen. You or anybody else. The boy is going to live with me.'

'If he is to live with anybody, he should live with his mother.' Breuning was red with anger.

'How dare you say that to me, Steffen? Leave my apartment now. I insist.'

Breuning tried to placate him. 'I am sorry if I offended you, Ludwig. I am merely trying to point out . . .'

Ludwig got up and walked to the sideboard, where he poured himself a glass of wine. He was of half a mind to go through with his threat and order his friend to leave but he knew he needed his support. It would not be easy having Karl to live here, he knew that: Steffen was right to be concerned. But his mind was made up.

'I have a housekeeper and a cook. I will employ a tutor. The boy will receive an even better education that way. Czerny will continue to give him piano lessons.'

'Ludwig,' Breuning said, drawing up a chair and articulating with extra care, 'he is a sensitive boy. He has had a lot of difficulties to overcome. His father's death when he was so young, then that operation. Now he knows about this dreadful breach between his mother and his uncle. It is all having a profound effect on him. You will be gentle with him, won't you?'

Ludwig found Nanette in sombre mood. He lifted her hand and brushed it with his lips, careful not to touch her other arm, which hung in a sling. 'When will you be free of this?' he asked.

'Soon. But it does not matter. There is no more pain. Ludwig, I heard of your intention to –'

Ludwig thrust his hands over his ears. 'No, Nanette, I do not wish to hear.'

Nanette gestured to a black sack in the corner of the room. 'Your laundry is ready, Ludwig. Andreas told me you were coming this morning.'

'Is the Englishman here?'

'With Andreas in the music hall. You know your way through.'

Ludwig took the short corridor to the room Streicher had built to exhibit his models. He saw the two men by one of the pianos along the back wall. They were talking animatedly, Andreas standing beside the instrument, the Englishman sitting on the stool, his hands over the keys.

For a moment Ludwig considered leaving. A stranger. *How will he speak?* The man was hitting a single note now, softly at first, then with increasing pressure.

Ludwig looked at the piano, its polished wood given a burnished hue by the pale rays of sunshine that penetrated the tall windows. Such a handsome instrument. *My* instrument, which produces *my* language.

He walked towards the two men. Andreas greeted him. 'Ludwig. So good of you to come. This is Mr Thomas Broadwood Esquire, famous piano-builder of London and head of the firm Broadwood and Sons.'

The other man smiled modestly and held out his hand. Ludwig looked at it, then bowed curtly.

'So honoured, Herr Beethoven, though your name is so familiar to us in London, I feel I know you already.' Broadwood was small, prematurely balding, the skin of his scalp stretched tight and reflecting the sunlight as he moved his head. His voice was higher pitched and more forceful than Ludwig had expected.

'We were talking about the pianos of London and our own pianos,' Andreas said brightly. 'Explain to Ludwig, Thomas, the one crucial difference between them.'

The Englishman leaped up, and peered inside the piano. 'Do you see here, sir? The hammer action. There is a problem. Rebounding. Strike the key hard –' He reached round with his left hand, still keeping his head in the body of the piano, and struck a note several times. 'It rebounds. The note is not clear.

Do you hear, sir?' He did not wait for a reply, suddenly aware of his ill-judged question. 'You cannot play a quick sequence of one note, because the hammer . . .'

Ludwig gazed at the wires and hammers, and struggled briefly to assimilate what Broadwood was saying. All this talk of action, hammers! He wanted to sit at the piano and play it. That was what the instrument was for. Then Broadwood said, which he both heard and understood perfectly, 'Would you play something, sir, so I can watch *how* you play?'

Andreas gestured to the stool and Ludwig sat, looked for a moment at the keys, the ivory picking up the light that still streamed into the room. How inviting they looked, willing him to release the sound they could produce.

He played the huge C minor chords that began the Pathétique sonata. The sound vibrated through his body before it penetrated his ears. He played the second sequence of chords, trying to force himself to hear them as he played. The third sequence, *sforzando*, he played harder, and harder still, and then the mighty run in the right hand ending on an unexpectedly gentle octave E.

He felt Andreas's hands on his shoulders. 'The Pathétique. You know, Broadwood, my wife and I were the first people in all Vienna to hear those chords.'

'Really, sir? And now they are known across Europe. Your friend Herr Ries,' Broadwood said to Ludwig, 'has made quite a name for himself performing your music.'

Ludwig was allowing the words to float around his head like so many butterflies, not attempting to listen to them or make sense of them. He became aware, though, that the Englishman was trying to communicate with him.

'Mr Ries, sir. A friend of yours. He sends you greetings from London. I saw him just before I left.'

At last Ludwig gave Broadwood his attention. 'Will you take a message to him? He invited me to come to London with two new symphonies. But I cannot come. I haven't begun work on them. Tell him I have been ill.'

Broadwood nodded. 'He assumed you would not be coming, since he hadn't heard from you. Do not worry, sir. He is a patient man, and the London Philharmonic Society, I understand, will renew its invitation at some future date. Now, sir, let us talk about pianos. Can you imagine an action heavier than this? Would it not suit you?'

Ludwig had no trouble hearing Broadwood's words. He

nodded. 'The chords need more weight. They must sound as if . . .'

This time he played a different sequence of chords, in the major this time and higher up the keyboard. They were the same chords he had played in his room on Streicher's piano, which had resulted in the broken wires. He recalled a touch he had added last time and repeated it now: a fleeting single quaver on low B flat, the home key, as if to launch the sequence of chords into the air.

He played them again, this time extending the little finger of his right hand on the fourth chord, the first of two quavers, to E flat. It created a fleeting discord. 'Yes!' he said, under his breath, playing them again and accenting the discord. He sang, as he played the chords yet again, this time higher up the keyboard. He wanted to play on. The chords needed a contrasting theme to set them in context. It would come to him easily, he knew, but it would need work. This was not the moment. He was aware again of Broadwood's voice. '. . . precisely the kind of forceful playing that suits the heavier action.'

Ludwig wanted to be alone in his apartment, seated at the piano composing. He stood up and bowed formally to Broadwood, then more perfunctorily to his old friend. 'Gentlemen, a pleasure. I have work to do.'

'Ludwig,' Andreas said quickly. 'A glass of wine before you go. I have a bottle I prepared specially for my guest.'

Reluctantly Ludwig allowed himself to be led through to the house, where Nanette had already laid out glasses and sweet biscuits. Moments later the wine brought relief to Ludwig's head, which still resounded with music and words . . . Broadwood was speaking to him again.

'Mr Beethoven, sir. It would do me a great honour if you would accept one of my pianos as a gift. I shall build it especially for you and my firm will arrange to ship it to you here in Vienna. Will you accept it, sir? There will be no cost to you. My firm will bear the expense of the shipment. As I say, sir, it will be a great honour to the firm of Broadwood and Sons.'

'Come, Karl, we will walk. Are your legs strong?' Without waiting for a reply Ludwig took his hat and coat off the stand and made for the door.

'My wound hurts. From my operation.'

But Ludwig was insistent. Outside he put out his arm and hailed a passing carriage. 'Währinger cemetery. And be quick.'

He said nothing as the carriage rumbled across the cobbles of the city centre. Darkness filled the small compartment when it passed under the mighty Bastion wall at the Schottentor Gate, and headed into the open countryside on the other side of the Glacis. Eventually he said, his voice softening, 'You know what today is, don't you? The anniversary of your father's death. We were close, your father and I. Not always. We had our disagreements, as brothers do. But we understood each other.'

Ludwig was aware of the sullenness behind Karl's dark eyes. He expected the boy to speak, to say, perhaps, that he knew his uncle was misrepresenting his relationship with his father. But the boy said nothing.

Ludwig watched the countryside roll past until they entered the village of Währing, site of Vienna's principal cemetery. Ludwig took his nephew's hand firmly and led him through the gates of the cemetery and along the path that ran round the perimeter.

He stopped in front of a grave with a small rectangular headstone, which was white and unweathered.

CARL VAN BEETHOVEN
1774–1815

CITIZEN OF BONN IN THE RHINELAND

BELOVED FATHER OF KARL

'You changed it,' Karl said, his eyes filling with tears.

'Your name is on it now. There is no need for any other. Your father was proud of you.'

'My father!' Karl almost spat out the words. 'What did he ever do for me? We were always miserable, Mother and I. He hurt her hand once with a knife. She still has the scar.'

Ludwig heard him clearly and wanted to slap him down, not just for what he was saying, but because he was deliberately speaking loudly, in a way he knew Ludwig would be able to hear.

'Come over here. Sit on the bench.' Without looking at Karl, Ludwig began to speak. He had practised the words in his head a number of times because he found it difficult to say exactly what he meant. 'You are a Beethoven. You carry the name of Beethoven. You are the next generation. It is important you understand the responsibility you bear. The world will know the name of Beethoven. Not just now but for generations to come. Do you understand?' Karl nodded slightly. 'You must understand that everything I do for you, my concern for your welfare, is with that in mind. One day the world will talk of you the way it does now of me. I have no doubt of that. There is a vein of greatness that runs through our line. You did not know your great-grandfather. He was a great artist. You do not have a choice. You, too, will be an artist.'

He turned to Karl, who was staring into the distance. 'Are you listening to me? Do you understand?' Again Karl nodded, but his face was blank, his mouth hanging slightly open. 'That is why I am taking you out of school. It is what you wanted, isn't it? You will live with me and have a private tutor. Czerny will continue your piano lessons.'

Frustration mounted in Ludwig at the boy's passivity. Why would he not respond? At times, Ludwig had to confess to himself, he simply did not behave like a Beethoven. The mother's fault. The damned mother's fault. *I will not let that spoil the boy or hurt the Beethoven name. I will not.*

'Come on,' he said, standing. He felt drops of rain on his head. 'We can't walk. We will get too wet. We'll take a carriage back.'

BOOK SIX

Chapter 1

Ludwig pressed the ivory keys and relished the weight under his fingers. He could not hear the sound, but it did not matter. He ran his finger along the wooden edge of the piano. Mahogany, deep burnished brown, so deep it was like liquid. He stood back and looked at the body – longer, more tapering than on any piano he had seen. The legs were curiously feminine, wide at the top like thighs, rounded and tapering to ankles so thin it was remarkable they could sustain the weight they had to carry.

He studied the wooden board that ran along the back of the keys and read the words inscribed on it: *Hoc Instrumentum est Thomae Broadwood (Londini) donum, propter Ingenium illustrissimi Beethoven.* And close by it, in less sure script, a signature: *Ferd. Ries.*

He looked at the keyboard: it extended further into the bass register than he had seen before. The deep, mellifluous bass. He sat and played a simple phrase, beginning on D below the stave, descending to A and ending on deep F sharp. He could feel the vibrations as soon as he stroked the keys, which required more pressure than he was used to, but it suited him. How right Broadwood had been!

Straightening his back, he played the same sequence of chords he had played for the Englishman. They were grand, almost magisterial – such a contrast to the phrase he had just explored in the bass.

'Karl! Karl!' he called. 'Come here. Come to your uncle.' He waited before turning, giving the boy time to enter the room. Why, he wondered for the thousandth time, was the child's face so melancholy? 'Can you not smile, boy? I have some momentous news to tell you, and you shall be first to hear it. I will compose a new sonata for this noble instrument. And I shall name it after the instrument in whose honour it is written. The piano. The *Klavier*. The *Hammerklavier*.

Do you not think it is a good name? Listen to the opening. Listen.'

He played the chords again, preceded by their fleeting quaver.
When he turned, he saw that Karl had left the room.

Reluctantly Ludwig climbed the stairs of the Amalienhof
to Archduke Rudolph's rooms. Conversation was becoming
increasingly difficult for him, even with close friends like
Zmeskall and Breuning. The Archduke always strove to make
him feel at ease, even when chiding him gently for not coming to
the Hofburg enough to teach him composition. But inevitably,
talking to the brother of the Emperor was not as carefree as
conversing with Zmeskall in the Alter Blumenstock or the
Goldene Birne. He considered carrying some paper in his
pocket so communications could be written down, but it was
so undignified. It made him look more of an invalid than poor
old Prince Lobkowitz and his crutch.

The Archduke greeted him, sombrely. Ludwig immediately
indicated his left ear. 'In here, sir. Loudly. I can barely hear
any more.'

The Archduke directed Ludwig to a chair, summoned a
servant who put a tray down with carafe and glasses, waved
him away and poured the almost orange-coloured wine. 'Thank
you for coming, Herr Beethoven. I have to tell you – and
I suspect you will not be sorry to hear it – that I must
suspend my musical studies for a while. The appointment I
have dreaded is soon to come to pass. It is an unquestion-
able honour. I should be grateful. The Church saved me
from a career in the military but now it is to take over
my life.'

'What do you mean?' Ludwig asked, sipping the wine with
some contentment.

'I am to become Archbishop of Olmütz, in Bohemia. It
requires a lot of study and instruction.'

'Why? To learn to pray? Anyone can pray.'

'I shall not bore you with details. But two years of intensive
instruction, to begin in the spring. In a year I will be appointed
to the archbishopric, with my enthronement taking place nine
months after that. A long affair, and then, once enthroned, I
shall leave Vienna to tend my flock.'

Ludwig could not contain his laughter. 'Shepherd Rudolph!'
he said, knowing even as he said it that no other commoner

could have used such language in front of the Emperor's brother.

The Archduke sipped his wine delicately. 'Are you composing, Herr Beethoven?' he asked firmly.

'I have ideas for a piano sonata. And you, sir? You should always have a work in hand.'

'I am attempting to compose a trio, for clarinet, cello and piano.'

'For *what*?' Ludwig burst out. 'Clarinet, cello and piano, did you say? Well, why not? Shock the audience, sir. Give them what they least expect.'

'I regret you are freer to do that than I. My aim is to complete it soon and perform it on my name-day in two weeks' time. In front of my brother and Her Imperial Majesty. Would you . . . would you do me the honour –?'

'My ears have failed me. You will have to stop talking. Here. I have a gift for your name-day.' He sat at the piano and played the chords that would open the Hammerklavier Sonata, repeating them. Then he played the sequence again, singing this time: '*Erz-Herzog Rudolph! Erz-Herzog Rudolph. Feierlicher Namenstag!*'

He paused, to let the vibrations leave his body, then played the haunting sequence low in the bass. For a moment he was lost in thought, as he played a quaver accompaniment in the right hand. Remembering the Archduke, he played the opening chords again, then stood and returned to his seat.

'I am honoured,' the Archduke said, articulating clearly, 'to have heard the seeds of what will grow into a great work. Now tell me, Herr Beethoven, how fares the uncle with his nephew?'

'Father!' Ludwig snapped. 'I am the boy's father. That is how I behave to him. But he does not always behave like a son. He will learn. It will come.'

'You need to spend time alone together. To get to know each other. Take him away for a while. Let him continue his studies in the tranquillity of the countryside. You love nature. You can work more easily away from the city. It will be good for both of you. That way you can live like father and son.'

Ludwig stared blankly at his patron. How wretched I am. I cannot talk to Karl as a father would. If he speaks to me I cannot hear him. How can I tell him of my hopes for him, for the future? If I could make him listen to my music, maybe then he would understand . . .

'It would be impossible. We would need –'

'Take your servants with you. You have servants, don't you?'

'Servants? A useless pair. An old housekeeper who complains about everything and a cook who is fatter than Schuppanzigh.'

The Archduke smiled. 'Rent rooms. Take them with you.'

Ludwig shook his head.

Stephan von Breuning's letter caused tears of rage to leap into Ludwig's eyes.

My dear friend

I applaud your actions, knowing as I have always known that at the bottom of your heart there lies nothing but kindness. How else could you have become the great artist that you are?

The young lad spent only a little time with his mother, taken there by your housekeeper who waited patiently in an anteroom, but it allowed a true bond to be rekindled between mother and son.

As a father I applaud you. My own wife and children join me in greeting you.

Your friend
Stffn v.B.

Chapter 2

Ludwig directed the four men, straining against their leather aprons, as they manhandled the piano up the stairs. 'Take care, damn you. This is a valuable instrument. Sent to me from London. By ship to Trieste and then over the mountains. And you will ruin it on a single flight of stairs.'

He wondered where Karl was. At least he was safe here in Mödling, away from the clutches of his mother. He had confronted the housekeeper – old Frau Dorling – and she had admitted taking Karl to see his mother. He had threatened to sack her, had only relented after her lamentations of poverty.

It was some years since Ludwig had been in Mödling, and although it was here that he had composed his First Symphony it evoked little nostalgia in him. But Mödling was only two hours south of Vienna, just off the main road to Baden, set in beautiful countryside, and Nanette Streicher had established that rooms were available for the summer in the house of the master potter on the Herrengasse. On Ludwig's instructions Andreas had arranged for the Broadwood piano to be moved there.

He was pleased to get away from the city. He had never recovered completely from his last illness. His stomach and bowels plagued him; the colic was always ready to strike; sometimes the dirt and dust of the city seemed to lie in his lungs, making even the simple act of breathing difficult; and then there was his deafness – worse than ever, a deep heaviness in his head that he could actually *hear* with the whistles, buzzing, crashings a constant threat.

Only after drinking liberal quantities of wine did he gain any relief from his deafness.

'Come on, Karl. Up past the church to the edge of the woods. I remember it. You'll like it. It's called the Hinterbrühl.' Ludwig strode past Othmar's church and up the slope, gentle at first then rising sharply. He knew the boy was having trouble keeping up with him, but he wanted him to exert himself. 'There. Look. Isn't that a fine view?' Ludwig stood at the top of the rise, surveying the landscape. In the distance, shimmering in the early-summer air, stood Vienna, surrounded by its dark Bastion wall, like a solid belt, protecting its inhabitants and hemming them in. The wide grass-covered Glacis stretched out from it, tiny knots of people just visible running this way and that. Soldiers were drilling: an occasional glint of sunlight flashed off a bayonet. And towering above everything, waving crazily to the eye so that it seemed about to collapse, the great Gothic steeple of St Stephansdom.

Ludwig threw himself to the ground at the base of a tall tree. 'Come. Sit!' he said. The boy's face was flushed and he was panting. His eyebrows were angled upwards under a frown, giving a look that reflected sadness more than anger. Ludwig patted the ground and was pleased that the boy sat beside him rather than wandering off to be alone. 'Now you know I won't hear you if you speak,' Ludwig said. 'My ears are singing from the climb. Playing an entire symphony in my head,' he said, smiling. 'I want to talk to you. Don't interrupt me.'

Karl wiped his sleeve across his damp forehead. Ludwig waited for his own breathing to steady. 'You won't do it again, will you? You know what I am talking about. You mustn't. Remember, the court made a ruling. You must not go against it. It is the right decision, otherwise the court would not have taken it.'

Karl glared at his feet.

'I am your uncle, Karl, but you must think of me as your father, treat me as your father, and I will always seek the best for you. I will not let anything bad influence you. You know what I mean by that, don't you?'

Ludwig thought he saw the faint trace of a smile. Encouraged, he continued, 'As you know, I have entered you in the school here run by the village priest, Pater Fröhlich, for the summer. You will be in class with other boys. That is good. You need friends. I want you to be the best in class, so that everyone says Master Beethoven is the cleverest boy in Mödling. You will do that for your uncle, won't you? For your father?'

The boy's eyes had wandered off into the distance. 'And no more nonsense with the housekeeper. If she tries to instil any evil into you, I will dismiss her.'

After a few moments' silence, in which Ludwig tried to think of something more to say, an idea came to him.

'Karl, I want to talk about music to you. Will you listen?' To Ludwig's delight, his nephew turned his face towards him and nodded, albeit unsmilingly. 'I am working on a new piano sonata. It will be a big work. Will you let me play it for you? No, maybe I had better not. I will hit too many wrong notes because I cannot hear properly. But when Czerny comes down to give you lessons, I will ask him to play it. But, Karl, listen to me, I have another idea, and I want you to be the first to hear it. I want to compose a work that contains voices. Not an oratorio, or an opera, but a symphony. A purely orchestral work, with voices as instruments. No one has composed such a work before. But I . . . I believe . . . Karl, do you understand what I am saying?'

'No,' Karl said, with sudden force. 'I want to go back now.' He jumped up and ran off down the slope.

Ludwig took his fingers off the keys. Where was Karl? He should have returned from school by now. He stood and walked to the door. He would go to the school, which was housed in the building alongside the church, and walk home with his nephew. But as he moved down the short corridor he saw that the door to the kitchen was half closed. This was unusual – Peppi, the cook, always opened the door wide, propping a bucket against it, probably to allow a through-draught to carry off the cooking smells.

He looked in and saw Peppi and Karl standing on the far side of the kitchen table. They were engaged in animated conversation: it occurred to Ludwig that he had never seen his nephew speaking so volubly before. They must be plotting.

Suddenly Peppi thrust her hands into the pockets of her housecoat and brought out some paper bags. She shook the contents on to the table. There were bonbons and small chocolate animals. Karl grabbed them, nodding his thanks and smiling broadly.

Ludwig found himself smiling, too, at the innocence of the scene. He carried on down the stairs and into the main square.

It was only later in the day that doubt began to gnaw at him. What started it, he could not say. Perhaps it had been the slightly frightened look on Peppi's face.

Ludwig soon became convinced of a conspiracy. He summoned the housekeeper.

'Frau Dorling, you have been to see the boy's mother, haven't you? You or the cook. One of you. Come on, woman, I want the truth or I will dismiss you both.'

'No, sir. As the Lord is my witness, no, sir.' She made the sign of the cross.

'Where did Peppi get those bonbons? There is no shop in this village that sells such frippery.'

'I – the Lord bless me, sir, I do not know. I shall question her, sir. But I assure you, sir, she is a loyal servant to you, just as I am myself.'

Later that day Ludwig told Karl to come to see him in his room. 'Where did that girl get the bonbons, Karl?'

Ludwig regretted his words immediately as tears started in the boy's eyes. He pulled a handkerchief from his sleeve and handed it to him. For once he felt sorry for his nephew. 'All right. I shall not ask any more questions. How is school? Are you progressing well?'

Karl wiped his eyes, smiled briefly and muttered something unintelligible, then disappeared.

Ludwig was working on the new piano sonata. The first movement – uncorrected – was complete. It was huge, a vast exploration of the opening sequence of chords, with their falling thirds at the end. He was working on the second movement, a Scherzo, which would be followed by a slow movement to balance the opening movement in size. The Scherzo had to sit between these two large movements almost as a punctuation mark.

Already he preferred the Broadwood to any other piano he had played. The heavy action allowed him to invest the notes with more power, more passion. Also, to begin with, he could hear the notes, if imperfectly. The firmer strings Broadwood used, more tightly strung, let out more sound and greater vibration.

The Hammerklavier Sonata. The words stood proudly at the top of the first page. How they would ridicule the title! Piano Sonata, that is all it means, the publisher would say; it has no significance. Yet to Ludwig it was perfect. It summed up exactly what he wished to say. Yes, a sonata for the king of instruments.

* * *

One morning he received a note from Pater Fröhlich asking him to come to the school after classes at four o'clock.

Fröhlich's face was long, with no hint of a smile behind the full beard. 'Please be seated, Herr Beethoven,' the priest said, in a firm, deep voice. 'I am aware of your affliction and will speak as clearly as I am able. Do you hear me satisfactorily?'

Ludwig nodded.

'Your nephew –'

'My son. He is like a son to me. His father –'

'I am aware of the family history, sir. It is not for me to comment, but he is a disruptive boy.'

'A what?'

'I used the word disruptive, sir.'

'That is a lie, sir. A calumnious lie. Karl is the gentlest creature I know.'

'That is how he may be when he is in your company, Herr Beethoven, but it is not how he behaves when he is in my class.'

'What do you mean, Fröhlich? Explain yourself.'

'He incites the boys to disobey their parents. He is mischievous, but beyond the normal good-natured mischief of a boy of his age. I understand he does not see his mother. That you have forbidden him –'

'I have done no such thing,' Ludwig roared. 'There was a ruling by the Landrecht and I am obeying it.'

'I am aware of that. It is harsh on the boy and, of course, on his mother.'

'I am not going to discuss it with you, Fröhlich. I am not here to be given a lecture on how to conduct my affairs. I engaged you to teach my son – my nephew. Kindly carry out your duty.'

Ludwig left the building, with the priest's words ringing in his ears. He started to cross the square towards the Herrengasse, but changed his mind. The late-afternoon air was warm with summer sun; groups of children, their day's classes over, played in small clusters around the trees. Ludwig saw their mouths open in silent shrieks of joy. The only sound in his head was the whistle, which came in waves of varying intensity. He shivered – the portent of another illness, another fever?

He walked to the bottom of the square to the bath-house. The sudden damp heat swept over him as he entered and the strong smell of sulphur almost choked him. The baths were smaller than in Baden, the chief spa town of the area. There were just three, all – he noted gratefully – empty. He chose the one from which the most steam rose and sank into it. He let out a deep sigh of pleasure as the hot water flowed over him.

He wanted to think about Karl but as he relaxed and his eyelids closed, his head filled with music. He heard the stirring chords that opened the new sonata, and in his mind he played through the entire first movement. His head moved in time to the furious tempo, he saw his fingers on the keys . . .

The Scherzo he left for the moment; he knew it was fully formed. But the slow movement, the great Adagio; ah, yes, he thought, unlike any other adagio I have written. He wanted it to be different, formless, abstract almost. He heard the theme that would act like its anchor, but played – he knew now – by the right hand, crossing over the left, deep in the bass, then repeating it a moment later in the high treble. In his head he heard it all.

And to follow the Adagio? He smiled at the audacity of the idea that came to him. A fugue! A massive fugue – not for two voices but three!

He sank his shoulders lower in the water then sat up quickly, allowing the hot water to flow over them and down his body, before sinking deep again. The Hammerklavier Sonata. Archduke Rudolph would have the dedication – let him claim the opening chords as a name-day gift. Was there a greater champion of Ludwig's music in Vienna than the Archduke? Prince Lichnowsky and Prince Lobkowitz were both dead now. And the Archduke was more than just a patron. He had always seemed to understand Ludwig's music.

And now he was to leave Vienna. Sadness swept over him, which brought him back to contemplation of his nephew. What *was* the matter with the boy? Is he destined always to be such a problem?

The sadness gave way to loneliness. *If I had a wife, if I had children of my own* . . . The words of Jeitteles' poem floated into his mind:

> To the distant pastures grazing
> Where first, my love, we kissed.

Chapter 3

Frau Dorling and Peppi were whispering together. Ludwig watched their faces. The old housekeeper's was stern and unyielding as she berated Peppi, who looked scared.

Ludwig decided that for the moment he would say nothing, and turned his attention to Karl's behaviour. The sullenness had gone, leaving in its place a certain recklessness. At first Ludwig had been pleased to see the boy's character strengthen, but now there was something disturbing about his demeanour: he would hurry into a room, look dartingly around, then hurry out again. For the first time, Ludwig recognised the boy's father in him.

What was it Carl had been called by those who did not like him? A hyena – Ludwig had seen prints of the animal in Artaria's in the Kohlmarkt, standing on the African plain, its head jutting forward, its rump dropping sharply away as if to present its enemies with less of a target.

He decided it was time to speak to Pater Fröhlich again. Clearly it was the school that was at fault, and Fröhlich should be told so. But before he had time to put his plan into effect, he received a note from the priest asking him to see him urgently.

'Herr Beethoven, it is with great regret I have to tell you that I can no longer allow your nephew to remain in my school. He is a bad influence on my other pupils.'

The priest's voice was strong, but Ludwig had to listen hard and watch his lips to understand what he was saying.

'He says evil things about his mother to the other boys, and encourages them to revile their own mothers.'

'His mother is an evil woman, Fröhlich,' Ludwig said, with a trace of triumph in his voice. 'I confess myself somewhat pleased young Karl recognises it.'

'It is not for me to make judgements, sir. Even a bad mother is still a mother. But there is more to it than simple insults, Herr

Beethoven. When I challenged Master Karl about his words, he told me you encouraged him to use such malicious tones. I have to tell you, sir, as a man of God, I cannot condone such behaviour.'

Ludwig felt his cheeks heat with rage. '*You* do not condone such behaviour. You have no right to speak to me like that. You will not meddle in my affairs. I pay you to teach the boy, and that is all I require you to do.'

'No longer, sir. No longer. The boy is dismissed from my school forthwith. I am not prepared to discuss the matter any further.'

Peppi asked Ludwig if she could take Karl to Baden for the day. The boy was miserable at losing the few friends he had made at Fröhlich's school and an outing would raise his spirits. Ludwig agreed straight away; he needed time to think about what to do next.

Should he return to Vienna and put the boy back in Giannatasio's school? He rejected that idea immediately: he had rented the house until September – another two months – and he still harboured the belief that living with Karl away from the city would draw the boy closer to him.

Maybe he should teach the boy himself. For a full hour he drew up a schedule of classes on a piece of paper, but knew even as he did so that the plan would never work. By the time he abandoned it, the floor around him was littered with crumpled balls of paper.

He went to the piano and played part of the fugue that would form the final movement of the new piano sonata. It would be a mighty fugue – so much more work to do on it. By the time he got up, the late-afternoon sun had given way to evening and he could smell cooking. Peppi and the boy must have returned. He walked to the sideboard by the window and poured himself a glass of wine. Even though he had felt rather than heard it, the music had soothed him and the wine increased his unexpected sense of well-being. Let Karl enjoy the remaining weeks in the countryside, he thought, and on returning to Vienna he could resume his studies with a tutor.

What was more important than anything was that Karl was here with him in Mödling and would be living with him in Vienna, away from his mother.

He put down the glass and walked towards the kitchen. The

door was open and he stood rooted to the spot as his eyes took in the scene. Peppi – her eyes open wide in greed – was dropping coins one by one on to the table. Frau Dorling was watching her, counting. To the side of them, paying no attention, was Karl. He had two bags of bonbons, one of which he was untying; he poured the sweets on to the table and began to count them in imitation of Peppi.

Ludwig grasped instantly what the tableau meant. A tight feeling constricted his chest and he stamped his foot as hard as he could. Peppi jumped and turned hastily to tend the pot simmering on the stove. 'Damn you, women! Damn you for your insolence and disobedience. Do you think I do not know what you are up to?' He turned to Karl, who pushed back his chair and dashed past him out of the room. Ludwig wanted to order him back, but he knew the boy would not obey.

Ludwig looked from one woman to the other. 'You, you elephant, you took Karl to his mother, didn't you? You didn't go to Baden, you went to Vienna, didn't you?'

Peppi gasped in fright. Ludwig could see that Frau Dorling was speaking to him. 'Don't try to explain, woman,' he shouted at her. 'There is no explaining to do. You are both evil, conniving women, taking advantage of a man who is deaf and whose only concern is the welfare of his nephew. You are both dismissed. This instant. Get out of the house. Now!'

He moved forward and swept the coins off the table. Peppi ran to the older woman's side. 'Go on. Out of this house! Before I call the police.'

Ludwig went back to the piano room and stood at the window until he saw Peppi and Frau Dorling, each carrying a large bag, emerge on to the Herrengasse and hurry towards the village square. Then he went to Karl's room and tried to open the door, but it was bolted. He nodded. Safely inside, in no danger. That was best.

Back in the piano room he poured himself another glass of wine and drank it slowly. He needed advice, someone who would listen sympathetically and be able to make practical decisions for him.

He swallowed the last mouthful of wine and smiled.

Nanette Streicher put her hand unselfconsciously on his. 'I came as soon as I read your letter, Ludwig.'

'People are always taking advantage of me, Nanette. Servants, especially. They spy on me, they do things behind my back.'

'You mustn't think that, Ludwig. It's not true.'

Ludwig's ears howled as if trying to block out the unwelcome words. 'Nanette, do not lecture me. My ears won't stand it. I need new servants and I need to know what to do with Karl.'

'He should return to school in Vienna.'

'Not his schooling, Nanette. His behaviour. If he is disruptive – if this fool of a teacher is right – how do I make him behave properly? He sneaked off with that idiot of a cook to see his mother. *Against the court order.*'

Nanette put her hand on his again. 'Calm yourself, Ludwig. On the matter of servants, it is trivial and I have already solved it. I have hired a new housekeeper for you, a cousin of my own housekeeper. She will look after your apartment, as well as cook for you. She will bring me your dirty laundry and I will take care of it.'

Ludwig was mollified. 'Thank you, Nanette. But that's in Vienna. What shall I do here in Mödling?'

'Why don't you return to Vienna early. You –'

'No!' Ludwig said sharply. 'I don't want him to be anywhere near his mother. I am keeping him here.'

'I will find someone for you. Do not worry. Now, can we talk about Karl?'

'Nanette, whatever you have to say will not make me change my mind.'

'Ludwig, you should consider entering Karl for a school in Vienna. Not a private tutor. He needs the company of boys his own age. He is too isolated if you –'

'He had that here, and look what happened.'

'He will be more settled in Vienna. And his mother – she is allowed to see him once a month, isn't she?'

'I'm not putting him into that Spaniard's school again. The woman used to go there in disguise.'

'Ludwig, send him to one of the city schools. It will be less expensive.'

'A city school? Like a Gymnasium?'

'Yes. I know it will be good for him. In fact, Ludwig,' she moved closer to him and spoke clearly, 'Andreas and I discussed it at length. We took the liberty of putting his name down for the Akademische Gymnasium. It is close to your apartment. It was fortunate we did. If we had waited any longer, there would have been no place available.'

Ludwig let Nanette's words sink in. A public school, with other boys from less elevated circumstances. But . . . maybe that would help the boy, make him feel more at ease . . .

'I need to confirm his place as soon as I return to Vienna,' Nanette said. 'Andreas and I are sure it is the right course of action. Karl will be among boys his own age, he will receive good instruction, and he will come home to you every night.'

Ludwig walked to the sideboard and cursed to see the carafe empty.

'There is one matter,' Nanette added. 'He will have to take an examination. Not difficult, more a formality. But he will need a tutor who knows the syllabus. I have found one and spoken to him, and he is prepared to come here to Mödling to teach Karl. Twice a week is sufficient. Then, in mid-August, you will bring him back to Vienna to take the examination.'

Ludwig took a deep breath. 'You are a good friend, Nanette, and I am grateful to you.'

Chapter 4

Ludwig rested his hand on the frame of the Broadwood, grateful it had survived the journey back to Vienna intact.

'Play the Adagio for me, Czerny. Remember that the keys need more pressure.'

Ludwig saw the fatigue in Czerny's face, but ignored it. 'Just the opening. As far as the second subject.'

'Sir, will you forgive me if I decline? I have already given lessons for twelve hours today, and the same yesterday, and nearly as much tomorrow. I have had no time to practise my own playing. I would not do justice to your sublime music.'

Ludwig had not heard clearly what Czerny had said, but the younger man's raised eyebrows and slight shake of the head conveyed his meaning.

'Damn you, Czerny. Lessons, did you say? You're like Ries. You'll be forgotten as soon as you die. What use is teaching?' He played the chord that opened the huge slow movement of the Hammerklavier Sonata, and the small turning phrase that followed it. He sang aloud: 'Laaa-laa-laa-laa-laaa.' He stopped playing. 'You'll tell me F sharp, modulating to A major,' he said, turning to Czerny with a grin.

'F sharp minor, sir,' Czerny said, with a wink.

'Hah!' Ludwig exclaimed. 'I compose a work of genius and you reduce it to a ten-finger exercise. Then tell me about this modulation.' He played the mysterious chords of the first subject that gave way to a totally unexpected phrase in G major, stopped and turned again to Czerny.

'Beautiful, sir. But not allowed, if I might humbly say so.'

'God, Czerny, it is a good thing I am deaf or I might have to scold you.' Then Ludwig became serious. He turned to the keys. 'Is the opening of the Adagio too abrupt?' He was speaking quietly, as if to himself. 'It may need . . . No.' He shook his head. 'Now tell me . . . But first some wine.' He poured a glass for

Czerny and more for himself. 'My nephew. Is his piano playing progressing? Does he have genius?' He leaned towards Czerny with a frown of concentration.

'He is competent, sir. He does the exercises I set him.'

'Exercises, Czerny. I don't care about exercises. Can he play any of my music?'

Czerny smiled weakly. 'No, sir. Not yet. I'm not sure he'll ever –'

'He's a clever boy, you know. He passed his examination into the Gymnasium. I'm very proud of him. Does he talk to you, Czerny? Does he ever tell you about himself?'

Czerny cast his eyes down, clearly caught in a dilemma. He swirled the wine in his glass. 'I – I am not sure he likes his new school. I think he preferred the one he went to before. The Spanish teacher's school.'

'Has he ever talked about his mother?' Ludwig looked eagerly at Czerny and could see him wrestling with himself. Fearful of what the young man might say, Ludwig went on hurriedly, 'Bad influence on him. He's better away from her. Will you keep me informed of his progress?' Then he had a thought. 'Let me put an idea to you. It came to me in Mödling. I told Karl about it. A symphony with voices. What do you think?'

Czerny spluttered. 'I – I'm not sure – I have never –'

'You'll tell me it's not allowed, won't you, Czerny?'

Ludwig received a note from Leopold von Schmerling, asking him to come to his offices on the Kohlmarkt. He resented the interruption: he was making sketches for the new work and had not yet decided how the voices would feature – probably not until later in the work. But how? And what words?

His mind full of music, he was not prepared for the shock of Schmerling's words, and assumed at first that his ears were deceiving him. 'You'll have to write it down. I can't hear you. All this damned noise on the street outside.'

Schmerling scribbled, 'Your sister-in-law has again petitioned the Landrecht for guardianship of your nephew.'

Ludwig read the words several times. 'What does this mean?'

Schmerling spoke clearly and firmly. 'She has the right, but I do not think she will succeed.'

Ludwig's head swam. Only minutes ago, it seemed, there was nothing to come between him and his composition; now, the most dreadful prospect loomed before him.

Schmerling went on, 'Let me explain, Herr Beethoven. Your sister-in-law has applied to the Landrecht to have Karl admitted to the Royal Imperial Seminary, where he would have educational instruction as well as board and lodging. She says the fact that she pays half her pension towards Karl's education gives her an equal say.'

'That means he would —'

'May I ask you, sir? You took the boy to the country with you. Did anything happen that might —?'

'That damned man Fröhlich dismissed Karl from his school. Without reason. Without justification.'

'That explains it. Frau Beethoven must be using it as a pretext to change the boy's education. He is now in the Gymnasium, isn't he? Is he happy there?'

Ludwig's face clouded. 'He has told his piano teacher he does not like it — but he is just a boy. What can he know?'

'He must have told his mother too. He sees her once a month, doesn't he?' Schmerling observed.

The wretched boy! Ludwig thought. Did he not see he was ruining his own future?

'If he has spoken like that to his mother,' Schmerling said, 'we will have to argue in court that his childish judgement must be ignored for his better welfare. But with the mother arguing as well . . .' He trailed off. 'They will demand to see his school report, and they might ask for a statement from the teacher in Mödling. I have to tell you, Herr Beethoven, we might have a struggle on our hands. You might lose sole guardianship of your nephew.'

Ludwig bent forward in the chair, trying to ease the pains in his stomach. Every time he ate his stomach revolted. Nanette had insisted on calling in Doktor Malfatti and Ludwig did not protest.

Now Ludwig swallowed Malfatti's thick white potion, sucking in his cheeks at the unpleasant taste. For a while it seemed to work, then his stomach plagued him again. His misery was compounded by a sore throat and a hacking cough, which made his head ache.

Nanette instructed the new cook on what to prepare, and Ludwig derived some comfort from the thick chicken broth. He tried to console himself by playing the piano, but it only made his head worse.

When he realised that Karl was rarely in the apartment, Nanette told him the boy was staying with her and Andreas. Ludwig did not believe her, but did not have the strength to argue. Karl was seeing his mother, there could be no doubt of it. His despair was absolute. He was about to lose the one living being who mattered to him. He had fought so hard, and now it had all to come to nothing. At night the tears came, of rage, frustration and sadness.

On 7 October the Landrecht dismissed Frau Beethoven's application. The boy's uncle, it ruled, being of noble birth and a musician of the highest reputation, was to remain his sole guardian – unless there was any material change of circumstances, in which case the court would review its decision.

The weather in Vienna was icy. There had been snow in October and by late November the elderly and very young were succumbing. Carts draped in black made their way slowly through the streets, carrying bodies to the cemeteries in outlying villages. The horses' breath emitted from flared nostrils in great solid shafts of white. People went out as little as they could, and when they did they were wrapped in coats and scarves, hands thrust in coat sleeves and feet encased in bundles of cloth.

Ludwig ordered the cook to have hot soup ready for Karl each day on his return from the Gymnasium. He wanted to talk to him, but the boy would go straight to his room and bolt the door. Ludwig decided to do nothing to alter this schedule. There was a small fire in Karl's room and he made sure it was lit before his return from school. At least he would be warm while he did his homework. And when Karl was in his room, Ludwig had the comfort of knowing where he was.

As Ludwig grew to accept his nephew's rejection, his health improved. The cold – dry, crisp, invigorating – cleared his head. He made more sketches for the new symphony with voices, but was displeased with them and put the project aside, in the knowledge that one day he would return to it. Instead he went on with the monumental fugue that ended the Hammerklavier. He still wasn't satisfied with the opening to the Adagio. Was it too abrupt?

During the night of 2 December there was a sudden change in the weather. The people of Vienna awoke to milder temperatures, the cobbles glistening treacherously with melt-water. That morning Ludwig rose later than usual, his sleep improved by the more temperate weather. He was in an equable mood until the cook informed him that Karl had not taken breakfast.

'Why didn't you wake him, woman? He'll be late for school.'

Ludwig hurried to Karl's door and banged on it. 'Unlock the door, Karl. It is late.' There was no response. He beat on the door again. 'Let me in, Karl!' He turned the handle and, to his astonishment, the door opened. There was no sign of Karl.

Even before Ludwig read the note that the cook held out to him when he returned to the kitchen, he knew what had happened.

> Brother-in-Law
>   My son Karl has returned to me, his mother, of his own free will. You should not try to fetch him. His health is not good, due to neglect. I shall care for him, as a mother should.
>
>   J. v. Beethoven

Ludwig threw a coat round his shoulders and hurried to the Kohlmarkt, slipping on the cobbles, cursing as he fell heavily on his hip.

He was breathless when he pushed past the assistant into Schmerling's office. 'The boy's run away, Schmerling. To his mother's. We must get him back.'

'I feared something like this,' the lawyer said. 'It will not turn out well, I am afraid. Let me get the papers and we will go to the police.'

He opened a drawer and took out a file, which he tied with ribbon. He put on a long black coat and tall hat, and motioned to Ludwig to follow him. At the police station in the Graben he demanded to see the senior officer, explained that a court order had been violated, and asked for two officers to accompany him to the residence of the widow Beethoven on the Rauhensteingasse.

Ludwig hurried along behind the three men, wiping his forehead frequently with a handkerchief and coughing with the exertion.

Schmerling used the silver top of his cane to bang on the door of the apartment. Ludwig stood behind the small group, his heart hammering.

He was outraged at the look of triumph on Johanna's face when she opened the door.

'Frau Beethoven,' Schmerling said, 'the boy Karl, whom we believe to be here, is in breach of the Landrecht order. You must return him to the guardianship of his uncle forthwith, in compliance with the order.'

Ludwig's head throbbed from the effort of the walk – and the emotional pressure of the whole affair – but he knew Johanna would make sure he could hear whatever defiant words she was going to deliver.

'The boy Karl?' Johanna's lips curled in contempt. 'If you mean my son, kindly use those words.'

Ludwig wanted to reach through the three men standing in front of him, grab his sister-in-law by the shoulders and shake her – shake the smugness out of her, wipe the look of victory from her face, make her understand the evil of what she was doing, and how Karl was suffering as a consequence.

Ludwig saw with dismay how Schmerling's shoulders sagged as he cleared his throat nervously. 'Master Beethoven, your son. I must ask you to admit us so that he can be returned to his guardian, in compliance –'

'You are not coming in here, any of you!' she spat. Her face coloured and tears sprang to her eyes. 'You are so cruel, all of you.'

It's a trick, Ludwig thought indignantly. She's using her feminine wiles to get round them. They must not let her succeed.

'Frau Beethoven,' Schmerling said, 'the court order is clear and I have the authority,' he gestured to the policemen standing on either side of him, 'to impose it. However, if you can assure me you will comply before nightfall, that will be acceptable.'

Johanna's head dropped as she stifled her sobs with the handkerchief. When she looked up the defiance had returned. Her eyes fixed piercingly on Ludwig's.

'I will bring my son to the police station at four o'clock this afternoon. But do not think this is the end of the matter.'

Chapter 5

Why had Steffen brought his son? Ludwig wondered irritably. But he knew the answer. The pair were inseparable. Gerhard was five now, with an angelic face and enquiring eyes. He looked adoringly at his father, nodding at Steffen's every utterance as if to add his own weight.

His friend seemed careworn. Ludwig noticed the grey circles under his eyes and the dullness of his hair. The lively youth he had known in Bonn, and with whom he had climbed the Drachenfels, was now a weary middle-aged man.

'You look dreaful, Steffen,' he said. 'Are you ill? Is your wife chastising you?'

'Just a little tired, Ludwig. There is always so much work to do. I never seem to be able to get through it.'

'Will you have some wine?'

Stephan refused, then said, 'I have to return to the Hofburg. A pile of papers to sort through by this evening.'

Ludwig held out the wine to Gerhard. 'A small drink, Hosenknopf? No, I think your father would not approve.'

'Ludwig, I have to go soon, but I must talk to you seriously for a moment. Gerhard, run into the kitchen and see what Cook has got for you. Maybe she will make you a gingerbread man.'

Ludwig took a deep breath. 'Steffen, I do not want to talk about Karl, or his mother, or anything to do with the matter.'

'Ludwig, please listen to me. Why are you hurting Johanna so? Do you realise that by hurting her you are hurting Karl too?'

'No! Stop it, Steffen. It has nothing to do with you.'

'Ludwig, I have known you for longer than anyone else. We grew up together. Have you forgotten that? I knew you when you were just a poor boy, struggling to have your music heard. If it had not been for my mother . . . Have you forgotten all that, Ludwig?'

'Steffen, you are trying my patience. Worse than that, you are hurting my ears.'

'Damn it, Ludwig! Do you only *ever* think of yourself? *Do you have any idea of the pain you inflict on others?*'

Ludwig gulped his wine. He wanted to end the conversation. It was not the first time his old friend had berated him like this, and it brought out all the old resentment he held against him – his smugness, his desire to do what was right and proper, his reluctance to say or do anything that might go against the rules, however ridiculous and petty those rules might be.

'You complain of a pile of papers waiting for you at the Hofburg,' Ludwig said, an edge to his voice. 'Do you ever wonder why you have not progressed to a more exalted position? You, a former officer in the Teutonic Order. You were, weren't you? Look at you now. The Order must be very proud of you.'

He saw the hurt on his friend's face and he wanted to stop, but he could not; it had gone too far. He had not asked him to meddle in his affairs. 'Remember, Steffen, I have a court order . . .'

The words dried on his lips as Breuning looked up sharply. 'All right, Ludwig. You have said enough. Listen now to me. I will say only a few words and then I will leave. If you continue to behave like this with Karl you will regret it, believe me. Also, although I know it will be of no consequence to you, you will lose my friendship once and for all. I suspect that will hurt me more than it will you.' He stood up and glanced once more at Ludwig. 'Do not forget my warning, Ludwig.' He strode out of the room to collect Gerhard.

Ludwig felt sad that the boy did not come in to bid him farewell; he liked the chirpy little fellow and his impish face.

Schmerling was solemn. 'I have grim news for you, Herr Beethoven. What I have to say is important. You must tell me if you do not hear me properly, and I will write it down.'

Ludwig wanted to stall him somehow, but he knew it would make matters more difficult. Better to get the whole business over with. He waved his hand dismissively.

'Your sister-in-law has made a new application to the court, citing the fact that Karl ran away as evidence of a material change of circumstances. I have a copy of her affidavit here. She makes a strong case.'

Schmerling's words did not surprise him. After Breuning's warning he had been expecting something like this. He had tried to talk to Karl, but the boy would say nothing. He had suggested that they went away together, maybe to Linz to see his uncle Johann, but the boy would not listen, the sullen look etched on to his features as if nothing short of a mason's chisel would remove it.

'She says she was denied the access to her son to which she was entitled – that is to be expected, and I think we can rebut that – and she says that if he remains under the sole influence of you, his guardian, he will suffer physical and moral ruin.'

Ludwig gasped, but before he could speak, Schmerling continued, 'She says, "The Beethoven brothers are eccentric men, my late husband and his brother so often at odds with each other that they might better be called enemies than brothers." And she says the codicil to Carl's will made it clear –'

'Eccentric, did you say? What do you mean, Schmerling?'

'Not my word, Herr Beethoven. But words such as that will not carry weight with the court. What concerns me far more . . . Allow me to ask you something. Your nephew Karl. Did you notice anything physically unusual about him before he ran away?'

Ludwig was bewildered. What was Schmerling getting at?

'According to Frau Beethoven, Karl had frost-bitten hands and feet. You remember how cold it was in the city? She also says he had no warm clothing and had not taken a bath for a long time. Karl corroborates all this. It will be difficult for you to deny it.'

'I tried to speak to him, but he –'

'And worse still,' Schmerling continued, 'her lawyer has obtained a statement from the teacher Fröhlich in Mödling. He refers to the "physical and moral degeneration" of the boy while in your care.' Schmerling sat back.

'It is all nonsense,' Ludwig spluttered.

'The boy will be called on to testify. It is unlikely he will deny any of that. Even if he does, even if he were to say nothing, there is still the fact that he ran away. That is the most powerful evidence of all.'

'Schmerling, are you going to let them get away with these lies? Are you on their side?'

'No, sir!' the lawyer snapped. 'I have a duty as your legal representative to make the facts known to you, and advise you accordingly. My advice is that you should not allow this to come to court.'

'Give in. Is that what you are saying, Schmerling? After all I have done for the boy!'

The lawyer held up his hands. 'There is one other matter, Herr Beethoven. I have spoken in private with your sister-in-law's lawyer. That is a perfectly proper course of action. It is for lawyers to try to prevent litigation wherever possible – though many people, I admit, might dispute that. He informed me that if you persist in your action, he will reveal to the court some information of a highly personal nature, which will settle the matter once and for all in Frau Beethoven's favour.'

Ludwig struggled to understand what Schmerling had said. 'What did you say, Schmerling? Explain it again.'

'Your sister-in-law appears to be in possession of certain information which she believes would be highly embarrassing to you if it were to be revealed in court. Do you have any suspicion of what that might be?'

Ludwig's mind was blank, his face expressionless. 'She is fooling you, Schmerling. You, her own lawyer, everyone. Can't you see that? She will stop at nothing to get her son back.'

Ludwig was summoned to appear before the court. Schmerling had explained to him that the panel of judges would hear Karl first, then him, and Johanna last. Each would be heard alone, with neither of the other two in court, so the evidence would not be influenced by anything that was said.

Ludwig had thought long and hard about what Schmerling had asked him. Finally, it came to him. The only thing it could be was that that mad woman Josephine Stackelberg had claimed again that her child was his. And it was untrue. He was going to lose his beloved Karl because of a lie.

When Ludwig walked into the courtroom, he nearly lost his footing as his body seemed to revolt. A sharp pain shot through his stomach, communicating directly, it seemed, with his head, which was now throbbing. The familiar screeching in his ears would begin at any moment.

He sat, for what seemed an interminable length of time, while Schmerling addressed the judges. He did not attempt to listen.

As last he was asked to rise and he took the oath on the Bible, then strained to hear the judges' questioning through the noises in his head.

'What were the circumstances of your nephew Karl's departure from your apartment?'

'He can act of his own free will. I do not impose restrictions on him.'

'And he chose of his own free will to return to his mother.'

Ludwig realised his mistake immediately. 'His mother put interminable pressure on him.'

'Do you have evidence of that?'

'She is a wicked woman. A convicted criminal. If you –'

He felt Schmerling at his side and heard his urgent whisper. 'Do not talk of her. Confine yourself to what you know.'

'He left me a note. I assume his mother ordered him to leave.'

'Can you give us details of the education you provide for him?'

'He has the best schooling, the best tutors. Czerny – a pupil of mine – teaches him the piano.'

'According to our papers, the schoolmaster from Mödling, Herr Fröhlich, disagrees.'

'Mödling?' Ludwig repeated. 'I had bad servants. They conspired against me. I was forced to dismiss them.'

'We are not inquiring about your domestic arrangements, Herr Beethoven, but the educational instruction you provided for your ward.'

'Fröhlich conspired against me too. It was a conspiracy.'

'Your sister-in-law applied to us to have your nephew admitted to the Royal Imperial Seminary. Why did you object?'

'I will not allow her to decide on my nephew's education. She is an immoral woman,' Ludwig said, anger mounting in his voice. 'You know that. She was convicted of theft.' He felt Schmerling's hand on his arm.

'And what institution do *you* intend sending your nephew to? I understand he is temporarily at school in the Landstrasse. Mmmh?'

Ludwig's mind raced. 'The Theresianum,' he blurted out.

The judge's face settled into a smug smile. 'The Theresianum. Yes, a fine school. For children of noble birth. Exclusively. Herr Beethoven, are you of noble birth?'

Ludwig felt a prickling sensation on his forehead. He scratched it. He turned to Schmerling. 'My ears. What is he asking?'

He saw that Schmerling's face was pale and he flinched as the lawyer whispered urgently into his ear. 'I warned you they had hold of something. You must answer them. Are you of noble birth? If the answer is no, it will go badly.'

Ludwig stared at the judges, all of whom returned his gaze. Before he could answer, one of them spoke. 'The prefix to your name. It is "Van", is it not? Not "Von".'

Ludwig nodded almost imperceptibly. 'Dutch,' he half whispered.

'And in Holland the prefix "van" does not denote nobility, as the prefix "von" does in the empire of Austria. Your father was a musician in the employ of the Elector of Cologne, and dismissed from service due to drunkenness. That is correct, is it not?'

Ludwig closed his eyes as the dreadful sounds invaded his head. He could not shut them out. Nausea swept through him. Why were they trying to destroy him? *That is their aim; they want to destroy me. I will not let them. I will not let them destroy me.*

'My grandfather was Kapellmeister. He was organist at Malines in Flanders, before entering the service of the court at Bonn. My birthplace.'

The judge in the centre of the panel picked up a gavel and banged it on the bench. 'This case is dismissed from the Royal Imperial Landrecht and handed down to the lower court of the city magistrate.'

'The case is as good as lost,' Schmerling said. 'The lower court always favours the so-called aggrieved party. And it will go against you that you allowed the case to be heard by the Landrecht in the first place, without admitting that you were not of noble birth.'

The hearing was set for 11 January 1819. The Magistrate's Court agreed to a request from Schmerling that, due to his client's deafness, it would allow him to state his case in the form of a document, rather than appear in court.

A week later it ruled that the musician Ludwig van Beethoven was to yield guardianship of his nephew to the boy's mother, the widow Beethoven.

BOOK SEVEN

BOOK SIX

Chapter 1

Ludwig thought he was going mad. He looked at the pile of papers on the table in front of him. Words, words, words. Do this, do that. Anton Diabelli, publisher and composer, invites you, along with fifty other Austrian musicians of distinction, to compose a variation on his own waltz theme which he has the honour to enclose. His Imperial Highness Archduke Rudolph informs you of his appointment as Archbishop of Olmütz, and requires you to compose a solemn work for the enthronement in nine months' time.

Who would help him? Stephan von Breuning had severed their friendship for ever; Nikolaus Zmeskall was on extended sick leave from the Hungarian Chancellery; Schuppanzigh was in Moscow; Ferdinand Ries and Ignaz Moscheles were in London. Czerny had a full teaching schedule. There was, as always, Nanette Streicher. But Ludwig had sensed a withdrawal on her part while the saga of the court case continued.

He poured himself a glass of the rough wine and gulped half of it in one mouthful. Another piece of paper lay on the table top, smaller than the rest and written in a clear immature hand. He picked it up and read it yet again, searching for the words he knew were not there. All he asked was some sign of affection, not even love, just some sign . . .

The ungrateful wretch, he thought, tears stinging his eyes. The boy is a monster. *No, no.* How can I blame a thirteen-year-old boy? It is the mother's fault, no one else's. That monster of a mother. He is ruined, ruined by her. If only I had treated him differently, made him respect me, even perhaps love me, he would have become a fine Beethoven. Now, what does the future hold?

He looked again at all the papers, then swept them to the floor. He gulped down the rest of the wine.

The noises in his head were increasing by the second as if in league with his mood. He sang aloud to try to smother them. He paced the floor, driving his heels into the wooden boards. Had the moment come? That moment for which he had prepared himself ever since that fateful stay in Heiligenstadt, so many years ago, when he had written his last will and testament, his declaration to mankind of his deafness.

He was aware of someone else in the room, a dark shadow. 'Out! Get out!' he thundered. The shadow quivered and disappeared. Air, the smell of trees, of plants, that was what he needed. He pulled on a coat and went down into the street.

It was several moments before he realised his folly. It was night. Pitch black. He looked up at the house. Only a single candle burned in the window on the first floor. It must have been the landlord who had come to tell him he was making too much noise in the middle of the night.

With a toss of his head he stalked off down the street that led away to the fields. Mödling. Why had he come back to this place – to the same house even, that he had shared with Karl the year before – with its painful memories? But he had needed to get away from Vienna after the trauma of the court case. The humiliation of it! Thrown out by the Landrecht and made to apply to the common magistrate. It was scarcely credible.

Soon he was surrounded by darkness, the outlines of the trees barely visible. A million stars glistened and twinkled. He gazed into the blackness. Not a light was to be seen.

His breathing steadied and he concentrated, opening his eyes. Something was different. What was it? The shock of realisation hit him like a thunderbolt. No noises in his ears. Utter quiet. It had been so long since he had been able to enjoy silence.

From somewhere deep in his head a gentle sound began, the sound of angels singing. There were no words, just the soft soprano voices caressing his poor head, which suffered so much, and easing the pain in his aching limbs.

Antonie's face swam into his mind. Had she not loved him? Had she not told him of his worth? He felt tears again, the tears that came so easily now. Soon the sobs racked his shoulders. Would no one ever love him the way Antonie had?

He stilled his sobs and waited for the dreadful sounds to return. But they did not come. The angels' voices had gone, and there was nothing again. Tomorrow all the pain of living will return. But I will compose. I *will*. I still have so much to say. And I *will* say it.

He lifted the end of the bed and dragged it round so that the head was under the window. He lay down and a cool breeze wafted round his neck. He could see nothing but the stars, some bright and still, others twinkling like minuscule candles.

Who had put the stars there? Who had given mankind such marvels to wonder at? Who had created such beauty? *Who has given me the ability to express divine truths in music?*

After a while he got up and pulled the bed slightly to the side so that he could stand in front of the window. He looked down at the street and felt the rumble of the floor as a solitary carriage, pulled by a single, weary horse, approached. The driver was slumped forward, probably half asleep, his whip held at an angle. Ludwig watched it pass below, the rumble intensifying then fading.

He had heard nothing. Not the sound of the wheels creaking on their axles, not the horse's hoofs on the cobbles, not the dreadful sounds in his head. He had heard nothing. His hearing might be deteriorating still further, but could it also be possible that the noises that had been his uninvited companions for twenty years were abating too?

Thank you, Lord. The words formulated in his head. *Thank you, Lord*. He went to the table and lit the candle, shielding the flame with his hand until he was sure it had taken. He picked up a sheaf of papers.

Kyrie eleison	Lord, have mercy on us
Christe eleison	Christ, have mercy on us
Kyrie eleison	Lord, have mercy on us

The opening words of the Missa Solemnis. He read on. The Gloria next, *Glory to God in the highest*. Yes, he thought, as he read the thanks of mankind towards its heavenly father. Then the Credo, the solemn affirmation of faith. How many times had he heard it as a boy, when he was Gottlob Neefe's assistant organist in Bonn? The words had floated over his head; he had never stopped to think about them – until now. *And on the third day he rose again . . . and his kingdom shall have no end*.

A rush of music entered his head as he contemplated the Sanctus. *Holy, Holy, Holy, Lord God of Hosts*. He heard the sounds, jumbled, chaotic – but sweet. He closed his eyes. The voices of angels again.

Emotion welled in him as he read the simple lines of the Agnus Dei, the lines that closed the Mass.

Lamb of God, who takest away the sins of the world,
  have mercy on us.
Lamb of God, who takest away the sins of the world,
  grant us peace.

He put down the papers and walked again to the window. The Missa Solemnis sent to him by Archduke Rudolph. Yes, he thought, I will set it to music to be played at his enthronement. But it will not be just for him: it will be my own thanks to God for the great gift with which He has endowed me. The gift of music.

The notes would not come. They simply *would not come*. 'Ky-ri-e! Ky-ri-e!' he sang at the top of his voice, on a single high note. And there it rested, as if held in place by some great weight.

He scribbled phrases on a scrap of paper, fragments that seemed to bear no relation to each other. In his mind he kept seeing the face of his nephew, brooding. How can I work with all this in my head?

He went to the sideboard where a plate of food lay. There were two flies on it and he waved them away angrily. He picked up a piece of meat and tore off an end with his teeth. It was hard and cold and he spat it out.

He went back to the table and scratched out the most recent fragments he had written. He turned to where the piano had stood the previous year. He should have brought it again, his wonderful gift from Thomas Broadwood, but several strings had frayed and Andreas Streicher had taken it to his workshop to repair it.

'Bring me food!' he yelled.

A man hurried into the room. 'Quiet, Herr Beethoven. It is after midnight. It is too late for food. The cook has gone to bed.'

Ludwig rushed at him, grabbed him by the shoulders, propelled him out of the door and slammed it after him. Then he took the plate of food, opened the window and hurled it out into the night.

The next morning the same man, in formal attire, stood in

Ludwig's doorway and handed him a letter. He refused to move until Ludwig had opened it and read it.

> Herr Beethoven
> Your unsocial behaviour makes it impossible for you to continue to reside here. You must leave at the end of the week. If you fail to do so, I shall speak to the authorities. Kindly sign your agreement at the bottom of this page.

Ludwig realised the man was serious. He dug into his pocket and pushed several coins into his hand. Then he gave him more. 'I shall eat in the tavern from now on. At least there they have a decent cook,' he said.

Credo in unum Deum, Patrem omnipotentem, Ludwig repeated quietly to himself. In his head he heard his own voice quite clearly. He said the words a little louder, stressing the syllables as if they were written in two-four time.

As he lifted his head the heavy dullness returned and the movement around him was like a rough but silent ballet. Waiters moved quickly between tables, plates piled high up their arms. Carafes of wine clanged noiselessly against each other. Diners' mouths opened and shut, to accompany extravagant gestures, but with no sounds.

Isolated in my own private world, Ludwig thought. He sat back and looked at the multitude of faces, none of which returned his gaze. Most were laughing, some were serious, chewing and speaking at the same time, so keen were they to get their point across. Heads shook or nodded. All so involved, so intense, yet do they not realise that everything is transitory? They think what they are talking about is so important, yet in a year's – a month's – time they will have forgotten it and be talking about something new.

My work *is* for all time, for eternity. My ideas are for future generations, because I am dealing in eternal truths. I am an artist, put on this earth by God to give art to mankind. A benevolent God, who loves what he has created.

And a cruel God, who can make a man suffer. Why did he ordain that *I* should suffer?

A man in an apron pushed a menu towards him.

'Veal,' Ludwig said, without looking up.

'There is no veal,' the waiter responded.

'And wine,' Ludwig continued, reading the text of the Mass.

'I said there is no veal.'

Ludwig was aware that the man was still standing there, stabbing the menu with his finger.

'Veal. Are *you* deaf too?'

The man's mouth moved.

'I cannot hear your words,' Ludwig said, through tightened lips. 'I ordered my food, damn you, man. Just go and get it.' Ludwig waved his arm, which caught the waiter's apron. He staggered back, then steadied himself and hurried away. Ludwig shouted after him. 'Bring the wine now. I have waited long enough!' Faces turned towards him, but he took no notice and went on mouthing the words in front of him.

'*Credo in unum Deum . . . Credo in unum Dominum Jesum Christum . . .*'

He jotted notes on a scrap of paper, crossing them out angrily almost as soon as he had written them.

Now another man stood opposite him. 'My waiter told you there was no veal, sir, and you assaulted him. Sir, I am the proprietor. I have noticed your behaviour before. I shall have to ask you – sir?' He jabbed Ludwig on the arm.

'*Filium Dei unigenitum –*' he broke off. 'Who are you? Go away. I am working.'

The man's fists were clenched, his knuckles white. 'There is no veal,' he articulated loudly. 'Now you must leave. I will not have you upset our staff – or our patrons,' he added, looking round the room, which had fallen silent.

The words penetrated. Ludwig pushed the table hard, sending the man reeling back. He brushed past him, threw off the arm that tried to hold him back and strode out into the street. The air felt cool on his flushed cheeks. He wanted to walk; he needed to walk. But he was suddenly tired.

With a sigh of resignation he crossed the street and went back up to his apartment.

'*Credo in unum Deum . . . Credo in unum –*' He pulled out a pencil from one pocket and delved into the other to bring out the text. Damn. He had left it in the tavern. But the thought of all those faces turning towards him, the anger of the proprietor . . .

He felt the floor vibrate. Someone was coming up the stairs to his apartment. The landlord. Now he would have to confront him too. His head slumped forward on his chest and he drew his sleeve across his eyes, then turned to the door. A stranger was standing there. The man appeared to be in his mid-twenties, though his erect bearing – ramrod straight back and one arm hooked behind him, head held at an upward angle – gave him the demeanour of a man ten years older. He wore a pair of round, rimless spectacles on a nose with an extraordinarily thin bridge which broadened out, almost comically, into a bulbous end with flared nostrils.

Ludwig saw immediately that his left hand was extended, a sheaf of papers clutched in it. 'Thank you. Very kind.' He moved forward, took the papers and returned to the table. He assumed the man would leave immediately but moments later a piece of paper was pushed towards him. He read the neatly written words.

Master. I witnessed the unseemly behaviour towards you. A great artist should not be treated thus. May I be of assistance to you? I am a student of law with musical aspirations. I am prepared to devote my time to your well-being, so that you may give mankind the fruits of your genius unimpeded.

Anton Felix Schindler

The man's eyes were directed at a point on the opposite wall, as if he did not want to influence Ludwig's response.

'Will you put these papers in order? And I am hungry. No one will give me food.'

'If you will permit me, Master,' Schindler wrote, 'the bath-house serves excellent food. Its speciality is veal. I have taken the liberty of telling them you are on your way to dine there.' Then he resumed his distant gaze.

'I am deaf, Herr Schindler. You will have to . . . But you know that.' He raised his eyebrows at his naïvety.

Schindler wrote again. 'There is no greater disciple of your music, Master. When I heard of your impediment, I made it my life's ambition to be of assistance to you.'

'If the bath-house serves veal, then you have made a good start, Schindler.'

Chapter 2

'Your former colleague, Herr Ries, informs you that he received your addition to the opening of the Adagio of the sonata you called the Hammerklavier the very day before engraving began,' Schindler said.

'Two notes. Just two notes. People will ask why. The answer is so obvious.'

'Of course, Master.' Schindler shuffled some papers.

Ludwig took a deep breath of satisfaction. He knew practically nothing about this man Schindler, nor had any desire to, beyond the fact that he was from Moravia and had come to Vienna to study law. He had described himself as a competent violinist, but had not offered to demonstrate this to Ludwig and Ludwig had not asked him to. What was clear was that, as he had promised, Schindler was prepared to sublimate all his personal requirements to help Ludwig. Unlike former assistants, such as Ries, Gleichenstein, Moscheles, even Czerny, he was not interested in trying to establish his own career. As far as Ludwig could tell, he rarely went to the law school to study. Where his finances came from, Ludwig had no idea; perhaps he had inherited enough money to be able to live as he pleased. Certainly he had never asked Ludwig for payment.

Another factor endeared Schindler to Ludwig. He had a way of talking that engaged his attention, to the extent that after a few weeks he found he could understand what the young man said. He did not hear the voice clearly, but with a combination of voice and hand movements Schindler made himself understood. Furthermore, he protected Ludwig from other voices. Anyone who wished to speak to Ludwig had to speak first to Schindler, who provided a notebook and pencil for the question or remark to be written down.

In short, Ludwig found that he was relieved of the irksome task of straining to hear voices, and of having to explain his impediment. Schindler took the weight of all that off his shoulders.

Now Schindler reached into his leather portfolio. 'His Imperial Highness Archduke Rudolph wishes to be informed of progress on the Mass for his enthronement.'

'The Gloria is sketched. Apart from the *Gratias agimus tibi*. Glor-or-or-or-or-oria,' Ludwig sang, in a raucous rising voice. And again, 'Gloria in excelsis.' He went quickly to the piano, played a swift rising sequence and sang to it. He played on, quavers in the base, picking out the chorus's line in the treble. 'Gloria! Gloria! Then *piano* –' He lowered his head and almost whispered the incantation: '*Pax hominibus, hominibus . . .*'

He allowed his fingers to roam up and down the keys almost at random, but always with the *Gloria* theme identifiable. 'And then . . . minor key for the *Gratis*.' He played a chord, softly, feeling its vibration in his body and hearing it in his mind.

Finally he stood up and poured a glass of wine. He turned and was momentarily startled. 'Schindler, I forgot. Wine?'

'Thank you, Master, but no,' he said, tears of pleasure in his eyes. 'I cannot tell you what a great honour I feel to have witnessed –' He gulped.

'Can't hear you, Schindler. The Gloria will be finished soon. Then I will turn to the Credo. The central part of the whole work.'

'May I speak, Master? Can you hear my voice?'

With a thrill of joy, Ludwig nodded.

'Master, we are nearly at the end of the year now and the enthronement is in March. The work will be a large one. Will you complete it in time?'

'Tell His Imperial Highness, His Worshipful Grace the Archbishop, His Rudolphness, that he will have his Missa Solemnis for his enthronement. Now what else do you wish to plague me with, Schindelberg, Schindelmeister, Schindelkopf?'

'You have received a letter from your brother, Master. Herr Beethoven in Linz.'

Ludwig felt a pang. How long had it been since he had heard from Johann, or even seen him? Johann had visited Vienna occasionally on business, but never with time for more than a cursory greeting. He had sent the odd letter too, saying that he was in good health and his business prospering, but no information beyond that. Ludwig remembered Johann had once written in a letter that his wife could have no more children, but the fear lurked at the back of his mind. 'They have not had a child?'

Schindler shook his head. 'No, Master. He writes solely to inform you he has purchased a country estate near Krems on the Danube. At a village called Gneixendorf. He says he goes there to be alone and enjoy the peace and solitude. He invites you to stay there any time you wish to leave the city.'

'He is a fool, but a rich fool. Does he say he is coming to Vienna?'

'Yes, but he does not say when. "I shall see you in Vienna before too long."'

'And no mention of a child? Are you quite sure?'

'Quite sure, Master. I am sorry, Master.'

'There is only one Beethoven of the next generation. He is my nephew but I feel as if he is my son,' Ludwig said quietly. 'They took him from me. I know he did not wish it.'

'Master, will you forgive me if I speak out of turn?'

Was Schindler now about to say something that would alter the balance of their relationship, as so many friends had in the past? Ludwig wondered. He hoped not. He had come to rely on the man and he did not want to have to dismiss him. But if he, too, were to start criticising the way he had behaved towards his sister-in-law . . . 'If you want to talk to me about my nephew, you had better choose your words carefully. Or, better still, say nothing.'

Schindler wiped an imaginary bead of perspiration from his forehead. 'I shall say just a few words, which I hope might bring you encouragement. If I offend you, I ask in advance for your forgiveness.'

Ludwig saw his earnestness and could not bring himself to still the man's words. He gave a small nod of approval.

'Master, as you know, I am a student of the law. I have taken the liberty of reading the documents relating to the litigation involving your nephew. It is my firm belief that you have been denied justice. The ruling of the magistrate's court, Master. The lower court did not have the jurisdiction to overturn the ruling of the Landrecht.'

It took a moment or two for Schindler's statement to register. 'You are saying that the lower court does not have the power . . .' Schindler was nodding. 'But,' Ludwig continued, 'that is too simple. If it does not have the power, how was it able . . . ?'

Schindler smiled. 'The law, Master, is not like music. It does not obey rules. It professes to, but in practice it does not. What might appear obvious to you and me, does not appear so to lawyers. If it did, there would be no work for them to do. Lawyers earn a living by disagreeing with each other. On purpose. The law is the law. It should be that simple. But if they argue, they earn money.' He held his palms outwards as if to emphasise the self-evidence of what he had said.

'But what can I do?'

'You can take your case to the Court of Appeal. It is your right. And I believe they will find in your favour.'

Schindler was a student of the law, he must know what he's talking about, Ludwig thought. 'What must I do?' he asked.

'Leave everything to me, Master. I will take advice from some colleagues. But, in the first instance, I will draw up a document, detailing your arguments. I will stress the immoral character of the boy's mother, and how his own character will suffer if she is allowed to keep him. Also, his schooling has suffered since he left you, hasn't it?'

Ludwig nodded vigorously. 'He is at Blöchlinger's establishment on the Kaiserstrasse and I have heard nothing but bad reports. Blöchlinger has written to me, as he is obliged to do, and he informs me the boy is not making the progress he should. He blames the mother.'

'Excellent. It will be good to have him on our side. It will help rebut the other school-teacher. The one in Mödling. Fröhlich.'

The very name made Ludwig wince. 'The man is an ignoramus. He knows nothing about schooling and teaching.'

'Do not worry, Master, it will not be hard to discredit him. Will you allow me to begin work on the documentation?'

'My dear Herr Beethoven,' Archduke Rudolph said, 'if I tell you this is one of the saddest moments of my life, you will know it comes from the heart, won't you?'

A dull ache in Ludwig's chest had darkened his mood. He had not wanted to answer the summons from the Archduke, but Schindler had convinced him of the worth of remaining on familiar terms with a member of the Imperial royal family.

'Sir, I am unwell. My hearing plagues me, my stomach plagues me. People plague me. Not you, of course. But more and more I want people to leave me alone. My own company is all I desire.'

'I shall not detain you. Come, sit down.' The Archduke poured a glass of wine and handed it to Ludwig. 'I leave the city in a week.' He spoke directly into Ludwig's left ear.

'For a considerable period of time?' Ludwig enquired.

'For ever, Herr Beethoven, although I will return from time to time. My residence will be the Archbishop's palace in Olmütz. In two weeks from now I will be Archbishop and not Archduke.'

Ludwig sighed. 'The Missa Solemnis is not complete. I thought I would be able ... I have had other matters on my mind.'

'I understand, Herr Beethoven. You are taking legal action again concerning your nephew, are you not?'

'My nephew is the most important human being on this earth. He is a Beethoven.'

'His mother, I am sure, feels that way too.'

'No! I will not talk about it. No one understands. No one. Except Schindler. Without him I would be lost.'

'Forgive me. You are right. It is not for me to express an opinion.'

There was a moment's silence. 'I apologise for my tone,' Ludwig said. 'It was not appropriate. But this is an important matter. The Court of Appeal is to make a judgement shortly. If I lose ...' He was loathe to continue.

'As I was saying, I leave in a week. I wanted the opportunity to say farewell personally.'

Ludwig sipped his wine. 'Vienna will be the poorer for your absence. And I am sorry that the Missa is not ready.'

The Archduke chuckled. 'I shall be honest, Herr Beethoven. I did not expect it to be. As soon as I learned that you were planning a large work, I made other arrangements. I originally expected just a single piece. The Gloria alone. Or the Sanctus, perhaps.'

'I want to set the whole Mass. A single piece would not stand alone.'

'No, no. Of course not. I understand. I have no doubt that the finished work will stand with the greatest settings of the solemn mass. Mozart, Haydn, Bach, Cherubini —'

'Bach's is the greatest. The B minor. But mine will be different.'

'Your music always is, Herr Beethoven. I recognised that from the earliest days. Do you remember the dominant sevenths of the Symphony in C?'

Indeed Ludwig remembered well how the young Archduke at not more than twelve years of age, and in the company of his mother, the Empress, had attended the benefit concert at the Burgtheater and professed himself enthralled with the opening chord of Ludwig's First Symphony. 'You have been good to me, sir,' he said quietly. 'I shall miss you.'

'And I you,' the Archduke replied. 'Your music has been a formative part of my life. There has been no music like it before, nor will there be after you have gone. You are greater than Bach, Mozart, Haydn. You have given something to mankind for which it will thank you a hundred years from now. Two hundred. And,' he smiled as he spoke, 'my name will be known for the sole reason that you have attached it to so many of your great works.'

'Then I shall attach it to one more. The Missa will be dedicated to you. If God gives me enough years to finish it.'

Chapter 3

'I am pleased for you, Ludwig,' Nikolaus Zmeskall said, 'though goodness knows, it was a long business. Come and sit over here.' He gestured with one of his two walking sticks, then hobbled painfully to a chair, collapsed into it with a great sigh and laid the sticks beside him.

'With your legs and my ears, Nikola, there is not a whole man among us. How bad is it?'

'It's my joints,' Zmeskall explained. 'My knees and hips. The damp weather makes them worse. The doctors say there is nothing they can do, short of cutting off my legs below the knees. That still leaves the hips.'

Zmeskall gestured to the carafe of wine on the table. Ludwig poured two glasses, then took a notebook and pencil from his pocket and passed it to Zmeskall, who wrote, 'What influenced the Court of Appeal? Why did they reverse the judgement?'

Ludwig set his lips. 'Damn fool woman. Condemned herself. An illegitimate child. It just confirms what I have always said about her.'

'Impossible for her to hide it. Everyone knew.'

'She appealed personally to the Emperor. He refused to intervene, of course.'

The two men sat in silence for a few moments. Zmeskall picked up the pencil hesitantly, then scribbled, 'Sad news. Josephine is ill. They say they can do nothing for her. She has lost her mind.'

A pit opened in Ludwig's stomach. 'She has had a sad life. What about her children?'

'Stack took his,' Zmeskall wrote. 'Back to Estonia, I believe. Her children by Deym are in M'vasar with her family. The little one, Minona, is with Therese, somewhere in the country. But she fears Stack will come back for her.'

'She should go back to Hungary to be with her family.'

'Won't leave Vienna. She'll die here.' Then Zmeskall flung down the pencil and asked loudly, 'What are you going to do with your nephew?'

'He's at Blöchlinger's. At least he is away from his mother there. It is best for him. Czerny says he is progressing well on the piano. He will be a fine musician.'

Zmeskall raised his eyebrows quizzically.

'He will be!' Ludwig remonstrated. 'I will make sure of it. He just needed to be away from that woman. And now, my friend, if you do not cease to question me, I shall become even more deaf than I am – and I shall also lose the ability to read!'

Ludwig could not sleep. He tossed and turned until he lost patience, threw off the bedclothes and went to the piano. There he played the opening movement of the first of his new set of piano sonatas. Serene, gentle, flowing like a stream, pressing on urgently but never in doubt as to its destination. The vibration of the notes tingled in his body but he could not tell how loudly he was playing. He bent his head low to the keys but it did not make their sound any clearer. He knew it was deepest night, that he would be in trouble with the landlord again. Never mind, Schindler would sort that out. Thank God for Schindler.

Without a break he went into the second movement, the Prestissimo, more fury now. Typical Beethoven, they will say. Always angry, always tempestuous. Then let them listen to the third and final movement.

Gesangvoll, mit innigster Empfindung, he had written at the top of the page. Full of song, yet with the deepest feeling. On he played, his fingers barely stroking the keys for the hymnlike theme that was the basis of the movement. And then the variations that followed it. Ah, he thought, how I love writing variations. As he played he recalled that the publisher Diabelli had asked him, along with other composers, to write a variation on a theme he had composed. He had refused and set it to one side. Well, maybe, he thought. But not yet. Not in competition with other composers. Charlatans, who know nothing of what it means to compose from the heart.

The next two sonatas were already sketched out and, like the first, as different from the great Hammerklavier as it was possible to be. Small works, almost intimate. It will give them something to argue about. The experts will discuss my motives. Ordinary people will just listen. That is all that is necessary.

In the days that followed Ludwig felt progressively unwell. His throat hurt constantly, as though it were lined with rough, splintered wood. The sweat on his forehead alternately burned and chilled him.

The wretched fever again, but this time it was different. The dull ache in his chest – more precisely in the hollow area between chest and stomach – affected his breathing. His knee was swollen and tender to the touch. Soon he found he could not walk without excruciating pain. His elbow hurt too.

Could he have caught the pox? Had the past come back to pay him his dues? He sat long hours contemplating the dreadful possibilities that lay ahead.

Schindler was solicitous; he wanted to call the doctor. Ludwig thanked him, but refused. 'Just make sure I have enough wine in the cupboard and leave me alone for a week. It will pass.' He did not believe it when he said it and by the end of the week he was very ill. He did not want to see Malfatti, with his doom-laden face and dire predictions. More than anyone he wanted Nanette, with her kindly face and comforting words. But he knew he could not call on her. Like Stephan von Breuning, she had disapproved of his behaviour towards Johanna and he had not seen her since the Appeal Court ruling.

Ignoring the pain in his leg he went to the piano, shuffled through a pile of manuscript papers and found the sheet he was looking for. On the top he had written the single word *Arietta*, little air. A simple tune of dotted quavers, lasting no more than seven or eight bars, though he had not yet written in bar lines.

He played it, exaggerating the rhythm of the dotted notes, nodding for the beat and playing off it. He picked up a pencil and wrote 3/4 at the top of the stave, knowing that it was wrong. He scratched it out and wrote 9/4, then 9/8. Then scratched them both out.

How can I tell other pianists what I am trying to say? Such a simple theme . . . Yes, just as I did in the Hammerklavier . . . as if drawing breath and saying, '*Now listen* . . .' He played two falling intervals, C-G, D-G, then the *arietta*. Then he saw that those two intervals were more than just drawing breath: they were the stimulus for the theme that followed. He snatched up the pencil and wrote 9/16. Now the theme flowed, oh, how it flowed.

In syncopated semiquavers, he played a variation of the

theme and, laughing, wrote 6/16 on the paper. Descending demi-semiquavers, syncopated not dotted again, deconstructing the two simple descending intervals with which the *arietta* began. This time he wrote 12/32.

As if his fingers had taken over from him, he began a trill in the treble. Above it and below it the simple descending intervals. He looked at his own fingers, marvelling at how they moved. Louder and louder he trilled, in both hands now, the *arietta* of dotted quavers still clearly discernible. Then, the trill high in the treble, with the falling intervals lower in the treble and furious demi-semiquaver runs in the bass.

Faster and faster he played, knowing even as he did so the sheer folly of what he was doing. Abruptly he stopped, his hands in mid-air. In his head he could *feel* the notes – *oh, why can I not hear them?*

He pounded the keys and felt several go slack. Inside the piano strings curled and quivered.

He wrote down the trills. This is what matters most, he thought. Not the piano, which cannot withstand what I ask of it.

He buried his head in his hands, the dampness of his tears between his fingers.

Doktor Malfatti was prodding his knee. The skin around the joint was red and swollen. He gestured at Ludwig to fold up his sleeve. More gently this time, he felt around the elbow. Ludwig gritted his teeth and cried out as the pain lanced up his arm to his head. Then Malfatti felt his forehead and peered into his mouth, depressing his tongue with a wooden spatula. 'Your throat is inflamed,' he intoned, 'and you have a fever that has gone to your joints.'

Ludwig glanced at Schindler, who repeated into his ear what Malfatti had said, and that Ludwig must remain in bed until it had passed.

Then the doctor put his long face close to Ludwig's, the heavy bags under his eyes almost touching his skin. 'This is a serious fever. It has attacked your joints. The name for it is rheumatic fever. In itself it will pass, but the danger is that it will lead to something worse. If that happens you will become very seriously ill. Do you understand?'

The anger and frustration within Ludwig yielded to self-pity. He thought of the piano sonatas, which still needed so much work; of the Missa Solemnis, the great sacred work he intended as a tribute to the Almighty.

'You must restrict your intake of wine,' Malfatti continued. 'It is affecting your liver. See here . . . when I press.'

The dull ache that had sat in Ludwig's chest flared into pain. 'Stop, Malfatti. You will make me worse.'

'That is your liver. It is affected by too much alcohol. No more wine. Not until you are completely better.' He glanced up at Schindler who nodded.

'Leave me,' Ludwig said weakly. 'No, Schindler, you wait here. I have letters to dictate and ideas I want you to write down. You will not stop me working, Malfatti. If I cannot work, you will no longer have a patient. He will be dead.'

Chapter 4

Nikolaus Zmeskall sent Ludwig a note informing him that on 31 March 1821 Josephine Stackelberg had died.

> . . . the poor angel was alone and unloved. Her family in Martonvasar did nothing to ease her suffering. Her children were not brought to comfort her. It is said in her last breath she spoke the name of her youngest, Minona, the child whom she hardly knew.

Poor Josephine. A tremor ran through Ludwig. What would have become of him if she had consented to marry him when he had asked her? He remembered the humiliation of calling at her house on the Rothenturmgasse and being told by the servant she was unavailable, or had left the city for the day.

What tragic choices she had made. Deym and Stackelberg, both wretched men who had lived off her and treated her cruelly. Deym's premature death had at least rid her of him but she had thrown her life away on an even worse man.

Had she regretted turning her back on himself? he wondered. Her sister Therese had once hinted so. He remembered the single time they had made love. She had been like a woman possessed, but as if possessed by something he was not and could never be.

Oh, poor Josephine. His eyes filled with tears. I should have gone to see her, he thought.

Later in the day Schindler came to see him. 'Master, can you hear me, or shall I write down what I have to say?' he asked grimly. He studied Ludwig then picked up the notebook and pencil that lay on the table.

'Your nephew Karl has run away from Blöchlinger's institute to his mother. But B. went to fetch him and the mother handed him over.'

Ludwig exhaled. Would this torture never end? He pressed on his chest where the pain was. 'Why did you take away the wine?' He gave Schindler a shove.

Schindler stood his ground. 'It is important that you look after your health, Master. You owe it to the public. To the world. So your genius can continue to create masterpieces.'

Again Ludwig did not hear the words, but Schindler's expression conveyed the message. 'Get me wine now, Schindler. I have this pain. Only wine will relieve it.'

Schindler wrote, 'You must obey the doctor's orders.'

Ludwig hurled the pad into Schindler's face as hard as he could. Schindler executed a small bow and left.

Josephine, Karl – *my music.*

He stumbled over to the window and threw it open. The cool evening air washed over his hot feverish face like a soothing balm. It was dark outside, probably around nine or ten o'clock.

He slammed the window shut and took a coat from the stand by the door of the apartment. He thrust his arm into the sleeve and swore when it came out of a hole at the elbow. He put it on and tried to do it up, but there were no buttons. Why had Nanette not repaired it? He saw a box in a corner tied with string, which he undid then tied in a knot round his waist as a belt. He found his hat and scooped a few coins into his pocket.

He left the apartment and hobbled along the Landstrasse, turning right before he reached the Stubentor gate and on to the towpath that ran along the Donau Arm, now the Donau Canal. The water was black and still, smelled pungent, and the lights of houses near by reflected in it. He could not hear the bargeman shout as he almost collided with a horse, plodding along the towpath, but his head was full of his music.

'Cre-do, Cre-do!' It was a short affirmative phrase that he knew would form the opening to the Credo section of the Missa solemnis. It would be sung first by the bass chorus, then picked up in canon by the other voices, developing into a fugue before the soloists came in with the *Incarnatus est.* 'B flat major.' He wanted to jot notes on the scrap of paper in his pocket. Then he saw the inviting light of a tavern.

Inside, he rubbed his hands at the warmth. 'Wine. A small carafe.' He tossed some coins on the counter and took the wine to a small table where he pulled out the paper and scribbled a short phrase. Dotted minim, crotchet, minim, minim. Cre-do, Cre-do. He pushed the paper back into his pocket, drank the wine in a single draught and left the tavern.

He was on a bridge crossing the canal. Ahead he saw a great dark mass, and walked down a broad street towards it. The Augarten public park. For a moment he considered walking along the linden-lined alley to the pavilion – the pavilion in which he had performed his music so many times – but instead he went further along the canal, finally leaving it where it curled away from the city. He limped on to the Glacis then on to the wide Währingerstrasse, which led north out of the city.

All the time he walked he heard his music, exultant, in glorification of God. Occasionally a carriage rumbled by and he felt the vibration of its wheels against the rough road.

Soon, he knew, he would be in Döbling. His breath was laboured now and he feared that when he stopped the pounding in his head would return – some wine would still it.

At last in the distance he saw a tavern. When he entered it, the heat in the room hit him forcefully. He sat at a table with his wine and quaffed it thirstily. When he went to the counter for another small carafe, the landlord spoke to him. 'Ten minutes. Then we close.'

Ludwig sat down again and took out the paper, but the sounds in his head were jumbled. The lights from the candles danced in front of his eyes. Slowly, with increasing intensity, the pain in his chest grew. He wanted to cry out, to beg it to stop. The landlord was gesticulating at him, pointing towards the door. Ludwig drank his wine then stood up, moved unsteadily out into the night.

The air was icy cold against his face. He needed to find a carriage to take him back to Vienna, but that was hopeless. He peered into the darkness. He was on a narrow road in the middle of nowhere.

He slumped against a tree and slid to the ground. The damp earth felt cold through his coat and trousers. His head throbbed and the pain in his chest with it. So much pain. He stayed where he was for a little while, then forced himself to get up and walk on. Eventually he saw flickering lights and headed towards them.

Soon he was close to the lights and vaguely recognised his surroundings. He walked along the street. Candles shone in windows and he peered into one, then another. There was no sign of life behind the lights. He knocked on one window, then at another. No response.

Suddenly he started as he felt a firm hand on his shoulder. A lantern dazzled him and made the pain in his head worse. He saw from the tall shiny black hat that the man was a policeman.

'I am Beethoven,' he said hoarsely.

The man's mouth moved again. Ludwig caught the stale odour of his breath.

'I am deaf.'

'Hah!' the man cried. 'You're not Bethoffen. You're a tramp.'

Ludwig tried to break free, but the man's grip was firm and he was propelled along the street, then thrust through a door and marched along a short corridor. At the end the man pulled a large bunch of keys from his pocket and unlocked a heavy door. Inside there was just an iron bedstead.

'You're under arrest,' the man said, then repeated it in a loud voice. 'Under arrest. You'll be seen by the magistrate in the morning.'

'I am Beethoven. Where am I?'

'Heiligenstadt,' the policeman said. 'Don't pretend you don't know. We don't like scoundrels like you on our streets.'

The policeman turned his back and walked towards the door, holding the key that would lock Ludwig in the cell. 'Seyfried,' Ludwig said suddenly. 'Kapellmeister Seyfried. Bring him here. He will tell you I am Beethoven.'

The policeman stopped and turned. The look on his face had changed. 'Herr Seyfried? Do you know what time it is? I cannot disturb anybody. It is the middle of the night.'

The man's words reverberated off the walls, hurting Ludwig's ears but mercifully allowing him to hear them. 'Go, man, hurry. Get Seyfried. He will not mind. Tell him Beethoven is here, and that I am ill.'

He must have slept, because the next thing he knew Seyfried's face was peering into his.

'Seyfried. Thank God.'

'Herr Beethoven. Can you hear me? I am so sorry to see you are unwell. I did not know you were in Heiligenstadt. If I had known – Come, I have explained who you are. There will be no charges against you. You can sleep in my house, then I will arrange a carriage for you in the morning.'

BOOK EIGHT

BOOK THREE

Chapter 1

'I am going to die soon, Schindler. My health is failing.' Ludwig shut the tattered book.

'No, Master. No. It is not true.' Schindler smiled, but his eyelids sat low over his eyes, robbing the smile of any warmth.

'I feel it here.' Ludwig pushed his fist into his chest, in the hollow between his ribs.

'It is the effects of the jaundice, Master. The doctor said the pain would remain.'

'Pour me a glass of wine, Schindler. A glass of my medicine.'

'Master, I cannot. The doctor –'

'Damn you, Schindler, pour me wine now, or I will get it myself.'

Ludwig gulped it thirstily, relishing the taste in his dry mouth. He could no longer remember when he had last felt well. The rheumatic fever had been followed by jaundice, causing him pains in his head and chest that he knew now would never completely leave him.

Doktor Malfatti had blamed the jaundice on the stress of Ludwig's arrest, and that he had walked for hours in the chill night air. As news of the incident had spread across Vienna, Schindler had protected him from a stream of inquisitive visitors. Ludwig instructed him that if either Stephan von Breuning or Nanette Streicher called, he was to admit them. But they did not.

Ludwig opened the book again, creasing the pages carelessly. 'Listen, Schindler.' Schindler said something but his words made no impression on Ludwig's ears. 'Get the trumpet, Schindler.'

He held the battered instrument to his ear and Schindler's voice penetrated the invisible blanket. 'Peters in Leipzig asks for compositions. Are you prepared to let him have any?'

'Give him the Piano Sonatas. The three.'

'They are already with Schlesinger in Berlin.'

'Then give him the Missa Solemnis. And the set of Baga-telles.'

'Master, the Missa is promised to Simrock in Bonn and also Herr Schlesinger. I –'

Schindler jerked back as Ludwig swept the air with the trumpet. 'I do not know, Schindler. Organise it. Give it to them both. Whatever earns me more money. I need it, for my beloved Karl's education.'

'That is correct, Master,' Schindler said. Then he wrote, 'Schlesinger notes that the sonata in C minor, the last of the three, has no final movement. He asks when it will be ready. And he says the trills make it impossible to play.'

'Tell him to go and fish in the Danube – maybe he will catch a movement. There will be no third movement. I have finished with the piano. It is no more use to me.' Ludwig emptied his glass and gestured to Schindler to refill it. 'Listen to this, Schindler.' He read from the book,

> '"Embrace each other, Oh ye millions!
> His kiss to all the world he gives!
> Brothers – see beyond the stars
> Is where our loving father lives."'

He paused to reflect on the words. 'Schiller. Do you know the poem, "An die Freude", To Joy?' He carried on more to himself, '"Beggars became the brothers of Princes . . ." He changed that line . . . "Alle Menschen werden Brüder", "All mankind will be as brothers". It's better. The poet puts it better than the priest. The Mass. It is nothing compared with this poem. When I was younger I intended setting it to music. Now it is too late.'

Freu-de schö-ner Göt-ter Fun-ken Toch-ter aus Ely-sium.

Ludwig scribbled notes on a stave and wrote the disjointed words underneath, then screwed up the paper and threw it on to the floor to join the several other pieces. He walked to the piano – the Broadwood that he had once loved so much but which now showed signs of neglect. The frame was chipped and snapped wires curled under the lid.

He sang the words to himself, then aloud. The sounds

jangled inside his head. My voice, he thought, is the only sound I can hear. He sat again at the table, staring at another sheet of manuscript paper, its staves standing empty and challenging. He scribbled more notes. Dotted crotchet, quaver, crotchet. Daa-da-dum. Daa-da-dum. With clenched fists he beat the rhythm on the table . . . and put a line through the notes.

'Why will the pain in my chest not go, Malfatti?'

'Because you drink too much wine, Herr Beethoven.'

'And if I do not drink the wine, the pain is worse. How do you explain that, Herr Doktor Genius?'

Malfatti smiled lugubriously but said nothing. He was putting away his instruments. 'Your body is tired of the abuse you subject it to,' he wrote. 'Drink less. Eat regularly. Sleep at night, like everybody else.'

'I am dying, aren't I?'

'No!' Malfatti almost shouted. 'You are not dying. You have no illness that could not be cured if you behaved differently. Even your hearing would improve. But you will not take advice.'

Crotchet-quaver, crotchet-quaver, crotchet-quaver. *Freu-de schöner Götter-funken* –

'No, no, no!' He strode to the window, threw it open and bellowed out his frustration into the night.

The next morning Schindler brought him coffee and cakes. 'The landlord asks me to tell you that he has had complaints about noises in the night,' he wrote on a piece of paper, and pushed it timorously towards Ludwig.

'What am I going to do, Schindler,' he asked rhetorically, 'if the music will not come?' He blew on his coffee. Schindler was writing again. He did not want to read the words, but Schindler's optimistic expression overcame his reluctance.

'Herr B. 's complaints about Karl's fees have been answered by this timely letter.' Ludwig unfolded it and read:

9 November 1821

Monsieur!

I take the liberty of writing to you, as one who is as much a passionate admirer of music as of your talent, to ask if you will consent to compose one, two or three new string quartets, for which labour I will be glad to pay you what you think proper. I will accept the dedication with gratitude. Kindly give me the name of the bank to which I should address the sum you require. The instrument I am cultivating is the cello.

I beg you to accept the assurance of my great admiration and high regard.

Prince Nikolas Borissovich Galitzin

'Who is this Galitzin?'

'I have made inquiries, Master,' Schindler said, into the trumpet Ludwig held to his ear. 'He is a Russian of the highest reputation, with connections at the Hofburg Palace.'

'Tell him I cannot compose any more. I have finished composing.'

'No, Master. I will tell him no such thing,' Schindler declared.

Ludwig's heart leaped at the sight of his nephew but he did not at first recognise the tall individual standing beside the boy, dressed in a blue frock-coat with brass buttons, white cravat and light corn-coloured trousers. He wore grey linen gloves, of which the fingers were too long and hung loosely at the ends. On his head was a large hat, at a rakish angle. It was the man's eyes that allowed Ludwig to identify him. His heart sank.

'Johann. You are in Vienna. Karl, my boy! Come to your father and embrace him.'

Karl stepped forward smartly, brought his heels together and bowed briefly. 'Good day, Uncle,' he said firmly.

'Come now. Embrace me.' Ludwig held out his arms but Karl bowed his head again and retreated to his original position.

'Fine boy, our nephew, isn't he?'

'*Our* nephew?' Ludwig spluttered. 'Do not call him *our* nephew. He is *my* nephew. My son. What have you ever done for him, stuck out there in the wilderness?'

Johann ignored his outburst.

'I have bought an estate at Gneixendorf. A beautiful house set in its own grounds, with vineyards all around running down to the Danube. And I have brought in an artist from Bonn to paint the Rhine on the walls, to remind me of our home.'

Ludwig's chin sank on to his chest. The Rhine! The ache of nostalgia swept over him, but Johann was talking again. 'I have come to see you to invite you and Karl to stay with

Therese and me. My wife will make you most comfortable.'

The sound of his sister-in-law's name brought him out of his reverie. 'And your wife's bastard daughter?' he asked, enjoying Johann's discomfiture.

'There is no need for such language, particularly not in front of the boy,' Johann said, peeling off his gloves. 'And particularly since you are now in my debt.'

'What do you mean?'

'Your man spoke to me. Schindler. It appears you are short of money, despite being the greatest composer on earth. I have made a loan across to you.'

'I am not!' Ludwig exploded. 'A Russian prince has commissioned new works from me.'

'It is still not enough to cover Karl's school fees and your own rent and living costs. But do not worry, I shall not ask for repayment until you are ready. I am glad to be able to help. Now, will you and Karl come and stay with me at my estate?'

Ludwig glanced at Karl, but the boy's attention had wandered. 'No. He needs to be here, where his education can proceed and Czerny can give him piano lessons. Karl? Are you practising, as Herr Czerny has instructed you?'

Karl said nothing. He looked quickly from one uncle to the other, bowed and left the room.

'A fine boy. He will be a fine man. A Beethoven,' Ludwig said.

Johann leaned towards him. 'You were right about the mother. Bad reputation. She is free with her favours, from what I hear. Therese's brother lives here in Vienna. He is a baker. He hears things in his shop. It is rumoured that she had a child, maybe two, by different men. She gave them away, so it is said. Just rumours.'

Ludwig nodded. 'It is why she lost the boy.'

'It is likely he has heard the talk. He told me his mother is not a good woman, and that he is grateful to you for caring for him. He is shy. He will not tell you himself, but I know he is grateful.'

Chapter 2

Freu-de schö-ner Götter-funken Toch-ter aus Ely-sium.

Ludwig looked at the stave. He sang the rising and falling theme. Was this the theme for which he had been searching? The theme that he would use to combine voices and instruments? A Grand Symphony, with a final chorus on Schiller's poem 'To Joy'?

'Schindler!' he called. 'I need you. Is the piano repaired?'

He knew even as he bent to pick up the ear trumpet that the faithful Schindler would be standing, formal and erect, black frock-coat tightly buttoned, hands clasped in front of him, a folder in his hands to take notes. 'Well?'

Schindler inclined his head. 'The strings are all replaced, Master. Some structural work still needs to be done to the frame. The repairer's advice, Master, is to play it with less force.'

Ludwig walked to the piano, lifted the lid and rejoiced at the sight of the taut wires. 'Streicher? Did he come?'

Schindler shook his head. 'It was the repairer from Schanz's in the Wallnerstrasse.'

Ludwig used the trumpet to mask his disappointment. 'Fetch Czerny. Tell him I want to see him.'

'Czerny, Master? I am sure he will be very busy with his pupils.'

Ludwig waved the trumpet angrily. 'Get Czerny, I said, Schindler. Are you as deaf as I am?'

Schindler half opened the folder he held. 'Of course, Master. First, may I draw your attention to this letter that has come from Herr Diabelli. The publisher. You may remember, he asked several composers for a set of variations –'

'Yes, yes. He will have them. Get Czerny.'

'See here, Czerny,' he said to his former pupil, who now stood before him, smiling, 'the secret of my happiness.' He

led Czerny into the bedroom, where, on a shelf above the
washstand, stood a line of dark glass jars. 'The magic potion
that has washed away my pain. One full jar every twenty-four
hours. A devilish concoction, prepared by His Eminence Signor
Malfatti, to maintain my intestines in good order.' He saw
Schindler, standing patiently as ever, faint disapproval directed
at Czerny. 'Out, Schindler. This is a time for musicians to talk.
Not lawyers. Leave us.'

Schindler bowed, sent a last warning glance to Czerny and
left the room.

'So, young man,' Ludwig said cheerily, putting his arm round
Czerny's shoulders, 'are you earning a living teaching your
students how to play scales and arpeggios and broken chords
and chromatic runs and key signatures and counterpoint and
fugue and how many quavers make a crotchet and . . . ?'

Czerny threw back his head and laughed. 'I fear, sir, you have
me condemned for the pedagogue I am. I still believe there is
no substitute for practice. Without the basic skills . . .'

'Your words, Czerny, are emitting from your mouth wrapped
in a thick woollen blanket, which they do not shed before
reaching my ears.'

Czerny reached swiftly for the ear trumpet, which lay on
the table.

'No!' Ludwig barked. 'I do not need it today. I only use it
when I do not want to hear what is being said. Now, there is
something I want to play you. I need your help. But first, you
didn't answer my question. How goes your teaching?'

Czerny leaned close to Ludwig's ear and said distinctly, 'I
cannot complain, sir. It affords me a living. And I have one
particular pupil who I believe is the best young pianist I have
heard. I believe he is possessed of rare genius. Would you do
me the honour of listening to him?'

Ludwig paused a moment to take in his words. 'No, Czerny,'
he said, smiling. 'You forget. I cannot listen. I do not hear what
is being played. I only feel it.'

'Nevertheless, sir, it would greatly honour me to have your
opinion. He is a young lad from Hungary who –'

'No! Now, Czerny, I want you to listen. Do you remember
this theme?' Ludwig walked to the piano and played the rather
naïve waltz theme Diabelli had sent to him and around fifty
other composers throughout Austria, to develop one variation
each, the result to be published and proceeds to go to war

widows and orphans. He concentrated on the sound in his ears. Silence. He stretched his arms towards the keys and again played the waltz. The sounds reverberated in his head and through his body. He knew he was not hearing them directly from his fingers and the keys, but his head *knew* what the sounds were.

'*Maestoso!*' he called, playing the theme in a series of *fortissimo* chords linked by a fleeting quaver. 'And now *allegro. Vivace, allegro, vivace,*' he sang, as the theme metamorphosed under his fingers, loud one moment, soft the next; chords, then chromatic runs; a flurry of wild notes, then soft notes separated by rests. On and on he played, '*Presto . . . moderato . . . andante . . .*' Finally his fingers slowed and he lifted them from the keys, praying to God to keep all unwanted sounds from his ears.

He turned on the stool, started slightly to see Czerny then got up to pour wine. He handed a glass to Czerny, ignoring his protestations, and took one for himself.

His breathing was now steady and he looked at Czerny, who said something. Ludwig reached for the trumpet and put it to his ear. 'Again, Czerny. Into this infernal contraption.'

'Miraculous, sir. That you can do so much with such a banal theme.'

'Simple, Czerny. Not banal, simple. Did you like the variation in the style of the immortal Mozart? In homage to him. He taught me the greatest lesson of all, Czerny. The simplest themes contain the most profound implications. Complicated themes contain nothing but themselves.'

'Will you publish it, sir?'

Ludwig smiled mischievously. 'That is what I wanted to see you about, Czerny. I want you to notate it for me.'

Czerny's jaw sagged. 'All of it, sir? But it was so long. Surely, just four or five variations –'

'Twenty, maybe, Czerny. Or twenty-five. Or thirty. I will sketch it out, then play it for you and you can notate it.'

Clearly Czerny considered a change of subject was necessary. 'I received a letter from Ferdi Ries, sir. He tells me he plays your works often and arranges concerts. He is having great success with your Hammerklavier Sonata. The reason, he says, is that so few pianists can play it! He told me how you added two notes at the last minute to the opening of the slow movement. May I ask why, sir?'

'It was necessary. What else does he say?'

'He asks if you have any new composition. He says the

Philharmonic Society of London has put the matter of the overtures behind it and has expressed an interest in a new work.'

Ludwig put down the ear trumpet and thought for a few moments. 'Get Schindler to draft a letter to him, I will sign it. Tell him I am working on a remarkable new symphony that will include voices. Ask him what the Society will pay me for it.'

'I will, sir. I am very pleased to hear you are composing. I have more good news for you. Our old friend Schuppanzigh is returning from Russia soon.'

A wave of pleasure flowed through Ludwig and he got to his feet. He hopped from one foot to another. 'Schupp-Schupp-Schuppanzigh . . . Schuppanzigh-is-a-Fat-Man, Schuppanzigh-is-a-Fat-Man,' he sang, before dropping heavily into the chair again.

He gulped the wine and shook his head. 'The body does not allow you to do everything you used to. But still no noises, Czerny. It is good news, is it not? You will work on the variations, won't you? For your old teacher? And I will do you a service in return. You can bring this pupil of yours to me. This *Wunderkind* from Hungary.'

Chapter 3

'An opera, Schindler, Herr Schindlerberg, Herr Lumpenkerl, Graf Hauptlumpenkerl! Shall I not compose another opera?'

Ludwig enjoyed seeing Schindler's eyebrows arch above his unsmiling face as he allowed the mildly insulting epithets to wash over him.

'Master, the variations for Diabelli need correcting and there is the commission for His Excellency Prince Galitzin to fulfil. Also, I have received word from Herr Ries in London. He writes that the Philharmonic Society is prepared to pay fifty pounds for a new symphony.'

Ludwig took the trumpet from his ear, spun it on the table and watched it as it fell to the floor. He bowed in exaggerated gratitude as Schindler picked it up. 'Fifty pounds? Generous. Five hundred florins, or thereabouts. Tell them I accept. They shall have their symphony and I shall go to London and conduct it.'

Schindler made a note, then said, 'Master, I should remind you Herr Czerny is coming this morning with his pupil. He will be here shortly.'

Schindler's words were finding their way through the heaviness in his ears today, which contributed to Ludwig's unusual good humour, but it was not its sole cause. The medicine Doktor Malfatti had prescribed in large doses had eased his stomach pains and regularised his bowels. He had to admit to himself that it was a long time since he had felt so well. Perhaps this marked the beginning of a turn in his health?

'This man Grillparzer is making a name for himself, is he not?'

'Yes, Master. A fine playwright. But he upsets the authorities. The censor forces him to alter what he has written.'

'It happened to Mozart too, with something as innocent as *The Marriage of Figaro*. And it happened to me. My *Fidelio* was censored. One day there will be no more censorship. You cannot censor ideas, Schindler.'

'No, Master. Now, if I may, I will prepare –'

'Maybe I should speak to Grillparzer. I made his acquaintance once. I stayed in the same house as him and his mother in Heiligenstadt. He was little more than a boy. Shall I ask him for a subject for a libretto?'

'Master, as I said, you have a lot of work ahead of you. Perhaps after that.'

Ludwig nodded. 'Pour me wine, Schindler. And mix me some powders for my head.' An ache had developed behind his eyes – a mere trifle that would pass by noon.

The disdain with which Schindler ushered in Czerny and his young pupil was evident. Ludwig heard him say '. . . no more than fifteen minutes.' He thought of countermanding him, but decided against it. Although he did not exactly like the dry, humourless Schindler, the man was devoted to him – and Ludwig needed him.

'Come in, Czerny, come in. And you, young man. Come here and tell me your name. Speak loudly – as loudly as you can. Into this trumpet, which helps a deaf old man hear a little bit.'

'Ferencz Liszt, sir. I am called Franz.'

'Where are you from, boy, and how old are you?'

'Raiding in Hungary, sir. I am twelve.'

'Fine age, isn't it, Czerny? So much ahead of you. Were you not that age when you were first brought to see me?'

'Yes, sir,' Czerny said, warily. 'And I still recall how nervous I was.'

But Ludwig was watching the boy and didn't hear him. 'So you are learning to play the piano, are you, young man? What can you play?'

'Sir,' Czerny interjected, 'if I may answer for my pupil. I am preparing him for his first recital in Vienna. He will play from Bach's Well-tempered Klavier, as well as – as –' he stammered, '– your piano concerto in C major.'

The ache behind Ludwig's eyes was still there and he wanted to close them. The light streaming in through the first-floor window seemed unusually bright and he turned his chair so that his back was to it.

'Now, boy, you play the Well-tempered Klavier? Let me hear you. If my damned ears will allow it.'

The slight figure, with long straight fair hair that reached almost to his shoulders, walked to the piano. He stroked the wooden backboard, which bore the signature of Ferdinand Ries. Ludwig saw him peer briefly over the top into the body of the piano, as if to check that the strings were in good order. He suppressed a snicker.

Franz sat on the stool, arranging his tail-coat so that it fell neatly over the back. He sat, head held high, contemplating silently for a moment. Ludwig thought, The boy is putting on a performance, but there's nothing wrong with that – as long as he has the talent to justify it. He half closed his eyes and braced himself for the sounds that he prayed he would hear without distortion.

As the music reached him, he closed his eyes fully, not knowing whether it was Franz Liszt playing or the sounds in his head that he remembered so well from his own youth.

How many times had he played the Preludes and Fugues for his teacher, Gottlob Neefe? And when he had first come to Vienna, this was the music – the Preludes and Fugues in all the forty-eight keys – that had gained him *entrée* into the salons of the nobility. Baron van Swieten, Prince Lichnowsky, Prince Lobkowitz . . .

He opened his eyes so that he could see the boy's fingers. They moved with seamless grace across the keys: their thinness belied their strength. All the time the boy held his back straight and his head erect, never once looking at his fingers.

It was some moments before Ludwig realised he was hearing what Franz was playing. The notes were not clear, but it was as if they were willing their way through to his brain.

Liszt completed the C minor fugue with a flourish, raising his hands and holding them suspended in the air, lowering his head as if in homage to them. Finally he placed his palms on his thighs.

Ludwig did not want to speak – words would violate the space in his head that was still taken up with the glorious music. But he knew he had to. 'Bravo, boy. That was fine playing. Remember, Johann Sebastian Bach is the master before whom we must all prostrate ourselves. He is the father of music. Now,' he said, a testing look passing over his face, 'that last fugue, the C minor. Can you transpose it to another key? Say, an interval up. D minor.' He saw anxiety in Czerny's eyes.

The boy nodded eagerly, turned back to the piano and, after

a moment's pause, stretched out his fingers and played the fugue – note perfect – in D minor.

'Ha!' Ludwig exclaimed. 'A devil of a fellow. The boy is a young Turk!'

'Sir!' Liszt exclaimed. 'Will you allow me to play something of yours now?'

Ludwig laughed: he had heard the boy's words and knew that he would take it as a sign of assent.

'I will play the first movement of your concerto, sir. The C major,' Franz said, emboldened by Ludwig's approval.

He played the gentle solo opening of the concerto – a turning phrase of crotchets and quavers; more turning quavers in the treble accompanied by simple chords in the bass. Then the demi-semiquaver triplets and the crotchets that end the phrase.

Ludwig nodded for the three-beat pause before the soloist's first real test: a huge descending arpeggio run of semiquavers. He saw the boy's fingers flash across the keys. A second run, a third run, turning semiquavers in the bass and grace-note staccato crotchets in the treble, another run, then an abrupt change of pace – quavers and crotchets – a *crescendo*, before another series of runs closing with descending triplets that end the soloist's first section.

Ludwig found he had been conducting, and was now automatically counting the seven-bar rest before the soloist re-enters. He saw that Franz was nodding to exactly the same beat, before his right hand played the swift rising chromatic scale that began the development section.

His skin tingled and his chest was tight as the years evaporated and he saw himself as a boy playing before Wolfgang Mozart. How scared he had been that at any moment the great man – in ill health, with a thousand worries – would turn on his heel and leave the room.

This boy's talent was remarkable, though, of that there was no doubt. Only occasionally did he miss a note, and that was when his small hand was unable to encompass the leaps Ludwig had demanded. But most of all the child was observing the dynamic markings. Where Ludwig had written *piano*, he played *piano*; where he had written *forte* he played *forte*. Most importantly of all, the *crescendos* were scrupulously observed.

Ludwig knew that much of the praise was due to Czerny,

with his meticulous teaching methods – such a brilliant tech-. nician, thought Ludwig, but where was the inspiration? Franz was now, just before the end of the movement, playing the cadenza Ludwig had written some years after the actual work, encompassing the octave leaps with ease. The trill that was the cue for the orchestra to re-enter, and then . . . The piano was silent for the remaining bars of the movement, but Liszt played the orchestra part, ending with a flourish on the single octave C major, the home key.

Ludwig gripped the sides of his chair and stood up, steadying himself until the moment of giddiness passed.

He walked across to the piano and put his hands firmly on the boy's shoulders. 'Go, now. You are one of the fortunate ones. You will bring joy to many people. There is nothing in this world better or finer!'

Ludwig waved a clutch of papers in the air. 'Come here, Schindler. Do you know what this is? I have been elected to the Royal Academy of Music of Sweden. Sweden. Hah! By the personal order of His Majesty King Charles . . .' he consulted one of the sheets '. . . the Fourteenth. And do you know who His Majesty is?'

Schindler, a weary look on his face, shook his head.

'None other than the former General Bernadotte of the French Imperial Army, who had the good sense to turn against his leader, the upstart impostor Napoleon Bonaparte.'

'Bonaparte is dead, Master. It is said he was poisoned by the English. Will you compose a piece in his memory?'

'I already did, Schindler. It is there in the symphony that was to have been his.'

'The Funeral March, Master? The Adagio Assai?'

Ludwig flapped the papers again. 'Sweden, Schindler. Sweden. Shall I go there to receive the honour? No, I will freeze to death. Draft letters, Schindler. One to the Wiener Zeitung, the other to the Beobachter, announcing the honour. Otherwise no one will know. You have to blow your own trumpet, Schindler, because no one will blow it for you. My grandfather told me that, when I was just a child.' He walked towards the wall on which the old portrait hung, above the piano as always. 'Look at that face, Schindler. Is it not the finest face you have ever seen? If only he had known . . . But I believe he did.'

Schindler touched his shoulder to gain his attention. 'Sir, this note has come for you.' He held it out hesitantly, as if he would rather not pass it over.

Ludwig snatched it from him and his heart leaped with joy. Ignaz Schuppanzigh announced that he was back in Vienna and asked Ludwig to join him as soon as he received this note. 'I am going to the Schwan, Schindler, to drink their disgusting wine. First, mix me some powders. This damned pain in my eyes will not go.'

Less than half an hour later Ludwig alighted from the carriage and walked through the Neuer Market. It had been some time since he had visited the Schwan, once such a regular venue for the Rhinelanders-in-exile. With the end of the war people had less time for leisure, concentrating on building up businesses and earning a living. Also, Ludwig's health had kept him away, and many of his drinking companions had either left Vienna – like Ries, and, until now, Schuppanzigh – or were still avoiding him because of his behaviour towards his sister-in-law.

For a moment he stood in front of the fountain depicting the Danube and its tributaries, the naked bodies of the figures glistening with the water that cascaded off them. Then he walked into the Schwan and the smell of stale beer and wine sent his mind back to years gone by. Where was Gleichenstein now? Freiburg, wasn't it? And Ferdi Ries, married and in London – ah, how I mistreated that boy – and brother Casper Carl, dead at forty-one.

At the counter he took a filled pipe from the rack and glanced towards the corner where the Rhinelanders had always sat. But the wall was not where it had been. Everything was smaller. The tables were fewer and closer together. He felt a pang of nostalgia for what had been – and could never be recaptured.

Schuppanzigh was gesturing to him, holding up two carafes of wine. Ludwig walked over to him and the two men embraced.

'Schuppi. Good to see you. Schuppanzigh-ist-ein-Lump,' he sang. 'Schuppanzigh-ist-ein-Lump, Wer kennt ihn, wer kennt ihn nicht . . .'

Schuppanzigh chortled with glee. '"Lob auf den Dicken",' he said. '"In Praise of Fatness". For three solo voices and full choir. Duration, thirty seconds. By Ludwig van Beethoven, to ensure the immortality of his old friend Ignaz Schuppanzigh. And do you see, Ludwig? I am still somewhat on the large side? Well, I have a reputation to keep up!'

Ludwig brought out the ear trumpet and dropped it on the table.

'Well, Schuppi, where have you been?'

'Moscow and St Petersburg. Playing at court. Quartets by a certain Herr Beethoven. Sad, you know, the name of Razumovsky is forgotten. Does anyone ever see him here?'

Ludwig shook his head. 'He is a recluse. Still in the city somewhere, but no one sees him. The fire broke his spirit. Sad.'

'But tell me *your* news. Are you composing?'

'To my own surprise. You know, Schuppi, I thought my deafness would end it, but I have written more piano sonatas, variations, and I am working on a new symphony. A different symphony, with a chorus in the final movement.'

'Interesting. Ah! Yes! There! Turn round, Ludwig.'

Ludwig was horrified at the sight of the figure making its way across the room towards them. The man's thick hair was snowy white, the face beneath it now drawn and grey. His body bent forward and his bony hands, the knuckles white with strain, held two walking sticks. His mouth was drawn wide into a smile, but seemed more a grimace of pain.

Ludwig hurriedly poured a glass of wine for his old friend and Zmeskall nodded his thanks. His lips puckered and trembled as he brought the glass to them.

'Welcome home, Ignaz,' he said, holding his glass towards Schuppanzigh. 'Will you show us your Cossack dance? Go on. Down on your haunches.'

'With great pleasure, Nikola. Only you will have to hand my wine down to me. I will never be able to get up again.'

'And Ludwig,' Zmeskall said. 'Most high-born genius of music. Though not as high-born as the Landrecht thought you were.'

'Nikola,' Ludwig said, investing his voice with what he hoped was a hard edge, 'I have one inestimable advantage over you. If I don't want to hear what you say, I don't have to.'

The other two laughed and Ludwig joined in. He drained his glass. 'Aaaargh! I swore never to touch the Schwan's wine again. Swan's piss!'

Zmeskall turned to Schuppanzigh. 'Ignaz, I shall have to rename you Falstaff. Look at you, sitting there with your stomach straining to escape your belt. You certainly did not starve in Russia. Too many dumplings, I would say. Now, tell me about music in Moscow. Do they play the composition of our esteemed friend?'

'Indeed they do.'

'In Sweden too,' Ludwig said, enjoying the surprised looks on his friends' faces. 'I am a member of their Royal Academy of Music.'

'Excellent. Let us toast your health,' Zmeskall said. They raised their glasses again.

'What of our friends?' Schuppanzigh asked. 'Breuning and Streicher? And is there word from Ries in London?'

Ludwig saw Zmeskall dart a quick look at him. 'Stephan works too hard,' Zmeskall said. 'It is taking a toll on his health. He has two lovely children, a son and a daughter who –'

'Hosenknopf,' Ludwig said. 'I call him Trouser Button. He is a fine boy.'

'His real name is Gerhard,' Zmeskall said. 'Ludwig, you should –'

Pain suddenly intensified in Ludwig's forehead. 'No, Nikola! I will not talk about it. I have heard things. Things you do not know. About the boy's mother. She –'

'Steffen's wife?' Schuppanzigh asked innocently.

Ludwig pressed his fingertips against his forehead. It felt as if a hammer lay behind his eyes hitting them in time to his heartbeat. He tried to focus on his friends' faces but they seemed to be moving and the brightness – as if the sun were shining directly at him, which it was not – dazzled him. He shut his eyes and tried to stand, but the table seemed to be moving. Then everything swung around him and the ceiling – dark brown, sticky with tar – was where the floor should have been.

Chapter 4

The small house on the corner of the Rathausgasse in Baden suited Ludwig's needs. He took the first floor, which consisted of a narrow entrance hall, a bedroom and a study. He told the landlord to put in a second bed: Karl was coming to join him.

Doktor Malfatti had told Ludwig that he would take no responsibility for his well-being unless he stopped drinking. His collapse in the Schwan was due to his body being saturated with alcohol, which had caused his vital organs to cease functioning. He told Ludwig that the alcohol had affected his eyes and that he was in danger of losing his sight as well as his hearing. He should stay in a darkened room during the day and cover his eyes with a bandage at night.

Ludwig informed him that he was taking rooms in Baden to work on his new symphony. Doktor Malfatti warned him that if he worked too hard and continued to drink, there was every likelihood that he would not see Vienna again.

Joy consumed Ludwig when Karl stood before him. 'My boy. My nephew. My son! Come, let me embrace you.' He flung his arms round the young man's neck.

Karl's remained by his sides. 'I cannot stay long. I must return to Vienna to study for the university entrance examination.'

'What are you saying, Karl? Remember, your old father is deaf. Sit here. Now, write down what you want to say. It is better.' Karl scrawled a few words. It took Ludwig a few moments to decipher them. 'Yes. University. You have finished at Blöchlinger's. We must drink wine to celebrate. How old are you now?'

Karl wrote '18', paused, the pencil poised in the air, then added 'next month'.

'Eighteen! Good. Go to the sideboard and pour us both a glass. It is local wine, from the vineyards of Baden. Malfatti will have no complaints. It was the filthy stuff at the Schwan that made my body revolt. This wine is pure. It soothes my stomach and helps me to hear. Who can object to that?'

Karl put the two glasses on the table. He said, 'My mother has been ill. I thought you should know.' Then with a sigh at the tedium, he wrote it down.

Ludwig's stomach churned. The raw flavour of undigested wine came up his chest and he coughed, his eyes watering. He dabbed at them with his sleeve and turned his chair away from the window as the light suddenly seemed harsh. 'If your mother's been ill, it's her own doing,' he observed.

'No!' Karl's palm came down hard on the table. Ludwig looked up: the boy was staring at him accusingly.

'I will not talk any more about it,' Ludwig blustered. He thrust his head towards Karl and watched as the boy's lips quivered and tears came into his eyes. He wiped them with his sleeve, then passed it under his nose.

'Come on, no tears. You're eighteen. You're behaving like a girl,' Ludwig reproached him, but tenderly. 'You're a good nephew to me, Karl. A good son, as you would have been to your own father. You are a Beethoven, and I am proud of you. Now, I want you to help me while we are here in Baden. My new symphony. See? I have already sketched out the movements. Now I must put flesh on the bones. Especially for the final movement. Voices *and* instruments, Karl. It will cause a revolution in music. A revolution with no guillotine!' He laughed at his joke and was pleased to see the corners of Karl's mouth turn up.

In Vienna a conversation was taking place that would have astonished Ludwig, had he been aware of it. Stephan von Breuning, with Gerhard at his side, was sitting in the front room of the Streichers' piano factory, talking earnestly with them. 'It is not in my nature to speak ill of anyone, but I really do believe this man Herr Schindler is making our friend's life more difficult than it need be.'

'You are being too charitable, Steffen,' Streicher said. 'He is a self-centred, self-seeking, self-important –'

Nanette tapped her husband gently on the arm to calm him. 'He is a bad influence, of that I am sure,' she said in measured tones, 'but what can we do about it? Ludwig will not hear a word against him, apparently.'

Breuning nodded. 'Nikolaus Zmeskall tried to raise it with him, but he would not talk about it. I can see Ludwig's point of view – Schindler takes all the strain and worry off his shoulders, so he can concentrate on his music.'

'But to his detriment,' Nanette said. 'Does he know we have tried to see him? All of us? You have tried, haven't you, Steffen?'

Breuning nodded. 'After he collapsed in the Schwan. Nikola told me immediately about it, but trying to get past Schindler was like trying to breach the Bastion wall.'

'He'll think that we've deserted him,' Streicher said.

Nanette sighed. 'But that's true. Because of the way he behaved towards Johanna. You had words with him over it, didn't you, Steffen?'

'I'm afraid so. But if he is ill, seriously ill – and Doktor Malfatti believes that is the case – then he needs his friends, however he may have behaved in the past.'

'Anyway,' Streicher said, with a sardonic smile, 'he's not entirely wrong about Johanna. She is not a woman of virtue. Two illegitimate children by two different men.'

'Enough, Andreas. Let us not speak about her behind her back. In any case, to keep a son from his mother cannot be right, whatever the circumstances,' Nanette said. 'You look tired, Steffen. You are working too hard. How is your dear wife?'

The breath caught in Ludwig's chest and he coughed. 'Wait, Karl.' He forced out the words through quivering lips, then saw a large flat rock, on which he sat down. When the spasm ended he wiped his forehead with a handkerchief.

Karl was standing over him, one hip cocked out in a manner that just stopped short of being provocative. 'Come on, Uncle. Look. Up there. We are climbing to the ruins.'

The whistling was painfully loud in Ludwig's ears and every time he drew breath he felt the catch in his lungs – yet they had not walked far. This was just the beginning of the Helenenthal with the familiar Schwechat rushing by.

He began to cough again. The phlegm rose in his throat and he spat it into the damp earth of the riverbank. The relief was immediate and he stood up. Karl was already climbing towards the Rauhenstein ruins. Ludwig wanted nothing more than to be back in his apartment, sitting in an easy chair and sipping wine, but there was nothing for it: he followed his nephew up the path.

'Darkness into light, Karl. Do you see?' With the palm of his left hand he tapped on the table top gently. With his right he beat a different rhythm. 'Da–daaa, da–daaa,' he sang. '*Pianissimo*, as quiet as it is possible to play. Mystery. Da–da–daa, da–da–daa. And then a *crescendo*. But not into light. Not yet. The wind players introduce the second theme. A question, begging for an answer. But there will be no answer yet. No, no. There will be many more questions. Come, pour your uncle some wine.'

Karl handed Ludwig a glass and wrote, 'I must return to Vienna to study.'

Ludwig gazed into his nephew's face, trying to read what lay behind the words, but before he could say anything, Karl, his face, it seemed, dragged down by sadness, wrote again, 'She promised me so many things that I could not resist her. I am sorry I was so weak at the time and beg your forgiveness.'

Unable to restrain himself Ludwig got up, took Karl in his arms and hugged him. 'My son,' he said, wiping tears from his eyes, 'it is good you understand. Now you know why I fought so hard for you. Your mother has chosen to go down a certain path, and you must have nothing to do with it. You are a Beethoven. Her other children are not. You must not associate with them. Where will you stay when you return to Vienna?'

'I have a friend. From the school. He lives in the Landstrasse. Near your apartment,' Karl scribbled.

For a moment Ludwig thought of the Streichers. Could he ask them to supervise Karl? He dismissed the idea quickly. His heart leaped as Karl wrote, 'I will see Herr and Frau Streicher.'

In Baden Ludwig's health slowly improved. He took the baths, and the pain in his lungs gradually subsided.

He was working on the symphony. The sounds he wanted to create were as clear in his head as if an orchestra was playing them. He had no piano to work on, which seemed almost a liberation. No struggling to hear the notes, no broken strings to remind him of his deafness . . .

There would be no Scherzo in this symphony. This would be a second movement unlike any he had ever written. *Molto vivace* and *fortissimo*. And what instrument would be the driving force behind it? The timpani! He gasped at his own audacity and wrote the dotted rhythm on the stave.

One morning Schindler came to see him, bowing from the waist and apologising ceaselessly for the interruption. Ludwig waved him impatiently to the small wooden chair.

'Herr Diabelli has published the set of variations you wrote for him, and wishes to know to whom the work is to be dedicated.'

Ludwig was pleased that he could hear Schindler's words but the man was so odiously obsequious that he had begun to dislike him intensely and hoped that the uncomfortable chair would encourage him to make his visit brief.

'I will think about it. Have you seen Karl?'

Schindler's face froze.

'What is the matter? He is all right, isn't he?'

Schindler nodded. 'Yes. But his behaviour –'

'What do you mean, man? What has happened?'

'I have heard reports, Master, that he is frequenting brothels. With friends, of course. They are forcing him, I am sure. But I have checked, and it is true.'

For a moment Ludwig considered telling Schindler he could not hear and bundling him out of the door. Instead, he said, 'I want you to have nothing to do with Karl, Schindler. He and I have spoken. He is a man now, you know. Eighteen. He will make his way.'

Schindler shuffled some papers, and extracted the one he had been looking for. 'On a different matter, then, Master, I do not wish to give you cause for concern, but your finances . . . Your rent, in Vienna and here, is due and Karl's fees at the university –'

'I cannot hear you, Schindler, so you are wasting your breath.'

Schindler moved forward and enunciated, 'Shall I speak to Herr Beethoven, Master, your brother, and ask him –'

'No! You will do no such thing. I will give a concert. Speak to the director at the Wien. Palffy.'

'Count Palffy, Master?'

'Count Swindler, who cheated me out of receipts for my opera. No, do not contact him either. I will give a concert outside this wretched country, where no one will try to cheat me. I will make enquiries in Berlin.'

Schindler licked the tip of his pencil and made a note.

'Leave me now, Schindler. I have work to do.' Ludwig waited until the man had stood up and was at the door. 'Is there any word from my friends, Schindler?'

Schindler mouthed some words that Ludwig could not hear.

'Come here and speak to me properly, you wretch. Now, have my friends tried to contact me?'

'I have heard from some, Master.'

'Breuning? Streicher and his wife?'

'They have asked me about your welfare, Master. I have kept them informed, and I have told them you are not to be disturbed, so that you can work on your symphony in peace.'

Ludwig looked at the imperturbable face of the man who had taken control of him and felt a deep loathing. Schindler seemed to think that he alone knew what was right and wrong for him. 'So tell me, Schindler, may I have your permission to break wind?'

Chapter 5

The Symphony in D minor, the ninth, was finished, Schiller's poem set for four solo voices and chorus forming the final climactic movement. The work was longer than any previous orchestral piece and would, Ludwig knew, take well over an hour to perform. More than anything, he wanted it to be performed, but he did not want complaints from players about its complexity, nor did he want criticism from ignorant musicians in Vienna who were jealous of him.

To Schindler's surprise, he persisted with his idea of performing the work in Berlin and ordered Schindler to draft a letter to the director of the Berlin Staatstheater. The response was immediate and favourable.

Eighteen twenty-four opened promisingly for Ludwig and he walked with a lighter tread. The completion of the symphony had an immediate and beneficial effect on his health. The awful incident in the Schwan became to him no more than a bad memory.

Then he received a letter from Antonie Brentano in Frankfurt. Her youngest child Karl, with whom she had been pregnant during that fateful trip to Prague and Karlsbad, had developed partial paralysis of the legs. He also suffered from fits. She had taken him to see a renowned physician in Paris, but to no avail. Her sole means of comforting him, she wrote, was to play the piano for him. Antonie . . . Tears formed in his eyes, but he was less saddened by thoughts of her than he had expected. It was past, over, yet he tried to think how he could help her. He wanted to write to her, but he knew the words would be wrong. Somehow he must show her that he had not forgotten their love. It came to him in a moment's inspiration.

'Schindler,' he said, 'tell Diabelli I want to dedicate the piano variations to Frau Antonie Brentano of Frankfurt.'

He was also heartened by Karl's progress. He was working

hard at his studies and had also resumed his piano lessons with Czerny. Ludwig had not forgotten what Schindler had told him, but the young man's face and manner bore no signs of debauchery, and he concluded that Schindler had merely been malicious.

He took new lodgings in the Landstrasse – a larger apartment so that Karl could live with him but enjoy a degree of independence. He was turning into a fine-looking young man. It occurred to him, too, that Karl might be seeing his mother but he found that the idea no longer filled him with horror. His nephew had been away from her influence for several years now so there would be no lasting damage.

On a crisp morning in early February, Ludwig took a carriage to Steiner's publishing house in the Paternostergasse, where he spent an hour discussing plans to publish the new symphony, as well as the quartets promised to Prince Galitzin on which he intended soon to begin work.

Afterwards he walked up to the Graben, drawn towards Taroni's coffee-house where he took a small table at the back of the busy room and ordered black coffee topped with whipped cream. He took out a notebook and was searching for a pencil when a familiar face – high forehead, long straight nose, but thinner and more drawn than he remembered – loomed so close that he could almost feel the skin.

'Hello, Steffen. You look ill.'

'Hello, my old friend. The tactful diplomat, as ever. No, I am not ill, just working to support a family. Like everyone else in this city.'

His words were distant and unclear, as if he were at the other end of the room. Ludwig took out the old ear trumpet. 'It will help a little but not for long.'

'I hear you have completed a new symphony. Zmeskall told me. He heard it from Schuppanzigh, who heard it from your secretary, Schindler.'

'I am going to perform it in Berlin, where it will be appreciated.'

'*Berlin?*'

'It is arranged. I will conduct it myself.' Ludwig sipped the coffee, wiping the cream from his upper lip with a handkerchief he pulled from his sleeve. 'Have you seen my nephew recently?

He is a fine young man. I am proud of him, as proud as a father could be.'

Ludwig saw Breuning's face cloud and, for a brief moment, he wished he had not mentioned Karl.

'Your sister-in-law has been ill,' was all Breuning said.

Ludwig waved the trumpet airily. 'I am sorry when anyone is ill. I nearly went blind from pains in my head.'

'We heard you had been ill. Nanette tried to see you. We have all tried to see you, but your secretary, Herr Schindler, is protective.'

Ludwig drank more coffee. 'He is useful to me, but I will get rid of him. After Berlin. Tell her I would like to see her. I will have words with Schindler.'

Ludwig held the letter with slightly trembling hands. 'Karl, my boy, help me understand this.' The truth was that he had understood the letter perfectly, but he wanted his nephew to see it.

'Read it to me, Uncle,' Karl said loudly, his head jutting forward as he spoke. 'Extracts, if you will, I am late for an appointment.'

Ludwig looked up in bewilderment.

'My friend Niemetz, Uncle. We are meeting at Taroni's, before going to the university library.'

'The boy is a bad influence on you.' Ludwig regretted the words as soon as he had spoken them. He had met Niemetz – a friend of Karl from Blöchlinger's institute who had moved on to university with him – and had no reason to think ill of him.

'Read me the letter, Uncle.'

'Very well. Just the sentences that matter. It is signed by nearly twenty illustrious names in the world of music and the arts. It begins with compliments to me, then says they speak on behalf of the whole of Austria. Listen: "Although Beethoven's name and creations belong to all mankind and every country which opens its heart to art, it is Austria which is best entitled to claim him and his divine works as her own." You see, Karl, they have heard of my intention to go to Berlin. I know that is what they mean. And they are jealous. Hah! It goes on: "We feel more than ever before that the great need of the moment is a new enterprise directed by a powerful hand, a new advent of the ruler in his domain. And so we beg and beseech you, in the name of our native art: do not withhold from us or our fellow countrymen

any longer the newest masterworks from your hand." Hah! They
flatter me, Karl. Beware of flattery. "The ruler in his domain." It
was not always so.'

'You will agree?' Karl asked impatiently. 'You will give them
their concert?'

'Let me finish. They talk about my mass, the Missa Solemnis,
"a grand sacred composition in which are immortalised the
emotions of the human soul, penetrated and transfigured by the
power of faith and super-terrestrial light." And the symphony,
"a new flower which glows in the garland of your glorious, still
unequalled symphonies." They say foreign art has taken hold of
our sacred soil and I alone – the foremost among living men
in his domain – can rescue it. This is how they end: "May the
year which we have begun not come to an end without the
opportunity for us to rejoice in the successful outcome of this,
our petition, and may the coming spring witness the unfolding
of your divine gifts and become a time of blossom also for us
and the world of art!" And then there are all the signatures.'

Ludwig folded the letter and moved over to the window.
Outside a steady stream of carriages was trundling towards the
city or leaving it for the countryside. Men and women walked
past impassively, bundles on their backs or under their arms.
'You know,' he mused, more to himself than to Karl, 'my
music will always be criticised. Musicians and players will attack
it. They will question why I have written this or that, and say
that such-and-such a work is inferior to another. But I have not
composed my music for them. I have composed it for those
people out on the street, with all their cares and worries. I
have composed it to give them strength and the courage to
overcome their troubles. My music is for all humanity. They
were right in the letter. It is for everyone.'

He was lost in contemplation of his words. All humanity.
Those ordinary men and women on the street who need art
to succour their souls . . .

He turned round and was startled to see Schindler standing
where Karl had been. 'Master, I –'

'Read this, Schindler.' He held out the letter. 'Draft a reply
of acceptance. Then make contact with Palffy at the Wien. I
am to give a concert in Vienna.'

Chapter 6

'Damn you, Palffy!' Ludwig shouted, and banged his fist on the table. 'I will have Schuppanzigh leading the orchestra, Umlauf conducting, and I will set the *tempi*.'

Palffy cast a despairing look at Schindler, who blinked hard behind his spectacles. 'I can order the orchestra to play under Herr Schuppanzigh, but I cannot vouch for the result,' Palffy said. 'They will expect Clement to lead them and Kapellmeister Seyfried to conduct.'

Ludwig swung his ear trumpet away from the Count. 'Schuppanzigh and Umlauf, Palffy, or there will be no concert.'

When they returned to Ludwig's lodgings, Schindler gestured to Ludwig to sit and wrote, 'I have important information to communicate.'

'Be brief, Schindler. Speak clearly and I will hear you.'

'Master, I have seen the Frenchman, Monsieur Duport, who now owns the Kärntnertor theatre. He would be willing for your concert to take place there, with Herr Schuppanzigh and Herr Umlauf.'

Ludwig smiled. He might have grown to dislike Schindler immensely, but there were times when the man's deviousness worked to his advantage. 'Then tell Palffy. That will frighten him and he will do as I wish.'

The next day Schindler arranged for Schuppanzigh and Umlauf to come to see Ludwig.

'Two works,' Ludwig said. 'The Missa Solemnis, then the Symphony in D. Both works for orchestra, chorus and soloists. I have asked for you both specifically. Umlauf, you know my music better than Seyfried, better than any other director. Schuppi, I must have you for the violin solo in the Sanctus – and Schuppi, you will rehearse the strings. Umlauf, wind sections, chorus and soloists. At the concert I will be on the podium with you, Umlauf, and I will give you the *tempi*. All understood?'

The men nodded. 'Now tell me who we should have for soloists,' Ludwig said.

Umlauf opened a folder and took out a sheet of paper. 'I have listed names here, Herr Beethoven. In my opinion they are the most accomplished singers in the city. With your permission I will speak to them. Soprano, Henriette Sontag, and alto, Karoline Unger. Both are known for their performances of Signor Rossini's music.'

'Rossini, did you say? Pfft! Music for the frivolous spirit of our time. He composes in weeks what a true composer composes in years. If their voices are used to *his* music, they will not be adequate for mine.'

'I assure you, Herr Beethoven, they are the very finest singers. The men also. Haitzinger, tenor, and Preisinger, bass. The chorus will be provided by the Musikgesellschaft.'

'Ludwig,' Schuppanzigh interjected, 'do you have a firm date?'

Schindler answered him. 'Most likely towards the end of this month. The twenty-third or -fourth. The twenty-fourth is a Friday.'

'Not long, then,' Schuppanzigh said. 'We must begin work.'

As the date neared Ludwig found, to his dismay, that his old problems recurred. Stomach pains debilitated him; the noises returned to his ears and his head pounded. He drank more wine, which at first provided welcome relief, but soon it stopped him sleeping properly and he began each day with worse pains.

Then a series of disasters struck, conveyed to him first by Umlauf and then Schindler.

'There is a problem with the singers, Herr Beethoven. The sopranos of the chorus say their high B flat in the Credo is impossible to sustain over three and a half bars, as you demand. They ask permission to drop it by an octave.'

'No! They will sing what I have written.'

'There is another problem, sir,' Umlauf continued, without a pause. 'Preisinger cannot sing top F sharp in the Symphony, in the solo bass entry. Also, I confess, his voice has deteriorated. I have substituted Seipelt for him. A fine bass. But, I regret, still no top F sharp.'

Ludwig had barely come to terms with the singers' difficulties when Schindler made his announcement. 'The Church authorities have objected to the performance of religious music in a theatre, and the censor has accordingly banned the Missa Solemnis from being performed.'

'But it is *my* Missa Solemnis, not the Church's. It is up to me if I want it performed or not.'

'I have taken advice, Master, and I am told you should write to the censor, Herr von Sartorius, stating that the sections of the Missa are hymns, so they will be accorded proper reverence.'

'They are *not* hymns!'

'And, Master, forgive my impertinence, but again I have taken advice. If you restricted it to three pieces – hymns – it would be more likely to satisfy the censor. Not the whole work, in other words.'

Schindler's face expressed his astonishment when Ludwig, after reflection, said, 'Yes. Maybe that will stop the singers complaining.'

With Schindler's help he drafted a letter to the censor. The reply was swift: there was to be no performance of any section of the Missa Solemnis.

Schuppanzigh reported that the musicians had spent so much time on the Missa Solemnis that the symphony was under-rehearsed and as for any work to replace the Missa . . .

Ludwig could scarcely contemplate the disaster that lay before him. His head hammered and his ears howled.

Schindler told him that Count Palffy had interceded with the President of Police, and he believed he could get the censor's ban overturned. But – 'Palffy says the orchestra have presented him with a final ultimatum. They will not play under Schuppanzigh and Umlauf. Master, for the sake of the concert –'

Ludwig's anger poured out, as if the dam had been finally breached. 'The concert is cancelled. I will not deal with these imbeciles. It is enough.'

Schindler, Schuppanzigh and Umlauf held an urgent meeting with Palffy. The Count lifted his arms in a gesture of helplessness. 'I should have known better than to try to deal with Beethoven.' He shook his head is despair.

'It's vital this concert takes place,' Schuppanzigh said. 'If not, I believe the humiliation will kill him. He might never compose again. This new symphony is one of his most extraordinary works. It *must* be heard.'

'What about the Missa?' Schindler asked. 'Have you had any success, Count?'

'I spoke to Sedlnitzky at police headquarters. He said he would overrule the censor, as long as the sections – no more than three – were described in the programme as hymns.'

'Then if that problem is solved, we must find a way of persuading him –'

'You have only one solution,' Palffy said, 'and that is to transfer the concert to the Kärntnertor. I know Duport would take it. It would mean a loss for my house, but it is clear that Beethoven will not compromise. No reflection on you, my dear Schuppanzigh – I am second to none in my respect for you – but on this occasion it would have made life easier for everyone if he had accepted Clement and Seyfried.'

Duport agreed to take the concert, but the only date available was Friday 7 May, little over two weeks away. 'It means the handbills will not have much time to circulate. I cannot promise you a full house, but I will do my best.'

Schindler conveyed the news to Ludwig, who was triumphant in his vindication. 'Do you see, Schindler? These people are nothing but charlatans. If you stand up to them, you can get your way. And two extra weeks for rehearsals will be welcome.'

Visibly bracing himself, then reaching for a notebook and pencil as if putting the words on paper would remove him from responsibility for them, Schindler wrote, 'And the Missa reduced to three segments?'

'You have to make compromises in life, Schindler. We'll play the Kyrie and Agnus Dei, of course, to begin and end. And the Credo, the central part of the Mass. The censor will only complain if we try to leave it out.'

'Indeed, Master. And Herr Schuppanzigh will be spared the solo in the Sanctus.'

'Hah! I could have had Clement after all!' An idea suddenly occurred to him. 'Where is Archduke Rudolph? Is he in Vienna?'

'I think not, Master. I believe he is in Olmütz.'

'Then we will invite the Emperor and Empress as guests of honour. Tell the Frenchman, whatever his name is, to announce it on the handbills.'

'Master, we cannot be sure His Imperial –'

But Ludwig's cheeks were burning with the flush of enthusiasm. 'Come. Now. We will go to the Hofburg and personally invite them. There is not a moment to lose.'

Ludwig's sudden optimism was unconfined. His new symphony would be heard. If this concert had been cancelled, who could tell if it would be performed in his lifetime? And with Umlauf and Schuppanzigh in control, the performance would be as accomplished as anyone in Vienna could make it.

At the Hofburg he and Schindler were told to wait in an anteroom at the back of the wide rectangular courtyard. Eventually a secretary bowed to them formally and agreed to convey their letter to the personal secretary of His Imperial Majesty.

A day later Ludwig's received a note from the Emperor's secretary, which stated that His Imperial Majesty and the Empress would be unable to attend the concert, due to a prior engagement, but that it was the intention of one of the younger archdukes to represent the Imperial Royal Family.

Chapter 7

Ludwig mixed water with the white powder and tossed it back in a single draught, willing the churning of his stomach to subside. 'Schindler!' he shouted.

Schindler, tension etched on his face, appeared in the doorway.

'I need my black frock-coat, waistcoat, black silk stockings and the shoes with the buckles.'

Schindler started to speak, but Ludwig pointed to the notebook. He scribbled for a few moments: 'You do not own a black frock-coat, Master. The green one will serve. It is dark and the lights will not be bright.'

Ludwig winced as he pulled the waistcoat across his stomach and fastened the buttons. Then he wetted his wide-toothed comb and tried to bring some order to his hair. 'Come on, Schindler. The public and the critics await us. One will love us, the other will not.'

The auditorium was full to the rear of the second parterre, but Ludwig was more concerned at the large empty box nearer the stage. 'Why is the Emperor's reprentative not here yet?'

'I am sure he will arrive just before the start,' Schindler said into his ear. 'Do not concern yourself. It is an excellent audience. You will make a great profit.'

Ludwig strode across the back of the stage, where the musicians were mingling before taking their seats. He looked at their instruments: violins and cellos dark and glistening, horns, trumpets and trombones reflecting the candlelight that flickered in dozens of glass-covered wall sconces. I am among musicians again, he thought. When they make the sounds come from their instruments they will be speaking the language I understand, and the language with which I will speak to people as yet unborn.

Unsmiling, he acknowledged their frequent bows, marks of respect towards the creator of the music they were about to play. He remembered past concerts, spoilt by the complaints of players and – he believed – deliberately poor playing, but there had been none of that for this concert. Schuppanzigh and Umlauf reported that in rehearsals the musicians seemed to have understood they were playing music of a different order from anything they had played before.

I was right to insist on Schuppanzigh and Umlauf from the start, he thought. Men who truly understand my music. Schuppanzigh's violin looked absurdly small in his great fleshy hands, while Umlauf was beating his baton gently in the air in time to some beat that existed only in his head.

He felt Schindler's hand on his shoulder. He turned and saw Nikolaus Zmeskall, his skin hanging loosely from his face, lifting himself on spindly arms from the seat on which he had been carried in and manoeuvring himself into a chair on the aisle. Ludwig watched his old friend as he settled down, the pain caused by the exertion evident in his eyes.

A stillness came over Ludwig, isolating him from the bustle around him. Zmeskall was sinking into a long, slow, inexorable decline.

Then there was a tug at his coat. He turned to see young Gerhard von Breuning smiling up at him and his father hurrying over. Ludwig was overwhelmed by the shining optimism in the boy's eyes at the world lying before him waiting to be conquered.

'I am sorry,' Breuning said, close to his ear. 'I tried to stop him. Good luck, Ludwig.'

'Your brother, Master,' Schindler said, into his other ear, and there was Johann's tall figure, once again dressed in that absurd blue frock-coat with brass buttons, his wide mouth set in an inane smile. Alongside him the tall, thin figure of Karl, the picture of boredom. Ludwig wanted to shake him by the shoulders and make him understand the importance of the evening. Instead he sighed and turned back to the musicians.

They were seated now, tuning their instruments. Schindler led Ludwig to the side of the stage where Umlauf waited, still conducting to his imaginary beat, his brow furrowed in concentration.

Ludwig closed his eyes against the howling in his ears. Soon the sounds of my music will flow out across the stage to the audience. My message to mankind. From my heart, may my music go to theirs.

Then Umlauf, eyes blazing, nodded at him and walked out on to the stage. Ludwig followed and the audience broke into applause. He turned quickly to the orchestra. In his head he already heard the opening of the Missa Solemnis, the huge D major chord that, after the introduction, would lead into the affirmation of the Kyrie. He grasped Umlauf's sleeve and gave him the beat with his arms. He wanted to remind him not to lose the pace on the sustained chords, but he could not trust his voice or his ears.

To the side of Umlauf and in front of him – almost a part of the orchestra – was a small chair, and Ludwig sat down it, shoulders rounded, head sunk on his chest. Moments later the music washed over him.

From behind the orchestra came the voices, chorus in unison and then the soloists. *Kyrie eleison . . .* He remembered what he had written on the top of the first page: *Mit Andacht*, with reverence; and then, as if to temper the devotional ring of those words, he had added, *Von Herzen – möge es wieder zu Herzen gehen!* From the heart – may it return straight to the heart!

This was the solemn Mass, but it must never be too solemn. He had written a religious work, but it was for the concert hall rather than a church. The censor in theory had been right!

Just three lines, *Kyrie eleison, Christe eleison, Kyrie eleison.* Yet I have created a whole movement, Ludwig thought. It does not require complicated words, any more than intricate themes, to make music. But wait, he thought, until my symphony is played. My music, and the words of Schiller, unified in a way no composer has done before.

The trombones, their great bells raised, gave out the unequivocal affirmation of the Credo. *Sforzando, fortissimo*, then sudden *piano*. Chorus and orchestra enter and the sopranos rise, inexorably – to top B flat. Ludwig started in his chair as, half-way through the sustained note, they dropped suddenly to B flat an octave lower! He glanced at Umlauf, whose eyes were directed over the heads of the players towards the singers. Already the music had moved on. The momentum was right, orchestra and voices blending perfectly.

Ludwig allowed himself a small smile. Did it really matter? The music he had written was there in the score, for perpetuity. One day there would be sopranos who could hold that top B flat.

The solo voices entered with the *Incarnatus est*, and the

statement of the Crucifixion. At first, only reduced strings –
he could hear Schuppanzigh's violin leading the turning phrase
of the *Incarnatus* and its development, before the juddering and
jolting rhythms of the Crucifixion with its diminished chords.

But the single note of G ushers in the Resurrection, the
central tenet of the Christian faith. The voices rise in unison.
Ludwig leaned back in his chair and folded his arms. Let them
have their Resurrection, he thought, and the restatement of the
Credo that follows it – the Credo uttered in hurried quavers by
the chorus.

He tapped his foot to the rhythm of the huge fugue, which
brought the Credo to an end – a fugue based around the single
word Amen!

Would Bach, or Mozart or Haydn or any of his predecessors,
have composed a fugue on the word Amen? No. But it is my
statement. The Missa Solemnis is not for the priests and bishops
alone, but for all mankind.

Agnus Dei – Lamb of God, who takest away the sins of the
world, have mercy on us. Back to the minor key. Will the men
of the Church try to reclaim the piece? He folded his arms
tighter. What will they make of the timpani in the middle
section, accompanied by *tremolo* strings and the bugle call from
the trumpets? Will they declare it as the Second Coming of
Christ? They will be wrong. It is music. Music among the words
of the Mass. Do not question why it is there or its purpose.

And how many people will recognise the quotation from
Handel, with which the fugue is launched? It is from the great
Hallelujah chorus of *Messiah. My tribute – not to God but to the
man whose name I first heard from my grandfather.*

Pacem, pacem, dona pacem. Umlauf cued the players for the final
fortissimo flourish, ending in the home key of D major. Then he
bent, took Ludwig's hand and pulled him to his feet.

Ludwig turned to the audience, but did not bow as Umlauf
did. He wanted to read their faces, try to understand how they
felt. He saw that for the most part they were serious, some
frowning. A number of people were crossing themselves. Good,
thought Ludwig, that will please the censor. The applause was
polite, restrained almost.

The work had left them confused What had they just heard?
A solemn religious work, or a concert piece? The problem for
them was that although the words belonged to the former, the
music belonged to the latter. It will take time, he thought.

But what of my new symphony? That is what matters most. If that fails . . . He closed his eyes tight, waiting for all the sounds in his ears to dissipate. Then, as he left the stage with Umlauf, he summoned the opening bars – the mysterious *pianissimo* triplets in the strings – of the symphony into his head.

'Master, you have created a work of great genius.' Ludwig heard Schindler's oleaginous voice in his ear.

Ludwig nodded. 'Get me some water. And wine to follow.' He turned to Umlauf. 'The symphony is important, Umlauf. I –' He was interrupted by Schuppanzigh who came towards him, violin and bow clutched in one hand, the other mopping his forehead with a handkerchief. 'Congratulations, Ludwig. Splendid piece.' His earnest, high-pitched voice found its way through the blank heaviness in Ludwig's ears.

'They did not understand it. It does not matter. You led well, Schuppi. Now there is the symphony.' He took the two glasses Schindler held out to him, emptying the water glass in a single draught then sipping the wine. 'Umlauf,' he said, turning to the conductor, 'remember not to let the pace slacken, even in the third movement. And in the Scherzo, the *molto vivace*, the timpani must enter like thunder. Sudden, do you understand?'

'The musicians are ready, sir. And the singers. I believe they will give you a performance to be proud of.' Schuppanzigh nodded in agreement.

A sudden thought occurred to Ludwig. 'Schindler, has the Emperor's representative arrived?'

Schindler looked apprehensive as he glanced to the other two for support. 'No, Master. The imperial box is empty.'

'Empty?'

'It is nothing, Master. And it is time. The symphony should begin now.'

Schuppanzigh went back on to the stage and gave the instruction for the players to tune their instruments.

The chair was still in place but Ludwig did not want it. He lifted it, looked around and was grateful when a pair of hands took it from him and bore it away. He positioned himself next to Umlauf so that he could be sure of giving him the beat. Umlauf was bowing to the audience and bidding the players to rise. Ludwig put his hands over his ears to keep out the harsh sound. Already in his head he could hear the *tremolo* opening of the first movement, the curtain that must be pulled back slowly to reveal what lies behind.

'Two beats, not four,' he said to Umlauf, cursing at the sound of his own voice in his head. 'Watch me.'

Umlauf smiled and nodded, looked around the players with his eyebrows raised, maintaining the smile as a signal of encouragement. Finally he turned to Schuppanzigh, who indicated that the orchestra was ready.

Ludwig lifted his arms and gave a beat of two. He saw the second violins and cellos play the triplet semiquavers – an eerie open chord, lacking the essential centre that would have made it conventional – and the first violins enter with the *pianissimo* descending fifths and fourths, the first chink in the curtain. At first the sound did not reach him and he closed his eyes to increase his concentration. Then, gloriously, he heard the notes – soft, gentle, *pianissimo*, exactly as he had written them.

He held his arms frozen in the air. The sounds were good – no whistling or rushing or howling. He sensed the movement of the musicians around him, the sawing of the strings at the first *fortissimo* in which the whole orchestra played in unison a double dotted descent.

He wanted to cry out that he could hear his music, that what he had feared for almost all his adult life had not yet come to pass.

Piano, *dolce*, the first hint of the great theme that is to come in the finale, played by flute, clarinet and horn, answered by oboe and trumpet – just six bars, but enough. A suggestion, nothing more. And soon the dotted rhythm again, to drive the movement forward. He crouched for the rising *piano* scales in the strings and jumped high for the *fortissimo* quavers and dotted semiquavers. Half turning he saw Umlauf's arms waving in time to his, his eyes wide and his face frozen in concentration. The players' eyes flitted from the scores to Umlauf, the strain and effort chiselled on their faces. They were playing – Ludwig knew – as they had never played before.

He turned to Schuppanzigh, whose exaggerated head movements exactly mirrored Umlauf's beat, so that the players could take it from him as well as from Umlauf. He held his violin high up on his cheek so that his ear was almost on the body; the flesh of his face quivered each time he brought down the bow.

In front of Ludwig the brass players' cheeks were ballooned and reddened, as they held the long-sustained note that led to the furious runs in the strings, before the return of the dotted rhythm and then . . . *pianissimo* . . . Ludwig crouched down, holding his arms out to the first violins, his hands trembling like leaves in the wind.

The return of the opening of the symphony, that eerie open chord, followed by the *pianissimo* descending fourths and fifths. What did it mean? Speak for me, Ludwig wanted to say to the players. Speak to the audience in my language.

The development this time, more concentrated, more complex . . . Ludwig held his arms still, listening to the music he had created. *It must never end . . .*

The strings were sawing the air with the double bowing that would bring the movement to an end. *Pianissimo!* No, no, too loud! He put his forefinger across his lips, waving the other arm at Schuppanzigh, who seemed to shrink into his chair. Now it was right. A gradual *crescendo*, step by step, ever higher, and then – *fortissimo* – great octave leaps from all the strings, first and second violins, violas, cellos and basses, still double bowing . . . a final statement of the dotted rhythm, truncated this time, from the whole orchestra, rapid ascending runs and five staccato quavers, unequivocal, absolute, the final two accompanied by timpani to emphasise their certainty – to end the movement in the single unison note of D.

Ludwig held out his arms unmoving. He wanted to nod approval at Umlauf; he wanted to take Schuppanzigh by the shoulders and thank him. More than anything he wanted to go and see the timpanist, hearten and encourage him, for he, more than any other player, would be responsible for the success – or failure – of the next movement, the Scherzo.

Suddenly the silence in his head became intense and before he could react to it he saw the violinists' bows flash in the light. The high *fortissimo* B and the instant drop to D reached his ears like a thunderous – but welcome – wave. Music again filled his head. He willed the timpanist to seize his chance.

There it was! D dotted crotchet to D quaver and crotchet an octave lower, instantly echoed by the strings. It was the launch for the swift development section that followed. Brisk, Umlauf, he wanted to say, just three beats in the bar, crotchets played with the speed of semiquavers, but each one firmly defined – that is why I wrote crotchets and not quavers.

He bent his knees, his arms out, just his hands beating. *Pianissimo, sempre pianissimo.* Now you can begin your *crescendo*, he thought. Slowly he raised himself up, increasing his arm movements. *Fortissimo!* He brought his arms down wildly for the first beat of each bar – he had written *forte* in every bar for this section – in case the musicians doubted it.

He reached in front of him to bring in the sustained minims in the wind, contrasting with the dotted rhythm of the strings. Now another hint – no more – of the great theme that was to come in the finale, so that when it finally entered there would be a spark of recognition in the audience.

The dotted rhythm again to push the music forward. The octave leaps in the strings leading . . . where? He thrust his arms out, palms outwards to bring the orchestra to a complete and unexpected halt. Now change the rhythm. Let the wind players carry the music on, to a *pizzicato* accompaniment in the strings, leading to . . .

The timpanist crashed his drums again, answered by the wind but cut off again by the timpani; the wind tried to speak, but the timpani interrupted, wind, timpani, wind, timpani, until finally they blended . . .

A strange noise assaulted Ludwig's ears, but even through the music he could tell what it was. The audience was cheering and clapping. There was an audible cry of 'Encore!' and another of '*Vivat!*'

He clenched his lips, driving the orchestra on like a team of horses. Timpani again! Dotted crotchet, quaver, crotchet at octave intervals. From behind the orchestra Ludwig saw the drumsticks in a blur of movement.

The sustained chord again, a brief restatement of the main theme, and then the Trio. Ludwig swung his arms across his body; like a country dance, he wanted to say to the players, let the music sway, oboe, clarinet and horn only. And what is this theme? Nothing more than another preparation for the great theme of the finale, only it does not rise as that theme will.

Other instruments joined in, as if more countryfolk were taking to the dance floor. Horns and trombones set up a sustained chord, around which the strings danced, until they, too, joined in a huge series of chords, after which a brief restatement of the dotted theme brought the movement to a *fortissimo* close of unison crotchets.

Ludwig held his breath. The last of the music left his head to be replaced by a wave of discord from behind him. It was a huge roar swelling from the audience.

'Timpani,' he said quietly to himself, then turning he directed the timpanist to stand. The man held his drumsticks pointing upwards and executed a deep bow. Ludwig turned to Umlauf, wanting him to quell the applause and continue with the music, but Umlauf was acknowledging it and it showed no sign of abating.

The applause, punctuated with more shouts of 'Encore!' and '*Vivat!*', was hurting his ears and banishing the last vestiges of the music. Would he hear the soft, gentle Adagio?

Umlauf must call the audience to order and ready the players. Suddenly a different sound reached Ludwig's ears. He glanced at Umlauf, who pointed to the aisle running down the middle of the parterre.

The Police Commissioner was shouting through his cupped hands: 'Silence! Silence! The music must continue! Silence!'

The clapping subsided as a wave crashes on the shore and is pulled back out to sea.

Ludwig mopped his brow. He knew he should be exultant at the reception the symphony was earning, but he was fearful that his ears would prevent him from reaching the end, that the symphony would be, for him, unfinished. In his head he heard the gentle opening of the Adagio, horns answered by clarinets, like a series of sighs, supported by low strings before the first violins take up the main theme. The tempo was good, not too slow; this was an Adagio, not a Marcia Funèbre. It was a moment before he realised that the sounds he was hearing were coming from the musicians, not his imagination.

The violins stated the opening theme – slow, stately, but gaining slightly in the upward phrase – answered in the wind. Such a simple theme! Four bars only and it was complete. Ludwig allowed the sumptuous sound of the strings to flow through his head. Gently they played their grace notes under the soaring clarinet, and he prepared himself for the move into the second theme. Sustain it, Umlauf, he thought to himself. B flat to D major! No break – allow one theme to dissolve into the other, to *become* it. Had he ever written a more unexpected, and more exquisite, modulation? Schuppanzigh's violin sang out, picking up the pace slightly, for the turning second subject, another simple theme that he knew would remain in the heads of the audience as if they had always known it.

The variations followed – semiquaver runs for the first violins of such complexity that the potential for catastrophe hung in the air. Ludwig gave Schuppanzigh an encouraging smile. His friend's fleshy flat-tipped fingers flew up and down the fingerboard and his bow gave out the long *legato* phrases. Behind him the other violinists used just the centre of their bows, fearful of missing one of the accidentals or the octave leaps that Ludwig had cruelly written in the middle of the passage. But Schuppanzigh's violin again sang out the notes, in such a way that always behind them hovered the simple opening theme. Ludwig closed his eyes again, ecstatic.

From the back of the orchestra the horns sounded their accompaniment – even the exposed solo rising scale was perfect. A short unison section, *sforzando* and *fortissimo*, led to the opening theme once more, and again Schuppanzigh's fingers flew up the E string allowing the turning triplets to sing out above the orchestra and up to a B flat trill.

Finally, in a *diminuendo* as faultless as Ludwig could have wanted, the entire orchestra descended to a *pianissimo*, before following Umlauf's ever-expanding arms to end the movement gently – but expectantly.

Barely a pause followed before Umlauf brought his arms down and out in a ferocious gesture. Ludwig stared at him, unseeing. The final statement. The message that must be heard.

The sound of the *fortissimo* wind instruments swept over him, buffeting him like a gale. Then the sudden stop. He looked to the right as the cellos and double basses – alone! – played an introductory recitative just seven bars long. The wind burst in again. Cellos and double basses again, shortened this time . . . and now . . .

Ludwig could hardly believe his own audacity. Each of the preceding three movements briefly quoted – the falling fourths and fifths of the first, the dotted rhythm and rising crotchets of the second, and the simple opening theme of the third, all reduced to just two bars . . . Each time truncated by cellos and basses, cut off brutally as if to say, 'No, you have had your moment, it is time to move on.'

Ludwig sensed movement and opened his eyes. Silently, their faces seemingly set in stone, the four solo singers walked on to the stage.

The cellos and basses sawed at their instruments in the furious *fortissimo* passage of accidental high sharps, themselves cut off this time by the wind. A suggestion from the wind of the great theme that was about to unfold, a descending run from the deep strings . . . and the moment had arrived.

Alone, the cellos and basses stated the theme of the finale, at which the earlier movements had hinted. A theme, it seemed to him now, that had always been in his head, needing only to be given life.

Violas joined the deep strings, with solo bassoon accompaniment above like a protecting bird. The slow *crescendo* and then Ludwig heard for the first time the full theme, in all its force and glory, played by brass and woodwind in unison, anchoring octave chords in the strings, and the timpani – quaver-crotchet, quaver-crotchet – marking the beat. He turned to his right and saw Umlauf increasing the pace, as second violins and violas swirled underneath the theme, then suddenly arresting it, before cueing the timpani to give the roll that brings the whole orchestra in with a reprise of the opening of the movement, leading this time to a sound that had never been heard in any symphony before.

Ludwig lifted his head to judge what he had created. To his left a solo baritone voice implored the music to cease its restless tones. Instead, it begged, let us raise our voices in more pleasing and joyful sounds.

How right he had been to use Schiller's words! 'Alle Menschen werden Brüder.' All mankind will become brothers. The forces of art, literary and musical, forged to utter an unalterable truth.

The image of his beloved grandfather floated into his mind, as if to acknowledge the great legacy he had passed on and which his grandson had so gloriously fulfilled. Now, behind the orchestra, the voices of the chorus sounded and then those of the other soloists, topped by the soprano Henriette Sontag, as clear in the air as the summer song of a nightingale. Round Ludwig the sounds swirled, a perfect blend of voices – solo and chorus – and instruments. His entire being was filled with his music.

> He who's known the great good fortune
> Of a friend, a friend to be.
> And he who's won a fair sweet woman,
> Let him join our Jubilee!

They were the same words that Florestan sings in the closing moments of *Fidelio*. But before Ludwig could contemplate the sadness the words held for him, the chorus raised its voices in a mighty exultation to God, ending on a sustained chord that suddenly shifted the key – an unmistakable signal to the listener that something unexpected was about to happen.

In the distance – almost, as it were, behind the massed troops in the Prater and the flags of the victorious allies fluttering in the breeze – a bass drum gave the beat of a Turkish march, joined moments later by cymbals and triangle. Ludwig thrilled to it. The unexpected, always the unexpected! And this Turkish march was nothing more than another variation of the main theme, as if to prove that every note in this final movement had its proper place.

Now it was the tenor's turn, and Ludwig could sense the slight figure of Haitzinger straining forward on his toes to give the words emphasis. The orchestra took over, Umlauf's arms duplicated by Schuppanzigh's nod for the fugue at the centre of the movement, allowing the chorus to gather their strength for the massive declamation of the main theme that followed.

D major, an unequivocal affirmation, full chorus and orchestra. The finale . . . that is what the audience will believe, Ludwig thought. But no. There is more to say yet.

The blast from the bass trombone resounded in his head as the male voices introduced Schiller's next verse, the recurring idea that was central to his great poem, soon joined by the other voices.

> Embrace each other, O ye millions!
> His kiss to all the world he gives!
> Brothers – see beyond the stars
> Is where our loving Father lives.

Ludwig tensed. The most complex part of the movement for the musicians and singers – *fortissimo* affirmation followed by *pianissimo* devotion, stresses off the beat, complex harmonies, voices and instruments going in different directions . . . And as if that were not enough, a double fugue – the voices themselves now going in opposite directions, underscored by intricate counterpoint.

Ludwig moved his arms but they were not the movements of a conductor, more the instinctive desire to respond to the complex sounds swirling around him. His symphony, exactly as he had conceived it.

At the climax the most difficult moment in the movement for the chorus – a top sustained A for the sopranos, while the altos and basses sing two contrasting themes and the tenors first support the sopranos then provide the inner harmony!

Fortissimo, fortissimo . . . but, as suddenly and unexpectedly as anything else in the whole symphony, *pianissimo*. Fragmented voices, slowly, inexorably, building to another climax.

Ludwig's breath quickened. It was the moment for the coda to begin. Drive them onward, Umlauf, he urged silently. After all that has gone before, the momentum must not be lost.

After a swirl of strings, an entirely new theme from the solo male voices, just a small turning phrase, but one which, taken up by the other soloists, and then the chorus, gives the music its driving force. Swift crotchets and quavers, the bows around him sawing at the instruments, their tips flashing in the light. But wait . . . one final unexpected moment of drama, but this time of quiet drama. The four solo voices, singing together for just eleven bars, with gentle orchestral accompaniment, proclaiming the central message of the whole work.

Alle Menschen werden Brüder, All mankind will become brothers, *Wo dein sanfter Flügel weilt.* Where your soft benev'lence reigns.

Then, in majestic unison, chorus and orchestra began the final *prestissimo*. There was nothing left, now, but to proclaim the message to all mankind, Schiller's message of hope.

This is what I want to say, Ludwig thought. *My* message to mankind. That there is hope. That if we look beyond ourselves, beyond the stars, we will see that God's most glorious creation is mankind itself. *I have given them the message I was put on this earth to deliver, the message that will reverberate down the generations for ever.* The sounds in his head began to mutate, the glorious sounds of music starting to jumble. Soon they would fade and the dreadful noises would return. He shook his head slightly at the raucousness that was, bit by bit, banishing the sounds he had created. He felt unsteady, buffeted by the alien cacophony around him.

Suddenly he gasped as a hand touched his shoulder. He opened his eyes, frightened at what he would see. He was dazzled by the light but slowly he recognised the smiling face of Karoline Unger. Gently, she turned him round. At first all he could see was a blur as the clamour intensified and swept towards him.

Then his lips parted slightly and the corners of his mouth

turned up. The audience – to the last man and woman – was on its feet, cheering, shouting, waving white handkerchiefs and hats in the air.

'Beethoven!' they roared. 'Beethoven! Beethoven! Beethoven!'

BOOK NINE

Chapter 1

'I want nothing more to do with Schindler,' Ludwig said in a surly voice. 'He swindled me out of receipts for the concert, and I will not tolerate dishonesty.'

'Sir,' Karl Holz said, 'I am sure that is not the case, though I do not wish to doubt your word. At any rate, I believe he has left Vienna for a while.'

'I will need you to help me, Holz. Will you do it? Schindler was a wretch, but he looked after my affairs.'

'With great pleasure, sir.' The young man, who was not much more than twenty-five with curly blond hair and a bright, open smile, pulled a chair closer to Ludwig. 'My position at the Chancellery is lowly and I have plenty of time to practise the violin. Herr Schuppanzigh frequently uses me as second violin in his quartet. It will give me great pleasure to be of assistance to a musician as distinguished as you, sir.'

'I will not be a musician for much longer if things go on as they are.' Ludwig wished that something would subdue the sharp pain in his stomach. 'First, I need a new doctor. Speak to Nanette Streicher in the Ungargasse. Tell her the Italian will not attend to me.'

Holz wrote in a notebook as Ludwig spoke. 'And I want you to keep an eye on my nephew Karl. Hah! He shares your name. He lives with a fellow student. I tried to stop him leaving, but he is nearly twenty. What could I do? I fear he will try to see his mother, and I do not want him to.'

'I will do as you wish, sir.'

'And, Holz, tell me about the Quartet. It failed, did it not?' As he spoke the whistle intensified in his head until he thought he would scream. Then, as suddenly as it had begun it subsided.

'The audience was unkind, but Herr Schuppanzigh says it was under-rehearsed. He has no doubt that it is a great work, worthy of its creator.'

'Let us hope the Russian prince thinks so too, or he will cancel the commission,' Ludwig growled.

'No, sir. I have spoken to him. He is pleased with the work and awaits the next.'

'Tell him he will have to wait. I do not know which will come first, a new Quartet or death.'

The pains in Ludwig's stomach became suddenly worse. His abdomen was tender to the touch and he all but lost control of his bowels. He observed, too, that he was passing blood. On the day that Doktor Braunhofer, general practitioner and professor of natural history at the university, came to see him, he coughed up mucus into a handkerchief and noticed to his horror that it, too, was laced with blood.

Braunhofer pressed two fingers on Ludwig's abdomen and Ludwig cried out in pain. 'Damn you, you will kill me!'

'Your intestines, Herr Beethoven, are inflamed.'

'I will soon die, won't I? Tell me, Braunhofer, then at least I will know. Shout, or I won't hear you.'

'No, sir, you will not. Your symptoms are distressing, but you are suffering from nothing that cannot be cured.'

'How will you cure me?'

'It will require iron discipline on your part. The body is a sensitive organ and responds to what we put into it. In your case I regret you have been putting evil substances inside it for far too long.'

Ludwig sighed. 'Stop drinking wine. You will tell me that, just as every other doctor has done. And I shall ignore you just as I did them.'

'Then your own prognosis will be very quickly proved correct.'

'Then tell me, Herr Doktor, what I should do.'

'No alcoholic drinks. That is a rule you absolutely must obey. No coffee and no spices. They upset the stomach. I will speak to your cook. I will give you powders to strengthen your bowels, but you will not need to take them for more than a week. *If* you obey my instructions.'

'I will be cured?'

'I will guarantee your full recovery, which, as an admirer of your genius, will cause me great satisfaction.'

Ludwig's stomach swelled into a balloon of pain. The cook,

under instructions from both Braunhofer and Nanette, restricted his diet to chicken broth and dumplings. For several days he vomited each time he swallowed the food and when he wiped his mouth his handkerchief was again stained with traces of blood.

Doktor Braunhofer came to see him daily, placing a silver trumpet gently on his abdomen and listening to it for several minutes at a time. He told Ludwig to stop taking the powders, to remain in bed and to continue to try to eat.

When at last the vomiting stopped, Ludwig found he could swallow some spoonfuls of broth, but each time he did so the sharp pains returned.

'It will take time,' Braunhofer told him one day, in the presence of Nanette. 'Sickness does not disappear in a day. Your body is ridding itself of the poison you have ingested.'

In the days that followed, Nanette sat for long hours in Ludwig's bedroom, tirelessly administering the soup and breaking up bread for him. Slowly the stomach pains lost their sharpness and when he spat saliva into a handkerchief it no longer contained blood.

But he also realised that the heaviness in his ears was greater than ever. He could not hear Nanette, Braunhofer or Karl Holz.

His nephew Karl, accompanied by Czerny, also visited him. By now he had accepted that he could no longer hear speech and he indicated the notebook and pencil on the table. 'Karl is becoming an accomplished pianist. He will show you,' Czerny wrote.

The young man went to the piano and Ludwig closed his eyes. When he finally opened them, Karl was standing before him open-mouthed, as if to berate his uncle for ignoring his playing.

Doktor Braunhofer smiled, his hands on his hips. 'A good recovery, due entirely to your obeying the instructions I gave you.' Ludwig pointed to the notebook and pencil. Braunhofer scribbled, 'Your deafness will improve as you recover.'

Ludwig's heart leaped when he read the words. So many doctors had told him the same thing, but Braunhofer's supreme confidence was new to him. And he had to admit that, as his strength returned, so did a feeling of well-being and determination. True, he had followed Braunhofer's dietary orders, as he had not followed Malfatti's, but they had consisted of more than simply renouncing wine.

'Can I drink wine again, now that I have recovered?'

Braunhofer laughed. 'You cannot! Under no circumstances.'

Ludwig waved away the doctor's move to write down what he had said: the message was clear. 'Even white wine, not red, diluted with water?'

Braunhofer picked up the pencil. 'Where do you like going the most to relax? Out of the city?'

'Baden. The Helenenthal.'

'Go there for the summer. Take the baths, but not on damp days. Walk in the valley. Tell the cook to continue your diet. But *no wine*!'

As the days passed Ludwig could feel his strength returning. He told Karl Holz to arrange accommodation for him in Baden. Before he left Ludwig summoned his nephew. 'I am going to Baden for the summer to recuperate from my illness. I need to begin work again. There are two more Quartets for Count Galitzin. I want you to come to Baden every Sunday to see me. We will walk in the Helenenthal together. Our favourite place.'

Karl was aghast: his mouth fell open in horror at the prospect.

'I want you to play the piano for me each time you come, so that I can judge your progress. According to Czerny, you have a great future as a musician.'

Karl appeared to be trying to pluck up courage to say something. Finally, visibly gritting his teeth, he snatched up the pencil and wrote on the pad. 'I am not going to be a musician. I want to be a soldier.'

Ludwig was exasperated rather than angry. Karl's intention was not unknown to him: Schindler had mentioned it months before, but Ludwig had dismissed it as a young man's fancy. Karl was unsuited to a military career: he was of slight build, not strong, with an open, almost feminine face. His character was equally unsuited to the rigours of the army. He was stubborn and had an aversion to obeying instructions.

'You do not have the makings of a soldier,' he said mildly. 'You are . . . We Beethovens are artists. That is what you must do.'

'Only you,' Karl wrote. 'Not my father or Uncle Johann.'

Ludwig wanted to berate him for his obstinacy, but he knew

that Karl would not change his mind. He knew, too, that opposition would make his own heart beat faster, he would have palpitations, and who could tell what that might do to his fragile health?

'You will visit me every Sunday. Karl Holz will be here, if you need anything.'

'Will you advance me a loan? My rent has been raised.'

Ludwig chuckled. 'You young men, you spend your money too readily. Tell Holz to advance you fifty florins, but no more than five a week.'

Karl wrote a few words on a new sheet of paper, tore it from the notebook and handed it to Ludwig. Without reading it Ludwig signed his name. Handing it back to his nephew with a benevolent smile, he gestured to a chair. 'Come and sit near me, Karl. I want to say a few words to you.'

Karl hesitated, then did as his uncle asked.

'You are a good boy, Karl. I have been very ill. I am cured for the moment, but I do not know for how long. My health is poor. It is important for me to know that you are well, that your studies are progressing and that you have what you need. You will soon embark on a career. It is my profound hope that you will become a musician. Your father was a musician, you know, before he worked at the Hofburg.'

Karl looked down at the table rather than at his uncle.

'While I am away in Baden it is important for me to know that you will not lapse into evil ways. Karl, you understand what I am referring to, don't you?'

The slightest inclination of Karl's head indicated that he did. His nostrils flared, but still he said nothing.

'I will not allow you to be corrupted, Karl. You saw your mother not so long ago – I allowed that. But that is enough. I have your moral well-being to consider. You are my nephew, but you know that you are as a son to me. I am a father to you. The truest parent you have.'

Chapter 2

The air in Baden was good, the familiar odour of sulphur lying over the town almost tangible evidence of the health-giving properties of the waters that gave the town its name.

Holz had arranged rooms in the Schloss Gutenbrunn, which was close to the largest bath-house in Baden. At first Ludwig was reluctant to use it, since it was always busy and he did not want to be approached by anybody. Soon, though, he realised he could achieve greater anonymity there than in the smaller baths he had frequented in the past. On a number of occasions he suspected that people wanted to strike up a conversation, but he never returned their glances and was soon able to enjoy the waters without fear of interruption.

He took the familiar walk into the Helenenthal, and up to the Rauhenstein ruins, but was dismayed at the effort it cost him. In the ruin itself he had to sit for a long while, waiting for his breath to steady and the strength to return to his legs. Once, a man and his wife came up to him, concerned, but Ludwig waved them away.

More than anything he craved wine – its familiar taste and calming effect that nothing else could replicate. He wrote to Doktor Braunhofer, imploring him to allow the occasional glass of diluted wine. By way of encouragement he wrote a four-part canon in the letter, set to words he had composed thanking the doctor for bringing him back from death's door.

Braunhofer's reply, which brought a wry smile to his face, contained a two-line verse on how a doctor may close the door to death, but how wine will always open it.

Ludwig had arrived in Baden in early May. Towards the end of the month the weather became unseasonably cold and wet, and Ludwig was forced to remain indoors. He wrote to Karl, asking why he had not yet come to see him. In a reply that arrived three days later the young man promised that he would come soon.

The weather did not improve. One Saturday morning, staring through the window-pane at the dark green of the Helenenthal shimmering in the distance, Ludwig heaved a sigh of frustration, then walked down the stairs to the front desk and ordered the clerk to have a carafe of white wine, and another of water, sent to his room.

Sitting at the table in his room he sipped the wine, only a little diluted, allowed it to run down the sides of his tongue and rest at the back of his throat before he swallowed it. Then he pulled the large blank manuscript book towards him and arranged a set of pencils alongside it. Across the top of the first sheet of paper he wrote: 'Holy song of thanksgiving of a convalescent to the Almighty, in the Lydian mode.' Working swiftly, he pencilled in a series of chords, long sonorous minims, linked by a plaintive phrase in the first violin. The movement, he decided, would form the central part of the new Quartet – the second – for Prince Galitzin.

As he wrote he heard the sounds of his music clearly in his head. The heaviness in his ears seemed almost to help. No extraneous sound could penetrate the thick blanket that normally caused him such misery. For the first time in his life, he was grateful for his deafness. Only the music he was composing filled his head, as clearly as if Schuppanzigh and his string quartet were playing.

The string quartet! How long ago was it that he had first tried to compose for this most sparse – and yet most perfect – of ensembles? All his life, he now realised, he had held the quartet as the highest form of musical expression. Not a single note can be wasted; each and every note must have its place.

Ludwig tapped his fingers urgently on the table. A high trill on the E string of the first violin would bring in the joyous section of the movement, away from the liturgical nature of the Lydian mode, one of the traditional church styles. *Neue Kraft fühlend*, he wrote. With new strength. Under the trill he put dancing quavers for the other three instruments, then taking the first violin up in a swift *staccato* run for a series of turning phrases punctuated by more trills.

The rain beat against the pane. Beyond it, the sodden trees stood motionless and resigned. Oh, to hear the sound of the nightingale, he thought. If the sun were shining brightly and the trees were alive with the song of birds *and I couldn't hear it* . . .

He scribbled on, as fast as he could make the pen move –

turning phrases of triple demi-semiquavers. They were illegible, some on the stave, some off it, to be tidied up later. But would they not bring the sound of summer into people's heads?

The plain chant of the Lydian mode must return. *Mit innigster Empfindung*, he wrote; the same words he had written on earlier compositions. Underneath he put two notes, middle C rising to A.

In his head he heard the interval and sang it. Here it would serve to introduce the final appearance of the plain chant. But even as he wrote the notes, he knew he would use them again – that yearning, pleading interval of a sixth.

Ludwig paced the floor. Why had he not heard from his nephew? Not even a note, and had he not made it quite clear that Karl was to visit him every Sunday? At first he had been tolerant, but it was over a month now. The weather had improved, they could walk together, climb to the Rauhenstein . . .

He went to the Marktplatz, just a stone's throw from the Gutenbrunn, and sat at a table outside a café waiting for Karl Holz to arrive. The square was bustling with people, admiring the fruit and vegetables on the stalls. Groups stood with packing cases, newly arrived from Vienna or preparing to return there. Steam rose from the horses' flanks. He no longer cared that he could not hear the noises of the market-place, that people's mouths moved silently. It was his fate to be deaf and nothing would change it now, whatever Braunhofer said.

He tilted back his face, so that the warm sun could caress it. He breathed deeply, the smell of sulphur curiously mixed with the inviting aroma of coffee. He clicked his fingers at a waiter, then waved him away as he saw Holz walking towards him. The man was annoyed, hesitated for a moment as if considering whether to remonstrate, but thought better of it and walked away.

'Sit here, Holz. What news of Karl?' He took out a pad and pencil.

'Coffee, sir, and water? The journey was hot.'

Ludwig clicked his fingers again. 'Coffee,' he said, then louder, 'Coffee! Be quick.' He turned back to Holz, eyebrows raised.

Holz wrote. 'He is well, I believe.'

'What do you mean, "you believe"?'

'He is often out, sometimes till late at night. The housekeeper told me.'

'Where is he?'

Holz shrugged. 'In the Alservorstadt, sometimes. At the taverns there.'

Ludwig's temper was fraying and he said, 'Stop. Not here. Come back to the Gutenbrunn.' He tossed some coins on the table and brushed past the waiter, who stood staring after them indignantly, the tray of coffee in his hands.

When they reached the apartment, he said, 'Write it down now, Holz.'

'I lured him into going to a beer-house with me to gauge if he drinks too much, but that is not the case.'

'Damn fool boy. How can he afford to drink anyway? Does he go to . . . places with his friends? You know what I mean.'

Holz wrote, 'I don't believe so, though he is constantly short of money. He asks me almost daily for money from you.'

'You must not!'

Holz shook his head. 'No money. Maybe you should give him a fixed sum periodically and he can keep account.'

'Is that what other students do?'

'He has asked the housekeeper for money. Also he has gone to his other uncle, who has given him money.'

Ludwig's eyebrows shot up. 'Johann? And he has given him some? That asinine, idiotic, worthless fool.' The colour rose in his cheeks and he could barely control himself. 'I have told Johann. I have told him *so many times*! He must not interfere in our lives. His wife is a whore and her daughter will become one!'

Holz timorously placed a hand on Ludwig's arm.

'Get me a glass of wine, Holz. I need it to calm me down.' Holz's face registered his surprise. 'Over there. Go on, man. In the cupboard.'

Ludwig gulped the rough red wine, savouring the sharpness and wincing as he felt it burn in his throat. He banged the glass on the table. Holz hurriedly moved the sheets of manuscript out of the way. Then, anxious to turn the conversation away from Johann's wife and stepdaughter, he wrote, 'I believe Karl has acquired his love of money from your brother.'

'Is Johann in Vienna? If he is, I will come straight back and tell him to his face.'

'Krems,' Holz wrote. 'He has written again, inviting you and Karl to stay at his estate.'

'The man is a fool. I want nothing to do with him. And I want Karl to have nothing to do with him.'

Holz nodded quickly. 'I will tell him you want him to come to visit you, sir,' he said.

Ludwig went to the sideboard and poured himself more wine. An empty feeling fluttered in his stomach. From the moment Holz had arrived there had been unspoken words in the air, hanging over everything that had passed between them. Ludwig knew he had to ask Holz the dreadful question, whose answer – he knew with utter certainty – would bring him nothing but pain.

He drank a mouthful of wine. 'Holz, has the boy seen his mother?'

Holz hesitated, then wrote, 'I'm not sure – I didn't ask him.'

Ludwig snatched up the book. 'Didn't ask? *Didn't ask?*' He flung it down on the table, and Holz lifted his arm protectively. 'Get out, Holz. You are as useless as all the rest. Go back to Vienna.'

After he had gone, Ludwig regretted that he had reacted so violently. He penned a note to his nephew, which he sent by the first stage the next day.

My Son

I am getting thinner and thinner and feel more ill than well and I have no doctor here, not even a sympathetic soul to whom I can turn – If you can manage to come on Sundays, do come. But I do not want in any way to interfere with your plans, if only I could be certain that your Sundays away from me were well spent. Indeed I must learn to give up everything I hold dear, and indeed will gladly do so, if only I could know that such sacrifices will bear good fruit –

Oh, does there remain any part of my being that has not been wounded, nay more, cut to the heart?!

Your faithful Father

Chapter 3

Ludwig embraced Karl, ignoring the way his nephew stiffened.
'Come, join me in some wine.' He poured two glasses, one
conspicuously less full than the other. 'Come and sit down and
give your father all your news from the city. But write it down.
My useless ears have given up the struggle.'

'Uncle,' Karl wrote. 'You are my uncle.'

Ludwig was hurt but he flicked his fingers as if to indicate it
was a trifling matter. 'Are your studies going well?'

'No. I lack books. I cannot buy them. No money. And my
clothes mark me out from the other students.'

'Why did you not tell me? You must not be short of books
and clothes. What do you need?'

Karl brightened and he wrote, '20 florins for books. Trousers
and jacket 58 florins. Or cheaper with cheaper cloth.'

'No, no. The best cloth. You must wear good clothes, but
only outdoors to make a good impression. Indoors wear older
clothes.'

Karl was astonished by his uncle's generosity.

'So,' Ludwig scribbled some figures. 'Seventy-eight florins. It
is a lot of money. Tell Holz to advance you that sum, but I will
expect to see you well dressed next time you come to see me.
Be sure to get a receipt from the tailor. And bring some of the
books so I can judge for myself how your studies are progressing.
What does Czerny say about your playing? Did he send a note
for me?'

Karl glanced round the room, relieved to see that there was
no piano. 'Prince G. asks how the quartets are progressing,'
he wrote.

'Tell him I am composing. By the time I return to Vienna
he will have his pieces.'

'How long are you staying?'

'Until the summer is over. And I want new lodgings in

Vienna. Tell Holz. Or Frau Streicher. I do not want to return
to the apartment where I nearly died.'

'You did not nearly die,' Karl wrote. 'How is your health?
Not as bad as in your letter.'

'It is worse than you know,' Ludwig said. 'The pain of being
a father is sometimes more than I can bear. Karl, you do not
know how much I love you and care about you.'

Karl held his uncle's eye but said nothing.

'Do not break the bond between us, Karl,' Ludwig begged.
'If you do, you will never be forgiven for your ingratitude.'

A mask fell over the young man's face and he shrank into his
chair. Ludwig was gratified that for once he had his nephew's
attention. 'Only suspicions, Karl. That is all I have. But someone
has told me you are associating with a person who is evil.
Wicked, Karl.'

Moisture came into Karl's eyes and he blinked to clear it. He
wanted to speak, that was obvious, but his lips did not move. He
looked at the notebook but his sigh showed that he had decided
the written word would not convey what he wanted to say.

'You must not, Karl. You must not associate with evil. You
told me you understood that. Do not go back on your word
now. Look at everything I am doing for you.' He jabbed a finger
at the paper with the figures written on it. 'Everything a father
would do for a son. You will not let me down, will you?'

Ludwig looked him in the eye and Karl did not flinch. Good,
Ludwig thought, strength of character. 'Come. Let us climb to
the Rauhenstein together.'

The second quartet, in A minor, was all but finished, with the
extensive Heiliger Dankgesang as the central movement. Almost
immediately Ludwig began work on the third quartet. The key
would be B flat major. He knew from an early stage that it
would be a very different piece from its predecessor. It would
be long – the sole quality the two would share – but it would
be . . . What was the word? It came to him easily as he gazed
through the window of the Gutenbrunn. Sunny.

As he worked on the two Quartets – completing one,
beginning the next – he saw that he was taking the form
into new regions, as he had for the Ninth Symphony. Why
did a string quartet always have to be just four movements?
These two would be five or six, possibly seven. Was a quartet not like a book of poetry, as a symphony was like a

novel? And was there some limit to the length of a work in words?

For the second quartet, the A minor, he had composed a short, lively movement based on a German dance. He knew even as he was writing it that it did not fit the mood of the piece. The solution was simple: it would sit perfectly in the new quartet instead.

At the same time as he worked on the opening movements, he wrote a succession of letters to Karl in Vienna. In contrast to the earlier ones they were free of doubt and suspicion. He enquired after Karl's health, sent him more money for books and clothes, asked whether his lodgings were satisfactory, described the dreadful food the cook was preparing for him on Doktor Braunhofer's orders. Occasionally he mentioned that it would be nice to see him, and forestalled any disappointment at not receiving replies by insisting that Karl did not waste time in writing back to him.

He thought a great deal about Karl and realised his dearest dreams had come true. He was turning into a fine young man with a mind of his own. There had been no more talk of joining the army, Czerny continued to send good reports of his musical progress and – of paramount importance – he had clearly accepted that the unfortunate circumstances of his parentage could be overcome. Ludwig felt a father's pride that he had achieved this much for Karl. The future, it appeared, boded well.

In between intensive sessions of composing he walked in the valley, relishing the heady scents of summer. Sitting under a tree, or on a rock by the Schwechat, if he closed his eyes he could hear the nightingale singing its joyous song to his command and in time to his beat.

Physically he was strong again, but less so than before his illness. He could no longer climb to the Rauhenstein ruin: the effort was too much.

His brother Johann wrote, again inviting him and Karl to stay at his estate. Ludwig tossed aside the letter contemptuously. 'Wretched ass,' he said under his breath. '*Asinaccio!*' The mere idea of exposing Karl to more immoral women was unthinkable.

Given his new-found optimism and strength, Ludwig was ill prepared for the arrival again of Karl Holz, his face drawn.

'What is it, Holz? Come and have some Baden sunshine and wine. Whatever ails you we will cure it. Will you take the waters too? Even on me they work their benefits.'

'Sir, I have news of your nephew which I know will upset you.' He reached for his notebook. Ludwig knew what he would say. His stomach griped suddenly, sending the pain straight to his head and a howling began in his ears. He stared defiantly at his guest.

'He has moved back to live with his mother. And his half-brother and -sister.'

'Damn you, Holz!' Ludwig shouted. 'Did I not tell you to look after him? To make sure he came to no harm?'

'Sir, he is living with his mother. That is not a crime.'

'Why do you think I fought in the courts all those years? For my own amusement? And what decision did the highest court in the land reach? And the Emperor? The Emperor, Holz. His Imperial Majesty took my side. And you sit there and tell me it is not a crime. Get the police, Holz. Go back to Vienna and get the police. Tell them to force him out of that – that whore's house. Do you hear?'

Ludwig glared at Holz. 'Why are you still sitting there? Get back to Vienna and do as I say.'

Holz found a clean sheet of paper, wrote a few words and passed it to Ludwig. 'He is an adult now, sir. He is entitled to make his own decisions.'

Holz's news sent Ludwig into a spiral of depression. His first thought was to hurry back to Vienna and take matters into his own hands, but he could hardly go to the woman's apartment and wrest her son physically from her. Holz, he knew, was right that Karl was now beyond the police and the courts. He also knew that any precipitate action would once again alienate his friends – and he needed friends like the Streichers and the von Breunings.

Was everything lost? All that he had striven for? His son – for that indeed was what Karl had become to him – whom he had nurtured, cared for, protected, fought for . . . Was he lost to him for ever? No, he said, time after time, *no, no, no, no.*

Soon, inevitably, all the ills that had plagued him for so long returned. His head thumped to every heartbeat, sharp pains pierced his stomach like arrows. The noises in his head doubled and redoubled. To try to relieve the abdominal pains he would grasp the flesh of his stomach and knead it – so hard that soon it was bruised. And it swelled. The puffiness travelled down from his stomach to his already swollen ankles. He could only just get his feet into his boots.

Should he send for Braunhofer? He knew the proprietor of the Gutenbrunn was worried about him: he cast Ludwig anxious looks as he came and went but was clearly reluctant to say anything. He decided against calling the doctor: his pain was not of a kind any doctor could cure. It came from deep inside. Soon he was drinking the local red wine in the same quantity as he had before his last illness.

Late in the evening at the end of a warm summer's day, the dying sun illuminating the ruby red of the carafe in front of him, his heart so heavy that he felt as if a rock hung in his chest, he wrote some notes on a piece of manuscript paper. Just two to begin with, B flat up to G, a rising sixth, that same interval that had beguiled him when he composed the *Heiliger Dankgesang*. The turning phrase that soon followed – a B natural below to disturb the intense calm – prepared the way for rising crotchets in the first violin, descending crotchets in the other three instruments to counterbalance them, and, unexpectedly, a *falling* sixth.

At the top of the page he wrote *Adagio molto espressivo*. He knew that he would pour into this movement for the four voices of the string quartet all the passion, anger and sorrow that consumed him. The instruments would sing like voices, each with its own lament yet each woven around the other.

Oh, Karl, my son. The wine swirled in his head and the music grew louder. The strings sang their lament for him. Sobs caught in his chest. Tears filled his eyes, making the pages in front of him swim. He rubbed them away with his sleeve; the coarse cloth dragged across the tender flesh of the lower lids which smarted.

He reached unsteadily for the pencil and wrote a word on the paper. *Beklemmt*. Tormented. He dashed off ascending quavers, semiquavers, demi-semiquavers, quaver rests in between – his sobs in notes – more semiquavers, always separated by tiny rests – the catch of the sobs in his chest.

He sat back, exhausted. The opening theme would return after the plangent weeping of the first violin, but *sotto voce*, so the listener would have to strain to hear the notes. Now they will understand my torment, he thought, when they listen to what I have created. Had any piece of music he had ever composed brought forth such tears of grief? It was a song, without words yet it contained more meaning than words could ever convey. *All that I feel – all the pain of my life – is in these notes, this movement.* He leafed through the pages until he found the beginning. Above the words *Adagio molto espressivo* he wrote in large letters, pressing firmly on the page, *Cavatina.*

Long walks again, while the *Cavatina* revolved in his head, developing from the ideas he had jotted down to fully formed musical phrases. Composition was draining his physical resources, he knew that. Yet he was not composing this music because he wanted to but because he had to. And when he wrote down the final *pianissimo* bar of the movement, he drew breath, drank wine, braced himself, and wrote another word on the page, a word that danced before his eyes, seeming to take on a life of its own, challenging him, defying him, daring him to use all the technical skills at his disposal . . . *Fuga.* A mighty fugue which, after the sorrow of the *Cavatina*, would contain all the fire and passion and force of which he was capable.

He walked faster and more determinedly along the floor of the Helenenthal valley; he climbed to the Rauhenstein regardless of the pain in his lungs and muscles, the throbbing in his head, and ignoring his swollen feet and ankles.

It would be, he knew from the start, the most immense fugue he had written. More than just immense, it would be a *double* fugue. Had anyone before him attempted such a feat? *If I can succeed, if I can create it . . .*

The notes spilled out. Page after page he covered with scrawled notes and punctuating rests. The music drove forward under its own impetus: quaver semiquaver, quaver semiquaver, quaver semiquaver, separated each time by a semiquaver rest. The all-important fleeting rest without which the fugue would lose its force.

He settled into a pattern. In the morning he would stride along the valley, the fugue reverberating in his head in time to the pounding of his boots. Occasionally, he would stop to make notes. Each day he climbed towards the Rauhenstein – sometimes turning back before he reached it, sometimes climbing the whole way, palms pushing on his thighs to give his legs added strength.

Around noon he returned to the Gutenbrunn. 'Food and wine,' he would call to the desk clerk as he climbed the stairs to his room, his leg muscles crying out in anguish at this final travail.

The wine quenched his thirst and sometimes he ate the food – particularly if it was fish.

After lunch he would lie on the bed fully dressed, breathing hard from the effort of creating sounds and transferring them to paper. The mighty, contrapuntal double fugue was growing in his head and on the paper.

All afternoon, sustained by a second carafe of wine, he wrote, referring to the notebook, scratching down more sequences, crossing out some vigorously, cursing when the paper tore.

It took longer than he had expected – weeks not days. There was no interruption: Holz did not come to Baden, neither did he – nor Karl – write, and he was glad to be able to work unimpeded. There could be nothing seriously wrong in Vienna: he would have heard. When he had finished the fugue, he would so back and take matters in hand.

The final return of the first fugue theme to end the piece. But he turned back the sheets and rewrote the opening. Too many notes. It must be sparse, the skeleton of a theme only, and the opening notes must cross the bar line, to give the fugue impetus from the start.

Unison, *sforzando*, a trill that hung in the air, and always the rests – the vital, unexpected rests that would give this fugue a character unlike any other ever written, including those by the master of fugue, Johann Sebastian Bach.

By the time he was satisfied – Czerny would tidy it up before sending it to the copyists – he had written a piece of extraordinary length, possibly the longest single movement he had ever composed.

How Schuppanzigh would complain! At the end of an already long quartet – six movements! – a fugue of unparalleled length. But how else to follow the Cavatina? After pathos, there could be only fury.

After completing the work, at the top of which he wrote Grosse Fuge, he remained a week in Baden. He continued his walks, but more slowly now and the chill of early autumn made him shiver. He did not climb to the ruin again – he feared his lungs would not stand it.

By the time he left his throat was sore and it hurt to take a deep breath. The muscles in his legs ached and although the bruising on his feet had gone they were unusually swollen and fleshy. Had there ever been a time when his body was not somehow causing concern? He'd call in Braunhofer. That was what doctors were for. Let him deal with it.

He gathered up all the papers carefully and put them in a folder, which he tied with string. Then he thrust his clothes into a leather bag and left Baden for Vienna.

Chapter 4

Ludwig climbed the broad ornate staircase behind Nanette Streicher and Karl Holz. On the second-floor landing he turned left to face a low broad door, its dull green paint lifted by the light that flooded through the landing window. Holz turned a key in the lock and the door swung open.

The two stood aside for Ludwig to walk in. He paused for a moment to allow his breathing to steady, then entered a narrow hallway off which lay a wide, bright room with two tall windows that looked back to the city allowing the daylight to stream in. He went to the nearer. Squinting against the bright light, he saw the wide expanse of the Glacis stretching before him, the dark wall of the Bastion looming beyond it and the busy Schottentor gate, through which small figures came and went. He could see clearly the great Gothic spire of St Stephansdom rising from the centre of the city.

'Both pianos in here, the Broadwood and the Graf,' he said. 'The bed against this wall.'

He saw Nanette look anxiously round the room and speak to him. Holz shouted into his ear, 'If this is the piano room, sir, the next room should be the bedroom.'

'Pianos and the bed in here,' he insisted. 'And my writing desk there, where the light falls. My grandfather's picture on the wall. So he can watch me compose and sleep.'

Nanette indicated to him to follow her to the back rooms of the apartment, which looked out on to a dark courtyard. She did not try to speak, pointing instead to the kitchen and the small room off it, the servant's room.

He knew he should thank her, express gratitude, but the words would not come. He was tired and felt unwell, and he wanted his pianos – the second had been lent to him by the Viennese piano-maker Conrad Graf – and the small amount of furniture he owned to be installed as soon as possible so he could resume work.

Then mischief overtook him. He looked down into the courtyard. 'What lies beyond that?'

'The beginnings of the countryside,' Holz said loudly. 'And then the village of Währing.'

'What is in Währing?' he asked. He saw understanding dawn in Nanette's face.

'The main cemetery,' Holz said guilelessly.

'My next residence, after this one,' Ludwig said.

The Schwarzspanierhaus, the House of the Black-robed Spaniards, derived its name from the Spanish Benedictine monks who previously occupied it. It was situated in the Alsergrund suburb, only a short distance from the apartment owned by Prince Lichnowsky in which Ludwig had lived for a time when he first came to Vienna, and an even shorter distance – just a minute's walk – from the Rothes Haus, in which he had shared the apartment with Stephan von Breuning.

It was not long before Breuning, accompanied by Gerhard, came to visit Ludwig.

'Hah, Hosenknopf!' Ludwig said, brightening visibly. 'And Steffen. You look as ill as I do. We will both soon go to Währing to join brother Carl.'

Breuning ignored the remark, looking round the room. He turned to his son, who handed him a notebook and pencil. 'Constanze has arranged for a cook and housekeeper for you. Should you not move your bed into a proper bedroom?'

'I work more at night than in the day. This way I can find my way around.'

Gerhard wrote, his face serious. 'You are in the monastery of the Spanish monks, sir.'

Ludwig chortled. 'Come here, Hosenknopf, and I will tell you a secret. But you must promise not to breathe a word to a soul.'

Gerhard looked fleetingly at his father, who nodded. He almost ran across the room to where Ludwig was sitting. 'When I was a boy of your age, I went to a school in Bonn – where your father and I were born – and the other children invented a nickname for me. Can you guess what it was?'

Gerhard thought hard. 'No, sir. The musician, maybe? The piano player?'

'They called me the Spaniard, because of my dark looks.' He opened his eyes wide and made a growling noise. 'But remember your promise and don't tell anyone. I do not want to be called it at the end of my life as well as at the beginning.'

Breuning was laughing. 'I had quite forgotten. Herr Beethoven is right, Gerhard. That is what they called him.'

'So, Hosenknopf, tell me. Are your piano studies going well?'

Gerhard wrote carefully, 'I have no musical skill. I will become a doctor of medicine when I grow up.'

Ludwig laughed out loud. 'So you have not changed your mind! You will do better than the fools I surround myself with. Pity you are not already qualified. I need your services now. By the time you are able to cure me, I will be long dead!'

'Stop, Ludwig,' Breuning said. 'Before we go, Constanze asks that you come and have dinner with us soon. You will do that, won't you? We are only a short walk. You can practically see the Rothes Haus from here.'

Ludwig heard his voice. 'I am poor company, Steffen, but it is good to have you as a neighbour . . .'

Breuning cleared his throat. 'We will leave you now, Ludwig. Constanze will be worried. Before I go, though, there is one thing I must say to you. Here . . .' He reached for the notebook. 'Karl is a good boy. He misses you. He waits to hear from you. Will you send him a note?'

Ludwig felt his heart leap with joy.

The next day Ludwig wrote to Karl, pleading with him to come to the Schwarzspanierhaus. He promised he would have no harsh words for him.

> For God's sake, my son, do not abandon yourself to misery. I will welcome you here as affectionately as ever. We will lovingly discuss what has to be considered and what must be done for the future. On my word of honour you will hear no reproaches, since they would in any case serve no purpose. All that you may expect from me is the most loving care and help – But do come – come to the faithful heart of your father.

After he had finished the letter, and while he was waiting for Holz to come and collect it, he dipped his quill in the ink again and wrote at the top of the page:

For God's sake do come at the earliest moment. If not, who knows what danger may confront you? Hurry. Hurry.

He watched the ink dry. Might the words have an adverse effect? No. *He will realise how much I care for him. My son.*

Karl came – though not until two days later – and walked imperiously around the apartment. He stood for a few moments in front of the portrait of Ludwig's grandfather. Then he turned to his uncle.

'Well?' Ludwig said. 'It is spacious, isn't it? There are too many rooms for me. I would be very happy . . . very happy –'

Karl grabbed the notebook and pencil from the table. 'Too far from the city. I must be near the university. I want to share rooms with a fellow student, but I cannot pay rent. No money.'

Ludwig looked at the words. Was Karl trying to say he was not living with his mother? He did not want to ask, for fear of discovering it was not so.

'I will speak to Holz. Also . . .' Ludwig decided the time had come to inform Karl of something else. 'I have purchased some bank shares in your name. For when you are older. They will mature and give you a certain –'

'When? How much?'

'You must be patient. But Holz will have the details.'

After Karl had left, carrying a note authorising Holz to advance him fifty florins against receipts, Ludwig went to the desk and opened the top left drawer. The envelope containing the bank shares lay there. He pulled out the drawer and put it on the table. In the gap at the back were his most treasured documents: the manuscript from Mozart, the Testament written in Heiligenstadt, and the tortured letter to Antonie Brentano. He placed the envelope on top of them.

He was about to replace the drawer when his eyes rested on one of the packing boxes standing against the wall. It had been damaged and the top of one of the sides hung down, barely secured with a nail. He went over to it and prised off the broken piece, the nail still in it. He pushed it to the back of the drawer space, where it fitted perfectly, hiding the documents securely behind it. Then he slid the drawer back into place.

Chapter 5

'Where are you living? Still with your friend?'

Karl wrote, 'I rent rooms from a Herr Schlemmer and his wife. Alleegasse. Short walk from the university. There is a carnival ball soon. Will you allow me to buy a ticket? The last event for students before the final exams.'

'Hah! A carnival ball. I shall accompany you.' Ludwig saw the look of panic flit across his nephew's face. 'Do you think I should not? I composed music for carnivals once. Back in the nineties. For Haydn.'

'I need money for a ticket. Also for more books. For the final period of study.'

Ludwig nodded. 'How are your studies progressing?'

'My tutor comes early, 8.30 to 9.30. Lectures from 9 to 12. In the afternoon lectures from 3 to 5. A further hour from 5 to 6.'

'That is hard work, but it is good for you, Karl. Shall we go for a walk? I would dearly love to spend time with you.'

Karl shook his head vigorously. 'I have to return to classes,' he wrote, and stood up.

'Hah!' Ludwig exclaimed, slapping his thigh. 'You do not want to be seen on the street with your eccentric uncle, isn't that it?' He laughed. 'You are excused. But, Karl, study well. You must pass your exams in the summer.'

Ludwig and Holz walked towards the Neuer Markt together. It was late March and the early-evening air was fresh with the promise of spring. Ludwig felt a little stronger than he had in the preceding months. Braunhofer's dietary instructions, which the cook followed scrupulously, seemed to be having a beneficial effect. He continued to drink red wine and Braunhofer had given up the struggle to prevent him. At the beginning of the year he had complained again of stomach pains and his eyes were red and sore, but both symptoms soon passed. The swellings in his legs and feet, about which Braunhofer had been inordinately concerned, had lessened somewhat but were still noticeable.

The most worrying aspect of his health, as far as Ludwig was concerned, was an increasing breathlessness and because of this the long walks in the country, which he so enjoyed, were now a thing of the past.

'Come,' he said, tugging at Holz's sleeve, 'sit for a moment at the side of the fountain. I need to catch my breath.' He closed his eyes, frowning at the ringing in his ears brought on by the walk. They would be a curse upon him until his dying day. 'And beyond . . .' he said quietly, his words almost inaudible above the steady sound of the fountain. 'If the Lord punishes me for the irreligious life I have led, he will cause me to be deaf even in Heaven. It is a thought I can hardly bear.'

He felt Holz's hand on his arm and turned wearily to him. 'Sir, come to the Mehlgrube. Hear your quartet. There will be a good audience. See, they have begun arriving.' Holz gestured towards the hall. Closer to Ludwig's ear, he continued, 'Rehearsals have gone well. Herr Schuppanzigh thinks it is your finest quartet. Though the *Grosse Fuge* makes more demands on us than any other music we have ever played!'

'For the whole of my life musicians have complained, Holz. They want music to be easy to play, so they do not have to work hard.'

'Oh, no, sir. I did not mean to complain. Will you come in, sir, and listen to it?'

'Did you say "listen", Holz? What would I listen with?' He did not give Holz a chance to reply. 'No. You go in and play my music with Count Falstaff and those other fine musicians, Linke and Weiss. Left and white. *Rechts und schwarz*. Right and black.' He chuckled at his joke. 'Holz, I ask you again to watch out for my nephew. I am worried about him. He spends money too readily and has nothing to show for it. Speak to his landlord. Tell him to ensure that Karl does not go out at night. I want him to stay in and study. And I want to know if he is seeing a particular person who has an immoral influence on him.'

Holz agreed wearily. 'I will report back to you. I believe your nephew comes easily under the influence of others. It is not his fault.'

'There is one student in particular. I forget his name. Maybe he is a bad influence.'

'Niemetz,' Karl reminded him. 'You are right. I established that while you were in Baden last summer. Do not concern yourself, sir, I will make inquiries. I will go in and join Herr Schuppanzigh now. Would you like me to report to you after the performance, sir? Where will you be?'

'Close at hand, Holz. Very close. Next door. In the Schwan.' He jerked his head towards the tavern.

As he sipped wine, Ludwig thought about his nephew. He was probably seeing his mother. He was certain that at least some of the money he was always advancing to Karl was finding its way to Johanna.

But Karl would be twenty-one on his next birthday. There was only so much a father could do to control a rebellious child. He sipped more wine, and took a sketchbook from his coat pocket.

Prince Galitzin's quartets were finished, but he was now composing a new one. He studied the simple lyrical phrase he had sketched some time before: rising minims, followed by a turning crotchet phrase. But look at the key – C sharp minor – and the accidental – B sharp! – in the very first bar. He scribbled *sf* under the unexpected A in the centre of the phrase – *So they know it is not a mistake*.

He sketched more fragments, illegible to anyone's eyes but his own. In his head the quartet already existed. He had known from the start that, like its predecessors, it would be a long work and he wanted it played without pause between the movements. *Ohne Bruch*, he wrote and underlined it twice.

Somehow, and he could not articulate it, the four voices of the quartet were providing him with exactly the means of expression he needed. Small, intimate, engaged in conversation, argument, discussion; interwoven, interlaced, and each one as important as the other. Perhaps he was escaping from the reality of his problems into the world in which he was at home.

By the time he saw a flushed Ignaz Schuppanzigh walking towards him, Holz close behind, the wine had calmed his fears. His ears rang still to the new quartet and were free of extraneous noise and pain. And the thought of conversation did not concern him. These people understood his deafness.

Schuppanzigh put more glasses and wine on the table and poured some for himself, Holz and Ludwig. He reached for the notebook Holz had put on the table. '*Succès fou*,' he wrote.

'And the fugue?'

A small frown passed across Schuppanzigh's brow and he waved his hand, as if to dismiss the question. 'Presto and Danza Tedesca encored,' he wrote.

Ludwig smiled. 'How many times?'

Schuppanzigh held up two fingers and wrote 'each'.

Ludwig gulped his wine. He had known those movements – slight, in comparison to the others – would be quickly appreciated. 'Delicacies,' he said. 'Just delicacies. The Cavatina?'

Schuppanzigh's face broke into an eager smile. 'I heard a sob,' he wrote. 'A lady clutched a handkerchief to her eyes.'

'Was she more "*beklemmt*" than you, my lord Falstaff?'

Holz took the notebook from him. 'The tears in the audience reflected the tears you shed when you composed it.'

Ludwig sat forward. 'And the Grosse Fuge, Schuppi. How was that received?'

Schuppanzigh and Holz exchanged glances. Holz wrote, 'One day it will be recognised as a masterpiece.'

Schuppanzigh took the notebook from him. 'It is so huge, it diminishes what comes before. Difficult for the players too, at the end of a long work.'

Could Schuppanzigh be right? Ludwig wondered. Poorly played, the Grosse Fuge would be in danger of dragging the whole work down. Even perfectly played, was it not in danger of smothering the pathos of the Cavatina? Before he could say anything, Schuppanzigh wrote, 'Artaria came to a rehearsal. He is willing to publish it as a separate work, if you give it an opus number. He will pay you separately. Write a new finale for the quartet. It would please the audiences too.'

'They are cattle. Asses,' Ludwig said, but there was no venom in his voice.

Schuppanzigh decided to change the subject and wrote, 'A young man was there. He idolises you. He composes songs.' He spotted him now at a corner table with a small group of friends. 'In the corner. Curly hair and glasses. Name is Franz Schubert. He is spoken of highly.'

Ludwig looked across at the young man, in his late twenties, with an unhealthy flush to his face probably brought on by the wine and the heat in the room. 'I have heard his name. Schindler once showed me some of his music. It was good. But I do not want to meet anybody. I won't hear them.'

*   *   *

Karl walked around the room, visibly agitated. Ludwig encouraged him to sit down. He wanted to put his arm round his shoulders and assure him everything would be fine – it was normal for students to be nervous when exams approached.

Finally Karl wrote something in the notebook. 'Not all students pass the final exams. If I do not, I will join the army. It is what I have always wanted.'

'Of course you will pass! No more talk of the army.' Ludwig tried to keep the note of displeasure out of his voice. 'How are your lodgings? Satisfactory?'

He saw Karl hesitate, then grasp the pencil again. 'I have fallen behind with rent. It is unavoidable. I must buy books for work.'

'Books. Always books.' Ludwig no longer tried to hide his exasperation. 'What else do you spend your money on? Mmmh? Frivolous things, I do not doubt, too much wine and beer and food and – and – carnival balls, when you should be working.'

Karl turned an angry face on him. 'Why do you always berate me? Always. Can I do nothing right?' He was not bothering to write anything down now, giving vent instead to his pent-up feelings. 'Even if I told you I won't see my mother you would still scold me.'

His harsh voice caused the ringing to begin in Ludwig's ears. 'Stop, Karl. You are hurting me. Do not shout.' Ludwig sat quiet for a few moments, then said, 'Will you come and live with me here? I have room. I can look after you.'

'Too far from the university,' Karl wrote. 'And I do not wish to die of suffocation.' He hastily crossed through the final words, turned the page and wrote carefully, 'My life belongs to me. If it becomes impossible I will take matters into my own hands.'

The noises howled in Ludwig's ears. 'Karl, you will surely cause me pain until the day I die. And all I have ever wanted is the best for you. To make you proud that you carry the name of Beethoven.'

Chapter 6

My dear Brother

Congratulations on the completion of your new quartet, which will surely stand among your highest works. Should you wish to send me a copy, I would gladly instruct the musicians from Krems in the finer points of interpreting the work of Beethoven. They play here regularly.

You should again consider coming to stay here with my wife and daughter. You may bring Karl, if it does not interfere with his studies.

Yr brother Johann
Landowner, Gneixendorf

Ludwig waved the letter at Stephan von Breuning. 'Is this not proof that the man is a complete imbecile? He thinks he knows my music. He knows less about my music than – than – a horse.'

Breuning patted his friend's knee soothingly. His children – Gerhard and *two* small girls now – were watching Ludwig, the girls with expectant smiles.

'If he is a landowner,' Ludwig said, 'I am a brain owner!'

There were peals of laughter from the girls and Gerhard, while Constanze, who was bustling around helping the maid to clear away the lunch plates, was smiling broadly. Only Breuning frowned. 'Ludwig, do not be unkind to Johann. He is your brother and he cares very much for you. Why do you not accept his invitation, anyway? The break would do you good.'

Ludwig crumpled the letter and thrust it in his pocket. 'Stephan, after all this time, have you not learned that you cannot talk to me as if I were a normal person with normal hearing? I can hear the delightful shrieks of your daughters. Your words – no doubt sober and reproving – are lost to me. It is just as well.'

Breuning sighed resignedly. 'Come, children, let us walk on the Glacis. Ludwig?' He pointed through the window to the expanse of grass that lay between the Alsergrund suburb and the Bastion wall.

Ludwig saw Constanze go up to her husband as he put on his coat. It was a warm summer's day, but she buttoned it up and wound a scarf round his neck. Ludwig could understand why: Breuning's face was drawn, he had an unhealthy grey pallor and had clearly lost weight.

The air felt good on Ludwig's cheeks as he strolled with his friend and watched the three children running on the grass. The girls had a hoop, which they passed between each other, running along, each with a stick in hand to propel it. Gerhard had a small kite, which he was trying in vain to get airborne. Each time he ran with it, it rose in the air not much more than twice or three times his own height, before twisting a few times and plunging to the ground.

'Stephan, do not try to talk to me – I will not hear you. But will you let me talk to you about Karl? I know we have had our differences in the past about him, but I am worried. I fear he is leading a – a – dissolute life. Despite everything I have done. He spends money. I do not know on what. He probably gambles at cards and drinks too much wine. I do not believe he will pass his exams in September. And then what?' He shrugged his shoulders and turned to his old friend.

Breuning walked slowly, his head bent, saying nothing.

'One solution would be for him to come and live with me again,' Ludwig said. 'I would be able to watch him and –' He felt Breuning's hand on his arm. His friend was shaking his head.

Ludwig passed him the notebook he carried in his pocket and Breuning wrote, 'You must let him go. Let him become a man.'

'I would,' Ludwig said, 'but I cannot allow him to become . . . He is a Beethoven, Steffen. He must never forget that. He is talking again of joining the army.'

Breuning could not see why that was such a grim prospect.

Ludwig sighed. 'You really do not understand, Steffen, do you? Sometimes I believe I am the only person who does. My feet are hurting. They swell when I walk. I will leave you. Thank your wife for lunch.'

*   *   *

Karl Holz was grim-faced. 'Sir, can you hear me if I talk loudly into your ear?'

Ludwig, annoyed at the interruption, thrust the notebook and pencil towards him. 'Schlemmer says Karl has disappeared. He left a note hinting at –'

'What, Holz? What, for God's sake? Can you not write quicker?'

'He wrote that no one would see him again.'

Ludwig's head dropped into his hands. Could he really . . . ? He roused himself. 'We must go to Schlemmer immediately,' he said. 'Where is his house?'

'The Alleegasse, near the university.'

Ludwig was already putting on his coat. It seemed to him as he did so that he was moving unnaturally slowly, as if he did not want the next few hours to unfold. It was a warm July day, but he wanted to look his best, for whatever eventualities this fateful day might bring. For the first time ever he noticed his coat needed brushing. With the palm of his hand he swept down the material. He left it unbuttoned as he reached for his hat.

'Come on, Holz. We had better find out what has happened.'

They found Schlemmer, a small man with impeccable manners whose naturally arched eyebrows gave him a permanent expression of concern, leafing through a ledger in his small, tidily furnished living room.

'Schlemmer? I am Beethoven. I have lost my hearing. Use this.' He produced his notebook and set it on the table in the centre of the room. 'What has happened to my son? My nephew. He lodges with you.'

Schlemmer bowed his head respectfully: he knew that he was in the presence of Europe's most renowned musician. He wrote, in a small, measured hand, 'I have not seen him for three days. He left a note saying he intended taking his life –'

'Where is the note, Schlemmer?'

The man opened a drawer and unfolded a piece of paper. Ludwig immediately recognised his nephew's spidery writing: 'I shall take my leave of you now. All of you. When you find me I will be free of all cares.'

'But that doesn't necessarily mean –' Ludwig said, knowing even as he uttered the words that he was deceiving himself.

Schlemmer carried on writing: 'He was behaving strangely so I spoke to his colleague, Niemetz.'

'And? What did he say? Come on, man. Write faster.'

Continuing in his precise script, Schlemmer wrote, 'N. said Karl had debts. And his studies were not going well. And he feared you would punish him if he failed. He told him he was going to Baden and the Helenenthal.'

Why would Karl choose the Helenenthal? A dreadful image – of Karl's body floating in the rushing waters of the Schwechat – filled his mind.

Schlemmer was still writing, in that irritatingly fastidious style. 'I searched his room to see if there were signs or clues. In his chest I found a pistol, already loaded, together with more bullets and powder. I hid it for safety. Then, two days later, he had gone, leaving this note.'

Ludwig gasped. 'Holz. You must go to Baden immediately. Find where he is staying and bring him back. He may be in the Rathausgasse, where he stayed with me once before. Inform the police if you have to, though. Whatever happens, he must be found.'

A sweet song of rest or song of peace.

Ludwig looked at his words, tears shimmering in his eyes. He wrote a simple turning theme, dotted crotchets to begin, quavers to follow. He looked across at the two pianos, standing curved end to curved end. There was no need to play any notes. He could hear them as clearly in his head as if four string players were sitting in front of him.

This movement is for you, my beloved Karl. Wherever you may be, whatever you have done, my love for you will not die.

He completed the theme and the small development that led from it. He would vary it now. Delve deeply into it to discover what lay behind the simple sequence of notes. Unlock the mystery they held.

But no. He held himself in check. Just a short movement and a small number of variations. The tears welled again. He did not believe he could stand the pain of writing many. And what would the other movements of this new quartet say? That would depend. He could not tell until he knew what had happened.

Holz stood before him, breathing hard. Trembling, Ludwig watched him write in the notebook: 'He pawned his watch to buy two more pistols. He discharged each one at his head. The first bullet flew past harmlessly. The second grazed his skull but did not penetrate. His life is not in danger. He has been found and taken to safety where a doctor is tending to him.'

'He shot himself but has survived?' Ludwig asked incredulously. 'But how?'

Holz wrote, 'He put only a little powder in each barrel. If he had used the pistol Schlemmer found, he would surely have died. It was loaded fully.'

Karl was alive! Ludwig did not know whether he was about to laugh with joy, or weep until he had no tears left. 'Where did it happen? Was he in the Helenenthal by the Schwechat?'

'In the Rauhenstein ruin.'

The Rauhenstein! He must have chosen it deliberately, Ludwig thought. Only I would realise the significance of it.

'I must see him. Where is he?'

Holz swallowed, pulled the notebook closer. 'He asked to be taken to his mother. He is with her.'

Chapter 7

Ludwig had told Holz to come with him; he did not want to confront Johanna alone. His heart beat in his chest like a hammer as he waited for her to open the door. What should he say to her? He did not know. He was sure of only one thing: Karl had to be moved into his apartment in the Schwarzspanierhaus as soon as possible. Had Holz really said Karl *asked* to be brought to his mother?

There it was: the head tilted defiantly. She had aged since Ludwig had last seen her, her cheeks hollower, the skin a little more drawn, her hair, pulled tightly back, was flecked with grey above her temples. Her mouth was closed tight, her eyes blazed, rendering words unnecessary, and her arms were folded across her chest.

'I must see Karl, my – boy,' Ludwig said, his voice harsh.

Johanna turned to Holz and her face softened. She nodded almost imperceptibly and Ludwig followed her in, his knees feeling as if at any moment they would no longer have the strength to support his body. A high-pitched whistle cut into his head as Johanna led him and Holz to the door of her bedroom – *her* bedroom – and pushed it ajar.

She and Holz stood aside. Ludwig stepped hesitantly into the room. Karl lay propped up on two or three pillows, his head swathed in a bandage, stained red at the right temple. His right eye was bruised and swollen.

An intense feeling swept through Ludwig – not, as he had expected, of tenderness, but of rage. He wanted to grab his nephew by the shoulders and drill some sense into him, make him understand the folly of what he had done. As he stood there he saw Johanna walk to the bed and stand protectively beside her son.

'How are you?' Ludwig asked, cursing the weakness of his words.

Karl's lips parted and Ludwig thought he was about to say something, but he closed them again.

'We . . . I will arrange for a doctor to see you. You must receive care.'

Johanna planted a small kiss on Karl's forehead and ushered Ludwig and Holz from the room. The three of them sat round the dining table in the centre of the living room. Ludwig took out his notebook. 'I will send for Doktor Smetana, who cared for him before when he needed the operation. He will be discreet. The authorities must not know.'

He saw Johanna and Holz exchange glances. Johanna took the notebook. 'I have already sent for a doctor. He is coming later today.'

Then Holz wrote, 'The police will have to be informed. The people who found Karl know he is your nephew. Word will quickly spread.'

Soon all Vienna will know, Ludwig thought. The name of Beethoven will be dragged through the mud. He was angry that matters had been taken out of his hands. 'You had no right to do anything,' he said to Johanna. 'I am in charge of Karl. The court decreed it. I will make the decisions. I will send for Smetana.'

Johanna wrung her hands 'No! My doctor is coming. He knows what happened. And he knows why.' She scribbled the words in the notebook.

'What do you mean?' Ludwig asked hoarsely.

Johanna stared at him briefly. Then she wrote, 'If you are in charge of Karl, why did he do what he did?'

Through Holz Ludwig learned that the doctor had ordered Karl to remain in his mother's apartment for a week, until the wound had healed sufficiently for him to be moved. He was then to be transferred to the General Hospital in the Alsergrund – a short walk from Ludwig's apartment – where he could be supervised. All wounds to the head were unpredictable and relapses common. He was likely to remain in hospital for a month or more.

While Ludwig was still trying to digest the full horror of Karl's action, Holz brought more news that depressed him even further.

'I had to make a full report to the police. An attempted suicide is an offence against the Church. They have ordered that Karl should receive religious instruction in hospital. They blame . . .'

he paused '. . . a lack of instruction in moral principles for what happened.'

Ludwig, hands thrust deep into his pockets, walked along the long white corridor, his head down. The odour of medicine caught at the back of his throat and caused him to take shallow breaths until he became accustomed to it. He did not know where Karl's room was but assumed that sooner or later he would find someone to ask. His shoulders felt as if they were crushed by an unbearable weight which he was powerless to shift.

He became aware that someone was watching him. He looked up. It was a young man dressed in a long white coat, buttoned up to the neck. A pair of small spectacles sat flatly against his face. His face wore a look of horror.

Ludwig saw the man move his lips, but all he could hear were the dreadful sounds in his head that swirled and eddied, intensifying with every beat of his heart. 'I am Beethoven. Take me to my nephew.'

The man gestured to Ludwig to follow him. He walked down another corridor to a desk behind which sat two nurses, their heads covered with billowing wimples tied tightly under their chins.

All three faces turned to Ludwig. One of the nurses spoke shrilly. Ludwig could just make out her words.

'Tramps are not allowed in here. You must leave.'

'I am Beethoven,' he said.

'You must leave.' He felt the doctor's hand on his arm.

The rage exploded in Ludwig. 'I am Beethoven the Musikus. My nephew is here. Karl van Beethoven.'

The nurse turned to her colleague. 'The suicide. This is his uncle. Herr Beethoven.' A flush rose in her face. 'We apologise, sir. The doctor will escort you,' she said loudly.

Ludwig was led down another corridor and into a small, airless room with a window set high in the wall. It took a few moments for his eyes to adjust to the dim light. Karl's face was turned away, the white of a new bandage standing out in the gloom. A dark bulk was positioned by the side of the bed – a monk, Ludwig realised, intoning from a prayer book, his head sunk into his shoulders.

'Out!' he shouted.

The man shot him a terrified look and scurried away. Ludwig closed the door, relieved that at last he was alone with Karl.

'Karl. My boy.' He had expected the words to come easily, but he stood there not knowing what more to say.

Karl gestured to him that he wanted to write. Hurriedly Ludwig pulled out the notebook and pencil. 'Do not plague me with reproaches and recriminations. It is past. Done.'

Ludwig shook his head as he read the words. 'I will not reproach you,' he said, ensuring – though it was difficult for him to tell – that his voice was low. He imagined the doctor and the monk standing on the other side of the door, listening. 'You do not blame me, do you?'

'I blame you, my mother, my professors, everyone. You all try to make me better and you make me worse.'

Ludwig sat on the monk's stool. The sight of his nephew lying there, his head swathed in bandages, was almost more than he could bear. Suddenly the heat in the room overwhelmed him and he felt faint. He put his hand on the bed to steady himself.

Karl was writing again: 'I cannot take my exams. I will still be in hospital. When I leave I will join the army.'

Wearily, Ludwig acknowledged that there was nothing more to be said.

The Breuning children stood by the window of the apartment in the Rothes Haus, jumping up and down excitedly. Even Gerhard had given up trying to restrain his sisters.

'There she goes! Look, Mama and Papa, there she goes!'

Ludwig stood next to Breuning watching the spectacle. He felt little interest, although all of Vienna, it seemed, was on the Glacis below or crowded into the Augarten and Prater, their heads craned upwards, hands shielding their eyes against the sun.

Madame Garnerin waved to the populace from the basket suspended below the balloon, which slowly lifted above the trees. The flags of Austria, tied around the rim of the basket, billowed out. Up and further up the balloon sailed, its ascent faltering every now and then as a gust of wind caught at it.

'Mama, Papa, what's going to happen?'

The figure of Madame Garnerin, now appreciably smaller, was suddenly raised above the basket as she clambered on to its rim. With one arm she held on to the rigging; with the other she gave a final wave – and jumped off.

The two Breuning girls shrieked; Gerhard clapped his hands over his face. For a few seconds she fell headlong towards the ground. Then a vast billowing sheet spread out above her: her parachute had opened, an immense protective dome over her head, and she floated serenely to the ground of the Prater, where she was swept up by the hundreds of excited people.

The Breuning children shouted and shrieked with excitement, and Ludwig forced a smile, but all he could think of was Karl.

'Steffen, what will I do?'

'Come into the other room and we will talk about it. Stanzi, *Liebchen*, will you look after the children? Ludwig and I are going into the study for a few minutes.'

Ludwig was pleased that his friend was prepared to talk to him and concentrated on what he was saying. He could hear his voice, through a combination of his intense desire to do so, and Breuning's practised technique of talking to him audibly.

'First, Ludwig, you must go away. You should not stay in the city. Tongues are wagging. People are saying unkind things about you.'

'But I –'

Breuning put a steadying hand on his arm. 'Rightly or wrongly, malicious things are being said. It is to be expected. Go away, into the country, and things will soon die down. Then you must decide what Karl is to do. Has he said anything?'

Ludwig nodded. 'He is still intending to join the army.'

'Why not? It will take him out of this city and all its wickedness. It is an honourable career. Ludwig, I am on the War Council at the Hofburg and I am acquainted with Second Field Marshal Baron von Stutterheim. His regiment is stationed at Iglau in southern Bohemia. Would you like me to talk to him?'

Ludwig nodded.

'Good. I will do so. Now, as I said, it would be better if you left the city. People forget quickly. Go and stay with Johann in Gneixendorf. He has already asked you, hasn't he? There you can be totally secluded. You need not see anyone you do not want to see.'

Ludwig digested the logic of his friend's words. Then Breuning added, 'As for Karl, you must be reasonable. He must be allowed to recuperate with his mother, who is best placed to look after him.'

Ludwig was unsure that he had understood properly. 'With his mother, did you say, Steffen? Are you so thick-skulled that you still believe . . . ?' He was shouting. 'If you believe I will allow that woman – that evil woman – to have any influence over my son –'

'He is *not* your son, Ludwig. He is *her* son,' Breuning hissed. His face was flushed with restrained fury in a way Ludwig had not seen before. Then, suddenly, it was drawn, almost haggard, the heaviness around his eyes darkening and his shoulders buckling under an invisible weight. In a matter of seconds he had transformed into an old man. His mouth hung slackly, then he mouthed something Ludwig could not hear.

A slight movement caught his eye. Gerhard had come into the room and was standing at his father's side, a serious look on his face. He pushed up his father's sleeve and put his finger on the pulse, mouthing the numbers as he counted.

Ludwig suppressed the cough that was building in his throat. Finally, as both father and son looked at him reproachfully, he said, 'I will go to Gneixendorf, but Karl is coming with me. He can recuperate there.'

BOOK TEN

Chapter 1

Johann beamed with pride. 'Well, Ludwig? What do you think? Does it not remind you of home?'

Ludwig walked slowly round the small room. A river had been painted on all four walls, broken only by windows and doors; the water was pale blue, flecked with white, and bordered on both sides by lush tropical plants. Palm trees rose, trunks curved, to a cloudless azure sky. Flowers blossomed along the bank.

'The Danube,' Ludwig said, pointing through the window to the river that lay at the bottom of the long slope in the distance.

'No,' Johann replied. 'The Rhine. Our river. Where we used to play when we were children. Everyone thinks it is the Danube. But it is not.'

'What is this waterfall?' Ludwig asked, pointing to a high cascading torrent of water that filled a panel of the wall.

'The Bingerloch. And that hill behind is the Rüdesheim heights. Did you not go there when you went with the Electoral orchestra to Mergentheim?'

Ludwig did not answer, but moved to the next panel. 'And this bridge? I do not recall a bridge.'

'Things have changed, Ludwig. It has been a long time since either of us has seen the Rhine.'

Ludwig's feet hurt from standing and he sat down to untie his boots. He wanted his brother to leave him in peace, but Johann sat at the table with him, pushing the manuscript books to one side. Ludwig took a notebook out of his pocket and put it purposefully on the table, but Johann began to speak, loudly and clearly. In the small room his words pierced the dullness in Ludwig's ears. 'You can have this apartment. Just three rooms, self-contained. You will not be disturbed. It faces east so you will get the morning sun. Karl will have a room on the landing opposite. I have assigned the son of one of my vine dressers to be your servant. His name is Michael.'

'Leave me alone now, Johann. I must work.'

'A few more things to tell you.' Johann pulled the notebook towards him and wrote, 'Breakfast is at 7.30, lunch at 12.30 and supper at 7.30. I have told the cook you particularly favour fish. Stay as long as you like, two months if you wish. The first two weeks will be gratis, after that I ask just 4 florins a day to contribute towards costs.'

I must pay my brother, as if he were a thieving landlord. Ludwig decided Johann's demand marked a change in the conversation and said, 'Your wife has continued in her immoral ways, hasn't she? I heard about it, even in Vienna. I do not expect to see her while I am here. Her or her bastard child. Is that understood?'

The lazy eyelid that drooped over Johann's right eye seemed to droop a little lower. He picked up the pen: 'My wife has surrendered her marriage contract. If she makes any new acquaintance I will require her to leave with her daughter. Meanwhile she keeps house. You will not see her, except for meals.'

'She must keep away from Karl. I want no evil influence to harm the poor boy. He is in enough distress as it is.'

The manuscript papers that Ludwig left scattered on the table were sketches, and whole passages, for the movements of the string quartet that would surround the aching slow movement he had already composed in Vienna. He had also decided to compose a new final movement for the earlier Quartet in B flat to replace the Grosse Fuge, which Artaria was to publish separately.

Johann had been right about one thing: the air of Gneixendorf was fresh and exhilarating. It was early October and Ludwig enjoyed long walks across the fields, weaving his way between the vines that covered the slopes and ran down to the Danube.

His head was full of the music he was composing. Unthinkingly he waved his arms in the air as he had for years past while walking in the countryside around Vienna. And, as in places like Heiligenstadt, Döbling, Mödling and Baden, the local people learned to ignore him. They knew who he was and what he was doing; the quizzical smiles that passed between them in the early days soon stopped.

Stories circulated in the single tavern in Gneixendorf and the many in nearby Krems, the large town on the banks of the Danube a carriage-ride down the long, winding hill. One of the local farm workers was roundly ribbed when he described how a man – 'He looked like a shabby peasant to me' – frightened his oxen with shouting and wild waving of his arms; the beasts had bolted down the hill and he had had great difficulty bringing them back under control. 'That was Beethoven the Musikus,' the man was told, and ordered to buy a round of drinks.

Michael, the vine-dresser's son, proved an invaluable help to Ludwig. He made the bed each morning and tidied his clothes. He gathered up the sheets of paper Ludwig had screwed up and thrown on the floor, keeping them for a day or two after Ludwig had once scoured the room for a sheet he had discarded. He made sure Ludwig was dressed ready for breakfast and reminded him of the time so he would not be late for lunch or dinner.

Meals were awkward. Ludwig could not follow conversation, what little there was, and the atmosphere between him and his sister-in-law was tense; her daughter Amalie sat for the most part with her head down, then helped clear away dishes.

On a number of occasions Ludwig persuaded Karl to go for walks with him. He tried to talk to him, to tell him how he was progressing with the quartet, but Karl said little. Ludwig noticed he was combing his hair forward to hide the scar above his temple where the bullet had left its mark.

With the cold weather of late October came a worsening of Ludwig's health. He still insisted on striding across the fields despite the pain in his feet, and went frequently down to the banks of the Danube – a walk of more than three hours. Soon his lungs hurt and he found he was again coughing up phlegm, particularly at the end of a walk when he sat on the edge of his bed trying to get his breath back.

More worrying to him, though, was the swollen state of his ankles and feet – and his stomach. It was distending gradually, although he had not noticeably altered his pattern of eating or drinking, and it ached dully as though an undigested lump of dough sat in it.

Secretly he ordered Michael to buy bandages in Krems, which he wrapped tightly round his abdomen, trying to pull it in. He dreaded the inevitable question from Johann about its size.

The quartet, to which Ludwig gave the opus number 135,

was completed and dispatched to the publisher. It was a lighter work than he had expected to write. Perhaps, he told himself, the yearning of the slow movement was of such intensity that it needed a lightening of tone on either side of it. Surprisingly, the final movement had given him the most trouble. He filled page after page of the sketchbook before settling on a simple three-note phrase to open it: dotted crotchet, quaver, minim, which would be reversed to provide the main theme.

The two phrases seemed to Ludwig to represent a simple question and its answer. Without thinking of the significance of what he was doing, he wrote under the first phrase, *Muss es sein?* Must it be? And under that the reply, *Es muss sein!* It must be.

He smiled at the words. What did they mean? Nothing.

When he was not out walking, Ludwig sat for long hours in the living room, staring at the mural of the Rhine. In his mind he could see the turbulent river, not blue and gentle as in the picture, but deep green and grey, harbouring the mysterious legends that were as old as the river itself. He saw the Drachenfels clearly, rough and rugged, not like the gentle hills of the mural or the impossibly colourful flowers with which the artist had bedecked the bank.

He began work on a replacement for the Grosse Fuge, but he could only work for a short time before he was overcome with tiredness and his eyes closed remorselessly. When he awoke his head throbbed and he invariably felt even more tired.

He ordered Michael to make sure there was always a full carafe of red wine in the cupboard. Increasingly only wine brought him relief from the pain in his feet, the ache in his stomach, the throbbing in his head. It was the wine – he was certain of it – that was making him sleepy. The stomach pains had their usual deleterious effect on his bowels. He wrote a note to Therese saying that from now on he would eat only soft-boiled eggs, and that Michael alone was to serve them to him.

His health inevitably affected his mood. At dinner one evening, still shivering after the walk from which he had returned at least an hour before, he noticed Michael was not helping to serve as he usually did. 'Where is Michael? Why isn't he bringing me my eggs?' Ludwig saw Johann and his wife exchange a glance.

'He had to be dismissed,' Therese said, taking the notebook from Ludwig. 'I gave him money to buy wine and fish. 5 florins. He lost it.'

Frustration and anger got the better of Ludwig. 'He is *my* servant. You cannot dismiss him without *my* permission.' He saw Johann's exasperation and added quickly, 'Here is five florins. Now get him back and tell him to bring me my food in my room. From now on I will eat there.'

A notion had been taking hold in Ludwig's mind for some time, based on a remark that Johann had made at the beginning of the visit. While he was composing it had remained just an idea to which he had not given his attention. Now it thrust itself forward and the more thought he gave it, the more it seemed a right and just course of action. Finally, his mind made up, he summoned Johann.

'Johann, your wife is a strumpet. You said so yourself.'

Johann's face betrayed his indignation. 'She is my wife, Ludwig. You will not use language like that.'

Ludwig could hear his words in the confines of the small room. 'You said so yourself. She has broken her marriage contract, you said.'

'That is between me and her and I do not wish to –'

'Johann, we have our family to consider. The Beethoven name is sacred and we must consider the next generation.'

'What do you mean?'

'You are not going to have children, are you?'

Johann paused for a moment. Finally, he said, 'She cannot. Her body was damaged giving birth to Amalie.'

'So there is just one son for the next generation. My Karl.'

'He is not *your* Karl. He is *our* nephew. And I still don't see what you are getting at.'

'Our brother asked me to look after him as a father, and I am asking you to name him as the sole beneficiary in your will, in place of your wife.'

Johann's jaw dropped.

'Johann,' Ludwig rushed on urgently, 'he is our only heir. He will inherit everything I own. I have bought him bank shares for when I die. It is the natural thing to do.'

'I have a family, Ludwig. I have a wife and child. I –'

'Your wife is wicked, just like that other woman, and the child is not yours. But look at this estate. You are a wealthy landowner. How can you not want that to pass to the next Beethoven generation?'

Johann looked down at his brother. 'I am sure Karl will be grateful to you for the bank shares, Ludwig. But he is unlikely to thank you for anything else.'

After that the two brothers avoided each other. It was mid-November: winter had come early and there was a hard frost on the fields. Ludwig walked more vigorously than before, ignoring his protesting feet, but his coat was not thick enough to keep out the cold. When he returned to his room he ordered Michael to light the stove, but it threw out little heat.

He had not seen Karl for some days. He questioned Johann, who wrote in the notebook, 'He goes to Krems for much of the day and evening. He plays billiards and drinks in the taverns.'

Ludwig decided it was time to return to Vienna. Although he refused to admit it to himself, he thought a visit from Doktor Braunhofer would not go amiss. And if Karl was slipping into bad habits, the sooner he was dispatched to Iglau to join his regiment the better. He summoned his nephew. 'We will return to Vienna. It is time.'

Karl wrote in the notebook, 'I am not ready. My hair has not grown long enough to cover my scar. It must be covered before I join the regiment.'

'How long will that take? I do not want to stay in this godforsaken place any longer.'

'Two weeks. Anyhow, I am happy here. I have formed a friendship.'

Even as he wrote the last word, Karl realised his mistake and tried to take back the notebook, but Ludwig grabbed it and read it. He knew instantly what had been going on. All his hopes, his dreams for Karl, once more shattered.

'Who?'

Karl looked his uncle in the eye for a moment, as if pondering whether silence was an option. Finally he wrote, 'Amalie'.

Ludwig tried to speak but emitted only a splutter. A mist came in front of his eyes. Before he could restrain himself he had struck Karl in the face.

Karl raised his hand to his cheek, his eyes wide in astonishment. Then he turned on his heel and left the room.

*   *   *

'Johann,' Ludwig said. 'We are returning to Vienna. Prepare the carriage.'

Johann's face was stern and unsmiling. 'The carriage is broken,' he wrote. 'It will take a week to repair.'

'I want to leave. *Now*, do you hear? I will not stay a day longer.'

'There is only the open carriage. You cannot use it in this weather.'

'Prepare it. Karl and I are returning to Vienna. Tell him to pack his clothes. We must leave.'

Chapter 2

Ludwig and Karl left Gneixendorf before dawn on Friday 1 December 1826. The air was raw, damp and icy, and there was no protection for them in the small open wagon drawn by a single horse with a reluctant driver, who sat huddled against the cold. Therese had given them each a blanket at the last moment but Ludwig, his skin burning, had passed his to Karl.

Daylight was sombre and gloomy, the air never shedding the early-morning frost and the sky a dull uniform grey. Ludwig shivered and trembled, the jolting of the carriage wheels hurting every muscle in his body.

Every hour or two the carriage driver pulled into a wayside inn for coffee and to water the horse. Karl drank thirstily, but Ludwig's swollen stomach would not accept food or drink.

'We'll stop at Tulln for the night,' the driver said. 'Another three hours. It'll be late, but there's nowhere between here and there.'

The brackish smell of the river made Ludwig feel nauseous as the driver turned the weary horse towards it. The wheels thudded with a hollow sound on the bridge as it crossed to the town of Tulln on the opposite bank. Ludwig saw candles flickering in the distance. A comfortable bed was within sight – and a warming glass of red wine.

The inn had only two small attic rooms. The driver said he would sleep on hay in the stables. Karl went to his room and closed the door without a backward glance at his uncle.

Ludwig entered his room and the cold air hit him like a hammer. The window was open and the wind howled through it. He forced it closed, then opened it again to reach for the shutters. There were none. He closed it again. He held up the candle and looked for a stove; there was none.

He sat on the edge of the bed, and put a hand to his forehead. It was clammy and burning hot. The pains in his swollen stomach were growing worse. He held his breath to try to suppress the pain, but to no avail.

He untied his boots and prised them away from his numbed and swollen feet, which prickled as the blood surged into them. He laid his head on the hard pillow, swung his legs on to the bed and brought his knees up high into his chest.

He drifted into a fitful sleep and awoke – it seemed only minutes later – as a dry, hacking cough rasped in his chest. He sat up dizzily, then stumbled to the door and called hoarsely down the stairs. 'Landlord! Bring me iced water.'

It soothed his parched throat like a balm, but set off pains in his sides that he thought would split him. He lay back, his hand over his eyes, head throbbing, and his sides feeling as if he had been stabbed.

He tried to sleep, but the short breaths he took to keep the stomach pains in check made it impossible. He longed to be back in his apartment in the Schwarzspanierhaus. How he wished he had never gone to Gneixendorf. What had it achieved? The reconciliation he had so hoped for between himself and Karl had not happened.

In the morning he staggered down the stairs, feeling weaker than he had ever felt. The pains in his abdomen had subsided but the nausea had not left him; the aroma of coffee and ham cooking on the stove, normally so welcoming, turned his stomach. He sat as far away from it as he could.

When it was time to leave he felt Karl's and the driver's hands under his arms supporting him. With a mighty heave they lifted him on to the carriage, where he sat in the seat, shoulders hunched, a single blanket around him, for the final four-hour drive to Vienna.

Sali the housekeeper bustled around the room. She brought in a small folding writing desk and put it on the floor by the bedside table so that Ludwig could dictate letters. She placed a handbell on the table so he could summon her. Time after time she came in to ask Ludwig if he would take some soup. In the end, regretting the sharpness of his tone, he told her to stay out of the room until she heard the bell.

Ludwig slept, fitfully at first, then more soundly. When at last he awoke the fever had subsided, and with it the pain in his stomach, although not the swelling. He tried to get up but his legs would not support him. He climbed back into bed, exhausted from the effort.

He rang for Sali. 'Where's Karl?' he asked, motioning to the notebook on the bedside table.

'He stays out with friends and comes in at night,' she wrote.

'He is living here?' Ludwig asked. Sali pointed to one of the rooms at the back of the apartment. She then wrote, 'He leaves for Iglau on 2 Jan. Under a month.'

'How long have I slept?'

'Nearly four days. Would you like soup?'

Even the sight of the word caused his stomach to turn, yet he knew he needed food to give him strength. Nevertheless he shook his head. 'Write to Holz for me. In my name, as if it has come from me. Call him Your Official Majesty. Say I should be greatly delighted if he would come and see me. Draw a stave at the bottom of the letter. Five lines. I will send him a gift.'

Her brow furrowed in concentration, her tongue darting out between her teeth as her lips mouthed the words, Sali composed a note to Karl Holz. Then, with something approaching relief, she took a ruler and drew a stave.

Ludwig sat as high as he could on the pillows she had propped behind his back and wrote a succession of notes – two phrases, each rising, the second beginning where the first left off. Under the notes, smiling as he did so, he wrote, '*Wir irren allesamt . . . nur jede irret anderst.*' Every one of us errs . . . though each of us in a different way.

'Thank you for my canon,' Holz said. 'D flat and A flat?' he asked, incredulously.

'I need to see Doktor Braunhofer. Will you ask him to come?'

Holz reached for the notebook. 'He has left Vienna.'

'I must see a doctor, though God knows . . . Speak to Nanette Streicher. And tell Breuning I am back in Vienna.'

A little later Gerhard came into the room. He was taller than Ludwig remembered, his head crowned with a mop of wavy fair hair. He walked purposefully to the end of the bed.

'Hah! Hosenknopf. I can hardly call you that any longer. You have grown.'

Gerhard walked round the bed and picked up the notebook. 'I am thirteen and a half. A boy not a child, and soon a man, so I can study to be a doctor.'

With a complete lack of embarrassment he leaned forward and felt Ludwig's forehead, then took his pulse. Without speaking he folded back the blanket and put his hands on either side of Ludwig's swollen stomach. He applied gentle pressure, then replaced the blanket.

'So, Hosenknopf, tell me my fate. I will die soon, but then we will all die one day.'

Gerhard wrote, 'You have dropsy. They will have to drain your stomach. Father is unwell. He, too, is in bed. Mother is looking after him. He works too hard. He sends his good wishes with me.'

'Thank you, Doktor Hosenknopf. Now you may tell Sali to bring me some wine.'

Gerhard frowned.

'Ludwig,' Nanette said, worriedly, 'this is Doktor Wawruch, professor at the General Hospital. Will you let him examine you?' Then she clucked and wrote the words in the notebook.

Ludwig looked tiredly at the man who stood before him. He had a round, kindly face, with hair that began half-way back on his head and fell in tight curls to his shoulders, leaving the front of his head exposed like a dome. He took the notebook from Nanette and wrote, 'Wawruch, sir. One who greatly reveres your name and will do everything possible to bring you swift relief.'

'Bring me wine, then, Medikus. Let the Medikus bring the Musikus wine.'

Wawruch smiled and wrote, 'Will you allow me to examine you?'

Ludwig assented and Wawruch felt his forehead then took his pulse. 'I know a young doctor you should meet,' Ludwig said. 'A quarter your age and just −'

Wawruch held his finger to his lips. Expressionless, he folded back the blanket and pressed Ludwig's stomach, as Gerhard had, but more firmly and in more places. Ludwig watched his swollen flesh yield under the doctor's hands. Wawruch pulled him forward by the shoulders and pressed round the base of the lungs. Gently he eased Ludwig on to his side and probed his back. Then he propped Ludwig up on the pillows, walked to the end of the bed, folded back the blanket and studied his feet, which were still swollen but less so than in Gneixendorf.

Finally he sat by the bed with the notebook. 'May I ask you some questions?' he wrote.

Ludwig nodded.

'Do you suffer from haemorrhoids? When did you last open your bowels?'

'Frequently, Doktor. The problem is the reverse. No haemorrhoids.'

'Have you ever seen blood from the rectum?'

Ludwig shook his head.

'Take a deep breath and tell me if it hurts.'

Ludwig did so, then said, 'It did hurt. Less now.'

'When did the swellings in your stomach and feet begin?'

'Before I went to stay with my brother. Last summer. It was worse while I was away.'

'Difficulty passing water?'

'Sometimes.'

'Do you drink wine?'

'Yes, and I am not going to stop, even if you tell me so.'

'It makes your stomach swelling worse.'

Ludwig said nothing.

'Your lungs are inflamed, your kidneys and liver damaged. You are seriously ill. You must follow my advice. I will give your housekeeper instructions. She must get certain medicines from the dispensary at the hospital and mix them for you. You must take them at two-hourly intervals. Also, instead of meals drink water with cream of tartar added for the next four days. Add sugar for strength. You must stay in bed and rest. Do not attempt to work. I will come to see you daily.'

Ludwig looked despairingly at Nanette, who hurried to his side and took his hands. 'You will get better, dear Ludwig, I know it. I just know it. You must follow Doktor Wawruch's advice. He is such a clever man.'

Sali set up a table close to the end of Ludwig's bed on which she placed an array of small bottles with stoppers, each containing a different liquid. In front of them stood several carafes of water, which she frequently replenished. At regular intervals, referring to a chart, she mixed a particular potion and handed it to Ludwig, waiting while he drank it.

Young Gerhard came often to see him. Each time he entered the room, Ludwig was disappointed that he was not Karl, but soon he looked forward to seeing the bright face of the growing lad, who took such an interest in his health.

Ludwig quickly settled into a routine of taking his medicines. He remained in bed and at first he felt even weaker, but knew that that was because he was not eating. On the third day he noticed that the swelling in his stomach was less.

He called Sali in and pointed out his discovery to her excitedly, seeking her confirmation. The young woman blushed strongly, nodding vigorously as she hurried from the room.

When he showed his stomach to Doktor Wawruch, the physician smiled reassuringly and wrote in the notebook that the regime was working and that he must continue to follow it.

Gerhard, though, was becoming more concerned for the man he regarded as his patient. 'You must eat, or you will become weaker. Your stomach will fill with fluid again and they will have to drain it.'

'I have two doctors and they tell me different things. For the moment, Doktor Breuning, I shall obey your senior colleague.'

On the seventh day after he began the new treatment, with Doktor Wawruch's encouragement, he got out of bed and walked around the room. His legs slowly regained their strength but his ankles swelled almost immediately and Wawruch hurriedly guided him to a chair. 'Little by little,' he wrote. 'Begin taking food. Soup, chicken broth. I will speak to the house-keeper.'

'And my stomach? Why is the swelling not going down more?'

'Patience. That is all that is required. I will come tomorrow.'

Ludwig sat between the end of the bed and the two pianos, looking over them to the windows and the Glacis beyond. In the distance he could see the sombre Bastion wall and the spire of St Stephansdom reaching up into the dark winter sky.

Occasionally he let his eyes rest on the burnished wood of the pianos. Why did he not feel the urge to sit at one of them and play? No, there was no more playing to be done. His deafness was complete – after all the years of struggle, the hopes raised then dashed, deafness had been the ultimate victor.

He turned in his chair to the wall that bore the portrait of his grandfather. In his mind's eye he could see his furious father, tearing the painting off the wall and striding out of the room to pawn it; and he could feel his own sorrow and helplessness as he watched the comforting face of his grandfather being taken away.

He looked into his grandfather's eyes now, as he had so often all those years ago. Then, they had inspired him, fired him. Now they were reassuring him, calming him, telling him his work was over and he must rest . . . and soon, soon, they would be together again.

He slept and it was dark when Sali came in, bringing with her the strong smell of boiled chicken. At first it nauseated him, then he allowed her to feed him several spoonfuls of broth. Its heat made him sweat, and Sali dabbed at his forehead. When he had finished, she followed it with a sweet-tasting potion.

Finally he let her lead him to the bed. His legs felt like sponge under him, his breath came in short gasps and his stomach felt heavy, as if the soup in it had turned into a glutinous lump. He put one hand under it protectively.

He climbed into bed, shivering as he felt the cold sheets through his nightshirt, and drew his knees up as high as he could without touching his stomach, then lay perfectly still, praying for sleep to come.

In the middle of the night he awoke with sharp pains. He cried out hoarsely, but there was a hideous movement in his stomach, which intensified with each second. Then his bowels collapsed and the stench that followed made him retch.

Tears poured down his cheeks, of anger, frustration and humiliation. How could he have sunk so low? Pain, dreadful pain, impossible to relieve. Legs pulled up, head propped on pillows, lying on his side, legs one on top of the other, first this way then that, more pain, more retching, and the awful stench that enveloped him . . .

'Out! Out!' he cried, with all the force he could muster, but Sali continued to clear up around him, wiping his face with a wet cloth.

Merciful sleep followed, but when morning came, filtering dimly into the room, Ludwig's stomach was more swollen than ever and raged with a searing pain. His feet were icy cold and when he looked at them he cried out to see how swollen they were. His ears rang with a cacophony of discordant sounds, like mocking laughter.

He writhed in pain, tears staining his cheeks and running down on to the pillows. He was hardly aware of the presence of Doktor Wawruch, feeling only his hands pressing on his stomach, which caused him to moan pitifully, then on his feet bringing sudden shafts of pain.

In a moment of clarity, so sharp that he wondered if he was really hearing the words or if his brain was on fire, Wawruch's voice came into his head.

'The situation is desperate. We will have to operate. The fluid must be removed from his stomach or it will burst.'

Chapter 3

Through a mist of pain Ludwig saw Doktor Wawruch and a stranger. Wawruch held the notebook in front of his eyes. 'This is Doktor Seibert, chief surgeon at the hospital. He will relieve the pains in your stomach. You will feel a pain in your side. Do not be alarmed.'

Ludwig felt wetness on his right side and smelt the strong odour of alcohol. Then an explosion in his head obliterated all thought. Hideous sounds screeched in his ears like shells on a battlefield. The searing pain in his side left him breathless. They had stabbed him.

All he could see was the dark ceiling, which seemed to be moving above him. He waited for it to clear, to be replaced by the blue sky of heaven, but slowly it became steadier. The hideous pain in his side was diminishing.

He became aware of bustling movements around him. Faces, drawn, were looking between each other and the floor and him. Wawruch's hands rested gently on his stomach. Sali floated this way and that, always with a large bowl in her hands.

Ludwig's breathing steadied now. His side was numb. He made a small twitching movement and pain shot through him. He realised that only by keeping perfectly still and breathing shallowly would the pain stay away.

An intense tiredness came over him and his eyes closed. A warm hand pressed on his forehead and he surrendered to his exhaustion.

'Do you see, Karl?' Ludwig said. 'The genius of medicine. My stomach fills with fluid and how do they get rid of it? They make a hole in my side so it can run out. All their studies and experiments and sophisticated techniques, and it comes to this.' He paused a moment to allow his breathing to settle from the effort of talking. 'Take care of the pipe. Disturb that and you will cause your old father to die in agony.'

Karl walked round to the left side of the bed, pulled up a chair and wrote in Ludwig's conversation notebook: 'I leave today for Iglau to join my regiment.'

Ludwig forced a smile. 'I have not seen you for a long time. What have you been doing?'

Karl looked away for a moment, then wrote for a considerable time. 'I have been here but you have not seen me. I had to make formal calls on my regimental commander, Lieutenant Field Marshal von Stutterheim, and his officers, who have been in Vienna for discussions at the War Office. I had to undergo a physical examination, which I passed successfully. I was fitted for a uniform. I also had to take an oath of service in front of the commanding officer, and afterwards my monthly allowance was fixed.'

'You are a good boy, Karl. It is the next stage of your life. How long will you be away?'

'I have leave after six months.'

'When you come back, I will take you to see the Rhine, where I grew up, where our family comes from.'

Karl looked at his uncle for a moment, then wrote, 'My uncle Johann says I should ask where you keep my bank shares. In case . . .'

'In a secret place. They are safe. I will give them to you when you return.'

Karl stood, tall and erect. He clicked his heels sharply and gave a formal bow, then turned and left the room, his stride long, his arms rigidly at his sides.

Ludwig lay in bed, free of the pipe that had been attached to him for two weeks. His stomach was still swollen, but considerably less so than before the draining. Doktor Wawruch had warned of the danger of further swelling, but it was impossible at this stage to tell if that would happen. He also recommended a small amount of soft food each day, since Ludwig's bowels had now stabilised.

Gerhard von Breuning was once again a regular visitor, his mien, it seemed to Ludwig, more mature with every passing day. 'They have attacked the symptom, not the cause. Your stomach will swell again, due to the state of your internal organs,' he wrote.

Ludwig slapped at him playfully, then winced at the pain in his side the movement caused. 'Is your father any better?'

Gerhard wrote, 'He insists on working although his health is poor. I fear for him.'

'Hah! The two boys from Bonn, sharing their illness. Tell him to recover quickly and we will return to Bonn and see the Rhine and climb the Drachenfels.'

Ludwig was frustrated at his impotence. His life was controlled by the doctors and his housekeeper, and he could think of no way to remedy the situation. The problem was unexpectedly and fortuitously resolved by a letter that Sali brought to him. She broke the seal and handed it to him.

Master!
   Will you permit me to enter your service again, in your hour of great need?

Yr servant
Anton Felix Schindler

Schindler quickly made himself indispensable to Ludwig, accompanying Sali each time she entered the room – Ludwig caught the look of resentment on her face – and even refusing to allow Doktor Wawruch to spend a single moment alone with him. He made sure there was always a notebook and pencil by the side of the bed, and Ludwig noticed one day that he had put an empty manuscript book there too.

With the swelling of his stomach reduced, Ludwig once more sat in the chair between the windows, overwhelmed by weakness but at least able to take small quantities of food.

Schindler brought messages from friends and colleagues. Karl Holz, now married, apologised for not being able to see him as often as before. Schuppanzigh sent reports of performances of this or that quartet, always enthusiastically received. Zmeskall suggested meeting in the Schwan, 'me in a wheelchair, and you, Ludwig, on a sedan bed'.

On the small round table that Sali had moved next to the chair, Schindler laid the manuscript book. Finally Ludwig picked it up and turned the pages. It was not, as he had thought, a new book: pages were covered with fragments and ideas. Each jotting sounded familiarly in his head. He remembered them all as they arranged themselves before his eyes. A new symphony, that had been the idea. He picked up one of the pencils that Schindler had laid alongside the book and made notes. He wrote new fragments and made adjustments to some already written. The opening theme – hymnlike, lyrical and sublime – he left untouched, allowing the sound of it, flute first, then oboe, to soar as if on wings through his head.

Soon he forgot the pain. There was a dull ache in his side, but if he did not move too much, it caused him little discomfort. Most importantly, in his head he could clearly hear the sounds of the music he was creating.

Suddenly, and without warning, the pains in his stomach struck again. When he cried out in agony, Sali hurried in, pressing a wet cloth to his forehead, holding a glass of water to his lips. For hours, it seemed, he could comprehend nothing. Through his blurred vision he saw images of Wawruch and Seibert and braced himself for the searing shaft of pain in his side. When it came he almost welcomed it, willing it to be the precursor of relief, as it had the last time.

He slept, and slowly his breathing steadied, the pain subsided. When, at last, he was able to sit up against the pillows Sali arranged behind him and take in his surroundings, a smiling Doktor Wawruch wrote in the notebook, 'A successful tapping. We drew out ten measures. More than before. Your stomach has diminished and you will feel better.'

Ludwig was able to resume his place in his chair and look again at the manuscript book. He began to eat but his throat was so dry he could hardly swallow. Wawruch explained that this would pass as his strength returned. But the dryness increased, until his throat was as parched as desert sand. It was as if a boulder sat in his throat, allowing nothing to pass it. He wanted to eat the broth Sali brought, but could not. He took small sips of water; the liquid brought relief, but it was outweighed by the pain of swallowing.

Depressed and tired, he looked up and thought at first that he was seeing a phantom. The long, lugubrious face that had looked down on him so often in sickness was looking down on him again, the head moving from side to side in a gesture of hopelessness.

'Malfatti,' Ludwig said, hoarsely.

Ludwig saw Schindler hand him the notebook and he wrote, 'My colleague Wawruch has allowed me to see you. I shall not interfere, but I recommend iced punch to relieve your thirst. Not more than a single glass a day.'

Sali handed him a large mug, rivulets of condensation running down the sides. The strong welcome aroma of alcohol wafted up to his nose and his senses responded instantly. The taste burst in his mouth like a welcome balm. Timorously he swallowed, then took another sip and swallowed again. The muscles in his throat relaxed.

Before he had taken many sips the alcohol was making him light-headed, confident about the future. He drained the mug and held it out to Sali.

Malfatti, his face longer than ever, held up a single finger.

'Schindler,' Ludwig said, a steely edge to his voice. 'Listen to me carefully. I am composing again. A new symphony. I have an idea for an oratorio based on the story of Saul and David. I feel better than I have for months. Why? The genius of the Italian. The punch that cools my throat, that nourishes my brain. Tell Sali to make more and to bring it to me. If you do not, Schindler, I will banish you from this room for ever more. Do you understand?'

Gerhard von Breuning looked anxiously at Ludwig. He picked up the notebook and wrote, 'Please, sir, do not drink so much punch. The relief is temporary. In the long run it will harm you.'

The light-headedness had brought about a total change in Ludwig's mood. 'Young doctor, you have much to learn but you have the years ahead of you to learn it. The country that produced Monteverdi and Cherubini has also produced the great Malfatti. Do you hear how strong my voice is? Do you see that my stomach is normal? Look at my ankles. Do you not see how the punch has soothed my pain and repaired my body?'

Ludwig demanded more punch, and Sali, clearly under instructions from Schindler, brought him jug after jug. Doktor Wawruch professed himself pleased with Ludwig's progress, but his face was a mask of concern.

'Why so grim, Professor Flesh-and-Bones, Professor Kill-or-Cure? Jealous that your Italian colleague has succeeded where you have failed?'

Wawruch's jaw tightened, but he said nothing.

Ludwig knew he was slurring his words, but he was unable to correct it. He tried to write notes on the stave, but the pencil would not move where he wanted it.

'Schindler!' he called out. In front of him he saw movement. There were faces, but they moved in strange ways, as if the skin was melting and forming into bizarre shapes. He tried to say something, but the sounds froze in his throat. He opened his mouth wider, but only air came out. He could not speak the words that formed in his mind, that he wished to transfer to his vocal cords. He coughed. He heard the rasping sound in his head. He tried to speak again. Nothing.

His breathing became erratic. 'Punch,' he tried to say. 'Ice.'

A hand was pressing below his ribs. He wanted to shout to whoever it was to stop. The pain pierced him. Why were they being so stupid? There had been no pain there before. Why couldn't they realise they were killing him by prodding and pressing?

He tried to cry out as the old pain in his side returned, but his head lolled on his shoulders and his lips moved wordlessly. He knew what was happening; his brain was able to connect the pain with the tapping of the fluid on his stomach, but he could do nothing to stop them.

All I need is the punch. It brings me relief. Just give me the iced punch to drink.

'The third tapping was a success,' Schindler wrote, a smile of encouragement stretched across his face. 'They have located the source of your illness. The key to your recovery lies in your liver.'

Ludwig was too weak to speak, but Schindler understood what he wanted to know. 'More medicines. Different potions,' he wrote. 'They have had discussions with your brother Johann. He will prepare new mixtures. You will also have a new diet. I regret no more punch.'

'Stupid,' Ludwig said, in little more than a whisper. 'They are all imbeciles.'

'Malfatti recommends steam baths. Sali will spread straw on hot jugs. You must lie on the straw. The heat will stimulate your skin and make you sweat. The evil disease in your body will flow out in the sweat.'

Ludwig howled in pain as the hot straw cut into his body. The sweat broke out on his skin but he shivered uncontrollably. Schindler and Sali exchanged anxious glances, lifted him off the straw and almost carried him back to the bed.

Doktor Wawruch ordered the steam bath to be dismantled and removed.

Chapter 4

Ludwig scribbled furiously in the sketchbook, occasionally sipping the iced water that stood on the table by him. His throat
was still dry and he had trouble speaking, but at least his voice
had returned. His stomach caused him little discomfort, apart
from the hour immediately after a meal. He had grown tired of
watching Wawruch, Seibert – even young Gerhard – nodding
with satisfaction at his progress.

Johann was a frequent visitor, his face showing his smug
satisfaction that the new potions were having the desired effect.
On one occasion, after pacing the room for a few minutes, he
approached his brother and wrote in the notebook, 'Karl's bank
shares. Where have you kept them? I should have them for
safe-keeping.'

Ludwig did not reply.

There was a lingering, steady pain in his side, where the tube
had been introduced three times, but Ludwig said nothing to the
doctors. He wanted no more fussing. In any case, perversely the
pain brought him some comfort: a reminder of what had been
and what, God forbid, could be again.

Schindler spent more and more time with him, keeping him
up to date and encouraging him to compose. On one occasion
he brought a letter from Ludwig's old boyhood friend Franz
Wegeler, now aged sixty, still living in Koblenz with his wife
Eleonore, and suggesting they all return to Bonn and visit the
scenes of their childhood. 'Write to him that I am unlikely to
see the Danube again, so there is little prospect of seeing the
Rhine.'

From London came a gift of the collected scores of Georg
Handel, and a letter from Ferdinand Ries saying he was
recommending that the Philharmonic Society of London make
a gift to Ludwig of one hundred pounds 'to be applied to his
comforts and necessities during his illness'.

'Write to Ries that they shall have the new symphony in return,' he told Schindler.

Schindler brought him a bound manuscript book. 'From a young composer who admires you greatly,' he wrote. 'Franz Schubert, writer of songs. He asks for your esteemed opinion.'

'How many songs?' Ludwig asked.

'Sixty here. He has composed more than five hundred.'

'Tell him he must wait until I have paid the respect due to Herr Handel. That alone will take me beyond the years normally allotted to a man.'

The pain in Ludwig's side grew worse, until he could not allow Schindler and Sali to lift him from the bed. There was no alternative but to show it to Doktor Wawruch.

As he knew it would, the pain cut through him when Wawruch removed the clothes from around the wound. His nightshirt was stuck to his skin. Painfully he turned his head and looked down. The sight turned his stomach. There was a gaping red wound in his side, the skin around it festering, and liquid oozed out as Wawruch held the nightshirt clear.

Ludwig threw back his head in agony. Suddenly the pain turned to fire. Wawruch was wiping the wound with a cloth dipped in neat alcohol. The smell threatened to suffocate Ludwig. He screamed hoarsely, knowing that if the pain did not stop he would lose consciousness.

He felt a hand on his stomach. It pressed, bringing more pain. Icy air swept round his feet as the bedclothes were folded back and fingers pressed into his soft, swollen ankles. He knew through it all what was happening. His stomach was swelling. They would have to tap the fluid again and he was not sure he could take it.

Gratefully his hands clasped the chilled goblet and the smell of the punch brought saliva into his mouth. He drank it thirstily. At last they understood, he thought.

He laid his head back and, within a few minutes, he felt the delicious numbing of sensation in his head as the punch took effect. He felt his hand being lifted and the goblet, newly chilled, was put in it again. He emptied it a second time.

His breathing steadied and he felt drowsy. He saw Franz Wegeler, as a boy, leading him up to the large house in the Münsterplatz. He could smell the perfume Steffen's mother wore, see the faces of her children as he played the piano for them . . .

His head jerked as a blinding flash went off inside it. His throat constricted as he gasped. The side of his body was on fire. They had introduced the tube.

He arched his back and held his breath, but hands forced him down. He laid his head back on the pillows but even with his eyes closed the room began to whirl around him.

He tried to turn his head and open his eyes, but it was not necessary. He could see the portrait that he knew was looking down on him.

Leave me alone. It is time for me to be with my grandfather.

The fight had gone out of him. He tried to speak, but the effort caused him too much pain. Sali brought him broth, holding his head forward with her arm and feeding him with her other hand. Each time, after no more than two or three mouthfuls, he shook his head.

The curtains hung across the tall windows. He wanted to tell Sali to open them so he could see the sky beyond, but he knew the light would hurt his eyes. In front of them sat the two pianos. For long hours he let his eyes rest on the dark wood of their surfaces. He could not see the keys. He was pleased: it would have brought too much pain. How he wished he could now just climb from his bed, walk across to one of them, sit at it and play. *His* music.

Would his fingers never again touch the ivory keys of a piano?

One day there was more bustling than usual. Figures moved in the darkness; heads leaned towards each other, whispering. Ludwig did not try to identify the faces, and in his head the blank heaviness was total.

Sali held the notebook close to his face. 'Close your eyes. I must open the curtains.'

Ludwig groaned at the effect of the light. He imagined the sun must be suspended directly outside the window, shining its full force straight at his face. After a few minutes his eyes adjusted to the glare, and he realised the sky was a dank grey.

He recognised Stephan von Breuning. His old friend's face was drawn, not just with anxiety but with age and the effects of his recent illness. His hair, which had once flopped over his forehead, was thin and grey; the high temples, which as a young man had given his face such dignity and charm, now stood out, emphasising the sunkenness of his cheeks.

Breuning leaned close to him, patted his arm. He put the notebook close to Ludwig's face. 'I have prepared your will. It leaves everything of yours to Karl and his legitimate heirs. You must sign it.'

Ludwig felt a twinge of resentment. They were manipulating him, taking advantage of him – as everyone always had. Publishers going back on their word, not paying what they had promised; theatre directors cheating him of receipts; friends using him for their own benefit . . .

He held out his hand for the pen. With the other he took the document and looked closely at it, moving it word by word under his eyes. He found the word 'legitimate'. Laboriously he crossed it out. He could not see – but could imagine – the intake of breath around him. With a huge effort, he wrote above it the word 'natural'. There, he thought, let them ponder on that.

He moved his hand down the document, where he saw his name printed in capital letters. Immediately above it he placed his signature. The nib of the pen tore the page slightly. He realised after he had written his name that he had not spelled it correctly: 'Ludwig van Bethoven.'

He gazed at it, wondering if he had the strength to cross it out and rewrite it. Then, with a sigh, he let the paper and pen fall to the bed.

Faces floated before him. Ignaz Moscheles, the dark hair tinged with grey. Carl Czerny, his tight black curls now receding from his forehead. Hummel came to see him; Ludwig stroked the rings on his fingers, wanting to tell him he was a great pianist and would have been greater if he had lightened his fingers by removing the rings. Instead he just smiled, hoping the smile would convey the message.

A man whose face was familiar, but whom he did not immediately recognise, sat by the bed. 'Ries?' he tried to say. The man wrote his name. 'Ignaz Gleichenstein, sir. And do you remember my wife Netty?'

Ludwig looked at the face of the woman behind him. Why did he not recognise them? Netty. Yes, the name seemed familiar. There was something . . . He could not remember.

He took the pencil and tried to write Ries's name. He

managed only an R, before dropping the pencil. Gleichenstein turned to Breuning, who in turn showed the book to Schindler.

Schindler wrote, 'Karl has been informed of your condition and is travelling from Iglau.'

Ludwig looked into a young face that gazed earnestly down at him. 'Karl?' he tried to say, but nothing came from his throat. 'Karl?' he tried again, wondering at the fair curls he knew Karl did not have.

'Gerhard von Breuning, sir,' the boy wrote. 'At your service and willing to care for you until the end.'

He saw Johann's anxious face. With his head he tried to gesture to the portrait on the wall. He wanted to say, 'You did not know him. I will tell him you are a successful man. But you are not a musician. Karl is not a musician. There will never be another Beethoven Musikus.' But all he could do was stare at his brother and hope he understood.

He felt a wet finger on his forehead make the Sign of the Cross. He saw a pair of white hands clasped close to him and looked up at the lips intoning silently.

He wanted to send the priest away, but he did not have the strength.

The light coming through the windows did not seem so bright and Ludwig found he could open his eyes properly. When he tried to speak he discovered that he could form words. He reached out his arm and rang the bell. Sali came hurrying in. 'Sit me up more.'

Sali hurried out and brought in more cushions. With a supreme effort she pulled him higher in the bed. He grimaced as the sores on his thighs and back rubbed against the sheet.

Later in the day Schindler came in, and behind him a servant pushing a flat board on wheels on top of which stood a box. Schindler wrote in the notebook, 'From Schott the publisher in Mainz, a crate of German wine.'

Ludwig tried to speak. There was a rasping in his throat. He tried again. Schindler bent down.

'Pity,' Ludwig said. 'Pity, too late.'

The effort of speaking had exhausted him and he closed his eyes. Dreams came vividly, in which he saw clearly the face of his mother. He felt her squeeze his hand. 'Can you hear me, Ludwig?'

He tried to nod. 'Can you hear me?' The words sounded clearly in his head. 'Squeeze my hand if you can hear me.'

Yes, yes, I can hear you. He felt a cloth on his face, wiping around his mouth. His eyelids were like lead and he could only open them a little way. A woman's face was close to his, her mouth moving slowly. *Nanette, is it you? Have you come to wish me well on my journey? My grandfather is waiting for me.*

He spoke to her clearly, yet he knew there was no sound in his throat. *Tell Johanna I forgive her.* Again no sound came out but through the blurred curtain of his eyelashes he saw Nanette nod. She understood.

He tried to open his eyes more, but slowly, heavily, darkness came down over him.

Gerhard von Breuning ran through the streets, oblivious of the rain that pounded in rivulets down his face and drenching his clothes. Flashes of lightning lit up the late-afternoon sky above him, followed by crashes of thunder that shook the buildings around him. He had never known a storm like it. He ran under the Schottentor gate, across the Glacis and along the Alstergasse, not pausing once for breath. He turned into Garnisongasse and ran across the small field to the entrance of the Schwarzspanierhaus. Inside the building, out of the rain, he stopped to catch his breath. He wiped his face with his sleeve, but water still poured from his hair down his cheeks.

He took a deep breath and ran up the stairs two at a time. From the moment he saw Sali's face he knew that he was too late. He opened the door and looked at the body of Ludwig van Beethoven, at peace, on the bed. His head was thrown back on the pillow, his hair spread out around it. His eyelids were stretched thinly over his eyes, which had swollen in death. His jaw hung slackly open. The skin of his face was pallid.

He heard a scratching noise and turned to see an artist sitting in the corner of the room drawing. He wanted to tell him to leave, but knew the man would not listen to a boy.

He walked closer to the bed, sensed that Sali was at his side.

'How did it happen?'

'There was a flash of lightning, followed by a violent clap of thunder. He opened his eyes and his right arm jerked up, with his fist clenched. He stayed that way for several seconds. The lightning illuminated his face. Then he fell back and was gone. I closed his eyelids.'

Gerhard thought for a moment. 'That is normal in liver failure, a spontaneous movement like that. Do not tell anyone, or they will attribute the wrong reasons to it.'

'Oh, no, young sir. You are wrong. He was raging at his fate. I heard them say so.'

Gerhard walked forward and took Ludwig's hand. It was icy cold. He lifted it and moved it across Ludwig's chest. Then he went to the other side of the bed and brought the other hand across. He joined them.

There was a cluck of irritation from the corner of the room. 'Will you leave him? I have work to do,' the artist said.

Chapter 5

Sali busied herself tidying the apartment, trying to shut the dreadful noises from her head. There was a constant hum of conversation, punctuated by sudden exclamations of surprise and an occasional harsh laugh. Frequently there were splashes of water and the sound of hands being rinsed and shaken dry. When she was closest to the door of the main room, she heard what sounded like a saw cutting wood. She continued to occupy herself, knowing that it was not her place to ask questions.

When the two doctors left the room, they were carrying a number of bags. 'You can call the undertaker now to dress the corpse. We have finished. Tell him we have cut out the auditory nerves for analysis. He will be able to hide the incisions with the hair.'

By midday Ludwig's body, dressed in a white shirt and dark suit, lay in an open polished oak coffin. His head was on a white silk pillow, the thick grey curls arranged around his face, surrounded by white roses. His hands were folded on his chest, holding a cross and a lily. On either side of his body lay more lilies. A black blanket, folded back to show the white underside, covered the lower half of his body.

The undertaker had done his best to secure the jaw, but because the temporal bones had been removed it hung slackly. He advised Sali to have the coffin closed: he did not want people to criticise his work.

The coffin stood on gilded supports in the room in which Ludwig had died, eight candles on tall stands burning around it.

It was 27 March, the day after his death. Stephan von Breuning had announced in the *Wiener Zeitung* that the funeral would be held in two days' time, and he had asked the Alser barracks near by to deploy a contingent of soldiers to control the crowds. He expected maybe as many as a thousand or more people to follow the coffin to the cemetery at Währing.

*   *   *

Four men – Breuning, Schindler, Holz and Johann van Beethoven
– stood in the corner of the room, whispering urgently, occasionally glancing at the coffin.

'Maybe the bank shares never existed,' Johann said.

'I know they do, sir,' Holz said. 'Master Karl told me, as he
told you. He would not invent that. He told me they were in
a secret place, but he did not know where.'

'We have searched everywhere. The desk, cupboards – there
is no secret drawer,' Schindler said. 'I shall make an inventory
assuming they did not exist.'

'And you will find the shares and tell no one. If you have not
already found them.'

'That is calumny, sir,' Schindler said. 'I am entrusted by our
late departed master to gather up his papers and catalogue them.
The shares will be no different from everything else.'

'Stop, both of you,' Breuning said wearily. 'It is unseemly to
argue like this. It is important we find the shares, or else there
is a risk of them being stolen while the apartment is being
cleared. Think, Holz. Are you sure he never said where they
were hidden?'

'The desk is the most likely place, sir. He never kept papers
anywhere else.'

'Except on the floor,' Johann said.

Breuning walked into the next room, followed by the others.
The desk top was open, its surface an untidy mass of papers. 'We
should look one last time here,' he said. 'Then that is enough.
We must all leave and continue preparations for the funeral. We
have only two days and there is a lot to be done. Holz, you have
been through all these papers?'

'*I* have,' Schindler said. 'And all the drawers. The shares are
not there.'

'But it was a secret place, wasn't it?' Breuning mused. 'It
wouldn't be anywhere obvious. We keep looking in obvious places.'

'How can there be a secret place in a desk?' Johann asked. 'It's
impossible.'

'Maybe behind the drawers,' Breuning said without con-
viction.

Karl Holz took out the drawers one by one, bending to look
behind them. 'Nothing,' he said, replacing the final one. Then
he noticed that the top left drawer protruded a fraction beyond

the front of the desk and gave it a push. It did not move. He pushed again. Still it did not move. Without saying anything he removed the drawer and reached to the back of the empty space with his hand. He withdrew his hand quickly. 'A rusty old nail sticking in the back. I ought to get it out, before someone else hurts their hand.'

He reached in again, grasped the nail, bent and twisted it this way and that until he was able to pull it clear. The piece of wood into which it was stuck came out with it. He looked in and saw some papers. 'I think we may have found the bank shares,' he said.

Schindler pushed him out of the way, reached in and brought out the papers. He put them on top of the desk.

'Keep away, all of you. I am in authority. I will examine the papers. You may watch, but you must not touch.' He opened the envelope on top of the small pile. 'The bank shares. Seven shares of bank stock. And letters. Here is a letter . . . The envelope says just "Aug' Gottes, K." He opened it, read the first few words and replaced it hurriedly. 'This is a private letter, which I will keep with all the other private documents, as my master instructed me. Another letter.' He unfolded a larger piece of paper. 'It is written to his brothers, but your name is not here, sir,' he said, turning to Johann. '"For my brothers Carl and . . ." there is a blank, then "Beethoven."'

'I shall take it, if it is directed to me,' Johann said, putting out his hand.

'It is not, sir. That is exactly the point. He has left your name out.'

'I insist!' Johann exclaimed.

'Stop,' Breuning said. 'Schindler will arrange all the papers and then the proper decisions can be made. Is that all there is, Schindler?'

Schindler held up some sheets of manuscript, covered in notes. 'A piece of music, but not in his hand. I will add it to his other papers.'

March 29, 1827, was a warm, beautiful spring day, the air tinged with the scent of early blossom. Stephan von Breuning, a weight on his shoulders he thought would be almost impossible to bear for the entire proceedings that were to follow, handed his son Gerhard a crepe band for his hat and another to put round his upper sleeve.

'That way they will know you are an official mourner,' he said. 'I fear as the coffin leaves that the crowd may separate us from it.'

A soldier came smartly to attention and clicked his heels. 'All is ready, sir. My men will line the route to the church, then during the service they'll take up new positions further along. I do not expect any disturbance, but with this number, you can never be sure.'

'How many do you estimate, Officer?'

The soldier looked over his shoulder towards the throng. 'Difficult to say, sir. At least ten thousand, and that could double as the cortège proceeds.'

Ludwig's coffin, adorned with a wreath of white lilies, lay on a bier in the courtyard of the Schwarzspanierhaus. Four black horses, each with a plume of white feathers fastened between its ears, stood ahead of it, shaking their heads. Two soldiers stood beside the lead pair, holding the reins.

Immediately behind the coffin stood Johann van Beethoven, his wife and step-daughter. Karl had not arrived in time from Iglau. Next stood Johanna van Beethoven, the breeze catching the black silk scarf that was wound round her head and neck. Her head was held slightly up, her eyes seeming to focus on the low sky in the distance. Behind her stood Nanette and Andreas Streicher, then Schindler and Holz.

Behind the chief mourners stood around twenty men, all dressed in black, with high black top hats. Each carried a tall candle wrapped in white crepe. Stephan recognised Carl Czerny, Kapellmeister Ignaz Seyfried, Ignaz Schuppanzigh, Johann Hummel, Ignaz Moscheles and the young composer who had so wanted to meet Beethoven, Franz Schubert, already being called his natural successor.

Satisfied that all was ready, he nodded to the officer, who gave an order to unlock the courtyard gates. A dozen soldiers moved out quickly, muskets ready to push back the clamouring crowd. The throng pushed forward and the soldiers struggled to hold them back. Slowly the mass of people yielded and they cleared a path through.

In front of the coffin stood a robed priest, holding aloft a tall silver cross. Behind him, their instruments catching the sun although they held them to their sides, stood four trombonists, followed by sixteen singers from the Burgtheater chorus.

The officer took one final look around, then nodded to the

priest, who set off slowly, followed by the musicians. With a tug the horses hauled the bier into motion – a jangle of chains and creaking of wood. The white crepe bands that hung down from it fluttered out as if trying to take flight. Two men in black top hats and black tail-coats hurriedly put out hands to steady the coffin and hold the lilies in place.

As the procession passed through the gates, someone cried out; handkerchiefs were raised in the air, then held to faces. As soon as the bier was clear of the gates the crowd fell in behind it. Johann and his wife were brushed roughly aside, Johanna and the Streichers with them, Breuning and Gerhard, too.

The officer saw what had happened and ordered his men to take action. His shout frightened the horses, who shied, causing the coffin to shift on the bier. The men in black put both hands against it to steady it, leaving the lilies on the ground where they had fallen.

More shouting as the soldiers pushed back the crowd. For a moment there was a look of panic on the officer's face as he feared a riot. His men were under strict orders not to fire their muskets without a command from him, and only him, and then straight up into the sky. But as quickly as the surge had begun, it ended. Order was restored and the mourners took their proper places; the bier swung slowly round and into the Alstergasse in total silence.

It was not a wide street and the distance to the Dreifaltigkeits-kirche, the Trinity Church of the Minorites, was not more than five hundred paces. But such was the size of the throng that the bier could not move at more than the slowest pace.

Suddenly the sun glinted off three rows of brass instruments standing by the side of the Alstergasse. On a downbeat from their director, the musicians played the Marcia Funèbre from Ludwig's Piano Sonata in A flat – the same funeral march Czerny had demonstrated to Ludwig on the table top at Luigi's café in Baden so many years ago. The sounds of the dirge were carried on the warm spring air, bringing more sobs and stifled cries from the crowd.

Breuning looked at the throng with amazement. There were heads on either side as far as he could see, crammed into every space on the street, between buildings, on balconies and where possible on roofs. These were not the official mourners one would see at an Imperial funeral, but ordinary people who had been touched by Beethoven's music, and who wanted to witness his final journey.

It was more than an hour before the bier came to a jangling halt in front of the church.

Swiftly the trombonists and singers took their places on either side of the church door, Ignaz Seyfried hurrying round to stand in front of them. While the bearer party of soldiers went about the task of removing the coffin from the bier and hoisting it on to their shoulders, they played. Seyfried had chosen one of the trombone *equali* Ludwig had composed for Kapellmeister Glöggl in Linz – appropriate, he considered, since *equali* were composed specifically for funerals. He had decided to arrange it for voices as well as trombones, and the doleful chords, alternated between the two, now sounded out.

Inside the long narrow church there was not a space free in the pews on either side of the aisle, apart from the front two rows reserved for the chief mourners. The coffin was placed on a catafalque in front of the high altar. The priest gave the blessing and the church choir intoned the *Libera me, Domine, de morta aeterna* from the funeral mass, again arranged by Kapellmeister Seyfried.

The journey from the church to the cemetery in the village of Währing was a long one. Breuning thought it would take as much as three hours, even if the crowd did not obstruct the procession.

In the event there was a slow thinning out of mourners as the bier moved away from the city; thousands became hundreds. Währing stood at the top of a long gradual incline. Soon the horses' flanks began to shine with sweat and they snorted noisily at the exertion of pulling the bier up the winding slope, as it left the city behind and houses gave way to fields. Breuning mopped his brow, wishing the day would end. But there was still another ceremony to come.

At Währing the coffin was carried into the village parish church, where two priests blessed it while the choir sang the *Miserere*, followed by the *Libera me*.

The procession that now covered the short distance to the cemetery was very different from that which had left the Schwarzspanierhaus. At its head was a boy in a white cassock, swinging a lighted censer, the smoke from the incense streaming out into the cool air. Next were the two parish priests; behind the coffin and to the rear of the family, friends and musicians, were the schoolchildren of the village, supervised fussily by their masters, anxious to put on a good display for the village.

And behind them were the village poor, their clothes ragged, their hair long and unkempt, grateful to be involved and aware that this was a funeral of unusual importance. The distinguished musicians who walked behind the chief mourners now carried new candles, still draped in crepe and burning brightly.

At the gates to the cemetery stood a small group. Breuning recognised Austria's leading playwright, Franz Grillparzer, whom Ludwig had known as a boy in Heiligenstadt, and alongside him Vienna's foremost court actor, Heinrich Anschütz, holding a sheaf of papers that fluttered in the warm breeze.

The original plan, to which Breuning had been party, had been for Anschütz to declaim at the graveside the oration Grillparzer had written. But someone in the Hofburg had told Breuning it was forbidden by law to make speeches on consecrated ground; only prayers were permitted.

And so, as the bier came to its final halt at the cemetery gates, Anschütz stepped forward and, one hand on his heart, the other holding the papers down to his side, he declaimed the funeral oration from memory. 'The last master of tuneful song, the organ of soulful concord, the heir and enhancer of Handel and Bach, of Haydn and Mozart's immortal fame is now no more, and we stand weeping over the riven strings of the harp that is hushed. The harp that is hushed! Let me call him so! For he was an artist, and all that was his, was his through art alone. He was an artist – and who shall arise to stand beside him?'

Breuning heard the words but found it hard to concentrate on them. In his mind was the face of the eager boy with whom he had climbed the Drachenfels, a boy who had fought against rules and regulations, arrogance and hypocrisy, privilege and authority. What would he make of what was happening now? He would wave his hand contemptuously at the words that were pouring forth – just words, he would say, flowery, meaningless words. There is only one way to describe me. *Through my music.* '. . . He was an artist, but a man as well. A man in every sense – and in the highest. Because he withdrew from the world, they called him a hater of men, and because he held aloof from sentimentality, they called him unfeeling. Ah, no. He fled from the world because he found no weapon to oppose it. He withdrew from mankind only after he had given them his all and received nothing in return. But in the end his heart beat warm for all men, in fatherly affection for humanity, for the world to which he gave his heart's blood. Thus he was, thus he died, thus he will live to the end of time.'

The soldiers carried the coffin round the right-hand path to the grave, which lay against the perimeter wall on the opposite side of the cemetery to that of Ludwig's brother Carl. There, sweating and red-faced, they lowered it on to a tarpaulin. Swiftly and expertly, with not a glance to the side, four gravediggers picked up the tarpaulin, lowered the coffin into the open grave, pulled the cloth clear and moved away.

The musicians carrying the tall candles stood beside the two long sides of the grave. At the foot stood Johann, his wife and step-daughter, also Johanna, and behind them Breuning and other close friends. At the head stood the senior of the two parish priests, who now uttered the final blessing.

Johann bent down, picked up a handful of earth and tossed it on to the coffin. His wife and Johanna did the same. Stephan, Nanette and Andreas Streicher followed, then Gerhard von Breuning. The crumpled earth landed with a dull thud and ran like dark beads of mercury across the lid.

On a given signal the musicians each took a snuffer from their pockets, held it in place for a moment, then put out their candles.

Chronology

1812 4 July Beethoven leaves Prague for Teplitz.

6 July Beethoven begins a passionate letter to an unnamed woman. In it he calls her his 'Eternally Beloved'.

Mid–late July Beethoven and Goethe meet several times. Late July Beethoven leaves Teplitz for Karlsbad to join the Brentano family.

Beethoven returns to Teplitz, where he meets Amalie Sebald. He falls ill.

September he decides to travel direct to Linz where his brother Johann has announced his intention to marry his housekeeper.

October Beethoven composes three *equali* for trombones for Kapellmeister Glöggl.

1813 8 March Karl Brentano born.

8 April Minona von Stackelberg born.

April Carl van Beethoven, seriously ill with consumption, declares that in the event of his death he wants Beethoven to be guardian of his son Karl.

21 June The English army under Wellington defeats the French at the battle of Vittoria in Spain.

Mälzel persuades Beethoven to write a piece in celebration of the victory for his mechanical instrument, the panharmonicon. The piece is later orchestrated and becomes known as the Battle Symphony op. 91.

28 August Gerhard von Breuning born.

12 August Austria declares war on France.

16–18 October Napoleon defeated by a combined army of Austrians, Prussians, Russians and Swedes at the Battle of Leipzig, the 'Battle of the Nations'.

8 December Beethoven and Mälzel give a charity concert at the Hofburg at which the Battle Symphony and the Seventh Symphony are performed in public for the first time.

1814 Beethoven agrees to revive his opera *Leonore/Fidelio*, asking Treitschke to provide a new libretto.

6 April Napoleon abdicates.

11 April Beethoven gives the first public performance of the Archduke Trio op. 97 with Schuppanzigh and Linke at the Römischer Kaiser; his deafness makes it a traumatic experience.

15 April Beethoven's old patron Prince Lichnowsky dies.

18 July *Fidelio* performed for the first time in its final form.

26 September *Fidelio* performed before several heads of state assembled for the Congress of Vienna.

October–November Beethoven composes a cantata, *Der glorreiche Augenblick*, for the Congress, and attends its first performance at the Hofburg on 29 November with the librettist, Weissenbach.

31 December Count Razumovsky's magnificent palace destroyed by fire.

1815 1 March Napoleon escapes from Elba.

May Beethoven abandons attempts to compose a Sixth Piano Concerto.

June Philharmonic Society of London commission three overtures from Beethoven for 75 guineas; he sends them the already composed opp. 113, 115 and 117.

18 June Battle of Waterloo.

14 November Carl van Beethoven, mortally ill, makes his will, stating his wishes over the guardianship of his son Karl.

15 November Carl van Beethoven dies of consumption.

22 November Carl's widow Johanna and Beethoven are appointed joint guardians of Karl.

28 November Beethoven appeals to the Landrecht, the court of the nobility, to exclude his sister-in-law from the guardianship of Karl, her son, beginning a legal battle that is to last for several years.

1816 2 February Karl is removed from his mother, and Beethoven enrols him in a boarding-school run by Giannatasio del Rio.

c. April Beethoven composes the song cycle *An die ferne Geliebte*. Czerny, on Beethoven's instructions, begins giving Karl piano lessons.

18 September Karl undergoes a hernia operation. The

Giannatasios take him to recuperate with Beethoven in Baden.

15 December Prince Lobkowitz, Beethoven's patron who previously had to flee Vienna to escape his creditors, dies at his estate in Bohemia.

1817 Persistent ill-health and problems with Karl make this the least creative year musically of Beethoven's life.

9 June Ferdinand Ries writes on behalf of the London Philharmonic Society, inviting Beethoven to London.

c. Autumn Beethoven begins work on what is to become the gigantic Hammerklavier Sonata, op. 106.

27 December Thomas Broadwood, having met Beethoven in Vienna, dispatches to him a new grand piano with the heavier English action which particularly suits Beethoven – and the new Sonata.

1818 24 January Karl leaves Giannatasio's boarding-school and begins living with Beethoven, studying with a private tutor.

19 May Beethoven takes Karl to Mödling for the summer months, enrolling him in the local school run by the village priest, Pater Fröhlich.

c. August Beethoven completes the Hammerklavier Sonata.

18 September Johanna van Beethoven petitions the Landrecht to obtain guardianship of Karl.

Autumn Beethoven makes sketches for a new Symphony that is to include voices.

3 December Karl runs away to his mother. Beethoven calls in the police to bring him back.

7 December Johanna again appeals to the Landrecht to remove Karl from his uncle's control.

11 December The hearing takes place; a week later the Landrecht transfers the case to the Magistrat, the lower court.

1819 11 January the Magistrat hears the case concerning Karl van Beethoven.

c. March Beethoven begins a set of piano variations for the publisher Diabelli, based on a theme Diabelli has composed.

April Beethoven begins the *Missa Solemnis*, intended for the enthronement of Archduke Rudolph as Archbishop of Olmütz the following year.

16 April Just before publication of the Hammerklavier Sonata, Beethoven sends Ries in London an additional bar of two notes to be inserted at the start of the slow movement.

22 June Karl enters Blöchlinger's institute.

2 August Johann van Beethoven buys a large estate at Gneixendorf bei Krems on the Danube.

c. November Beethoven works on the Gloria and Credo of the *Missa Solemnis*.

1820 7 January Beethoven, encouraged by Anton Schindler, petitions the Court of Appeal over the guardianship of Karl.

9 March Archduke Rudolph is enthroned as Archbishop of Olmütz; the *Missa Solemnis* is not ready for the occasion.

8 April Court of Appeal makes a final ruling in Beethoven's favour over the guardianship of Karl; Johanna appeals directly to the Emperor to intervene.

Summer Beethoven again sets the Missa Solemnis aside while he works on a new set of three piano sonatas.

1821 January Beethoven falls seriously ill with rheumatic fever.

31 March Josephine Deym-Stackelberg (*née* Brunsvik) dies.

Summer Barely recovered from fever, Beethoven develops jaundice.

5 May Napoleon Bonaparte dies in exile on the island of St Helena.

Beethoven completes the *Missa Solemnis* by the end of the year, though he is later to revise parts of it.

1822 Beethoven makes preliminary sketches setting Schiller's poem *An Die Freude* to music for use in a symphony combining instruments and voices.

Prince Galitzin commissions three string quartets from Beethoven.

The Philharmonic Society of London offers Beethoven £50 for a new symphony.

Beethoven, his health improved, accepts the commissions from both Prince Galitzin and the Philharmonic Society, and considers a collaboration with the playwright Grillparzer over a new opera.

Autumn Beethoven meets the young Franz Liszt, who is studying with Czerny.

Beethoven elected to the Royal Academy of Music of Sweden.

1823 Schuppanzigh returns to Vienna from Russia and resumes his friendship with Beethoven, who composes a canon *Falstefferel* to mark his return.

August After a sudden deterioration in his health, Beethoven goes to stay in Baden, where he works intensively on the Ninth Symphony.

Karl leaves Blöchlinger's institute and visits his uncle in Baden, before taking a place at the university.

1824 Beethoven makes plans for the first performance of the newly completed Ninth Symphony in Berlin.

Beethoven decides to dedicate the Diabelli Variations to Antonie Brentano.

February Vienna's leading musical names petition Beethoven – successfully – to hold the first performances of the *Missa Solemnis* and Ninth Symphony in Vienna.

The censor bans any performance of the *Missa*, a religious work, in a theatre.

7 May After a disagreement with Count Palffy at the Theater an der Wien, and a compromise over the ban, the *Missa Solemnis* and Ninth Symphony are given their premieres at the Kärntnertor theatre. Beethoven stands next to Umlauf on the podium giving him the beat. At the end of the Ninth Symphony, the contralto Karoline Unger turns Beethoven round so he can hear the applause.

Beethoven dismisses Schindler; Karl Holz, a young Chancellery official and violinist, takes his place.

Summer Beethoven again goes to Baden and turns his attention to Prince Galitzin's commission for three quartets.

1825 Beethoven's health again worsens; he is attended by Doktor Braunhofer.

Karl informs his uncle of his decision to join the army.

Summer Beethoven, in Baden again, works on the Galitzin quartets, composing the Heiliger Dankgesang, the Holy Song of Thanks, as his health appears to improve.

Beethoven learns that Karl is secretly seeing his mother, which puts a strain on their relationship.

Johann van Beethoven invites Ludwig and Karl to stay at his estate in Gneixendorf.

Distraught at learning that Karl is now living with his mother, and suffering from a marked worsening of his health, Beethoven composes the Cavatina and Fugue of Op. 130.

15 October Beethoven moves to his final lodgings in Vienna, the Schwarzspanierhaus.

Beethoven attempts a reconciliation with Karl, informing him that he has purchased bank shares in his name.

1826 21 March Schuppanzigh gives the first public performance of the String Quartet Op. 130. Beethoven agrees to compose a new final movement to replace the Grosse Fuge.

Johann again invites Beethoven and Karl to stay at Gneixendorf.

27 July Karl disappears from his lodgings, leaving behind hints of suicide.

28 September Beethoven and Karl leave Vienna to stay with Johann at Gneixendorf.

In Gneixendorf Beethoven composes a new finale for Op. 130.

1–2 December Beethoven and Karl return to Vienna. Beethoven falls ill in a cold village tavern where they spend the night en route.

Back in Vienna, Beethoven is attended by Doktor Wawruch.

20 December Beethoven undergoes an operation to reduce his abdominal swelling.

1827 2 January Karl departs for military service in Iglau in Bohemia.

8 January Beethoven undergoes a second operation to drain fluid.

2 February a third operation, as Beethoven's health rapidly deteriorates.

27 February a fourth operation, by which time the wound in Beethoven's side has become infected.

March Beethoven makes sketches for a Tenth Symphony.

*c.*22 March Beethoven receives the last rites.

26 March Beethoven dies.

29 March Beethoven's funeral. Twenty thousand people follow the coffin, in the largest gathering for a funeral ever in Vienna. At the Währinger cemetry the funeral oration, written by Franz Grillparzer, is delivered by the actor Heinrich Anschütz.

Postscript

It was estimated that twenty thousand people attended Beethoven's funeral – the largest gathering Vienna had seen. On 3 April, five days after the funeral, Mozart's *Requiem* was sung at the Church of the Augustinians in the Hofburg palace: by popular request the *Miserere* and *Libera me*, as played at the funeral, were repeated. Two days later, Cherubini's *Requiem* was performed in his memory.

Beethoven's auditory nerves, cut out by the doctors on his deathbed, were – according to Gerhard von Breuning – preserved in a sealed glass jar in the coroner's office for many years, before disappearing.

The post mortem performed on Beethoven at the same time described his liver as 'shrunk up to half its proper volume, of a leathery consistence and greenish-blue colour, beset with knots the size of a bean on its tuberculated surface as well as in its substance; all its vessels were very much narrowed and bloodless'. The likely cause of death was alcohol-induced cirrhosis of the liver.

In early April, in the same room in which Beethoven died, his personal effects were auctioned. According to Gerhard von Breuning, who attended with his father, 'A miserable collection of old-clothes dealers had found their way in, and the articles that came under the hammer were tugged this way and that, the pieces of furniture pushed and thumped, everything disarranged and soiled'.

On 5 November Beethoven's musical effects, including sketches in his own hand, autographs of printed works, original manuscripts and copied parts, were auctioned in rooms in the Kohlmarkt. The total intake was 1140 florins and 18 kreuzer. Beethoven's total estate, including cash, bank shares and personal effects, was valued at 9885 florins and 13 kreuzer (£1 equalled approximately 10 florins).

Beethoven's grave in the Währinger cemetery fell into neglect, and on 13 October 1863 his body – along with that of Schubert who was buried in a grave beside him – was exhumed and reburied. Before reburial a team of physicians compared Beethoven's skull with Schubert's, noting that Beethoven's was 'compact and thick', whereas Schubert's was 'fine and feminine'.

While the graves were prepared for reburial, Beethoven's skull was given for safe-keeping to Gerhard von Breuning, who writes in his memoirs, 'What stormy feelings passed through my mind evoking such powerful memories, as I had possession of that head for a few days, cleaned from it bits of dirt, kept it by my bedside overnight, and in general proudly watched over that head from whose mouth, in years gone by, I had so often heard the living word!'

On 21 June 1888 the bodies of Beethoven and Schubert were again exhumed and removed to the recently opened Zentralfriedhof, Vienna's main cemetery to the south of the city, where they lie today side by side – according to Schubert's deathbed wish – in the musicians' quarter.

In the years following Beethoven's death there was a campaign to have a monument to him erected in his home town, Bonn. Largely due to the efforts – and financial contribution – of Franz Liszt, this was finally achieved in August 1845.

A massive bronze statue, designed by an almost unknown sculptor, Ernst Julius Hähnel, showed Beethoven, one leg ahead of the other, both feet planted firmly on the ground, holding a pen in his lowered right hand and a notebook in his left; he is standing upright and staring ahead, brow knitted and features concentrating, abundantly thick hair framing his head.

Ignaz Moscheles said Hähnel had obtained 'an admirable likeness of the immortal composer'; Schindler that there was 'nothing to be seen there that conforms to reality'.

The statue was placed at the top end of the Münsterplatz, where it stands today, a little way in front of the house of Count von Fürstenburg, now the post office headquarters. A balcony had been erected on the front of the house for the guests of honour to witness the unveiling.

All Bonn turned out for the event; the small town on the Rhine had never seen a gathering like it. The guests of honour were no lesser figures than Queen Victoria of England and her German consort Prince Albert, King Friedrich Wilhelm of Prussia and Queen Elisabeth, and Archduke Friedrich of Austria.

The ceremony began with a speech from the music director at the university of Bonn, at the end of which the statue was unveiled to cheers from the crowd, the beating of drums, the ringing of bells and the firing of cannon – and the statue was found to be facing down the square, its back to the guests of honour on the balcony!

Karl van Beethoven left the army in 1832, marrying Caroline Naske in the same year. They had four daughters and a son, whom they named Ludwig. As the only Beethoven of the next generation, Karl was able to live comfortably as a private citizen on his inheritance from his uncles. He died at the age of fifty-two from liver disease. His wife outlived him by thirty-three years. Their only son Ludwig emigrated to America, where he found employment with the Michigan Central Railroad Company of Detroit. His wife, Maria Nitsche, was a concert pianist. Their only son, Karl Julius, who returned to Europe and fought in the First World War, was seriously wounded and died in hospital at the age of forty-seven, childless.

Johanna van Beethoven outlived her brother-in-law, with whom she had had such a stormy relationship, by forty-one years. She died in some poverty in Baden, aged eighty-two. There is no record of her ever saying or writing anything critical about Ludwig.

Johann van Beethoven lived prosperously on the proceeds of his apothecary business for the rest of his life. He frequently attended concert performances of his brother's music, always sitting in the front row, according to Gerhard von Breuning, 'all got up in a blue frock-coat with white vest, loudly shrieking Bravos from his big mouth at the end of every piece, beating his bony white-gloved hands together importantly.' Again according to Breuning, Johann proved to be 'as preposterous after his brother's death as he had been contemptible during his brother's life.' Johann died in Vienna in January 1848 at the age of seventy-one. His wife Therese died at Gneixendorf in 1828 of a 'nervous fever', aged just forty-one.

Stephan von Breuning, Beethoven's lifelong and most loyal friend, never recovered his health. He died barely two months after Beethoven's funeral. He had been ill with a liver condition and suffered a relapse, according to his son, after the trauma of attending the auction of Beethoven's effects. Gerhard believed the strain of his father's friendship with Beethoven broke his health. He was fifty-two when he died.

Gerhard von Breuning graduated as a doctor of medicine in 1837, worked first as a military doctor, then devoted himself exclusively to private practice. In 1874 he published his memoirs of Beethoven, *Aus dem Schwarzspanierhaus*, From the House of the Black-Robed Spaniards (Cambridge University Press, 1992), an invaluable and reliable account of the last years of Beethoven's life.

Ferdinand Ries gave a farewell concert in London in April 1824, before moving with his wife to Godesburg. He had accumulated considerable wealth from teaching and composition, but lost much of it when the London bank in which he had invested failed. About 1830 he moved to Frankfurt and in 1834 to Aachen, where he was appointed head of the town orchestra and Singakademie. But the duties of office did not suit him and he returned to Frankfurt two years later. He died after a short illness in January 1838, aged fifty-three. His father Franz outlived him by nine years. Ferdinand Ries was a prolific composer, leaving nearly one hundred and eighty works, including symphonies, operas, oratorios, chamber music, and solo piano pieces, none of which have remained in the repertory.

Carl Czerny earned a good living as piano teacher, his reputation assured by his closeness to Beethoven. He composed more than three hundred pieces, including masses, requiems and symphonies, but will always be known for his piano studies. He also published detailed instructions on how to perform each of Beethoven's major piano works. He never married and had no brothers, sisters or close relatives. He died aged sixty-six.

Franz Wegeler remained with his wife Eleonore (*née* von Breuning) in Koblenz where, as physician, he was a highly respected member of the community. They had two children. Wegeler never saw his childhood friend again after Beethoven left Bonn in 1792. In 1837–38, as reported by Gerhard von Breuning, the Wegelers returned to Bonn, and together with Franz Ries and Helene von Breuning they sat and talked of the young Beethoven they had known, though 'Frau Breuning had to be left out of these discussions, her mind having become feeble with age'. She was eighty-seven at the time. Wegeler was eighty-three when he died, Eleonore seventy.

Andreas and Nanette Streicher continued their successful piano-building business, passing it on to their son. They both died in the same year, 1838, after a happy marriage of forty-five years. Andreas was seventy-one, Nanette sixty-four. They are buried together in the musicians' quarter of the Zentralfriedhof.

Archduke Rudolph, Beethoven's greatest patron and a composer in his own right, suffered a fatal stroke when he was only forty-three. In accordance with his wishes, his heart was removed from his body and placed in a niche in the walls of the cathedral of St Wenceslas in Olmütz. His body lies with other members of the Habsburg dynasty in the family crypt in Vienna.

Antonie Brentano, Beethoven's Eternally Beloved, led a sad life. She outlived her husband and all but one of her children. Her son Karl, with whom she was pregnant in Prague and Karlsbad in 1812, was stricken with partial paralysis of the legs at an early age; at the age of four he showed signs of severe mental retardation, coupled with epileptic seizures and violent behaviour. During the last fifteen years of his life he was under the constant care of three attendants, and died at the age of thirty-seven. In later years Antonie found comfort in religion, and in her eleven grandchildren and thirteen great-grandchildren. At the age of forty-six she began to note down the names of her friends who had died; by the end of her long life the list ran to several pages. The first entry read: Beethoven, 26 March 1827. Antonie died at the age of eighty-eight.

Minona von Stackelberg, whom her mother Josephine believed to have been Beethoven's child, never married. She was only seven when her mother died, outliving her by seventy-six years. Her sisters, whom she also outlived, said she was always asking questions about their mother, in an attempt to come to know her better. She died in straitened circumstances in Vienna at the age of eighty-three.

The two most important written documents in Beethoven's life were the Heiligenstadt Testament and the Letter to the Eternally Beloved, both found in the secret drawer of his desk after his death. Anton Schindler, Beethoven's self-appointed executor, took charge of both.

The Testament passed from him to Beethoven's publisher Artaria and finally to Karl's mother Johanna. She in turn gave it to Franz Liszt to sell on her behalf. He brought it to London on a concert tour in 1840 and tried to sell it for fifty guineas, but there were no buyers. He finally sold it for less than that sum, making up the difference himself. The Testament passed through several more pairs of hands, before the composer Otto Goldschmidt, husband of the Swedish soprano Jenny Lind, presented it in 1887 to the Staats-und Universitätsbibliothek in Hamburg, where it remains today.

Schindler recognised the importance of the Letter to the Eternally Beloved, holding it back when he presented his collection of Beethoven's papers to the Royal Library in Berlin. It was not until 1880, long after Schindler's death, that it was reunited with the collection. Today it is held in the music section of the Staatsbibliothek Preussischer Kulturbesitz in Berlin.

The two pianos in Beethoven's possession at the time of his death enjoyed different, and ultimately happy, fates.

The Graf was taken back by its maker and sold. By some miracle it survived and was acquired by the Beethovenhaus Association in 1889. Today it stands in the house in which Beethoven was born in the Bonngasse. In 1967 the Austrian pianist Jörg Demus recorded the Sonata Opus 110 and Bagatelles Opus 126 on it. That was, as I was told, the last time its voice would be heard, since it was considered too delicate now to be played.

The Broadwood – by the time of Beethoven's death in a poor state due to his pounding on the keys and numerous repairs – was sold at the auction of his effects to an antique dealer for 100 florins. He gave it to Franz Liszt in 1846, who treasured it but never played on it. In 1874 he gave it to the Hungarian National Museum in Budapest, where it is today. In the early 1990s it was restored – a major task which involved virtually rebuilding it. Ferdinand Ries' signature was still clearly visible on the board behind the keys. Shortly after this it was transported briefly to England where the Malaysian-born English fortepianist Melvyn Tan performed on it. For this journey it was insured for five million pounds!

By fortunate coincidence Bonnie and I arrived in Teplitz from Prague on the same day of the year as Beethoven – 5 July – one hundred and eighty-five years later. Unlike him it took us a comfortable two hours, the road today skirting round the Waldtor forest where his carriage broke down.

Teplitz (Teplice in the Czech Republic) is Bohemia's oldest

spa town. Today it is an uncomfortable admixture of beautiful old buildings from the era of Empire and drab grey slabs from the era of Communism. It is hard today to imagine the royalty of Europe gathering there, but the Schlossplatz, with its castle and churches, has at least been preserved.

Again like Beethoven we were unable to get a room in the main hotel in the Schlossplatz (the Prince de Ligne) and stayed in a small hotel at the bottom of the hill. The Steinbad – Stone Baths – still stand in a small park opposite, still slightly run down. The town's main bathhouse – a beautiful and luxurious establishment on the same site off the Schlossplatz as two hundred years ago – is today named the Beethoven spa. It was built in 1825, thirteen years after Beethoven's last stay there!

The site in the Schlossgarten where Beethoven, walking with Goethe, insulted the Empress is marked with a small stone monument and a plaque set into the path.

Teplitz is proud of its association with Beethoven. It is the home of the North Bohemian State Philharmonic and is the venue of the annual Beethoven Music Festival.

The journey from Teplitz to Karlsbad, during which Beethoven reflected on what might have been as he gazed on the beautiful countryside, has a rather different effect today. The countryside is still beautiful, but it is a sad beauty. For kilometres on end a huge oil pipeline snakes alongside the road, *above* ground. Turn a bend and the view is suddenly dominated by a monstrous refinery, derelict, a skeleton of twisted and broken metal.

The low mountain range that separates Bohemia from Germany lies wounded – I can think of no other word. Its slopes have been stripped by heavy machinery, so that it resembles an arm from which the skin has been torn away. I turned to Bonnie as we drove, to find that the sight of such wilful destruction had brought her to tears.

There are signs of repair: in places new trees have been planted. But it will take decades, possibly even a hundred years, for the people of northern Bohemia to rid their beautiful landscape of the systematic rape to which it was subjected during the dark closed years that followed the Second World War.

Karlsbad (Karlovy Vary) has made more progress. It is the largest of the spa towns and a bustling tourist centre. The Auf der Wiese still runs along the river; shops, restaurants and cafés all do brisk trade. The town is dominated by the hideous oblong tower block that stands above the municipal baths – a gift to

the grateful people of the town from their Communist rulers
– but close your eyes to that and you can still imagine Karlsbad
as it was when the wealthy from all over Europe came to take
its waters.

The colonnade through which Beethoven walked with
Antonie Brentano still stands, and a few paces from where
the Aug' Gottes stood there is now the four star luxury Hotel
Pupp, home to the film stars who come each year to the
International Film Festival.

The journey south to Linz is a journey of contrasts. Southern
Bohemia is dotted with squat square grey concrete buildings and
as you approach the border with Austria you cross a no-man's-land
into which even today few Czechs venture, as if the memory alone
is enough. The barbed wire and machine gun posts have gone,
but there is still a darkness and drabness that suddenly lift as you
cross into Austria, with its neat little pocket handkerchief houses,
colourfully tiled roofs and floral curtains in the windows.

Linz is a bustling town on the Danube – keener to stress its
links with Anton Bruckner than Hitler, who attended school
there. By coincidence a chemist's shop stands on or near the site
where Johann Beethoven's apothecary shop stood. It is difficult
to tell precisely, because part of the river has been reclaimed and
there are no plaques or other mementoes to mark the town's
connection with the Beethoven family.

Johann van Beethoven's other residence, the estate at Gneixendorf, is a revelation. The house is still grand and beautiful, dominat-
ing the vineyards that surround it and run down to the Danube.
It is today in private hands, owned by a family that produces and
bottles wine.

Our unannounced arrival one Easter Saturday morning, when
the family was gathering for lunch, was welcomed in a way it
did not deserve. The lady of the house took us upstairs and
proudly showed us the small apartment in which Ludwig had
stayed, beautifully preserved. She showed us the mural of the
Rhine that Johann had commissioned and at which Ludwig had
gazed longingly as he worked on his Quartet. All the furniture,
she said, was either original or of the period.

After the Second World War Soviet soldiers were billeted in
the house, she told us, and used to build a small fire on the floor
of Beethoven's living room. The furniture, mural, apartment
and house all survived, but you can see the scratch marks on
the wall where they struck their matches!

We found it extraordinary that such an important site is not a museum, financed by the government. Given that, it is fortunate that the family that own it care for it as they do.

In Baden the small house where Beethoven composed much of the Ninth Symphony is now a museum – the first floor, that is. The ground floor is a rather inelegant antique and souvenir shop.

The Rauhenstein ruins have lost none of their menace, even if the woods that surround them are more tame than they were two centuries ago. The ruins are a favourite destination of weekend walkers, the winding path to them helpfully signalled by signs nailed to trees saying 'Beethovenweg'.

In Vienna the Amalienhof wing of the Hofburg palace, where Beethoven so often visited Archduke Rudolph, is today open to visitors. It is best known as the private quarters of Empress Elizabeth (1837–98) – Sissy – the tragic wife of Emperor Franz Josef. 1998, the centenary of her death, saw a permanent exhibition of her life in the Amalienhof, as well as portraits in windows across Vienna and a spate of books and souvenirs carrying her image; her beauty, informality, loathing of the stiffness and formality of royal life, and her violent early death so uncannily presaging our own Princess Diana.

The Razumovsky palace was restored after the New Year's Eve fire. Today it is a rather sorry sight. It stands like an ageing dowager, surrounded by upstart modern buildings. The garden that once swept down to the Danube is now small and overgrown, bordered on three sides by narrow streets. Today (1998) it is the home of the Geological Institute, but is in the process of being sold. Fortunately it is once again being restored, but is unlikely to resemble the palace the Prince knew.

Prince Razumovsky lived quietly and anonymously in Vienna until his death. The Razumovsky family lives there still.

The Römischer Kaiser, where Beethoven gave the fateful performance of the Archduke Trio (not to be confused with today's hotel on the Annagasse), stood on the corner of the Renngasse and the Freyung, opposite Prince Kinsky's palace. Today it is a faceless building housing a bank, with a plaque on the wall – to Franz Schubert!

The Schwarzspanierhaus, where Beethoven died, was taken over by the Cistercian Order of the Holy Cross in 1843. They vacated it sixty years later, and the decision was taken to tear it down. Despite protests from musicians, artists and cultural institutions across the world, Beethoven's last home was pulled down in 1904.

It is still a long uphill walk to the Währinger cemetery, which is today a small park with tennis courts, surrounded by blocks of flats. The original gravestones of Beethoven and Schubert still stand against the perimeter wall, unnoticed by people walking their dogs. The park is called the Schubert Park.

By contrast Beethoven's grave in the Zentralfriedhof – a replica of the original, just a simple obelisk and the name Beethoven, no dates, no eulogy – is a tourist attraction. You have to wait your turn to take a clear photograph of it. On the day Bonnie and I went to pay our respects to this man into whose life I had delved so deeply, there were fresh flowers on the grave.

As I stood contemplating this Titan among men, Bonnie wandered a little way off. After a minute or so she called me urgently. She had found another grave. It was the Streichers', and it faces Beethoven's. I saw Nanette's name in gold lettering.

'There you are,' I said, 'she's still looking after him.'

It is appropriate to end the story where we began – in Bonn. If you stand on the bank of the Rhine, you can see the Drachenfels looming in the distance, the jagged finger of the ruined castle atop it. (Try to ignore the tall rectangular glass tower that houses the offices of the Bundestag.)

There is an Italian restaurant on the bank, where we lunched. It is called Zur Lese, at the Place of Reading, a curious name which I did not think about until the proprietor told me it stands on the site of the Lesegesellschaft – the Reading Society to which Count Waldstein and Gottlob Neefe belonged.

Bonn's old cemetery stands on the outskirts of the town. Beethoven's mother, Maria Magdalena, lies there. Her gravestone reads (my translation): She was such a wonderful mother to me, my best friend.

The words are taken from a letter Beethoven wrote to Councillor Schaden in Augsburg in 1787 after his abortive trip to Vienna to meet Mozart. But the stone was only erected in the 1930s, and it is not certain that the grave really is Maria Magdalena's. It is not known where his father is buried.

Franz Ries, though – old Father Ries – does lie there. He died just nine days short of his ninety-first birthday.

But anyone who goes to Bonn's old cemetery today probably does so to see the graves of Robert and Clara Schumann.

What, then, is Beethoven's legacy? In the Cultural Revolution in China, the compositions of the 'capitalist musician Beethoven' were described as exemplifying the 'filthy nature of the bourgeoisie'. Yet, in the wonderfully twisted logic of Communism, the current regime in Beijing reveres him as a revolutionary.

The Soviet Union – as was – appropriated the fourth movement of the Ninth Symphony as 'the anthem of human freedom', performing it before the Supreme Soviet even as it shipped political dissidents off to the Gulags. How Beethoven would have trembled with rage!

A recent American university publication entitled *Feminine Endings, Music and Sexuality* wrote, 'The first movement of Beethoven's Ninth is dammed-up energy which finally explodes in the throttling, murderous rage of a rapist incapable of obtaining release.' I suspect Beethoven would have laughed and poured another glass of wine.

I prefer the testimony of the many readers who have written to me: the man who told me that Beethoven had saved his life – twice – but did not elaborate. Or the sixteen-year-old boy whose brother, a soldier, was ambushed and killed in Northern Ireland, and whose mother died six weeks later; now a middle-aged man, he says Beethoven's example gave him the courage to overcome adversity.

One theme is common to practically every one of several hundred letters: where there is weakness or frailty, Beethoven's music gives strength.

He was not a religious man: in all my research I never came across a single piece of anecdotal evidence of him ever having attended church voluntarily. But he was a man of enormous faith – faith in mankind. His music is his gift to mankind.

He was an artist – and who shall arise to stand beside him? He was an artist, but a man as well. Because he withdrew from the world, they called him a hater of men. But to the end his heart beat warm for all men, in fatherly love for humanity, for the world his all and his heart's blood.

Thus he was, thus he died, thus he will live to the end of time.

Other bestselling Warner titles available by mail:

☐ The Last Master: Passion and Anger	John Suchet	£7.99
☐ The Last Master: Passion and Pain	John Suchet	£7.99
☐ Mozart	Richard Baker	£12.99
☐ Schubert	Richard Baker	£12.99

The prices shown above are correct at time of going to press. However, the publishers reserve the right to increase prices on covers from those previously advertised without prior notice.

WARNER BOOKS

WARNER BOOKS

Cash Sales Department, P.O. Box 11, Falmouth, Cornwall, TR10 9EN
Tel: +44 (0) 1326 569777, Fax: +44 (0) 1326 569555
Email: books@barni.avel.co.uk

POST AND PACKING:
Payments can be made as follows: cheque, postal order (payable to Warner Books) or by credit cards. Do not send cash or currency.

All U.K. Orders	**FREE OF CHARGE**
E.E.C. & Overseas	25% of order value

Name (Block Letters) _____

Address _____

_____

Post/zip code: _____

☐ Please keep me in touch with future Warner publications

☐ I enclose my remittance £_____

☐ I wish to pay by Visa/Access/Mastercard/Eurocard

Card Expiry Date

_____